ROBERT L. SHUSTER

TO ZENZI

A NOVEL

New Issues Poetry & Prose

Western Michigan University
Kalamazoo, Michigan 49008

First Edition, 2021.

ISBN-13: 978-1-936970-69-8

Library of Congress Cataloging-in-Publication Data:
Shuster, Robert L..
To Zenzi/Robert L. Shuster
Library of Congress Control Number: 2020947940

Editor: Nancy Eimers
Managing Editor: Kimberly Kolbe
Art Direction: Nick Kuder
Cover Design: Kaitlyn Fisher
The Design Center, Gwen Frostic School of Art
College of Fine Arts
Western Michigan University

This book is the winner of the Association of Writers & Writing
Programs (AWP) Award for the Novel. AWP is a national, nonprofit
organization dedicated to serving American letters, writers, and
programs of writing.

Go to www.awpwriter.org for more information.

ROBERT L. SHUSTER

TO ZENZI

A NOVEL

NEW ISSUES

 WESTERN MICHIGAN UNIVERSITY

A universe of gratitude to my wife Laura, for always being that first reader (and enduring the pressure of it), and for her patience, support, and love

1

I begin, then, in 1945, in the late hours of March ninth, in central Berlin, a night of lingering winter chill and too much fate.

Thirteen years old, an assistant to the rotund air-raid warden Otto Köckler, I stood inside the doorway of a large underground bomb shelter, at the western edge of the Kreuzberg district, proudly clutching my kerosene lantern, and ushered the parade of anxious citizens down the steps into corridors of gloom. Though the city lay ruined in mounds and mounds of bricks and blackened timber, the British were attacking us again from the sky. The streets were just starting to erupt.

"You will all be safe," I shouted, having been taught by Herr Köckler to repeat certain reassuring phrases. "The concrete is thick, the enemy's assaults are losing steam, move to the back, be seated, breathe normally so that there's air for everybody, remember no smoking, the German people are strong and durable, we will emerge victorious, the toilets are on the left, the infirmary one floor down."

Dozens marched past me, many of them regulars. A solemn elderly couple, who dressed as if going to the theater, who carried thick books, candles, and a carafe of ersatz coffee, greeted me, as usual, with a Latin phrase about peace. Next came the mad widow Frau Seiler, wearing nothing but dirty bloomers on her lower half, making the familiar claim about a great shoulder of pork sadly left in the oven even though the gas lines had been destroyed long ago and the only meat you could get anymore came from horses. Soon after, a group of boys from the Führer's youth army surrounded me and cracked their same old joke: "Herr Ober! Herr Ober! A party of six! And a table by the window!" They howled like wolves because of my uniform. Modern military ones, permit me to explain, were in short supply. Though theirs came from the previous war, at least the cloth was field-gray. Mine, dug out of a closet, was an old post-office jacket, dark blue with gold buttons, much too large, drooping to my knees like a frock coat. When I first tried it on, stamps from the Kaiser years fluttered out from a pocket.

Now, from behind me, a whisper went right into my ear. "A pfennig for my passage, Charon." Instantly I knew the voice belonged to Kreszentia Fuchs, who was nicknamed Zenzi and who spoke with that bouncy southern accent, a Munich accent, which had a singing quality that I found both endearing and a little ridiculous. She pushed a coin into my palm, squeezing my hand. I heated up, all blushed out. It was one thing to be mocked by the boys, but quite another to have a curvy, know-it-all, fifteen-year-old girl show affection for me while I performed my duties. Black-haired and tall, with a delicate dented chin and round spectacles and breasts the size of 75mm shells, Kreszentia always wanted to impress you with the scholarly things she'd learned, myths and literature and opera, and even algebra and trigonometry. I had first encountered her in a typing class that my father had forced me to take—Vati despised the war and had an idea that clerical skills would keep me away from the front lines if I were ever called up. Zenzi, who sat next to me, clattered away at the keys without effort to produce poems she'd memorized by German masters or silly ones she wrote herself, never with errors, of course, and exhibited to anyone who would look. "Will you ferry me across the Styx, Charon?"

"Leave him alone, Zenzi," said her pale, withered mother, a schoolteacher before the schools had closed. "He's busy."

The origin of her flirting was not over my looks—I was underweight, with a sharp nose and blond eyebrows you could hardly see, and only came up to that chin of hers—but all due to her rabbit Einbrecher. The public shelters did not allow pets. Yet a few weeks before, on another night of loud bombardment, Zenzi had come in cradling the creature under her bulky coat and because I had a liking for animals and because Herr Köckler had not seen it, I made no mention of what she concealed.

Now I tried to locate the animal's lump, to make sure he was well hidden, but really I was making an excuse to stare at the bulging of her 75mm shells. Despite my disdain for all her high-flown talk, I could not resist imagining myself inside that coat, too. I envied that rabbit.

"Please find us after you're done with your rounds," she said, "because I have a gift for you, Herr Koertig."

The promise turned me red again, for it seemed to acknowledge my lust. I tried to cool off by returning Zenzi's formality. "Thank you for your kindness, Fräulein Fuchs."

Zenzi's mother shooed her away. Her father, a balding teacher of mathematics, scowled and sucked on a pipe he never lit, and then pointed back toward the waning moon that sat on the black sky like a slice of melon. "Without its light for guidance," he said, "those bombardiers might drop their loads on anything." I knew this already and nodded with impatience, but his observation, it turned out, was an omen.

Finally Herr Köckler ordered me to close the heavy door. This he no longer did himself, for the last time he tried, his gray tunic—one size too small, at least—had split along the spine. But I didn't mind, since the task involved a certain daring. You never knew what could come flying through the air—bomb shards, red-hot bricks, a porcelain sink. Once a department store's mannequin, its fashionable dress on fire, had soared past like a disgraced angel. Another day a melted dog almost tumbled inside. Therefore I used a long iron rod to push the door closed from a distance, then rushed up to bolt it.

"Very good, Tobias," Herr Köckler said. "Tell me, is there plenty of kerosene in the lantern?"

"All filled up." I lifted the light to show him and I saw his eyes rapidly blinking, his lips twisting and contorting. I wondered if the booms above, louder now, were giving him gas trouble, as they sometimes did. Herr Köckler had been studying at a seminary when the war started, and this interest in godly things explained to me his delicate constitution. A sweaty sheen, like lacquer, had spread across his brow.

"Be very thorough with your inspections tonight. I've been having more complaints about behavioral disorders." When he spoke the formal term, die Verhaltensstörungen, his bulk trembled, his jowls darkened. Officially, my duty after closing the door was to provide water to the thirsty, but Herr Köckler, diligent member of the Reichsluftschutzbund, had also instructed me to look out for smoking or black-market deals or seditious jokes or radios tuned to the BBC. Now he mostly wanted me to report on nudity, especially flesh meeting flesh. The destruction of the world above was bringing many young people together into last-ditch pleasure.

Bulbs in the ceiling didn't work because the electricity had been knocked out weeks ago, so with my lamp I followed the marks of glowing green paint on the floor and walls. My progress was slow, as I tried not to step on those sitting in the corridors. Many were living in the shelter now because their homes were nothing but rubble or dust. The crashes above pushed me to my knees. The stench, a humid stench, also made it difficult to move forward, it rose thick like fog, it filled me up like poison. It came from the clogged toilets, from oozing wounds and unwashed bodies and death itself, sweet and gagging. Another of my duties was to check for the dead, often suicides, the bodies could sit down here for days. Babies were hard to detect, the lifeless ones I mean, who had been too distressed to take the milk. The mothers still swaddled them and held them close.

I turned into the first room, where my own mother would go. Someone was chanting a prayer, a few others sang for children. My lantern light found Mutti seated against the wall, a rag held to her mouth. She was wearing, as usual, a huge pair of men's shoes, which she insisted were best for scrambling over bricks.

"Tobias, there you are, sit with me," she said into the cloth, her words muffled as if through a bad phone connection, "it's a bigger one tonight, I'm afraid for you. There's no need to run around here." Of course it greatly chagrined me, an assistant to the warden, that she said such things in front of everybody. "I'm worried about your father when it's like this," she added.

At the beginning of the war, Vati had joined us in the shelter. But a fear of looters gripped him and he started hunkering in the basement of our villa, in the Tiergarten neighborhood, to make sure no one found his costly paintings and sculpture. He had made a career dealing art—"Meisterstücke und Schund," masterpieces and trash—to the wealthy, and in the last decade he had exploited the Nazi fat cats, selling them the heroic nonsense they liked, even though he despised the regime and its Chancellor, "das laute ekelhafte Arschloch," the loud, disgusting asshole. Some of what Vati owned had been officially forbidden—prompting numerous private rages—so in addition to stopping thieves he wanted to make sure it all stayed out of sight. The bombs had come close to him, a nearby apartment had collapsed and another's upper floor had been reduced to cinders, but our building remained whole. He spent the hours there, I knew, listening to records of a favorite composer, Poulenc, whose melancholy works for piano gave him a pleasant nostalgia for the days before the bombing—those days when we would take the trolley to a bakery in Potsdamer Platz and gobble Pfannkuchen and then press our thumbs on the red-and-white Villeroy & Boch plates, on their country scenes, to pick up the last grains of sugar. Those were, I will say it for the record, the best days of my life.

"He'll be all right," I said to Mutti before scooting out—but in truth, I did worry. Not so much about my father's safety from the bombs but about his mood. In the last year, the war had given him long-lasting bouts of sadness. Some days he hardly spoke a word to us, and I had begun to wonder if he stayed in our basement to be alone.

The next rooms, packed shoulder to shoulder, flickered with eerie shadows from shallow candles, the Hindenburg lights. "Water!" I said, "water for those who most need it!" I filled a few cups from my canteens, and then headed to a descending stairwell, where Herr Köckler's newly stenciled slogans glowed in that green paint: *High Morals Preserve Our Stamina, Do Not Forsake Victory for Pleasure, Hedonism Is Cowardice.* In a certain area down there, I knew I would find plenty of "die Verhaltensstörungen." Just a few days ago, I came across a woman who was, dearest God, nursing her half-starved father.

Now, at the bottom of the steps, already I detected the orange tips of cigarettes and odors of beer and, I was sure, anti-

Führer laughter. I had heard many of the jokes from my father and his artist friends and had come to know that quiet but biting cackle. I never reported any of it, of course, for I was no informant, but especially since I did not want Herr Köckler venturing down here himself and disrupting what occurred further on, in a particular room. I checked for the dead (none) and dispensed more water and then, with covert steps, I shuffled over to the doorway of that special room, the one without candles that I never entered. I held my lantern up and peeked inside, glimpsing the shadowy, writhing tangle of bare limbs and buttocks, hearing the familiar moans and grunts. I stared until my blood became too hotly thrilled, which did not take long, and then fled, ashamed as usual, into another corridor.

Soon a familiar voice called out, high-pitched and lilting, Zenzi again. "Tobias, hold still for a moment," she said, "here's my gift." She handed me a scrap of paper, scrawled with lines of verse. "Would you like me to recite it for you?"

In front of her parents and everyone else? I could think of nothing more embarrassing and blurted, "There's no time for anything like that."

She bowed her head in disappointment, which was clear because her spectacles were gleaming in my lamplight. Immediately I wanted to soften my harsh reply, since in truth I was trying to imagine her nude. All that witnessed flesh in the abnormal room had boiled up my awkward desires for this girl. "I promise to read it later," I added.

Her mother yanked her arm. "Kreszentia, you will leave the boy alone." After another big rumble above us, she said to no one in particular, "It's heavier tonight. God save us."

The father set aside his pipe. "Is it true that the Russians have taken Danzig?"

Often I got such questions because of my uniform. But my

geography was very poor. And I did not know much about the progress of any front because my father refused to let me read or listen to any battle bulletins. So I gave Herr Fuchs the answer that Herr Köckler had taught, "The Russian invasion is already falling apart, our men are bravely defending the homeland, the Mongols will never cross the Oder." To be honest I did not remember where that river ran.

I continued on, emptying the canteens, and made my way back to the entrance. Not seeing Herr Köckler—who despite the rules was probably having a smoke in a storage closet he used for an office—I took out Zenzi's poem, recorded in her precise hand, and discovered a tribute to me from Einbrecher himself. Dearest God! By the time I reached the last line, that thankful rabbit was covering me with kisses! I stuffed the paper deep into my pocket.

The bombs kept falling, vibrating the floor and walls, boom after boom. My mother and Zenzi's mother were correct, tonight felt gigantic. Dust was bursting from the ceiling in candle-lit clouds. Around me, there was more and more sobbing and panicked shouts and the screeching of children. I could hear now the *thump-thump-thump* of the flak guns on top of the bunker in the zoo, not far away, and I imagined several British bombers spinning down in flames.

To busy myself, I brought out a little notebook, filled with my sketches. I had become quite good at drawing things. The famous Frau Kollwitz, whom Vati knew, had praised my skills during a few lessons some years before. Because Vati had banned me from making pictures of Messerschmitts and Panzers, lately I had concocted adventures in space, of the kind in novels I had devoured by Von Hanstein and Jules Verne. I went to work on a complex starship, and was about to surround it with a dense meteor shower, when without warning Herr Köckler's shiny face was looming above me, like an unexpected moon.

"What's the report, Tobias?"

I snapped shut the notebook, jumped up, and saluted. I stammered, "All is in order. I inspected all the corners, and everything was quiet."

He spread his arms and a satisfied expression came to his lips. "Ah, then, my slogans are working! You see, you do not always have to fill citizens with fear, as some believe. Appeal to their instincts for the noble act, and they respond! Resist our wanton desires, and we can all turn back that Bolshevik flood."

I stood there nodding and did not remind Herr Köckler that above us the explosions were coming from British bombs, not Russian.

"Relax, Tobias, I have no further tasks for you at the moment. But I do wish to speak with you about another matter." Otto Köckler smiled, grasping my shoulder. "You are a fine assistant. Obedient and intelligent. I would, of course, hate to lose your services here. But I must remind you—it is my duty to do so—that Germany is looking for strong boys like yourself to help defeat once and for all this Mongol threat."

"But I am not old enough, Herr Köckler."

"Ah, Tobias, your age is no longer a barrier. Our call to arms has expanded. In any case, you are quite mature." Another nearby crash shook the walls, and he winced, ducking. A thicker sheen had developed on his forehead, speckled with dust. He never wore his hat because it was also too small. "Perhaps you will consider it."

Like all boys—going back, I must guess, to ancient Egypt—I had dreamed of being a warrior, I had concocted skirmishes in my bedroom, I had revered the heroes (the dashing flying ace Galland and tank commander Wittmann, to name my favorites), but of course I knew that Vati would never allow me to volunteer for any military service. He had prevented me from joining the Führer's youth regiments, even though they were largely mandatory (his high connections had allowed the exception), and it had taken me months just to convince him to let me work for Herr Köckler. I fidgeted, I looked at the floor, and then said, "I will need my father's permission."

"Certainly. But he must understand, I'm sure, the extent of our needs now." Herr Köckler smiled again and patted his paunch. "And I should mention, Tobias, the food they serve the boys, it's rich and plentiful. Bread with every meal."

The thought of plentiful bread made my stomach rumble, and, as if cued by my hunger, the single long note of the all-clear siren began to wail. It was a little sour, since without electricity it had to be operated by a hand crank now, but what a relief to hear it every time!

The crowd shifted, as eager to leave as they were to enter, to breathe outside air, to see what had happened, to find food.

"Let the boy open the door," Herr Köckler yelled at the sea of heads behind me, "don't push, be calm, form a single file, you can all return to your homes, there's no need to hurry."

I ran up the stairs to release the bolt, then pulled open the door.

In an instant, super bright light flooded our cavern, hot black particles swarmed inside like insects, white dust swirled, and thick heat rushed at me with the force of wind. I staggered down as gasps and shouts leapt from the crowd. Some lurched backwards, some lunged forward, a great panic began to grow, a knot of elbows, arms, and hands. "Be calm!" Herr Köckler ordered, "please exit in a single file!" But he like many others began to choke and lost his words. I got mashed up against a wall, pressed so hard a gold button popped off my coat. We were jammed in, hardly able to move, speckled in soot. There was another surge upward. This one kept momentum and the people began to spill out into the fierce orange glow like sinners tossed into hell. The dust was stinging my eyes, they were full of water and blur, and I did not recognize my mother until she spoke.

"Tobias, Tobias, I don't know what's happening, I don't know but it must be terrible. It must be dangerous." She pressed the rag to her mouth, her eyes held a shining fear. "Stay down here until your father or I come back for you, promise me, promise me."

"But I don't need an escort. I will join you when I am finished with my duties."

"No, please listen, please obey. I don't want anything happening to you."

"What's going to happen? The bombers have left."

"Tobias! All that fire!" Her voice had broken, I had never heard it quite so screechy. "I must go, I'm too worried about your father. Stay here until we come back!"

Now I said nothing, and dearest God, it is to my deep and deep and deep regret that I gave her just a petulant scowl before she scurried away.

Forgive me once again, Mutti, forgive me.

Stupid stupid youth!

The grief still comes to me like a knife.

I returned to the lower rooms, discovering a death, an older man, possibly a suicide from poison. I had seen plenty of bodies before, but the sight of his lips, which held an eerie trace of a smile, sent me hurrying back up the stairs. I made my report to Herr Köckler, who asked a number of questions, what I had observed in the old man's section and so forth, because Herr Köckler did not want to run a bomb shelter known for despondency. Finally he released me from further duties.

I did not of course wait for my mother and father to return, I rushed out the door into the cauldron. The air clutched at me, stung me, foul and bitter. Flames curled everywhere. A fog of white ash went into my mouth and nostrils. Yes, everyone had been right, the bombing had been worse than ever. It was 4am but the light shined like noon. The fires and smoke confused my knowledge of the city. Squinting, I could not see very well. More walls had come down, cascades of stone. At first I didn't know which way to go. Others were scurrying around in confusion, too. I darted past youth-army boys acting as firemen and aiming hoses that seemed to hold no water. A uniformed man shouted into a megaphone: "Assemble here for fire duty! Assemble down the block for recovery duty! Assemble there for damage clearance..."

I scrambled over bricks and the curlicue tops of fallen lamp posts and past a blackened trolley turned sideways like a roasted pig, and found the Landwehr Canal. We lived close to it, we used to stroll along its banks, so I jogged down one side, following the path of the water shimmering orange. Our street ran parallel more or less to the canal and, cutting over, I saw the solid sign, still standing, with the heavy script and the little profile of a bear on top, and I nearly cried. It was not far now to our villa.

But buildings had come down here, too, and the further I went the less I recognized. At one point I doubled back, sure I had made a mistake. No, the sign said it was our street. Bricks everywhere, a big iron oven had tumbled down from a kitchen, and half a bed, and a pile of underwear, plus a body face down on rubble. I pushed through a small crowd that had gathered, including the city police, and I bolted for our building. I jammed in the key. It would not turn. I tried it a dozen times, in and out, back and forth, knowing something was wrong. I ran back into the street to question the crowd and I could see that many were giving me strange expressions, open mouthed. Then I looked more closely at the body on the pile of bricks—a woman whose dress was rumpled up so that you could see her underclothes in the leaping fire shadows, and also on her feet a pair of clunky men's shoes.

It took me a while to absorb the explanations from the nervous crowd, to understand what had happened.

A bomb had hit our apartment building, right on top. The key would not work because I was trying a door across the street, I had become so confused. It was our oven in the street, our bed. Of course I had not recognized that, either. My father was underneath all those bricks, flattened, not alive. Even so, my mother had rushed up to find him, using those big shoes to climb over bricks. Close by, an old man, a member of the Auxiliary Police on guard duty, he had only just learned how to fire a rifle—well, he mistook my mother for a looter and killed her with a single bullet to the neck, a dumb luck shot.

Not so surprising, I went into a little craziness. From that pile of underwear in the street, I scooped up a scorched pair, maybe my father's, and started waving it around my head, shouting obscenities, demanding to see the man who had killed my mother. He had in fact scurried off, ashamed of his act, and I would never learn his name. But what did it matter? I never knew the crew who had dropped the bomb, either. When several people tried to calm me down, I became louder, whipping the underwear around in a frenzy and telling the crowd they were trespassing, they did not belong here. I climbed atop the bricks, near my mother's body, and picked up a handful of shards and hurled it in their direction and that sent them running. A few frail members of the Auxiliary Police still insisted on removal of the bodies, but I threatened them with a plank of floorboard, and because more ghastly trouble elsewhere required their attention, they left me alone.

For the next few hours in the cold I shivered on the rubble, though not freezing because the smoldering fires, deeper down, sent up warmth. I apologized to my mother over and over for my rudeness, holding her bluing fingers, and peered into the orange embers below for any glimpse of Vati. Once I thought I heard his music playing, and then I worried that if anyone discovered it was French they would not allow a proper burial. I imagined that the souls of my parents had risen into heaven but wondered if the next batch of planes, the Americans, who bombed during the day, would bother them up there. My brain was flipping over and over. The sun rose, scavengers emerged from basements, sleep grabbed me. In a dream I smelled sweetish smoke, it reminded me of calmer days in the cafés with Vati. And then in chilly sunlight I looked up to see Herr Fuchs, balancing himself on the bricks, the pipe stuck in his mouth, this time lighted. "We heard about what happened," he said, "and we are all deeply sorry. Why don't you come with me. Someone will take care of your parents. The American planes will be on top of us soon and it won't be safe outside."

And so I followed the pipe-smoking man across the rubble, to another life.

2

Spring for me is the gloomiest season. March and April and May should be about rebirth, but instead, when I see daffodils or hear the nighttime peeping of the frogs, I can think only of the dead. In my worst moments, I send myself back in time to make an alteration: the three of us, my parents and I, sit in our Berlin basement together and we listen to Poulenc's charming music and chat about art and eat a little snack and then we all die, together, together, under that bomb.

It took the fire brigade an entire day to dig out Vati's remains. They cut a small passage, hauling up debris in buckets, which I inspected for any family token. I did find the Mickey Mouse doll, made by Steiff out of velvet and now with a melted head, that my mother had bought for me long before the war, but I somehow soon lost it, to my great dismay.

The burial took place in the Tiergarten. We used to stroll here on Sundays, down paths crowded with greenery. The place had become a sloppy wasteland, reminding me of photos I had seen of the earlier war. There were craters everywhere, like giant soup bowls. Lots of trees were only stumps and the surviving ones had been amputated for firewood, just sad gray poles. Herr Fuchs and his wife, as well as Zenzi, accompanied me, and we found a spot near the park's edge, near other graves, at the end of Graf Spee Strasse. The fire-brigade men carefully tapped the earth for any unexploded bombs, then grunting they dug a shallow ragged rectangle full of roots and laid my parents in there. We had no coffins, only planks wrapped with sheets. They told me my father was found intact, but the lie revealed itself when newspaper stuffed in a shirt-sleeve slipped out. I pretended I had not seen it, and the men threw the dirt to fill the hole.

I kneeled, pushing my hands into the earth. I knew that Vati would be angry that the war had finally killed him. He had complained about it since the beginning, hating the blackouts and the disappearance of taxis and the owlish watchmen on street corners who called you on the slightest error. "Last night that little prick on Schützenstrasse," I remember him saying, "he told me not to polish my shoes because they could reflect light into the sky! I would have murdered him if there had not been witnesses!" Every time he tore off ration coupons he would seethe. One of the worst moods came to my father when, from some official order, toilet paper disappeared from the stores. "Göring, that bastard, has hoarded it all to wipe his gigantic ass!" In spiteful exasperation, like others, he tried using torn strips of the Nazi newspaper, *Völkischer Beobachter*, and of course they clogged the pipes. Only after he called the plumber did he realize his protest might be discovered. Therefore I was ordered to sit on the toilet behind the closed door and moan in false sickness, preventing the bewildered man with the wrenches from entering. Vati's rages had become tiresome over the years, but now there was nothing I wanted more than to hear his slashing curses.

I marked the grave with bricks I had transported in a toy wagon from the rubble of our villa, then remained kneeling, too stunned to say or do anything more. Frau Fuchs wept and shivered, Herr Fuchs gestured with his pipe and uttered a brief eulogy that floated out on clouds of breath. Zenzi whispered to me, "It's a terrible thing that happened, but we will take care of you." She reached for my hand but discovered mud on my fingers and jerked away. Einbrecher, frightened, leaped out of her coat to hop around, and as Zenzi chased the fat rabbit into a crater, Frau Fuchs shouted after her in great wildness—"You will soil your dress! Don't step on any bombs!"—and ended the ceremony.

I followed the Fuchs family back to the Schoenburg district, to the shadowy basement of their building, where for the next week, I hardly ate, talked, moved, or even wept. I had lost everything, I did not even possess a single photograph of my parents. I was floating in a big nothing, it seemed, a dark void. Hour after hour, I slumped in an armchair that had been taken down from their third-floor apartment. Though all the rooms upstairs remained undamaged, Zenzi's mother feared the planes too much to live there. Herr Fuchs said he no longer wanted to use the public shelters, especially Otto Köckler's, because they were all filthy and disgraceful, and so we endured the raids in the basement, too. The four of us shared the space with an elderly couple, Herr and Frau Buchwald. When not doting on his white-haired wife, who seemed to be sick, the husband waved his bandaged hand and insisted that the Americans and British would soon start bombing the Russians instead of us when they realized where the real terror lay. "The Mongols are raping our women, throwing infants into bonfires. Remember what they did in Nemmersdorf! Nailing girls onto barn doors! Right through their hands and feet! Crucifixion! I've heard the stories! Depravity! They won't stop until they've killed every last German."

Even these outbursts failed to stir me. I was becoming more and more listless. I ignored the daily lessons in mathematics and German literature, I made no sketches. When Zenzi grasped my hand and whispered tender remarks, my interest only sputtered. I did not consider going back to help Herr Köckler. I did not even think to contact my one remaining grandparent, Opa Erich on the maternal side, to give him the news of Mutti's death. But he lived down in Stuttgart and the phones didn't work and I didn't want to see him anyway because he was loud and drank schnapps all night.

In addition to the meager rations—bits of fatty sausage, moldy cheese, stale bread—Herr Fuchs provided us with some beer, for he claimed it contained nutritious elements. Each night, while he and his wife read to us from Schiller and Goethe, we all shared a bottle or two, which kept old man Buchwald quiet and put me into a woozy state that sometimes let me hear—I was certain—the ghostly voices of my parents, calling out my name.

Then a certain event, permit me to explain, yanked me out of my thick grief. Herr Fuchs liked to take naps in his bed during the day, between raids, on the third story. You could set a clock to the American bombing, 9am and noon, and so despite his wife's protests he went up there at midmorning for snoozes, always returning, I noticed, refreshed and not so serious. One day, the mother and I, as well as the old couple, were watching Zenzi perform an awkward dance. She kept pausing to wind up a damaged phonograph that was playing some shrill symphonic music. In all of this dancing and winding, we had forgotten about the time and at some point heard the familiar drone of the bombers and the *thump-thump* of the flak. The recording's honking trombones had covered up the siren, or maybe it had never sounded. In any case, Frau Fuchs began to shriek as we heard the bombs start to fall. "He's still upstairs! He'll be killed! He's a very heavy sleeper!" Zenzi volunteered to wake him, but her mother was too terrified to let her go. Now, finally, I had a purpose again. I leaped up, insisting that the planes would not bother me, and raced up three flights of stairs.

Explosions in the distance shattered things, you could hear pieces of the city falling, splintering. I shoved in the key and burst into the apartment. "Herr Fuchs, the American planes!" I shouted and ran to the bedroom. There I found him, under blankets. He jerked up like a marionette and gazed at me with horror, then jumped out onto the floor, holding his hands over his pale mid-section, for he was naked. From the other side of the bed, giving me natural astonishment, another man tumbled, also without clothing. Bulkier than Herr Fuchs, and quite hairy, he knocked over a bedside table in his hurry.

Just as they reached for their clothing, an American bomb fell in the next block and a giant wind surged into the room— everyone kept their windows open during raids to prevent these forces from shattering the glass—and the three of us flew backward, knocked onto the floor, where I lay between two naked men with trousers around their ankles. Only bruised, they dressed and then we all galloped down the stairs. The bulky man fled into the street and Herr Fuchs grabbed me before I descended into the cellar. Trembling, he said, "Not a word about this to Frau Fuchs or Zenzi or anyone else. We don't want to upset them any more."

"Yes, yes, of course not."

"We are all a little crazy now."

The others embraced us, and thankfully, asked no questions about why Herr Fuchs clutched his balled-up underwear.

So a truth came to me that afternoon in the basement, as I sat there eating a slice of sausage: We are all a little crazy now. To have witnessed another example of it, in Herr Fuchs of all people—well, I experienced great relief, a kind of fellowship. My hunger returned, I started drawing pictures of spaceships again, and I participated in the daily lessons, even for the bewildering algebra. Zenzi resumed her know-it-all comments—"X equals 4, not 6, Tobias, and even if you forget to divide by 2, how do you get 6?"—but I didn't mind because the studies, and our occasional arguments, kept my mind away from death.

Restless after all those dispirited days, and tired of the basement, I found any excuse to venture into the streets—fetching water from a street pump, standing in line to buy rations, gaping at the most recent damage. One day in late March, on a trip to get bread, Zenzi and I encountered a crowd screaming profanity at a rooftop. We looked up and saw, to our amazement, a British crewman sprawled near a chimney. He had bailed out of his plane and landed there. A large white cloth stained a vivid red hung over the gable, his bloodied parachute. It was hard to tell if he was already dead or not, but grief and furor surged into my throat, and I started yelling things, too, with greater and greater force.

"It's too horrible," Zenzi said, pulling me away.

"He might have been the one who killed my father!"

"But what good will it do?" She clung to my hand, hurrying me past several blocks, so we could no longer hear the crowd. Then she stopped and whirled around, like a dancer, to face me. The lenses of her glasses gleamed in the sun like two coins. She wiped away my tears with her thumbs. "I have an idea, somewhere we can go that isn't about the war. I haven't been there in a long time, and I think it's still open. The zoo! Come on. The gorilla will make us laugh."

We wandered inside the gates, past wrecked cages and craters. A few other visitors shuffled around, but we had the place pretty much to ourselves. Following signs, we came upon Rosa the hippopotamus and her baby Knautschke. On a dirt bank, Rosa lay as still as a junked and rusting boiler. She was dried up, her hide cracked and covered in sores. Morose, she watched Knautschke slop around in a small muddy pool.

"She's like my mother," Zenzi said. "Sick with worry, while the child just wants to enjoy things."

Further along, the elephant Siam trumpeted his anger and stomped. I did not blame him, for he no longer resembled his species but rather a large sad creature forced to wear a gray suit ten sizes too big. His skin drooped, as loose as burlap. We moved on, sullen ourselves now, to Pongo the gorilla. He did not cheer us, either, as Zenzi had hoped. Gaunt, he slumped on a rock without moving and we thought he was dead until we saw a finger twitch. Soon after, we scurried out, settling on the southern bank of the canal.

"The poor things," Zenzi said. "The Red Cross should rescue all of them and take them back to Africa. They're starving."

"We should give them British bomber crews to eat."

"I don't think there are any carnivores left. Did you hear what happened to one of the tigers? He escaped after an air raid and ended up in a chocolate shop. He ate everything and then died. The owner tried to sue the zoo for his losses."

It occurred to me that if I had to die in Berlin that was how I might wish to do it, eating chocolate. Hunger pinched at my gut. I watched an older gentleman, not far from us, patiently fishing, and wondered if we should try our luck sometime...but Zenzi was trying to ask me something.

"Tobias," she said, and with a nervous habit pulled at the brocaded collar of her blouse, "did you hear what I said?"

"Switzerland?"

"Yes, please listen—my father thinks we should leave Berlin. He wants to go to Switzerland, like Furtwängler."

"Who?"

"The conductor of the Philharmonic! Well, he used to be."

"That's desertion. If you were a soldier, they would shoot

you." I had been too harsh, for the corner of Zenzi's mouth contorted, so I added, "This is our city. We can't just let the Russians have it."

"I don't think we can stop them now," she said. "They just keep coming, like angry bees."

I craned my neck to peer into the shadow at the top of her blouse, where she was still fiddling with the cloth, worried about something, it seemed. "We have new weapons. Huge guns and special bombs."

Just as I made this claim, the fisherman belched, and Zenzi and I both jerked in surprise, then fell into hysterical laughter. We had managed to find something to cheer us up, after all. Calm again, Zenzi asked, "Would you come with us, Tobias? You're part of the family now."

"Where?"

"Switzerland! Why stay here? There's nothing left."

"I don't know." A small oblong object now emerged in the canal, further down, just before the water bent out of sight. "That looks like a canoe."

"No, a man—you can see his shoes."

"I think you're right." I squinted at the water. A man with a dark jacket, floating on his back, certainly dead. I knew that pale, bluish tint of the skin, I had seen it so often.

"The poor thing didn't even get a burial."

"But he gets to make a journey. Maybe that's better than being under the dirt."

"If he keeps going," Zenzi said, "I suppose he could travel all the way to the North Sea."

"Don't you think we should get that bread?" I pushed my eyes up, toward the sky. "The Americans are coming soon."

Zenzi plucked out a wristwatch from her coat. "We've got more than an hour. I don't think they ever come before noon."

"But the line will be long. And your mother always worries. She probably thought you'd be back already."

"Tobias, sit for another minute," she said. "I want to tell you a secret."

"About your mother?"

"Well, yes, sort of." Now she whispered: "Do you know what Mischling means?"

I ventured a joke. "Something the animals do in the zoo."

"No, don't be ridiculous," she said, and then leaned closer. "Do you?"

"Someone with one Jewish parent."

"Yes. Or a grandparent."

"That's the secret?"

"Some still live in Berlin. But they're afraid the police will round them up one day."

"I know all that," I said, which was not exactly the truth. Vati had explained such things to me once in somber tones, but I had not remembered the details. The frenzy of hate against Jews, many who were Vati's clients and friends, had given him severe agony of the heart, and it sickened him, I believe, to talk about the subject. The information had not been repeated.

"Tobias, that is not the secret." Zenzi looked down and away. The fisherman tugged on his line. "This is it: I am a Mischling."

I felt a pleasant kind of stinging in my throat to hear a bit of dangerous news confided so close to my ear.

"Second degree," she whispered. "Mischling, second degree. My mother's grandmother was Jewish. You can't tell anyone."

"I promise."

"That's why we don't have much food. We have trouble getting rations. If they know, people keep their distance. It's lucky about my mother's hysteria and my father's back trouble, because a lot of Mischlinge were sent to the bomb factories. When Otto Köckler found out, he wouldn't let us in his shelter. What a fat pig, writing all those stupid slogans, half the words are misspelled. My father had to bribe him. Of course that moron told us that he was letting us stay because he'd gone to the seminary and had the charity of Jesus. But I knew what was going on. My father finally got tired of him, so that's why we're back in the basement."

"Herr Köckler never said anything to me."

"No, he does not want to be accused of giving favors to people like us." Zenzi groaned. "My mother's grandmother! She was born in 1865, and she died before I was born. I didn't even know until my father told me last year. Anyway, that's the reason, besides the Russians, he wants to go to Switzerland. He's afraid we'll be taken away. He thinks the Jews were not just sent to Poland. He thinks they were killed."

"Well, maybe the criminals, I mean the ones who did something awful. Murderers."

"No, everybody. He let it slip out one night, by accident when he was angry, and then tried to pretend he didn't remember saying anything. But that's what he thinks, I'm sure."

"Everybody? Now *you* are ridiculous."

"He listens to a radio sometimes after we go to sleep. The BBC. He hears things. I bet your father knew about it, too."

"He would have told me."

"It's too terrible. Our parents are trying to protect us. Maybe they're also ashamed."

"The British are probably lying," I said.

"Well, why were the Jews sent away in the first place? What did they do to deserve it?"

"They were moved to Poland for their protection. From the mobs."

"Who told you that?"

I looked away, knowing the answer would be ridiculed. "Herr Köckler."

"Köckler! That pig says nothing but lies. Don't be so naïve!" Zenzi's voice rose out of its whisper into a biting tone. "If only that bomb had worked!"

I winced, chastened by her rebuke, and glanced at the fisherman to see if he had heard the shouted lament. I knew, of course, what she meant, and remembered how Vati had wept and wept when he had learned on that July evening of the previous year, from the Führer's radio announcement, that Stauffenberg's bomb had not succeeded.

We watched the canal water slosh for a few minutes. The body floated past us and Zenzi covered her eyes. Then she flung her head around to glare at me, seizing my wrist. "Tobias, do I look Jewish?"

"I don't think so. But it doesn't matter to me."

"My dark hair? I have some on my arms, too. Look."

I looked, and could not help but imagine other places where it might be. "Lots of people do."

"You're not afraid of me, then?"

I bunched up one eye, a miniature shrug. "Only when you try to teach me algebra."

She grinned, then went serious again. "Tobias, I would like to kiss you."

No girl had ever made such a statement to me and I felt unsteady. "Now?"

"Of course."

"But what about the bread," I stammered with idiocy.

"Do you think I'm going to take all day doing it?"

I glanced again at the fisherman jiggling his line and hoped that he would not look over, but before I had much chance to worry, Zenzi launched her wide face. Streaming all that hair, it came at me like some kind of comet. Her lips touched a spot near my right eye. A warm flush spread over my neck and, it must be admitted, my private part began to lift off. Zenzi pulled back to gauge my interest, closed her eyes, and zoomed in again. This time, feeling brazen myself, I turned so that her target became my lips. Immediately I heard and felt what I thought must be love's immense roar. I was vibrating. The fisherman was vibrating, too, jerking all over, and then I watched him topple headfirst into the canal, as if a shark had caught hold of his hook. Now the roar changed pitch, it came from somewhere above us, and I saw a bunch of greenish shapes emerge from the sun, they looked at first like birds but weren't. I grabbed Zenzi's arm, yanked her up, and together we ran across the street toward a burned-out taxi.

"The Americans?" she screamed.

"No, no, Russian!"

Above the crumbled shells of buildings across the canal a dozen planes swooped up and banked, then plunged to hammer with their cannons anything on the street. A horse exploded and two women spun and collapsed. Zenzi and I crouched behind the taxi, clutching hands. The planes—all of them green, all flashing the familiar red stars on their wings—crowded the sky, swarm after swarm. The flak guns started up, thundering *thump thump thump* very close to us from the zoo. They were firing low, shattering everything around us. We flattened ourselves onto the ground and closed our eyes.

A few minutes later, the roar was gone. The shooting stopped. Zenzi and I, nearly deafened, heard a muted human wailing. We raised our heads, checked the sky, and then sprinted home, breathless, past ponds of blood. We did not stop—forgive us—to investigate any of the terrible cries. A shift had occurred, we knew, one that put us in a panic. That regular schedule of attacks, a schedule we had relied on, would no longer apply. Somewhere out there, a greater catastrophe was pushing toward us.

In the basement we were met by anger. Zenzi's mother yelled and yelled, straining her voice. The muscles on her thin neck stood out like rope. We should have been home an hour ago! Where had we gone! We forgot to get the bread! Everyone else was bringing home fresh loaves! Herr Fuchs tried to calm her, explaining the attack. "We should be thankful they are alive."

"Why didn't they get the bread?"

Even old man Buchwald, always ready to pour forth invective himself, seemed perplexed by the mother's behavior. Frau Fuchs spent the rest of the day sobbing, despite her husband's whispers and the cradling of her head. Zenzi said matter-of-factly to me, "She is falling apart."

Around dusk, Herr Fuchs asked me about the planes. He chose a time when Zenzi had gone to use the toilet, a bucket we kept in a tiny storage space off the main corridor. "You're certain they were Russian?"

"Yes," I said. "I saw the markings. They came from the east, too. Sturmoviks, I think."

"Barbaric." He stared at the pipe in his hand. "They're closer than any of us want to believe." Now he looked at the old man, who snored with a grotesque noise and leaned on his plump and silent wife. "He's correct about what happens after the battles. The Russians are raping entire towns. It doesn't even matter what age. Someone who fled from Graudenz told me the most horrific story, every female in the household, even the grandmother...no word to Zenzi about this, please. She's a sensitive girl."

He seemed to have forgotten that I was younger than his daughter. Probably she knew more about rape than I did. But the thought of such indecency, added to the fresh vision of those planes and their killing, was twisting up my gut. "We will counter-attack," I said, raising a fist. "We have special bombs in the factories now. They just have to get them to the front. Then we will flatten those bastards."

My curse had emerged like a belch, and I was embarrassed at having said it in front of Herr Fuchs. But he did not seem to have heard me. He was pointing to a map of Berlin and the surrounding area.

"It's simple algebra, Tobias, a classical problem. If the Russians begin here"—he touched a spot east of Berlin—"and advance at X kilometers per hour, and we try to leave the city, here, at Y kilometers per hour, how long do we have before we are overtaken?"

"We won't let them," I insisted, but my tone was not so forceful as before.

"I'm sure we'll put up a fight. But I'm afraid it will only delay what's inevitable. If we leave soon, I think we might have a chance, even just on foot."

Herr Fuchs continued to study that map, leaning over candlelit Berlin, the roads and parks and waterways in a soft glow, calm and ordered and neatly colored, all without rubble, all pristine. Well into the night he traced and measured routes, scribbled numbers, sighed and mumbled. Next to him, his wife slept, jerking every so often in a spasm. Zenzi, having avoided any mention of what we had seen after the raid, retreated to her mattress to read a book of poetry, then fell asleep herself. On my bed, I remained awake, unsettled. My skull was a stewpot, its contents a steaming mix: Zenzi's kiss and the dying Jews and the fearful Fuchses (Mischlinge!) and the invading Russians and the poor zoo animals and the Allied bombers and fits of wrath that made my eyes ache, and so I tried to concentrate on that kiss, remembering the joy of it, and hoping that I might soon feel another before the city disappeared, before it became only a memory on a map.

3

The rising of the sun brought enormous hunger. The bread Zenzi and I had not picked up was supposed to have thickened last night's watery soup, so now we suffered for our mistake. From my hollow belly, the sharpest of pains knifed up and down, into my ribs and bowels. A boy's appetite, if you have forgotten, is voracious, it is all consuming. I could think of nothing else but Pfannkuchen and the red raspberry jelly oozing into my mouth and I was about to run into the street to search for a bakery, I would run blocks and blocks to find one, when a booming knock shook the cellar door. I thought at first it was gunfire.

"Open up!" sounded the voice on the other side. "Berlin Defense Force!"

Herr Fuchs rose to let in a large uniformed man who wore a helmet and carried a rifle, not as a soldier would, but like a crutch. He stood in the doorway to our dim room, shadowed, his features vague.

"Gentlemen, ladies, children of all ages, I request your immediate and unwavering attention! I speak for the Berlin Defense Force! Yesterday's attack by the Mongol planes, an immoral and cowardly attack upon innocent civilians, was the surest sign yet that the Bolsheviks want to destroy Germany, want to kill every last citizen of our country, to forever eliminate our culture and our heritage. They will stop at nothing! Their methods are medieval! Their morals are those of the Neanderthal! They are brutes, the lowest form of creatures put on earth by God! Gentlemen, ladies, children of all ages, I ask you to defend Germany, defend Berlin, with all your might, against this terrible evil!"

The style and the voice I recognized—this was Otto Köckler, former student of theology, and my former superior. I felt instant shame at never having returned to explain to him my absence and my circumstances, so I hunkered down and hoped that he would not notice me in the shadows.

"You are right, they must be stopped!" shouted Herr Buchwald in response, waving his bandaged hand like a flag. "Animals! Disgusting animals! Rats and mongrel dogs! Fight their brutality with our own brutality!"

Otto Köckler, taken aback by this outburst, shifted the rifle to his other hand, cleared his throat, and continued:

"If any one of you here has not yet joined the defense of Berlin, either because of age or health, we are encouraging you to do so now, in this hour of need. We have tasks for everyone, but we are, in particular, looking for the young and energetic."

"There's a boy sitting right here," said the old man. "He's ready to fight."

"Yes?" Otto Köckler stepped further into the room. "Where is he?"

I could not flee, I could no longer hide. Without rising, I said, "I am here, Herr Köckler."

"Who is that?"

"Tobias Koertig."

"The same one? Ah, yes, I see. So it is. Koertig." He banged the stock of his rifle on the floor. "And how do you explain yourself? Leaving your post without permission. Dereliction of duty! It is lucky you weren't a soldier, you would have been hanged as an example."

Herr Fuchs now stood, waving his arms. "With all due respect, he is just a boy."

"But a boy," Otto Köckler answered, "who had certain duties, official duties, and abandoned them. Are you his father? The damnable light in here! I can't see a thing. Why did you allow this to happen?"

"No," I began, "my father—"

"His father," Herr Fuchs said, "was killed in an air raid. Hours later, his mother was shot to death by the police, who mistook the distraught woman for a looter. Tobias himself was almost killed yesterday by those planes. He's experienced enough tragedy. There is no need to bother this boy."

"Ah, I recognize you now, too, Fuchs." He turned back to me, using the familiar *du*. His voice lowered several pitches. "Well, you have certainly suffered. The grief is difficult, it pierces deeply, yet we must try to remain strong. Now is the time for action. Set aside your sorrows, for the fate of the nation is at stake. Avenge the deaths of your parents!" His voice rose, vibrating. "Avenge yesterday's terror! Take up arms! Join the defense of Berlin!"

"Tobias, you are too young," Herr Fuchs said. "There is no sense in it."

"No sense?" Otto Köckler pointed an accusing finger. "And what are you doing for the Reich?"

"I am on light work, rubble clearance. My wife is quite ill, and I have lumbago myself."

"You have the signed exemption, then?"

"Do you think I am lying? Do you think my interests in the welfare of Germany are any less than yours?" He had plucked a slip of paper from his pocket and now held it up. "There is your exemption."

"Then why do you try to prevent a boy from joining this great moral fight? Some might call that treasonous."

"That's absurd."

"Be careful with your remarks, Fuchs. Your stature among us is low."

Zenzi, stroking Einbrecher's fur, shouted from her spot near her mother, "Why are we trying to defend Berlin when Goebbels tells us we will push the Russians back across the Oder?"

"Don't be insolent, young lady."

"Let the boy join!" bellowed the old man. "He's healthy, he's strong. I fought in the last war and we had boys then, too. If I were younger, I'd grab a gun myself and try to pick off those dirty Bolshevik scum. I may do it yet."

Otto Köckler let the mood settle, took a pause, then began again, softer: "Tobias, we do not get very many opportunities in a lifetime to accomplish great things. But here you are, at a historical threshold, able to make a profound difference. Now is your chance! Grasp it! Help ensure our victory! There is nothing more important. You are young, it is true. But you will become a man very soon."

His words, it must be admitted, were having an effect on me, an effect made stronger by my lightheaded, Pfannkuchen-craving state. Bright visions came to me. Might I become another Michael Wittmann, war hero, recipient of the Knight's Cross and the Oak Leaves? Might I, too, perch in the turret of my massive tank and destroy the Russian armor? Surely Vati, looking down from his seat in the cosmos, would applaud my effort in helping stop the

Bolshevik invasion, which could, as Herr Köckler said, shred German culture, shred all the art that my father had so cherished! But if my hunger was inspiring fantasy, it was also leading me to think of something much more likely, for now I remembered Otto Köckler's promise to me, over a month ago, of the youth army's provisions: rich and plentiful, bread with every meal. That was enough to tip the scale, for my stomach had taken all it could bear. Your judgement may be harsh, but I stood, and with a tone I intended to be resolute but that emerged with a shaky sound, I said, "I will join."

"You have chosen the right path, my boy. You will report at ten o'clock to the Reichssportfeld."

"Today? This morning?"

"Yes, yes, there is no time to lose. Ten o'clock sharp. Do not be late. God be with you." Before marching off, Herr Köckler saluted with a triumphant flourish, mostly intended, I think, for Herr Fuchs.

Soon after, Herr Fuchs and the old man argued about my decision while Zenzi glanced at me now and then, saying nothing. She was tending to her mother, who was weeping again. The Sportfeld was almost nine kilometers to the west, and because I needed to walk—the trains and trolleys were too unreliable anymore—I did not have much time before I had to leave. The old man gripped my arm and gave me a blunt farewell, urging me to kill as many Russians as I could. Herr Fuchs, despite his disapproval, offered a bowl of the cold, leftover soup to fortify me for the trek, muttering a resigned "good luck." My cramps subsided. I felt less wobbly. Had I really meant to tell Herr Köckler that I would join? If I had not been so hungry, if we had picked up that bread instead of going to the zoo...but I did not know what to think. I wrapped myself in the post-office jacket. I stood in the doorway and waved to Zenzi as if I were going out for nothing but a chore. Finally she rose and shuffled over, then indicated that she wanted to speak to me outside. We went up the steps in silence. She had not put on a coat and she shivered in the morning chill, her hair not yet brushed, all splayed out like anxious thoughts.

"I don't want you to go," she said.

"Well, I said I would and now I have to do it."

"That doesn't mean anything. Herr Köckler is a pig."

"They could hang me now if I didn't show up."

"But you can come with us to Switzerland."

"I would feel too ashamed."

"Of what?"

"Of running away. Of being a coward. The British killed my parents and the Russians are doing terrible things to women and girls. Don't you think I have to fight?"

"Tobias, hold my hand."

I let hers come to mine. The warmth of her fingers gave me an ache at the bottom of my throat.

"Where will they send you?" she asked.

"I don't know. Somewhere out there." I pointed in the direction of the sun, where smoke spiraled upward, a fire not yet extinguished. "I guess they have to train me first."

"Tell them you're a cook. You can avoid the front lines."

"I've never cooked anything."

"You need to develop an imagination."

"Well, I better go," I said, withdrawing my hand.

Zenzi's mouth darted in like a swooping bird and she brushed her dry lips against mine, testing my response, then came back and held them there a little longer while those 75mm shells mashed up against my collarbone. "I don't know if I will see you again," she said.

"I promise to come back."

"But we might not be here."

"We'll write each other."

She gave me a quick nod with glossy eyes. "This is for you," she said, thrusting a small envelope at me. "Read it later." She disappeared back into the basement and I began, glumly, my walk to the Sportfeld. I would soon be a soldier, and everything would change once again.

4

There were blood tests and inoculations, an inspection of tongue and feet, a quick Prussian-style haircut, and a bowl of pea soup with a piece (though stale) of that promised bread, and then with dozens of other boys I stood on a playing field, where we had assembled for an appearance by Reichsjugendführer Artur Axmann, who ran the youth army. Resembling a salesman with his doughy face and thin lips, he stood behind the microphone and signaled for quiet, waving his stiff wooden arm, a replacement for the one he lost on the Eastern Front. A rumor went around that sometimes, to entertain his troops, he removed the arm and pretended it was trying to strangle him. Disappointing us, on this day he only gave a short speech with the usual encouragement and then led us to repeat several high-flown phrases in which we swore a sacred oath to the Reich.

We did not exactly return the seriousness. A giant group of boys is always prone to goofing around, and this one was no different. I witnessed plenty of laughter, jokes about the Mongols, and several minor pranks, such as the theft of hats and shoes. It felt like school again, and under the warming sun, my own mood had shifted toward some degree of happiness, helped of course by that pea soup. Even later, when we were shown newsreels intended to stoke hatred of the enemy, the lightheartedness continued. The projector clattered behind us, displaying bleak winter scenes of nothing but bodies, black, with peeling skin—women and children, the film's droning narrator informed us, killed and set aflame by the Russians. Obediently I cringed, but Klotz and Ryneck snickered, wondering in whispers if a frozen corpse might break in half if you dropped it.

That evening, our initiation concluded with a bonfire. Wearing new, baggy uniforms—a mix of styles collected from just about everywhere—we threw our civilian clothes into the flames. A bulky boy named Schwerdtfeger, draped in a giant Luftwaffe jacket, made us all realize what we had left behind. He started weeping about family photos, which were nothing but ashes now, for he'd forgotten to remove them from his old pants.

I had remembered myself to hang on to Zenzi's letter, and read it that evening in the crowded barracks. Another ode from her rabbit, I figured. No, Zenzi had written just a single line she said came from Schiller: *Kein Kaiser hat dem Herzen vorzuschreiben* (No emperor can dictate to the heart). Not understanding exactly what she meant, I tore up the paper, worried that it might get me in trouble. Then regret gripped my throat—I had destroyed the only thing that connected me to the only girl who had ever kissed me with real interest. I managed to find the ragged scrap that held "Herzen" and put it in my pocket.

The next morning, a pimply narrow-faced Kameradschaftsführer, no older than 17 and having a crazy look—his glassy eyes were off center, the tip of his nose was purple and sore—took charge of us. His name was Werner Fenzel.

After an endless lesson in saluting, he marched us around a field in an irritating mist. Our ill-fitting uniforms made it difficult to feel proud. I did not have a belt and the cuffs of my pants kept sliding down under my muddy heels. Schwerdtfeger wore boots two sizes too small, he was in agony with moaning, and Ducke could not endure the heavy cloth of a winter uniform and collapsed. Our field caps kept falling off because they were far too large, and picking them up made us get out of step, which brought Fenzel to scream things. Each time he did he wiped that purple nose, as he was very allergic (I learned later) to spring air. Finally, Fenzel arranged us in two parallel rows, facing each other. He explained the line-up:

"This is the first in a series of battle tests. Those of you who show a warrior's spirit will earn the honor of sending bullets up Bolshevik assholes! Those who show weakness will be dismissed and sent into trench-digging brigades, and given only a spoon! A spoon! Ha ha! I will demonstrate our first exercise with Ducke." Fair-haired Ducke was still drained of color from his faint. "On my command, soldiers will slap the man opposite. Slap with all your might! Ducke, straighten your back and look me in the eye."

I could see that Ducke was trembling and swaying, not really comprehending.

"A Russian soldier is advancing on you, " Fenzel continued. "Defend your country! Strike him!"

Ducke did not raise his hand, did not flinch, did not even make an attempt. Fenzel's big paw met Ducke's jaw with such force it lifted the boy off the ground, as if he was making a tricky reverse dive off a pier, and sent him sailing into the mud. He gasped when he landed, then lay on his side, twisted, not moving. The rest of us looked at him in terror, for we thought he was dead. The mist beaded on the enflamed and bloodied cheek. But then he started to wail incomprehensible things, which sent Fenzel into a rage.

Sneezing over and over in a machine-gun way, his pimples nearly bursting, the Kameradschaftsführer screamed so hard his voice cracked, "You are a pansy, Ducke—*ehzhoo!*—you are a Weichling, you are a little girl!" *Ehzhoo, eh ehzhoo!* "Get up and report to the barracks. You are not even worthy of digging trenches! You will sweep up the remains of civilians!"

Ducke staggered away sobbing and dripping mud. His disgrace filled me with fear. It was now our turn to receive a similar blow. The boy who stood opposite me, Albrecht Stalla, was a brawny 14-year-old with reddish hair, lips the color of blood, long arms, ears that stuck out like butterfly wings, and the full whiskers of a man. I would have to be quick if I was going to strike him at all. He grinned at me just before Fenzel gave the order, and sure enough, I barely managed to touch him, while his hand sent me reeling into the slime. Determined not to be like Ducke, I leaped back up, as did most other boys, even though my skin felt numb. Stalla shook my hand, apologizing in a whisper. Fenzel, alert to such things, overheard him and shouted: "When I give an order, you do not question it, you carry it out with lightning speed, and you never regret doing so! Each boy will now slap Stalla. If I see any of you not giving it the full force, you will be assigned to clean out the latrines of Bolshevik prisoners, to shovel Russian shit, day and night!"

By the end of his punishment, Stalla's face was a mangled piece of fruit, torn and leaking juice. Yet he still managed to give me a grin. Over a lunch of tasteless stew, Stalla told me the slaps were nothing compared to what his father gave him. "I joined up to get away from the arschloch. I'd rather meet the fucking Russians than see him again." Tipping the bowl to his mouth, Stalla sucked down the last of his brown glop. "You better finish yours. You've got the bones of a chicken. You couldn't throw a grenade three meters, I bet."

I tried to copy his sloppy manner of eating. "Where do you think they'll send us?"

"Somewhere near the Oder, right in the middle of it."

"How far is that?"

"How far? You don't know? Look at a map! Only sixty kilometers! They're on our ass!" He grinned again. "I'm looking forward to it, you know why? Farm girls! Hundreds of them up that way, big boobs, asses like fresh steaming rolls. They're wild about soldiers." Stalla, permit me to explain, was constantly imagining sex. He had already bragged to me of his semen production, claiming he had so much of it that he was forced to relieve the pressure four times a day, in one way or another. "I've got somebody right here in Berlin, an old maid except she's got a nice figure, lives in a place that hasn't been hit, has money and serves me real coffee. But farm girls are another thing. Hey, what are you writing there?" He looked over at a scrap of youth army stationary we'd been given for a letter home. I had been meaning to reply to Zenzi's note, but could not figure out how to begin, and so with an absent mind I had instead sketched a screaming Fenzel, his giant nose pouring out a river of snot. "That's pretty good. How did you learn?"

"A few lessons and a lot of practice."

"My only talent is cards. Schnapsen."

"I don't know it."

"I'll teach you sometime and we'll play for money. I can beat anyone. Except my mother. What a laugh, every time she wins, she shouts, 'Marmelade!' Something she learned as a kid. A funny old bird." Stalla shrugged, staring at the floor, and then, oddly, shrugged again. "She begged me not to join up. What about yours?"

"She's dead. My father, too."

"Well, at least you don't have to write them letters. It makes me crazy to try." He went back to studying my picture of Fenzel. "You better hide it or he'll hang you. What else can you draw?"

"Anything," I said.

"Girls?"

"Of course."

"I mean naked."

I nodded, though with little confidence.

Stalla squinted one eye. "I bet you've never seen one in the flesh."

"Of course I have. Twice." But I was not really giving the truth. On a schoolyard afternoon, a fierce wind had torn off Johanna Sauerbruch's skirt, revealing blue knickers and a thread or two of private hair. And in the summer of '41, wearing a frogman's mask—a gift from Vati to keep my attention away from our invasion of Russia—I was swimming to the bottom of the pool when Trudi Hellriegel clumsily dived and then struggled underwater to stuff her small white breasts, as pale as vanilla ice cream, back into her suit. I did not describe any of this to Stalla, but he shouted "Twice!" and laughed so hard that he began to wheeze. "Stick with me, Koertig, and I'll make sure you see what a girl's got underneath her dress."

Over the next week, the air raids came at their usual times, and though our area did not receive too much damage, I worried about Zenzi. I had sent her a few letters through the Feldpost—amusing pictures I had drawn of camp life—but I didn't know if they'd been delivered, for I'd heard that the censors had become quite strict. Nothing had come from her. Had she and her parents already left for Switzerland? I hoped to see her once again before we left Berlin, but we were not allowed to leave the camp even for a few hours. A rumor went around that we'd soon be at the Oder.

In fact, our training was becoming rushed, herky-jerky, one thing and the next. Fenzel had grown more agitated, he waved his arms like the city's traffic directors. He shouted and we obeyed. We crawled under rusted barbed wire. We stabbed pieces of rubber with knives. We simulated artillery by beating on each other's ill-fitting helmets with wooden clubs. We watched a demonstration of the portable Panzerfaust, cheering when Fenzel fired its missile at an old target-practice tank, blowing off the turret and sending a dummy commander, dressed in Soviet colors, spinning into the air.

One morning, with wild impatience, Fenzel ordered everyone to line up, stand at attention, and perform fifty synchronized salutes in a row with the familiar stiff arm at forty-five degrees, each time shouting our *Heils*. "Raise them high, do not let them tremble! Ryneck, straighten your elbow! Tuck the thumb under, Jansen, you moron! Do it again! And again!" He nodded his approval, his glassy lizard eyes flicking left and right. "A guest is arriving soon, SS-Hauptscharführer Drost. He will give a lesson in shooting. When you see me salute him, you will do the same, just as we learned now, all together with precision!"

A short time later, a Kubelwagen with a bulged hood resembling a pig's nose—an alteration made to accommodate a wood-gas engine, for gasoline was scarce anymore—roared and lurched across the field, and then stopped before us. Out came nubby-chinned Hauptscharführer Drost in a spotless, just-pressed gray uniform trimmed with a Göring-sized array of ornaments. He had a slight build with narrow shoulders and perhaps to compensate for this apparent weakness he strode toward us swinging his arms and kicking up a pair of silver-tipped boots, like a man shooing away a dog.

Nervous, we eyed Fenzel, and as soon as his hand flicked up for the salute, we raised our arms with crispness, we were perfectly synchronized. However, there had been a slight misunderstanding. One of the boys, earnest Horlitz, assumed that Fenzel had meant us to repeat what we had done for him, which was to salute many times over. So Horlitz, permit me to explain, raised his arm again, and the rest of us, afraid of making a mistake, lifted ours, too. Not just a second time, but another, and another! As we did this, saluting and saluting, shouting *Heil Heil Heil!*, looking like a dance troupe practicing a cabaret routine, Fenzel, who stood behind Drost, started to vibrate, his eyes bulged, his lips puckered, his pimples glowed red. Finally, after almost a dozen salutes, our arms grew tired, we lost confidence and came to a rest. Fenzel by this point was a stalk of quivering rhubarb. Drost glanced at him, then at us, to determine whether we had mocked or honored him. Unable to come to a conclusion, because all of us, including Fenzel, remained silent, Drost plunged into his lecture.

"Good morning, soldiers of the Reich. I am here to demonstrate to you the power of a bullet." He pulled a brass pellet from his pocket and held it between two fingers, where I could see the gleaming silver of his SS ring. "It is small but lethal. A single, well-placed bullet is enough to kill a man. A single one! I cannot emphasize this enough. A wasted bullet is a wasted chance to destroy the enemy. Always fire with accuracy, never do so until the enemy has come within the prescribed range of your weapon, whether it is a pistol or a tank! This will require courage and determination. Is this understood? Use your ammunition wisely." He now brought out a pistol from his holster. "Here you see a Walther PPK. Very simple and effective. It will kill a man just as well as a machine gun, just as well as the biggest bomb. Now, let me ask you, who among you has ever hunted rabbits or birds?"

A number of the other boys, including Stalla, lifted their hands, and I felt both jealous and ashamed. I had never touched a gun in my life. I had not killed anything except bugs! Stalla would laugh at me again.

"Well, it so happens," Hauptscharführer Drost continued, "that we have an animal for our demonstration this morning. An animal we call a rat! Which soldier would like to shoot our rat using my Walther PPK?"

Even though I had a fondness for animals, I had never liked rodents and I was also eager to impress Stalla, so before any other boy made his interest known, I spoke loudly, without hesitation: "I will shoot the rat!"

"What is your name?" Drost demanded.

"Koertig! Tobias Koertig!"

"Step forward, Koertig." He examined me, up and down. "You did not indicate your past experience with killing."

"No, Herr Hauptscharführer."

"But you wish to make the attempt now?"

"I am very capable!"

"Exactly the sort of enthusiasm I wish to see. Let us demonstrate the weapon."

Drost cocked the pistol and held it out, extending his arm toward the other half of the field. "You must relax your shoulders and your spine when you fire. Use only the tip of your finger to pull the trigger, since this gives you greater control. Now brace for the kickback." He fired off several rounds with little puffs of smoke like those from a toy, then replaced the clip. "You, Koertig, will do the same."

I took the pistol with a shaky hand and under his guidance popped off a few rounds—*pok-pok-pok*—feeling more confident with each one.

"Very good," Drost said. "Now you will shoot our rat."

He raised his left hand as a kind of signal, and from the Kubelwagen two other officers, of lesser rank than Drost, emerged holding an unshaven man with a bowed head, who wore shabby civilian clothes and had his wrists bound by a rope. This perplexed me a great deal, yet I assumed the scruffy man, maybe a French prisoner who had once trained animals, had the rat in his pocket.

Of course I was very wrong about this, as Drost now explained: "Soldiers, you see before you a traitor, a despicable enemy of the Reich. This man was involved in the pathetic plot to kill our beloved Führer last July, a plot that failed because our Führer was too strong for the miserable cowards who organized it, who committed the highest treason. For his crime, this man has been sentenced to death. Kneel, prisoner!"

"I am innocent!" the man said with a weak, scratchy voice as he dropped to the ground. "I was not involved. Let me live! I have two children!"

Drost stalked over to the man and kicked him sharply in the ribs, which quieted him down to a series of small moans. "There is your rat, Koertig. Aim at its head and shoot. Relax your shoulders. Remember to use the tip of your finger."

"I did not realize—"

"Position yourself, Koertig."

"I did not realize the rat was not a rat."

"Do not hesitate. The rat is a traitor. Now kill it. One shot to the head."

The Walther PPK felt like the heaviest of rocks in my hand. I shuffled over to the prisoner. He was murmuring a prayer, and when he saw me approach he pleaded in a whisper that I should spare him. This produced a dizzying effect on me. The prisoner's face became abnormally large, magnified, and I could see the individual beads of sweat on his head, the scab on his elbow, the dirt under his fingernails, the hair sprouting from his ear. He told me his daughters' names were Elke and Margret, which only made my head spin more. Hadn't there been a Margret, with a beak of a nose like the prisoner's, who once helped me, in geometry class, understand the difference between convex and concave figures? Who had even pointed out that her nose was a right triangle? I tried to lift the gun but couldn't, my arm had locked up and I felt at that moment that I wanted to run across the field, across Berlin, back to the basement and Zenzi. I would run all the way to Switzerland! The prisoner did it for me. I mean to say, there he was, sprinting away, for they had not tied his ankles together.

"Shoot him!" Drost ordered.

Panic surged through my veins, for of course I could not send a bullet into the back of a man who might be the father of a girl I once knew, but in my nervous stumbling I pulled the trigger nevertheless, aiming far to the right of the prisoner and bursting the Kubelwagen's rear tire. The recoil took the pistol from my hand, it landed in the mud, and I stood there dazed and mixed up, relieved that I had not committed murder but horrified that I had so miserably failed in front of the group. Hauptscharführer Drost marched over, I was afraid he would strike me, but he retrieved the pistol, wiped it off, and waited a few minutes until the other two officers apprehended the prisoner, who did not get far, and brought him back.

"Now watch," Drost said. "This is how you kill the enemy." He fired once, and the prisoner, kneeling again, toppled like an actor pretending to die, except that blood and other goo sprayed out from his temple. Then Drost fired the rest of the clip into the dead man's spine. *Pok-pok-pok-pok-pok.* "And that is how you treat a traitor. Take a good look at him. You will see much more of that. Fenzel!"

"Yes, Herr Hauptscharführer!"

"You are turning your boys into girls."

"Yes, Herr Hauptscharführer!"

"Damage to my vehicle will be subtracted from your pay. You will report to me immediately."

Drost marched back to the Kubelwagen, which limped off with one flat tire. The prisoner lay on the grass crumpled, the blood flowed from his head as thick as candy syrup. A moment ago he had begged me to save his life. I wobbled, feeling a little faint. If only I had spoken to him, if only he had known that I had not wanted to kill him...

But I did not have much time for regret or sorrow because after his meeting with Drost, Fenzel stormed at us, screaming so loud I could hardly understand him, and began his punishments. For our repeated salutes, all of us were ordered to collect rubble, place it in our haversacks, and run around a track until we fell over. Then Fenzel, citing my cowardice and my reckless shot, singled me out for a special task. He handed me a heavy old rifle from the previous war and ordered me to crawl with the giant thing from one end of the field to the other. In my misery all I could do was to think, over and over, that I should have listened to Herr Fuchs, I should have listened to Zenzi. Perhaps now I would be in Switzerland with them, sipping hot milk by a fire. By the time I had crossed the field's entire length, dusk had spread its gloom over me, my arms and legs were numb, my empty stomach was like a cauldron, my mouth hung open, so dry I could barely make a noise.

Now I watched Fenzel kneel before me and unfold a sheet of paper. I assumed it was some kind of official decree that stated the day and time of my execution by firing squad. But when he held it closer to my head I saw only a picture—the one I had drawn of Fenzel's nose, enormous and gushing.

"You are very talented," he said.

Through the roughness of my throat, I managed to push out a question. "Are you going to shoot me?"

"No, Koertig," Fenzel said, "it will be much more entertaining to see you die at the front."

When I finally staggered back to the barracks, my exhaustion was so complete that I did not understand, at first, the cheer that emerged from the other boys, who stood before me like a choir.

Then Stalla, grinning, presented me with a dozen pieces of bread—everyone had donated his share so that I could eat. I had won their admiration for surviving the torture. Surrounded by my comrades, buoyed by their goodwill, I stuffed that bread into my mouth as fast as I could, realizing that there was no turning back now, that there was no denying that I had become a soldier.

5

Soon after that episode, on April 13th, we heard some astonishing news. The American president, Roosevelt, had died—an event, many proclaimed with beaming joy, that all but assured our victory. Fenzel dismissed the need for such a "miracle" to win the war—"We'll do it all by ourselves, like true Germans"—then gave us an even more important announcement: we would be leaving for the front the next day.

   So it was, after a little less than two weeks of training, that we set off on a clear spring day for the nearest U-Bahn station, marching in ragged formation, in our droopy uniforms, to meet the enemy. Fenzel, determined to show off his troops, ordered us to goose-step into the train, and the pigeon-toed Paul Dohndorf, who was always tripping, accidentally kicked a woman in the shin. She cried until Fenzel gave her some cigarettes. The subway shuttled us to the zoo, where we were supposed to catch the above-ground train, the S-Bahn, and make our way beyond the city.

But at the zoo station, we discovered that our train would not be arriving for another five hours—mechanical problems with the engine as well as track damage from Russian bombs. So we were forced to sit around, hungry as always, with nothing to do except listen to Dohndorf pronounce all the station's signs in reverse, a longtime habit, he confessed. At some point the officers decided to march us to a bakery that was still operating. I sprang up, imagining Pfannkuchen, but Stalla told me, whispering, that he knew where we could get better food, not to mention entertainment, just a few blocks away.

I protested. "If we split off, Fenzel will hang us from a lamp post. He hates me, especially after finding that picture."

"But you said he wants to see you die at the front. Look, we've got five hours. They'll give us a few crumbs from that bakery and then march us right back here. Do you want to stay in this miserable station all day? Do you want to hear any more of Dohndorf's backwards crap? We'll say we were taking a piss and we didn't know where they went. We'll return in plenty of time to catch that train. Come on, I'll take you to see my old maid."

With hair and whiskers of a color that suggested fire, with those ears that stuck out and commanded your attention, Stalla possessed a certain energy, a certain confident authority that I found difficult to defy. So despite my apprehension, I agreed to this jaunt, adding a requirement: we would have to visit Zenzi, too.

We managed with little guile to slip away from the others and into the city streets. Stalla took me a little south of the zoo, to Wilmersdorf. More of the same here: smoking mounds of brick, a dead horse stripped of its flesh. The shells of burned-out buildings, like the ruins of castles, framed the gray sky with crumbling rows of window spaces. We tried to look important, keeping our helmets on, as if sent on an official errand. Few seemed to notice us. Being free of Fenzel, I felt almost jubilant. I followed Stalla to a residence that stood alone on the block, four stories all in a miracle without damage, each with a little balcony and French doors. From a pocket Stalla pulled a small jar of perfume and instructed me to dab it on my face and hands. Stalla also sprinkled a little into his pants. "She doesn't like it when you smell like a sewer."

We hurried up two dim flights of stairs and Stalla rapped on a door. We took off our helmets. A muffled voice answered and Stalla said, "Albrecht."

Now a woman stood before us, no taller than me, with brown curls and a flat oval face like a paper cut-out and teeth the size of tiny Pfefferminze that Vati used to keep in a dish.

"Oh my God, Albi," she exclaimed, kissing him on the cheek, "you really did it, you're a soldier. Look at you! Your hair! They've chopped it!"

"A little." He touched the sides and shrugged. "Tobias, this is Stefanie."

"Oh it's so sad," she said, "to see you in a uniform."

"What's the matter? We're going to send the Russians back to Moscow."

Stefanie looked at me with a half smile. This was Stalla's "old maid," she was probably in her late twenties, young but not young. I mean a tiredness clung to her. Dark-blue half moons spread below her eyes like a clown's painted marks. Still, she was elegant in a silky black dress covered in white polka-dots. She smelled of cinnamon. "So it's Tobias? And you're filled with the same kind of bravado?"

I nodded, afraid to speak.

Stalla clapped me on the shoulder. "He's shy around girls. But we've got a few hours before we go to the front and so I thought I'd bring him along."

Stefanie scowled, pushing creases all through her delicate skin. "They're not sending you outside Berlin, are they?"

"We're supposed to be waiting at the station for the train, but I wanted to see you."

Stefanie's lips, dry and cracked, closed over her small teeth, and she took a step back. "A few hours. Well, of course you must come in."

We passed through a tiny kitchen where something simmered in a pot, and then we entered a kind of parlor with lacy curtains and a fancy blue wallpaper of densely patterned leaves. Everywhere, porcelain figurines of ballerinas and horses cluttered shelves and tables. That smell of cinnamon again, stronger. We fell into red upholstered chairs. Nothing seemed to have been disturbed by the bombs.

Stefanie sat across from us, crossing her bare legs. The day had become almost warm, she had left a window partly open, the curtains fluttered in a breeze, I heard a bird go *crip-crip-crip*. "There's soup cooking," she said, "nettles and two potatoes, it should be ready soon. Some biscuits, too, and gooseberry jam. And beer." She shook a box and out fell several brown biscuits onto a silver tray. "I didn't think you would really join up."

Stalla flexed an arm. "I'm not a coward."

"Everyone tells me," she said, "that the Russians can't be stopped. They could be here in a week or two."

Stalla leaped up and mimicked a machine gun with his hands, going *ch-ch-ch-ch* and sweeping the imaginary weapon from side to side. "They won't get past *me*." He stood there grinning and Stefanie rose to kiss him again, this time on the lips.

"Let's eat the jam," she said, "and wash it down with beer." She unscrewed the lid and scooped out a greenish glob with a biscuit, and then pushed everything into her mouth at once. Stalla and I did the same, and I realized how hungry I was. When we ran out of biscuits, we used our fingers. It was only nine in the morning but we each sucked down a bottle of warm lager.

"So where are they sending you?" Stefanie asked me.

"Wherever the Russians are," I said, trying to prove that I wasn't so shy before a pretty girl.

"You don't have any guns."

I shook my head, instantly sheepish. "They'll give them to us when we get there."

Stefanie chewed, her small mouth pushing in and out, and stared beyond us at the blue wallpaper. Her eyes went liquid and blurry. "Albrecht," she said after another minute. "Your hands are sticky. Give them to me."

Stefanie clutched his fingers, shiny with the jam, and began to lick them. Her tongue, a little pink triangle, catlike, went from one to the next and she did not raise her head. Stalla kept his hands still, palms up, and looked at her with a soft expression.

Now the air-raid siren started its rising wail and I could hear the rough vibrations of an airplane engine in the distance, and then the *thud-thud* and the splintering of an explosion. I said, "The Americans," and looked at the other two. Stefanie stood before Stalla kissing his neck, and he was whispering something to her, making her giggle. "We are being bombed," I said. "Is there a cellar?"

While one of his hands gripped Stefanie's polka dots, Stalla gestured with the other toward the ceiling. "Don't worry, they never fall here. Stefanie's an angel. Here, take one of these," he said, displaying a vial the size of a large lipstick tube, "you won't be afraid of anything."

"What is it?"

"Pervitin. A vitamin. All the soldiers have it. You feel so much better."

I shook my head, but he and Stefanie each swallowed a gray tablet, then gulped their beer. Stefanie's miniature teeth gleamed with her smile. "Albrecht, my little devil."

The bombs came down, not very close, though at least one explosion made the curtains leap up like ballerinas. But I was not watching the curtains, I was gaping at Stalla, who was expertly unbuttoning that polka-dot dress. The black silk fluttered downward and Stefanie's white knickers were unhooked from her stockings and all of this also dropped around her feet in a kind of puddle. A naked, bony woman now stood before me with a boy's hips and breasts as flat as radio dials. Stalla was keeping his promise to me. My head seemed to wobble, a woozy state perhaps brought on by the beer but also by my amazement at the sight. Now Stalla turned to me and grinned before becoming naked himself. Then the two of them, giggling, singing, scampered into the bedroom, leaving the door open.

I remained near the window, smelling smoke now. The bombs had turned something into fire. I kept looking at the sky to search for any planes, but also glancing back—I could not help it—to the bed, where I could see, flashing into view, a thigh or a foot or a pale bottom. I could hear, too, breathy exclamations and the creaking of the bed springs. At one point, full of laughter, Stalla asked me to come inside their room, but I did not move, too afraid of them, too afraid of bombs.

Then the all-clear siren blared, and its noise sent Stefanie, once again inside the polka dots, rushing into the kitchen, yelling about the soup. But she informed us, with smiling relief, that it was only a little burned. She invited us to stay for lunch. Dressed again, too, Stalla fished a watch from his pocket and told Stefanie we couldn't stay too much longer because I still needed to see my girl and then we had to get back to the station.

"You shouldn't worry about the train," she said.

"It leaves in three hours," I informed her. "If we miss it, Fenzel will hang us from a lamp post with piano wire."

"Over in my neighbor's apartment," Stefanie said, "we

could find shirts and pants that would fit you."

Stalla, sniffing the soup, buttoning his trousers, shrugged. "We have everything we need."

"What I mean," Stefanie explained, "is that you could find civilian clothes."

"Why? We are soldiers."

"You don't have to be soldiers," she said.

Stalla gave her a fierce scowl. "What are you saying?"

"I don't want you getting killed."

"Who is dying? Not us."

"Albrecht, don't be foolish..."

"You want us to desert the army like cowards? Is that it?"

"Not cowards," Stefanie said with a touch of impatience. "Smart boys who enjoy life. The war is lost. Everyone sees that."

Stalla made a sneering sound, hating to be called a boy. His lips began to tremble. His face had become shiny. "Why are you saying these stupid things?"

I felt some ire of my own. "We have rockets now and other big things. Super weapons. The situation will change."

"Albrecht, both of you, listen to me. You know what happened. Stalingrad finished us. Ever since, no matter what we hear, we have been squeezed—from the east, the west, the south. From the sky. It's almost over. The German rockets are killing civilians, not armies. You are boys. You have lots of years ahead of you. Do you think these generals care what happens to you? Do you think Goebbels cares? They're tossing you into the fire. Don't go back to the station."

"So we should let the Russians march into Berlin?"

"Yes, yes, yes. Let them. Or go to the Americans. It's a matter of survival now."

"We are German," I stated. "Berlin is German."

Stalla, I could see, was tensed up, his arms like compressed springs. He was starting to stomp around. "We are not letting these murderers into our city!" he said. "Do you know how many of our people they have killed?"

"What do you think," Stefanie yelled, "we did to them?"

"They are murderers and rapists!" Stalla's lips were almost purple. His teeth were bared like an animal's. "They are criminals! I am German! I will not speak Russian!"

"I am talking about life!" Stefanie cried. "Life! It is better than lying dead in the mud!"

"Not if you are a coward."

I could see what Stalla was about to do, but I could not stop him, he seemed so taut and wild and full of danger—he gripped the handle of the soup pot and flung it at the wall the way he had thrown the practice grenades, with great force, with focused violence. The crash was like a small bomb. Porcelain figures shattered and the hot liquid with its bits of potato and strings of wet nettles splattered over the blue wallpaper. A moment of emptiness came after this, none of us spoke. A profound sadness filled my gut, for I was very sorry to know that I would not be having soup. Then Stefanie pressed both hands to her paper-cut-out face and began to sob, murmuring to us, "Please leave. Go play soldier."

On the street Stalla realized he had left his helmet in the apartment. "Fenzel will punish you if there's nothing on your head," I said, urging him to go back up. Too steamed, he just clenched his hands, still sticky with jam, and yelled about Stefanie. "Let the bombs fall on her! Let her starve to death! I don't ever want to see her again." I stood there dazed in the sunshine, wanting more than ever to see Zenzi after all that talk about lying dead in the mud.

We hurried east to Schoenburg. The sour smell of cooking gas leaking from underground sat in my throat, and we had to slosh through ankle-deep scum, for a water main had been torn open. On wooden barriers, painted signs warned of unexploded bombs. What a relief, then, to discover that the Fuchses' apartment building still stood.

I rapped on the cellar door and it was Herr Fuchs who answered. Weary-looking, unshaven, his hair long and scraggly where it still sprouted from his baldness, not sucking on his pipe, he squinted into the sunshine, not recognizing me in my helmet, and said, "If you are looking for an observation post, our apartment offers a very limited view. You are welcome to inspect it. Please be careful with the furnishings."

"It is me—Tobias Koertig."

"Yes? Yes?" He shaded his eyes. "Tobias. Ah, well, you're a soldier now."

"We are leaving for the front today."

"The front! But which?"

"Ivan," I said, trying to sound experienced.

"Ah, well." He squinted tighter and seemed to stare at my ear, lost in some thought. "I guess you'd like to say goodbye to Zenzi."

Stalla, sulking, told me he'd wait outside, so I followed Herr Fuchs down into the familiar dim room, where he called out to his daughter. It took a few seconds for my eyes to adjust. I saw the old man, silent for once, clutching his wife with his bandaged hand. He did not acknowledge me. Then I located Zenzi in the corner, a silhouette, near her mother. Sobbing came from there. I waited and waited, and no one said a thing. Finally Zenzi rose and moved toward me. "Let's go into the corridor," she said, somber. "My mother is not well. And Frau Buchwald is dying."

Outside the room, I said, "I'm getting on a train soon."

"Are you a cook?"

"I am just a regular soldier."

"But you don't have a gun."

"No," I said, embarrassed again by this fact. "Not yet. Did you get my letters?"

"No, nothing. I think the deliveries have stopped, like everything else." Zenzi glanced back to the main basement room, where the sobbing had grown louder. "At least you're going somewhere. I'm stuck here, with all this. She cries and cries. She doesn't want to eat. I'm always taking care of her and I don't have time to do anything else." Zenzi's black hair fell uncombed and knotted over her slumped shoulders. Her hands, in fists, hung low. "You look a little ridiculous in that helmet."

"It's too big for me," I stammered. I pulled at the strap under my chin and snatched it off. I moved a step closer, wanting to clutch Zenzi the way Stalla had done with Stefanie, but terrified of making the attempt. "I'm glad you didn't go to Switzerland yet."

"My father says it's too late. Now he's talking about finding the Americans."

"Wherever you end up, I'll find you. But we might win now. You heard about the American president, I guess."

"Tobias," she said and then stared at the floor.

How desperately I wanted her to demonstrate the kind of affection she had shown me before! My head began to float into that space between us, not really under my control, and my lips tried to connect with Zenzi's jaw. But they missed, touching her chilly ear, and she jerked away, slapping at my shoulder. Her glasses clattered onto the floor, and I knew this was the end, the end. She snatched them up, not looking at me, and I watched the girl, who not long ago had kissed me with great purpose, disappear into the basement, where I did not follow.

Outside, Stalla sat in the sun, morose, perched on rubble.

"Did you decide on a wedding date?" he asked with bitterness. I said nothing and we began to trudge over to the station.

Then there was a figure at my side, yelling my name, and I stopped—it was Zenzi in her bulky man's coat, breathless after having run to catch up. "Show them that you can peel a potato," she panted, dabbing a watery eye. "Stay in the kitchen and don't get shot."

I wanted to ask her when her father was going to take them to the Americans, and whether I would see her again, and I wanted to hold her one last time, but I did not have the chance, for she had scurried off, into the ruined street.

At the station, we found that our train had come and gone earlier than anyone had thought, bringing our group to the front without us. Another train, we were told, was due in an hour, so we waited with great worry as Stalla kept inventing excuses for us, each one more elaborate, that would somehow let us avoid another of Fenzel's punishments.

6

For the two hours it took to reach the first stop, Erkner—a journey of 30 kilometers made terribly slow by all the damaged track—Stalla and I mostly just stared, silent and a little dreamy, at the passing land. After the gray ruins and the gray air of Berlin, the sights on this mid-April day of trees bearing touches of green, and grass getting furry again, and a horse plowing a field with a hide that shined like bronze were no less than miracles.

But chaos greeted us at the station, where a swarm of civilians and soldiers pressed up to the train. Stalla and I elbowed our way past exhausted women clutching their children, past the brittle elderly with toothpick legs, past the screaming of officers, and headed inside to search for guidance on how to reach our unit. We did not have to look further than the lobby. There, seated on benches, were Horlitz and Dohndorf and Klotz and Schwerdtfeger, and there, above them, was the spotted knife-edge face of Fenzel and his sore nose. He spied us and in seconds we were accosted.

"Your absence was unauthorized! I could consider this desertion, punishable by death! They have beheaded men for less! Where have you been?"

Stalla uncorked one of his inventions. "Koertig was ill, he was vomiting, I think the mention of the bakery set him off, we had to find a place for him to do his business, and then we lost the group, and of course we tried to find you—"

"I don't care if you have typhoid," Fenzel said. "You stick with me. You obey my orders. Do not leave my sight. Where is your helmet, Stalla?"

"When I wasn't looking, one of the Volkssturm stole it for his soup."

"Never take it off your head! If I see anyone here removing his helmet, for soup or anything else, I will puncture his skull with a fork! As for Stalla and Koertig, they will be punished without mercy."

But the Kameradschaftsführer did not introduce us to any new tortures just yet. He seemed to be on edge, his thoughts elsewhere, probably already on the battlefield. While we waited for the next train, he paced and paced, cracked his knuckles, wiped his nose, and puffed cigarettes without pause. From this point east, the line ran with steam, but because a water tank had been hit by Russian fighters, there was another delay. I dared not ask about our next meal, and tried to lessen the sharp hunger ache by chewing on the strap of my helmet. Thankfully, a farmer offered us some spargel—white asparagus, an early crop—handing each boy a raw pale stalk. We nibbled on the pointed tips, working our way down, some even crunching the rough thick end. This lifted my spirits, and Stalla's, too, for he held the stalk in a sexual gesture. Even Fenzel ate one, attacking it with his fangs like a dog gnawing a stick.

Finally the train arrived, spouting steam and smoke, panting like some exhausted beast of burden, and soon we were chugging through dull, endless forest. While others settled into sleep, I whispered to Stalla, "The Volkssturm stole your helmet for soup!" and he flashed an impish grin. Then he leaned close and begged me to draw him some pictures of Stefanie, performing certain acts.

"I'll try," I said. "But Fenzel is watching." Our Kameradschaftsführer, refusing to sit, stood in the aisle, his glassy eyes drooping but open. "I thought you were done with her, anyway."

"We'll come back victorious and then she'll leap into my arms."

"Do you think so?"

"She loves me more than anybody she's ever known. We've had little fights before."

"I meant the war," I said.

"Are you giving up, too?"

"I'm just hungry. I would do anything for a raspberry Pfannkuchen."

Stalla tightened his hands into fists. "I should not have thrown the soup. She might not forgive me for that. I think it was that vitamin. Makes me jumpy."

"Well," I said, "you're right, when she sees us marching through the streets to celebrate the Russian surrender, she'll forget about the soup."

"Everything will be fine when we win, everything. When are those super weapons coming?"

"They're making them right now. It's only a matter of days or weeks."

"So tell me what they do."

I tried to remember what Otto Köckler had once described. Not sure if it was exactly right, I said, "There's one that has a special gas that puts the enemy to sleep but leaves German soldiers awake."

"That's good. Then we could just stomp on them with our boots. What's it called?"

I took a breath before inventing a name. "Wasserstoffmongolenschlafsäure."

Stalla, seated next to the open window, had collected cinders on his cheeks and forehead. They dotted his skin like freckles, making him look younger than he always seemed, making him look his real age of fourteen. His grin was full of that delight boys have with anything immense. "I'd love to see that stuff work!"

I wasn't sure if he believed me or not, but to preserve his grin, I tried to make my next idea even more powerful. "There's also a ray gun as big as this train, with a range of one hundred kilometers."

"Are you kidding?"

"It melts everything, tanks, towns, even a fleet of battleships!"

"Here's something I wish we had, too," Stalla said, perhaps suspecting my imagination. "A giant magnet. Just aim it, and all the Russian bullets and guns and tanks would fly over to our side!"

Jammed in next to me was Horlitz, who always wanted to be right but rarely was, and now, roused by our enthusiasm, he made his claim, too. "I've heard about a pipe full of wind that makes a hundred tornadoes and shoots them at the enemy."

Paul Dohndorf, who'd been mumbling more of his backward words, said, "It would be better to send out a fleet of armored steam rollers, Ivan would be flattened."

"Too slow!" protested pudgy Kurt Schwerdtfeger. "If we had cars that went a thousand kilometers per hour, they couldn't hit us, and we'd just shoot the Bolsheviks as we drove by."

As the train rolled through the dense green forest, our ideas began to spin from our mouths in greater wildness. The sleepers had awakened, and we all turned to face each other to hurl our inventions across the seats. We topped each weapon with a contraption even more ridiculous, we hardly let the next boy finish before offering another. We could not stop, we were caught up in a kind of whirlpool. Even the civilians, who had been slumping in their seats, now watched us with an amused fascination, some of them applauding our ingenuity.

"An ice machine that freezes men into statues!"

"A hypnotist who makes the enemy believe they're chickens!"

"A special U-boat that burrows underground and shoots torpedoes at Russian tanks!"

"An incredible glue that sticks soldiers to the ground so they can't ever walk again!"

"We'll sign an alliance with Martians!"

"No, with vampires!"

"How about a match that lights the air on fire!"

"A bomb as big as the moon that destroys the world and every human being on it!"

Gerhard Klotz, our best marksman, made this last suggestion, shrieking at the top of the frenzy, and prompting Fenzel to march down the aisle and slap Klotz's cheek. "Enough!" Fenzel screamed. "Are you in kindergarten? No, you are soldiers preparing for war! A war that is not a game! You will not speak to each other until we reach our destination! Anyone who disobeys me will be strapped naked to the front of the engine!" This last threat, which brought us dangerously close to laughter, was punctuated by an explosive, cannon-like sneeze—*ker-SCHPLOOZ!*—that sprayed several of the closest boys.

But exhaustion took hold of us, we became somber and quiet, depleted of jokes, and listened, for a long time, to the sniff and sniff and honk and sniff of the Kameradschaftsführer's allergies, and watched the vast stretch of trees march in the other direction like soldiers fleeing the front, soldiers we were replacing.

There was another change of trains at Fürstenwalde. Our new destination, north of us by a winding route, was somewhere near a place called Seelow, I had never heard of it. We left well after dusk and ran without lights. We kept our windows open so that we might hear the sounds of battle, but for hours it was just the *chug-chug-chug* of our engine. Somewhere, much later in the night, the train slowed, crawling and wheezing for what seemed like a million kilometers, and finally jerked to a stop. Not a station, but the middle of nowhere, the middle of blankness. Voices shot through the cars. Fenzel moved through the darkened aisle like a cinema usher, shining his blue light. "Everyone off! Maintain silence! No smoking! Honor your country and defeat the Bolsheviks with whatever means necessary!"

We stepped off the train into a breezy chill. The hunched and sleepy Volkssturm, who had traveled in a separate coach, were ordered into dimmed trucks, while most of the boys had to crawl onto wagons, pulled by thin, nervous horses. Stalla and I, along with Dohndorf and Klotz, settled into one filled with bitter-smelling hay. A single lantern revealed a farmer, not an officer, handling the reins, and his whispered commands to his animal gave me a moment of comfort, as if we had embarked on a magical little ride of the kind I had encountered at country fairs. We set off with gentle creaking, followed by other wagons carrying the rest of the boys and Fenzel.

Lightheaded from hunger and cold, I lay on my back, trying to sleep a little, hearing, as if in a dream, a thunderous rumble way off, and also, over and over, a weird birdlike call. Then it quit and there was nothing but the wagon's creak and the horse's clacking and Klotz's teeth chattering. Further on, my tired eyes went wide when we came around a small grove of trees and there were jagged flames rising in the distance, I could not tell how far. I thought,

We are really at the front. And then pink daylight came to the sky when a miniature sun appeared and floated down. "It is God," I said, half-believing it.

"A flare," said Stalla.

Dohndorf hissed with great drama. "Martians!"

Klotz gripped his helmet and said nothing, his teeth increasing their tempo.

The farmer brought us to his barn, where we would stay for the night. After the others arrived, we were served cooked eggs and boiled potatoes and soup with good chunks of meat, and a cup each of fresh milk, taken from the cow that stood near us. By lantern light we slopped it up in minutes. In all my days since, I have never tasted a meal so good. The farmer asked us if we wanted more and to our great disappointment, Fenzel sent him away, I wanted to kick his pimply face.

Then our Kameradschaftsführer wiped yolk from his chin and announced, "I have an urgent message!" He unfolded a sheet of paper and with a halting voice, as if reciting some required passage for school, he began to read a statement from the Führer himself, which guaranteed victory in a blood-bath of Bolsheviks and promised that anyone who retreated would be shot. "I expect nothing less than heroism from all of you!" Fenzel added. "Earn the Iron Cross! Think how proud you will be to wear it! Get all the sleep you can, because tomorrow we will proceed to our position and work all day to prepare it. I am staying outside because the hay is not good for my health. Anyone I hear talking will be stuck with a pitchfork."

I had great trouble sleeping at first, for we had no blankets and that distant thunder always made the cow moan. Then I heard the strange bird call again.

"Albrecht," I whispered. "Are you awake? What is that?"

"Yes," he answered after a while. There had been shuffling

coming from his corner, so I sort of knew what he'd been doing. "Artillery."

"No, the other one. Like a bird."

"Maybe it's one of our super weapons."

"I think you're right," I said. This possibility left me calmer and, after burrowing into the hay, I soon slipped into the solid granite of a boy's slumber.

7

The next morning, we discovered that Klotz had disappeared. Fenzel, holding a cup of porridge, dashed into the fields when he first heard the news and galloped around, yelling obscenities. "Desertion! Treason! When we find him, I'll cut off his head with a saw!" Fenzel put us on a search detail to comb the area, but we never found a thing. Dohndorf claimed Klotz had been taken by martians, insisting that the flare we saw the previous night was actually a spaceship. The conjecture intrigued me but I didn't have much time to indulge the fantasy because we were on the move again.

Furiously puffing a cigarette, Fenzel marched us double-time to a collection point and piled us into a halftrack, which clanked to our defensive position—the edge of another farm, where fields of silvery winter wheat met a small section of woods. Officers, most of them young, were directing boys and those sullen old men of the Volkssturm in the digging of trenches. In a whisper, Schwerdtfeger joked that they looked like gravediggers. Which maybe wasn't far from the truth, since there were Sankas here, too, which is what we called our field ambulances, really just trucks with grim, wounded soldiers piled in the back, all with dirty bandages. We peered at them as if on a trip to the zoo.

Fenzel led us to an ammunition truck, where we received weapons—long and heavy Italian rifles called Carcanos, not anything we'd seen before—and then pointed to the half-dug trenches near the road. "All of you, find a shovel and finish them. Dig deep. We can expect a bombardment any time now. Koertig and Stalla, you will come with me."

We followed him to a shed as fear grew in our bowels. Inside, old scythes and saws hung on the walls, and I thought, He is going to chop us up. But he pointed to two army-issue bicycles painted with greenish camouflage, each with two Panzerfausts attached to the handlebars. Ordering us to follow him, Fenzel mounted his own bicycle and with violent leg pumping he headed out into a gentle mist.

"Do you think he's forgotten about our punishment?" I said.

Stalla shrugged. "Or maybe he's taking us away to shoot us."

It turned out that Stalla's father ("a stupid man," Stalla reminded me) had never taught him how to ride a bicycle, so we both got on the same one—me pedaling, Stalla on the seat—and wobbled down the road, trying to balance the rifles, our shovels, and the fausts. We rode for a kilometer or two, just past a line of boundary trees with shiny half-grown leaves. Here, before other fields, a farmhouse and a barn sat in loneliness. Fenzel, waiting for us, shouted, "Why are you riding together?"

"The other bicycle was broken," Stalla told him.

"You must always say Herr Kameradschaftsführer!"

"Herr Kameradschaftsführer." Stalla had pronounced it as a child might.

Fenzel thrust out his arm, indicating the road. "This is the forward position. We expect the Bolsheviks to send their tanks through this area. The question is where. Koertig, tell me what you see in front of us."

I surveyed the fields. Tiny green shoots, all in a grid, were poking up carefully as if to check for Russians. "Sugar beets?"

"No!"

"Rutabagas?"

"Dirt, Koertig! The dirt is soft because of the rain, so they will not send their tanks across it. They will stay on the road. Now tell me, Stalla, where would you establish your emplacement?"

Stalla shrugged. "The trees."

"That is exactly wrong because that is exactly what they will expect. All generals know that you must always try to surprise the enemy. So instead of hiding in the obvious place, you will be lying in a trench near the road, you will destroy their tanks when they drive past. Just as Hauptscharführer Drost instructed, you must hold your fire until they are very close. That area," Fenzel said, sweeping a hand toward the middle of all those tiny shoots, "that is where you will dig the trench."

Stalla wiped mist off his face, squinted, and turned to look back from where we had come. "Don't you think it would be better, at least, to dig it further back, *near* the trees? That way they wouldn't be able to see us. Herr Kameradschaftsführer."

Fenzel sliced his arm through the air several times, as if he were trying to shake off a mosquito. "What you believe does not matter because you will obey my orders! You will dig where I say! I will not tolerate any more insubordination!" He stomped on his pedals and began to move off when he abruptly stopped and yelled once more: "Do not think of disappearing again. In front of you are the Bolsheviks. And behind you is execution. Because if I see either of you retreat from this position, I will have you shot. Shot full of holes!" Fenzel rode away, his stick-like figure dissolving in the mist.

"Well, at least he did not kill us," I said.

"No, he wants us to die here, in the forward position. But we'll get our revenge."

"How?"

"We will survive." He snickered and gave me a mock salute. "Maybe we'll both be heroes, too."

There it was again, Stalla's confidence, flaming up like a lighted match head, brightening my mood. Improbably, Stalla's joking prediction turned out to be pretty accurate, in a manner of speaking. Stalla! Stalla! Let me take a moment to thank this big-eared, sex-crazed kid for my existence beyond the war, and much more. Let me repeat his name with love—Albrecht Stalla!—a tribute to a friendship I have never found again.

While we dug the trench, throwing the dirt for almost two hours, my thoughts drifted to Berlin, where I imagined that I knew what Zenzi was doing at certain moments—forming a particular word in her mouth or writing the answer for an algebraic equation or pushing up her glasses onto her nose—as if we were connected by telepathic powers, the kind I'd seen in comic books. I would write her a long letter, I decided, when we had finished our duties.

The work was exhausting but in the end we were proud of our sculpted hole. Stalla even tore off a board from the barn and put it along the bottom for a runner, so we would not get our feet muddy. Resting, admiring our accomplishment, listening again to the distant thunder, we realized how overwhelming our thirst and hunger had become. We had forgotten to fill our canteens and in our haversacks we'd brought nothing to eat.

"That bastard is going to starve us to death," I said. "Let's signal them." We moved to the treeline but discovered that the rise in the land obscured all but the tops of our unit's trucks. We could not see them, and they could not see us.

Stalla picked up his Carcano. "We'll get their attention this way." He pulled the clip from his pocket and examined the bolt. "It probably goes in like this. Yes, that looks right. Now where do you think the safety is? That little piece near the end?" He pushed and turned a metal ring, then brought the rifle up at an angle and fired. *Crack!* We waited for a sign that they'd heard us. The mist collected on the tips of our noses. Nothing came.

Stalla now fired three shots, smoothly pulling the bolt each time. We waited again, and after a couple minutes, we got a response: an explosion. It sent us cowering, for amid the green shoots a hundred yards away, a shell had landed, sending up a cloud of mud. And then another, a little closer.

"The Russian bombardment!" I screamed.

"No no," Stalla answered, "it's coming from our side. Mortars. Fenzel is trying to kill us. What an arschloch!"

Two more shells landed in the trees. Branches spun toward us.

"Run to the house!" Stalla said.

"He'll shoot us if we retreat!"

"It's not backwards, it's sideways."

We sprinted across the road, through another muddy field, and tumbled into the house. We crawled to the windows and peered out as another few shells came down. And then the sky became quiet again, except for that far-away thunder.

We hurried through the empty rooms, hoping to find food. But they were bare except for drooping picture wire, a few dull magazines, and charred logs in the fireplace. Outside, a small shack built over bare ground was empty, too. The barn held only farming equipment. Behind it we found a pump and after vigorous work we got some clear cold water from the well and stuck our mouths under the spout. But our bellies still ached and we wandered around, moping, wondering if we could eat those green shoots or even the raw wheat. Then Stalla returned to that shack because he remembered seeing something in there: a trapdoor in the ground. Making happy exclamations he did not explain, he yanked on the handle. The door flew open to reveal a dark hole and a set of wooden steps. We were overwhelmed with a terrible stench, it rose like an invisible troll. There was no doubt: human death, human rot.

We recoiled, pinching our noses. "Who could it be," I said.

Stalla shrugged. "I'm going inside."

The odor filled me, top to bottom. My stomach couldn't take it and I tried to expel the gagging sweetness, heaving up bile. I lay there miserable. "But why?"

"There could be vegetables in there."

"What do you mean? That's human stink."

"I think it's a root cellar. I saw one in Austria once. Same kind of shack and door."

I stayed back while Stalla, squeezing his nose and holding his breath, descended the steps and disappeared into darkness. He emerged a few minutes later clutching a jar and a potato. "Two down there. Civilians, I think. Very dead. Let's see what's in the jar." He unscrewed the lid and sniffed. "Pickled beets. Koertig, we are going to have a feast. Lots more where these came from."

Through the shack's open door, I noticed someone on a bicycle coming down the road. "Fenzel!" I said. "Hide everything and close it up, we can't let him know, he'll take it all for himself."

We ran to the trench, but it was Dohndorf. He dismounted, carrying a small pot, and tried to give us an announcement:

"On the orders of Kameradschaftsführer Werner Fenzel, the scoundrels Koertig and Stalla will receive rations...no, no, will receive reduced rations as punishment for...for...Scheisse! I have forgotten exactly how he wanted me to say it...well, here is your dinner. I tried not to spill it. A little soup, but no bread, he ordered."

I looked at Stalla and gave him a small grin.

"Also," Dohndorf added, "I just remembered, Leznef wants a report about the shooting."

"Who's that," I asked, "a Bolshevik?"

"I'm sorry, I'm doing it again," Dohndorf admitted. "Fenzel."

"If he hears that," Stalla said, "he'll do the same to you, put your face where your ass is. Anyway, it was us. We thought we saw Russians, but they turned out to be wild boar. Who was trying to kill us with the mortar?"

"A nervous guy from the Volkssturm." Dohndorf scowled, considering our trench. "Why did you put it here? Anybody can see you."

"Fenzel's orders," I said. "He wants us killed."

Dohndorf scanned the fields. "You saw boar? Horlitz said one chased him while he was collecting wood. I wouldn't mind getting a look myself. Big tusks, right?"

"As long as your arm," Stalla said, smirking. "Keep your rifle ready."

"They haven't showed us how to shoot it yet."

"Any reports about the Russians?" I asked.

Dohndorf shrugged. "Nobody tells me anything."

After Dohndorf had gone, Stalla descended again into the root cellar's stench and retrieved several more jars of beets and carrots. We dug a shallow hole, started a fire inside it with hay from the barn and Stalla's lighter, and roasted everything to a blackened sweetness. Inside the house, we stuffed ourselves until we could hardly move. As dusk settled around us like a gas, we lay on the floor listening to the thunder in the east, but my mind came back to that terrible odor.

"Why do you think they died?" I said.

"Who?"

"The two in the root cellar."

"Executed. Traitors or spies." Stalla belched so loudly I flinched. "Or fucking deserters who tried to hide in civilian clothes."

"Maybe they owned the farm, maybe they did it to themselves. There's been a lot of that. Or they were Jews."

"All the Jews were relocated to Poland. Good riddance."

"We used to know a lot of Jews," I said, "Painters and musicians. I never saw them hurt anybody."

"That's because they sneak around. Slithering. Thieves and assassins."

I knew that Stalla was only repeating what he had heard, just like other boys, but I became hot and troubled. "I have heard that the Jews are being killed."

"We wouldn't waste the ammunition. Probably a rumor started by the Russians. The Bolsheviks are all Jews, you know."

"The killing might be true. Zenzi told me."

"That girl who said goodbye? Why would she know?"

I took a breath, remembering my promise to Zenzi but feeling cornered, and said, "Her father heard something on the radio. They are Mischlinge."

"Part Jew?" Stalla sat up as if launched by a spring. "What have you done with her?"

"A few kisses."

"You better be prepared. Jews are supposed to be wild in the sack. If you get a chance, I mean a real chance, don't miss it, whatever you do. You'll have to tell me everything. It'll be like doing it with a leopard. Koertig, you've got to draw me some pictures of Stefanie. Ugh, I'm all riled up now!"

Just then we heard a rumbling from the road. We rushed to the window, fearing the worst. A truck, open-topped, battered, missing a front tire and riding on the bare rim. But a German truck, coming from the east and heading to our main position. A red cross was sloppily painted on its wooden slats.

"Sanka," said Stalla. Even in the dim light we could make out soldiers sprawled inside, many topped with turbans of wrapped bandages, like circus swamis.

"I wonder how far away the Bolsheviks are now," I said. Neither of us ventured to suggest the distance. I spent the rest of the evening fulfilling Stalla's earlier request, drawing pictures of Stefanie, all nude, performing certain acts.

Nothing came to our advanced position on the second day, except for Dohndorf, who glided down just after sunrise to deliver a clip each of bullets for our Italian rifles, a pot of breakfast gruel, and another message, which he tried to speak again from memory: "On the orders of Kameradschaftsführer Fenzel, the scoundrels Koertig and Stalla will conduct reconnaissance by bicycle in an easterly....Scheisse! I have forgotten again...in an easterly...well, he wants you to ride until you see the Russians, and then come back and tell us how far away they are."

We had gotten up early simply to move our frigid blood, and also because we didn't want anyone to know we had stayed in the house. Now Stalla stood, and with a threatening finger, he pointed up the road toward our position. "Why don't you ask the wounded who came through here last night?"

"All they talk about is potatoes. Fenzel thinks they're pretending to be crazy so they don't have to fight." Dohndorf shrugged, and then kicked at the dirt. "I wish *I* could do recon. Fenzel has us digging another trench. I've got blisters. I'll take my time getting back, that's for sure." He mounted his bicycle, then turned to face us with a half smile. "I almost forgot, I have letters for you." Dohndorf retrieved two fresh, clean envelopes from his pocket. "We each got one. All from girls! Schwerdtfeger's is a real beauty. By the way, did you see any boar today?"

"Not yet, Frodnhod!" I said.

Dohndorf's smile became a giant grin, which exposed a few bits of porridge clinging to his teeth. "Tell me when you do, Saibot!" Then, emboldened, he saluted with the stiff arm and spit out, "Lieh Reltih!"

Naturally we assumed that Zenzi and Stefanie had written us, figuring that the censor had put their letters in blank envelopes to hide their origin, in case the Russians intercepted them. I danced as I tore open the paper, so thrilled that I couldn't focus at first on the written words, which ran something like this:

Dear brave Soldier of the Wehrmacht:

I hope you are not bothered to receive mail from a girl you do not know! A friend of mine told me many of you out there would like a note from those of us in the cities and towns, who are helping to keep things tidy for your return. I got your address from the Labor Service, where I work with others mending clothes for children. It is a beautiful autumn day, and perhaps you are enjoying it, too, looking up at the same sun, though I know life can be hard for you sometimes. But do not worry about us, we are quite content with our sewing, and the food is not so bad, even if there is no butter. I have enclosed a picture of myself, which I hope does not disappoint you, since I have not had my hair done in many weeks.

My best wishes,
Agathe

"What a lousy trick," Stalla said and cursed Fenzel a dozen times with expressions so foul I had not heard them before. "It's from some girl who doesn't even know my name."

"Mine, too," I muttered.

"Sent in October of last year! To the Wehrmacht! I bet that unit got wiped out, so some smart guy put these in new envelopes for us. Telling me how much she likes to watch birds! And what an ugly picture, too. Rabbit teeth. And yours! She's got a figure like a pickle barrel!"

But those ordinary photographs and bland notes started me longing again for a quiet day, without the need for a rifle, and I vowed again to write Zenzi a letter, as soon as we got back from our recon duties.

Heading east over the dirt road, we set off on our single bicycle, me pedaling and Stalla on the seat again, this time with only our rifles. At first, we entered what seemed like a tunnel. The dense trees on either side, no thicker than our legs but tall, arched above us. The tiny leaves let us see only a certain distance into the tangle, and I kept imagining human shapes.

"Do the Russians move quietly," I asked, "like Indians?" I remembered someone telling me that the Führer called them redskins.

"No, they're big and dumb, they stomp around like elephants. Stop worrying, there's no one here."

We continued in silence, except for the crackle of the tires and the toylike booming and popping of a battle somewhere far ahead. I calmed down a little after we stopped to munch on pickled beets. The sun had burned away thin clouds and the light coming through the trees painted stripes everywhere. Birds chattered, celebrating springtime warmth. Stalla and I pissed on rocks, aiming at bugs we imagined as Russian soldiers, who scurried away from our mighty blasts.

In a while we came to the edge of a clearing that sloped away from us, which allowed a far, stretching view. On a distant ridge, smoke was spiraling, and a bright orange flame sprouted in the shape of a tulip. We stared without speaking as planes cut in low, knives slicing the sky. Their guns went *spack-spack-spack*, like a coin tapped nervously on a table.

"Ours?" Stalla asked, shading his eyes.

"No, Sturmoviks," I said. "We have to make our report now. How far away is all that?"

"Ten kilometers, fifteen? I don't know."

"Do you think we have a position between them and us?"

"Maybe hidden in the valley somewhere." Stalla kicked his bicycle. "Where are our Focke-Wulfs?"

We watched the attacks continue in several waves. Stalla's hands tightened into fists. Then he ducked, flattening himself into mud. "Get down, get down!"

I figured he was mocking my earlier nerves because the planes were too far away to hurt us, so I remained standing, but his voice grew more urgent. "The enemy! Close by!"

I threw myself onto my stomach and he whispered, "Something's moving, a brown lump."

"A soldier?"

"Bigger."

Terror rushed down my legs. "What should we do?"

"I want to get a better look."

Stalla crawled forward, through long strands of yellowed grass, and I lay in place, inhaling the smell of dirt, praying that we would not come under fire. In a few minutes, he was back again at my side.

"It's a horse from another world," he said.

"What do you mean?"

"It's furry. And I heard it groan, something like *gaaaaah*."

"You're making a big joke."

"Look for yourself."

The possibility that creatures from outer space had landed

led me to unlock my legs and arms, and I inched forward on my elbows until I came within sight of what Stalla had described: a beast the size of a horse slumped on the ground, its neck strangely curved and covered in brown fur, its face like a sheep's but grotesque. Yet I recognized it, and after marveling at its presence for a minute, I returned to Stalla.

"It is a camel," I said.

"Who's joking now?"

"You can see the humps on his back."

"It came all the way up from Egypt? Don't be stupid."

"Ivan is using them for transport. I remember reading about it. I think maybe he's hurt."

Wary of some Russian trick, vigilant for any sign of soldiers, we approached the animal. There, on the camel's upper leg, a gash had leaked blood, turning the fur a dark red. We noticed, too, a pack still strapped to its middle.

"Who's going to shoot it?" Stalla asked. "I don't want him kicking me when I look to see what he's carrying."

"No," I cried. "We cannot waste the ammunition. And Ivan might hear it."

"Then I'll smash its head with a rock."

"Leave him alone."

"What's the matter? That's the enemy. It's dying, anyway."

"He does not know anything about being a Bolshevik. He is just a camel."

"Then you look in that fucking pack."

I crept up to this animal I had never even seen in a zoo, only in photos and picture books. "It's all right, boy, I am not going to harm you, I just want to find out what's in here." The hair on its head stood up as straight as a clown's wig. I held out my hands as if approaching a dog, for the purpose of being sniffed. Even with the distant booming on the far hill, I could hear a raspy breath. The blood had formed a gooey mass under his shoulder, he must have settled here a while ago. "Where did you come from, you probably wanted to get away from the guns." One of his small eyes peered at me, not with fear, but with an indifferent camel misery. He groaned with a "gaaaaah." Close enough now, I unbuckled the pack and reached inside, and came up with a handful of soggy grain.

"Check the other one," Stalla said.

It was the same in there, too, except that my hand, going a little deeper, found something hard. A bottle. I lifted it like a prize, and Stalla whooped.

"It has to be vodka," he said. "Some sly Russian stuck it in there."

"I could use it on his wound...."

"Now we can make our report and have a fine time in the house. What did you say?"

"I want to wash and sterilize it." I was already pouring water from my canteen on the camel's dirty blood when Stalla rushed over to grab the vodka. We tussled for a minute or two, falling into the grass with shouts. "You can't waste that on a stupid animal!" "He's suffering!" "If he heals, he'll go back and help the Russians!" "I'll take him to our side!" "Will you teach him tricks, too? What a moron!" Stronger, heftier, Stalla ended up with the bottle, brandishing it like a club, then walked back the entire way while I rode ahead on the bicycle.

Refusing to speak to each other, Stalla and I later made the report to Dohndorf, who delivered more of the thin soup, who marveled at our discovery of the camel, repeating his wish to travel with us. "I'll see if I can talk Leznef into it," he said. "By the way, he wants all trenches to have a parapet. Get a board and cut some notches in it for the rifles. He said he will make an inspection today."

Still silent with each other, we pulled boards off the barn and with an old rusty saw we cut the requested notches. Soon after, as promised, Fenzel arrived on his bicycle. A haggard look clung to his narrow face, his eyes were pink and full of water. Between orders for more trench improvements, he wiped his inflamed nostrils with his sleeve like a child.

"And you will conduct another reconnaissance mission tomorrow morning," he told us. "I want more details, precise numbers. Those wounded louts are making all kinds of ridiculous claims." He mounted his bicycle, started to head back, then circled around to us again. "If you fill Dohndorf's head with any more fantasies about camels, I will gouge out your eyes!"

Stalla and I looked at each other, and as soon as Fenzel had advanced far enough up the road, we started cackling. Our mutual contempt for the Kameradschaftsführer had mended our rift. We settled back inside the house and feasted on pickled beets and drank a little of that vodka.

"What luck we got punished, eh?" Stalla said with more laughter. He made an obscene gesture with his hand and his groin in the direction of the main position up the road. "The rest are digging trenches and listening to that affenschwanz Fenzel while we get drunk."

"But he put us here to die."

"Look, we're not going to sit in that trench like ducks. We're going to ambush the Russians, shoot them in the ass. If only I had one of those super weapons."

"I'm not sure if they exist. Maybe just in books. I'd prefer a time machine, anyway."

"What does that do?"

"You can travel to any year you want, in the past or the future."

Stalla considered this for a moment, rubbing his whiskered

neck. "What about yesterday, or the day before?"

"Sure."

"Well, I'd go back to Stefanie's place, and I would not throw the soup."

"I'd travel to a time when I was eating Pfannkuchen with my father. And then I would convince him not to stay in the basement, so I could save him, and my mother, too, because she would not get shot."

"Koertig, if the Russians don't come this way, we'll look for some of the local girls tomorrow. There's got to be another farm around here."

"After visiting my father, I'd go into the future, and take a rocket far into space, beyond Pluto, where everything would be quiet, and I'd stay there for a month and read all my favorite books."

Stalla shrugged. "They'd probably have a war out there, too."

Just then we heard a grinding sound that we first mistook for another Sanka. But it was coming from the sky. We rushed outside to see a biplane, a green one with a Russian star, moving slowly above the house. Stalla, drunk and yelling "Die! Die!" fired his rifle, *crack, crack, crack*. The double-winged creature, which sounded like an automobile in distress, banked and circled, still without urgency.

Then, permit me to explain, a strangeness occurred, or what I thought was one, the sky around the plane began to snow with giant flakes. Even for April snow, they seemed enormous, fluttering down in a very gentle way that I found beautiful. Of course I soon realized that these flakes were paper. Several sheets had blown near the house. We ran to inspect one as if it were a prize—a picture of a pretty woman, with a shiny fresh face, standing outside in winter weather. Above her ran the words "Wet! Cold! Put Nivea cream on your skin now!" We ran to the next, this one a drawing of an infant. "Loose, fine Nivea baby powder. Dries, soothes, calms." Everywhere we found them, it was the same, magazine advertisements for those blue cans of creams and lotions, with smiling fresh-faced women or roly-poly babies. The plane and its grinding engine disappeared in the eastern clouds.

"A stupid Russian joke," said Stalla. We used some of the paper to start a fire in the pit, where we roasted potatoes. Stalla, less angry after eating, cut up a few pages into small squares to make the 20 cards needed for Schnapsen, and he taught me the game, yelling *Marmelade!* every time he took a trick. In the house, I kept one of the snowy scenes at my side while I wrote a letter to Zenzi, telling her of the camel. Stalla took one of the Nivea girls himself, but to a separate room. Later, near twilight, we darted outside to carve our declarations of love—*Albrecht und Stefanie* and *Tobias und Zenzi*—onto either side of a wide tree, returning with hands made raw by the effort.

We probably should have taken that night's silence as a warning, but instead I felt at ease: there was no booming or high-pitched whine and I thought, the Russians must have gone in a different direction, or maybe they surrendered. I slept without any tremor.

8

A squawking bird woke me before dawn—not that funny distant sound I'd heard before but a real bird and a great relief. Another day, this one with a gentle, sparkling mist, had begun without shooting. The chilled smell of moist earth, rising into the house, filled me with lusts for romping and the like. Maybe Stalla and I could go in search of farm girls, after all. I went to the window, to see if I could spot the noisome creature—*spleek! spleek!*—and as I glanced around at the land, pale in the gray light, the trees began to explode. In that first moment I wondered if it might be a logging crew. Someone had ordered the construction of a barricade. But no, not that, for an enormous kind of thunder started crashing the air. It shook my brain and vibrated my lungs. Outside, the fields had become a brown ocean, churning with waves of mud.

Stalla rushed past me with his mouth flung open, I could not hear a word of what he yelled. He motioned me with a frantic arm to leave the house, and I shook my head No, and No again, certain that any exit would be crazy, the storm outside was deadly. The booming grew so loud it turned my innards into jelly. I kneeled, and then lay flat on the floor. I tried to crawl away but there was nowhere to go, the house did not have a basement and the crashing came from everywhere. Finally Stalla yanked me upwards and dragged me outside, and we managed to skitter across those leaping waves of earth and dive into that root cellar, pulling the trap door closed.

In the stench, we huddled, shivering. All around us the ground jerked and jumped. The remaining jars of pickled things toppled into splinters. The two dead civilians fell across my legs. I pressed my hands to my ears and discovered sticky blood. My stomach was melting, it seemed, running down my trousers. Mixed into the booming was that high-pitched whine, bird-like when I'd heard it from a distance, but now like a hundred U-Bahn trains rushing past my head.

I do not know how long this lasted. But just when our breaths had run out, when we could no longer put up with the stink, the crashing ceased. We waited a minute or two, and then creaked open the trap door. The shack above us had disappeared. We sucked in air that smelled of blackness, of burning and gunpowder and freshly massacred life, and then we poured out our guts into the heaved-up earth, retch after retch until our stomachs ached as if someone had punched us there. We sat stunned. The house and barn, also obliterated, were a pile of splinters that sent up spiky flames. The line of trees, too, were cut in half and burning, and craters now surrounded us, hills and valleys of mud. Smoke rose all over like fog, shrouding the sky.

A thirst like nothing I had ever known before gripped my throat. We began to crawl toward the well. Dizziness prevented us from standing. The great ringing in my head was like a siren. Down into a crater, and then up the other side. We moved as if in a dream. I tried to talk but my voice or my ears did not work, which I could not tell. The well pump, we found, no longer existed. Cloudy brown water was puddling the gouged earth like soup in a bowl, so we cupped our hands and gulped it.

Stalla, splattered with spots of brown, said something that I could not make out. I watched his mud-covered lips repeat it and I said, "There is something wrong with my ear."

He shuffled over, shouting, "They will be coming soon, I think."

I nodded, trying to wash my pants with more scoops of water, for they reeked of my own shit. "But the road is wrecked."

"They smash everything with artillery before they attack, just like everyone says. Look, they split our tree, right down the middle."

"Which?"

"The one we carved!"

"My letter to Zenzi, too." Despair came into my nostrils with the bitter smoke. "Ashes."

"Road or no road," Stalla said, glancing around, "they'll be here. One of us can go in the woods, what's left of them, while the other stays near the fire. The smoke is a good screen. That way we can cover the field. Which one for you? God, what a headache I have."

"I'm too tired." I listened to the remains of the house crackle, and to the *pop! pop!* behind us of sap as the trees became candles. "They've killed all the birds."

"Let me see your ear." He staggered closer. "Lots of blood, but nothing stuck in there. You'll feel better in a while. I'm going to see about the weapons."

We had left our rifles and Panzerfausts in the trench in case Fenzel stopped by to inspect. Stalla made his way back across the craters, and I watched him with little interest, instead wondering where all the wild boar went when the shells started. The mist sprayed my face, and this was all that kept me awake, for I wanted so much to lie down. Stalla, who had been digging in the dirt, raised both arms to display a rifle and a faust. We still had our weapons. I stood, then fell to my knees, then got up again, lurching toward the trench.

I asked Stalla, "Do you think those boar got away?"

He shrugged.

"I hope so," I said.

"Show me your ear again." This time he tried to wipe it, then peered inside. "Maybe shrapnel flew in there and pierced your brain! What is my name!"

"Albrecht."

"Why are we here?"

I thought for a second or two. "We have come from Neptune, traveling in time."

Stalla inspected my eyes, parted his lips, then broke out laughing when I cracked a tentative smile. My brain was all right. Peering back toward the burning line of trees, and toward the cratered young wheat beyond them, Stalla asked, "Do you think anyone else is still alive?"

"We can't find out," I said, "because if they are, they will shoot us on Fenzel's orders."

"You take the woods, I'll sit near the house. How many fausts do you want?"

"I don't think I want any."

"Wake up, Koertig! Here, you take one. After you shoot, hide up in the wheat, over in that big crater, and I'll try to join you. Let's hope they don't get that far."

"Wait! I don't remember how to fire it. Or the rifle."

Stalla rushed through the procedures—"Make sure about the safeties"—and then scurried off, carrying his own weapons.

Alone in the trench, I repeated to myself what he had just shown me, as if rehearsing lines for a school play. But the ringing in my head only confused everything, my concentration kept deflating. Dearest God, these things had become incomprehensible. I picked up the rifle, which felt enormously heavy, and lifted it to my shoulder, sighting the road. Then I went through the steps to arm the Panzerfaust. I removed the warhead, dropped in the fuse, replaced the warhead, held it in the correct position, flipped up the sight, and aimed at a burning tree, making a motion as if to touch the firing lever.

What happened next, permit me to explain, must have went like this: That safety pin had been jarred loose by the bombardment, my hand had a nervous spasm, the lever went down. In any case, a giant *FWOOOOSH* roared in my bad ear, hot gas nearly incinerated my trousers, and the weapon's toilet-plunger projectile shot forward 40 meters and landed in the mud. I stood shocked, but then realized it hadn't exploded. Hoping I might stick the missile back in the tube—an impossibility, but my mind no longer contained clear thoughts—I raced across the road to fetch it. Stalla, who had crouched behind the flaming house, was frantic, waving his arms at me, upset, rightly so, about my accidental firing. I scrambled over the mud, slipping with each step. Stalla continued to wave, annoying me now with his show of disgust at my clumsiness. "Don't worry," I shouted over and over until I finally noticed what he'd been trying to make me see along the torn-up road. It was a paralyzing sight. Three Russian tanks, I recognized them as T-34s, they were advancing on us. My bad ear had not heard a thing.

Terror kept me stuck until bullets started splashing the mud around me. I leaped up and headed for the trench. But I had become so confused I could not find it. I ran this way and that, I twirled, I went in circles, I hopped across gaping holes, I tripped and toppled, and it occurred to me that Fenzel was right, Fenzel was a genius, no one could see where we had dug. I suppose if not for the up-and-down path the tanks had to traverse in those craters, I would have died right there, but the bullets were not so accurate. Finally I flopped into the trench and grabbed the rifle. Before me, those steel behemoths were advancing through a dreamy blur of mud and mist. I fumbled with the safety, of course I had forgotten how to unlock it, and when I remembered, I fired once in a great panic, hitting only dirt. Because I did not want to witness my death or my killer, I ducked down into the trench, pulled the runner board on top of me like a child covering himself with a bedsheet, and pressed my hands over my ears and squeezed my eyes shut.

It is very possible that I fainted or blacked out from fright or even fell asleep. Things rattled and banged above me. Shouts of gibberish, a scream or two, a persistent trilling of something like a bell. A flashing so bright it came through my eyelids, a little thunder, and a smell of oily smoke. At some point it felt as if someone were running across my back. Then a comfortable peace settled, like those mornings in Berlin, years before, when I would lie in our small garden, my face surrounded by plants and weeds and the buzzing bugs, when the traffic sounds would magically recede, when I imagined that I had been transported to a new planet.

"Koertig!"

The word was repeated several times before I recognized it as my name. I rose into a crouch. Dirt clung to my eyelids, my vision had to adjust. More bright flames danced nearby. Coils of black smoke twisted upward. Around me lay dead men with strange wrinkled faces and thin eyes. The voice that had spoken my name continued but the alarm ringing in my head prevented me from understanding. I nodded, over and over, so I would not be impolite, and as I did I gradually understood that I was standing before a German officer, and he was accompanied by Fenzel, except that Fenzel had changed, as he now wore a square white patch in place of a nose. The smoke, it seemed, rose from Russian tanks. The bodies were those of Russian soldiers. Fenzel appeared to be angry, he was quivering, the skin surrounding that white square had gone crimson. But the officer was shaking my hand, pleased about something. What he said, what I managed to make out, sounded like "Our twentieth boy." Then he recoiled, covering his mouth, for I think he smelled my sewer reek.

9

"Where did you live in Berlin? What were the names of your parents? What color was your dog?"

"But we did not have a dog," I said to the bespectacled doctor, after satisfying him with answers for the other questions. Behind him, a gusty wind was flapping the canvas of a field-hospital tent. An insistent ringing filled my skull.

"Very good! Now who is Field Marshal of the Luftwaffe?"

"Hermann Göring."

"His middle name?"

I could not remember and felt the sweat of panic. "Johann?"

"Wilhelm," the doctor told me. "I don't expect every boy would know that. Tell me your favorite food."

"Raspberry Pfannkuchen."

"Excellent! You seem to be lucid. Follow my finger with your eyes. Good, good. What about your hearing?"

"There's a bell in my head."

"You have a perforated ear drum. It will take some time to heal. Such a sound is normal."

"Where are we?"

"West of the front line, ten kilometers or so."

A nurse, dressed in a maid's outfit or so it seemed, attended to other patients in a row of beds. I thought I recognized Ryneck, asleep with a bloodied bandage on his chest, Ryneck who had giggled loudest at the sight of corpses in those newsreels we'd watched back in training. "Is Albrecht alive?"

"Who is that?"

"Albrecht Stalla. A friend. He is fourteen."

"I don't believe we have anyone by that name here. Nurse? Do we have a Stalla, a boy? No? Well, there is another hospital further back, in the village, he might have been sent there."

I was trying my best to absorb all this. "You are German?"

"Yes, of course—ah, I see." The doctor patted my arm. "You have suffered a mild concussion, too. Some confusion is natural. But let me be the first to congratulate you on being selected to appear before the Führer himself."

I stiffened, my heart beat wildly. "To be hanged from a lamp post?"

"Just like a hero! Joking in his hospital bed. We are very proud of you, Tobias."

I stared at the doctor's eyes behind those mild-mannered glasses, trying to detect a trick, some sinister gleam. I wondered how much he and the others knew of my cowardice, and I began to explain. "There was a lot of smoke and fire and tanks—I tried to stop them, I fired my gun, I did not have anything else to shoot, so all I could do was lie down—"

"But two tanks!"

"Two?"

"Yes, the two you destroyed helped keep the enemy from

advancing. And three enemy soldiers. You must have shot them point blank, they were lying right at the edge of your trench, according to the report I heard. What a superb soldier, and so young! I think you'll be fine for travel tomorrow, so we can have you on a train for Berlin first thing in the morning." I began to tremble—memories of the bombardment and those advancing T-34s were swirling, flashing. But the doctor continued, "Not to worry, not to worry. After he pins the Iron Cross onto your tunic, the Führer might ask you a question, and all you have to do is answer it in a straightforward way. I have met him only once, but I can assure you that he is the kindest of men in such situations."

"What Iron Cross?"

"Second Class. Quite an honor!"

I did not believe a word of this, yet I worried that my brain had been damaged, that I was not understanding anything. I was determined to find out what was happening, what they really intended to do with me. On the doctor's orders, I was supposed to move around, and on my stroll—during which two nurses flashed me wide toothy smiles, offering their bubbly congratulations, more confusion!—I encountered Fenzel. He was sitting outside, on a turned-over crate, holding a map with outstretched arms so that he could read it while keeping his head aimed skyward. This was to prevent, I quickly understood, his juices from running out the middle of his face. The square bandage covering the spot where his nose used to protrude bore a yellowish red stain in the shape of a star, which looked, I thought, like the Russian one.

"Herr Kameradschaftsführer, I wish to speak with you," I said.

"Do not bother me," Fenzel answered. His words made a bubbling sound. He continued to stare straight up at the map. "I am busy planning our defense, so that I may keep morons like you from dying."

"I would like to know about Stalla."

"You mean dead or alive? That delinquent managed to remain amongst the living. Wounded in the ass."

"Was he sent to the hospital in the village?"

"Yes. Now go back to your bed and play with yourself."

"Herr Kameradschaftsführer, am I being sent to Berlin?"

"Correct. I will no longer have to put up with your stupidity."

"For a medal?"

At first he did not answer. His hands began to tremble, and a gurgling started in his throat, and then, as if a fuse had been sizzling inside him, he exploded. "Yes! Yes! An Iron Cross for Koertig! It's ridiculous! It's insane! I tried to stop it! I tried to tell Sturmscharführer Scheidenbach that you are incompetent!" He threw down his map and grabbed my jacket's lapel, yanking me close, keeping his head turned toward the sky. "Who expertly directed fire to drive back the invaders, who directed a flanking maneuver, who cut down three soldiers himself? Kameradschaftsführer Werner Fenzel! Werner Fenzel deserves the Iron Cross! Werner Fenzel did not receive some minor injury like yours, no, he sacrificed his nose! But they do not want a soldier missing his nose to appear before the Führer. No, no! They want some little sissy with blond hair and a clean complexion, no matter how much a coward!" By this time, Fenzel had turned to face me, I mean his head, too, so that those juices—a red and yellow goo—had begun to leak down both sides of his mouth, giving him the appearance of a sad vampire. "Admit that you did not destroy those tanks, Koertig, admit that you did not kill those soldiers."

Because I hated Fenzel and did not want to allow him any victory, because he would have me court-martialed and hanged if I admitted to being a coward, I said, "A concussion prevents me from remembering."

"Get out of my sight or I'll cut out your liver with a pen knife."

Later in the day, a slovenly member of the Volkssturm with gray teeth escorted me to the train station. He plopped me in his motorcycle's sidecar and drove so slowly that I could count the rocks in the road. On the way, shouting over the engine's roar, I begged him to take me to see SS-Sturmscharführer Scheidenbach, insisting that I had urgent information that could not wait. The train was not due for another several hours, so we poked along into the village, to the former Grundeschule, where Scheidenbach had set up his desk in the middle of a classroom, painted blue and still bearing, on one wall, the letters of the alphabet.

Heavy-set, balding, Scheidenbach sat at his desk like a teacher himself and sipped tea. I explained to him, without describing my own actions, that I believed it was Albrecht Stalla who really deserved the medal.

"And did you witness this boy destroying those tanks and killing those men?"

"No," I admitted, reddening, "I was lying in the trench. There was no one else except—"

"This Stalla is a friend of yours, I assume."

"Yes, Sturmscharführer Scheidenbach."

"So you would go out of your way to protect him."

"Yes, always."

"But a boy like Stalla, with such a low moral standing, is always in need of help. And to perpetrate a lie is a very grave offense."

"I am sure he was the one who did it."

Sturmscharführer Scheidenbach gave me a half grin. "Koertig, you know as well as I do that Stalla does not have his mind on warfare. That he is in no way capable of such decisive behavior. His pornographic interests and his lascivious tendencies are overwhelming any desire he has for fighting the invasion. We found several very explicit drawings of sex acts in his pocket. Disgusting in their detail, in their depravity! He admitted to having drawn them. I will not tolerate these sorts of distractions in the front lines, so he is being dismissed, sent back to Berlin for manual labor. Reprobates, cowards, and traitors will all be removed! Let me remind you that your sworn duty to the Führer and to this great country always comes before friendship. A fine boy like yourself should not be associating with dirty specimens such as Stalla, in any case."

"Yes, Herr Sturmscharführer."

"You are the twentieth and final boy chosen for this honor, Koertig, as our Führer wanted exactly that number. His belief in numerology is strong. His belief in our victory is strong. So you will take the train to Berlin today, and you will accept the Iron Cross from the great man himself on his birthday. Comb your hair and keep your nose clean."

10

The train rattled back the way we had come only a few days before. The stations were filled with a greater clamor. Civilians were begging to come aboard, screaming and pounding on the windows until SS officers tore them away. In a coach reserved for officers, a little dizzy from my injuries, dazed by the persistent flashes in my head of Russian tanks, I slumped in my seat despondent, my sympathy for these desperate people clouded with the fear and shame and guilt that my false award had given me. I had done nothing in that battle, nothing except hide, and now I was to be decorated by the Führer! What if he discovered the truth? I knew it now myself: before we left, I had managed to convince my Volkssturm escort to take me to the other hospital. There I had found Stalla with his fuzzy red beard, standing near his bed.

"How bad?" I asked, embracing him.

"They got me in the ass," he said. "I can still walk, but can't sit down, not even to crap. I'll have to stand all the way to Berlin."

"Yes, I was told they were sending you back."

"As soon as I get discharged from here." He pointed to his nose, then gave me half a grin. "I heard Fenzel won't be sneezing anymore."

"It's true," I said. "Lost his sniffer."

We quietly laughed and then, after glancing at my escort, who was chatting to a nurse on the other side of the room, I said, "You killed those tanks."

"They never saw me because of the fire and smoke. Boom, boom! Just like we saw at the Sportfeld. Best thing I've ever done in my life. I think our Panther got the third."

"And the soldiers, too?"

"They ran right into the trench! I knew you were there so I blasted them. Easy shots in the back. One took a while to die. I let him suffer. Why waste the ammunition?"

"I ran out of bullets, so all I did was lie there," I said, embarrassed, then got to the main point, dropping my voice: "But they think *I* did all that. The Führer's going to give me the Iron Cross."

Stalla nodded.

"You know? You didn't tell them?" I asked, incredulous.

"Scheidenbach is SS, I'm not going to say anything. He found you first. He decided on you. He was in a hurry. The only one to defy him was Fenzel. He killed some Bolsheviks, too, I heard, but all he does is brag about himself. Anyway, they think I ran away because I caught a bullet in my ass and they found shit stains in my underwear. What do they expect when there's no toilet paper? At least they could give me a new pair of pants."

I looked down at the fresh ones I had been issued, and felt a new wave of shame. "I tried to tell Scheidenbach that you were the one, but he didn't believe me. Why did you say that you drew those pictures?"

"I already got you in enough trouble by dragging you to Stefanie."

"If it weren't for you, I probably would have died..."

He shrugged, then scowled at me. "You don't look so good, Koertig. You're all pale."

"My head and ear got messed up." Now I saw my escort signaling. "I have to leave, but let's make sure to find each other in Berlin."

"Tell the Führer happy birthday from Albrecht. They've got me digging ditches or something, but I'll still find a way to fight."

By the time the train stopped in Erkner, I realized my woozy state was more than just my head and ear. I had fallen ill with a fever. The old man dragged me onto the S-Bahn, this time so jammed with the fleeing masses that the oxygen inside felt diminished. Chilled to my core and queasy, I went in and out of sleep, sometimes believing that I was lying in the villa's bedroom, where my mother sat, stroking my forehead, telling me not to worry about the Russians, and urging me to drink a glass of Fanta, which always filled our pantry, for Vati loved it. I could almost taste the sweet syrup on my tongue.

Oh I am aching at the moment for those days of the villa, of Fanta and Pfannkuchen...but I will continue...

My escort and I were supposed to have arrived the night of April 19th, a day before the Führer's birthday, but electrical troubles prevented us from getting to Berlin until the morning of the 20th. I stumbled out into the city. The old man strode ahead, keeping his distance, worried that he might catch my disease, and also afraid of punishment for delivering me late. Exhausted though less dizzy, I followed him between the hills of rubble, I staggered through the snaky paths while covering my mouth to keep out the thick yellow dust. We skirted the Tiergarten and then, when I thought I couldn't take another step, we arrived in the bleak government area of the massive stone facades and thick columns, cleaved and crumbled. I stood next to boulders that lay on the vast steps.

"Here is the Chancellery," the old man informed me, and then to the guard cradling his lead-colored machine-gun he said, "He is supposed to meet the Führer."

While the guard inspected my identification, I pleaded to my escort, who smelled of wine, "I would rather go somewhere else. I don't deserve the medal. Stalla should get it."

"Everyone is nervous when they're about to meet the Führer." Searching the sky, for the air-raid siren had begun to whoop, he scurried off and I was shown through massive double doors.

Inside, I found the nineteen other boys seated at a long table, chattering away as they ate breakfast. I could make out the sounds of bombs falling—probably a small raid in the distance, as no one seemed to care. I sat down myself and soon a serving woman rolled boiled potatoes on my plate and scooped out fried herring from a can. Oily brown slivers flopped down right under my nose. Ravenous, my queasiness fading, I sucked everything down in minutes, barely conscious of the nearest boy telling me that we were supposed to meet the Führer at noon. He asked me what I had done for the medal. He himself had delivered ammunition in a wheelbarrow while under enemy fire.

The herring had given me new energy. My chills had subsided. I did not want to be a coward anymore. The salty fish oil lubricated my voice. "I destroyed three Russian tanks and shot six of their soldiers in the back."

"You're joking!"

"I did."

I recounted the story in detail, as Stalla had described it but with my own exaggerations. The boy repeated my claim to another, and my concocted heroism soon spread around the table. Questions came to me in machine-gun style, too many for me to answer. Then I asked if anyone had a pencil and paper and soon someone produced both. Giddy on my full stomach and still a little feverish, I began to draw my exploits in great detail, in the curvy style of the comic *Zig and Puce*, whose characters I had adored until Vati hid the books because they were French. There I was, with a devil's grin, with muscles in my arms like rocks, creeping through shell holes, dragging two Panzerfausts and a rifle, stalking two tanks as shells exploded nearby and flames roared in the trees. The first frames circulated, and the boys begged for more. A young glum Unteroffizier with a sneering curl to his lips, our chaperone, smoked in his boredom and ignored us, engrossed with a magazine. He wandered away and returned several times, each time with an expression of greater disdain. Finally he informed us that our meeting with the Führer had been delayed until early afternoon. So I continued happily with my comic strip. Bucktoothed Russian soldiers charged across a field, coonskins on their heads, their tongues flopped out, crying like clowns for help, while others, fat and drunk, cowered in a trench just as I had really done. I drew myself standing triumphant in victory, silhouetted against fire and glowing smoke....

Now there came another announcement about another delay, an hour or two. I didn't care, I was a hit, I had almost forgotten about the Führer. Even though I felt myself fevering again, clammy all over, I asked the boys for more stationary. I sketched in a frenzy, now imagining Fenzel. The Unteroffizier had disappeared again somewhere and I became bold. I showed Fenzel screaming so loud his face was a gaping cave of teeth and tongue, his nose protruded like a wormy potato, his pimples bulged to the size of small balloons. As soon as he gave orders to attack, he was seized by a sneezing fit, yet his big *ker-SCHPLOOZ!* was so powerful it killed a Russian soldier each time. The room grew wild, the cackling had become a roar. "Now watch what happens to him," I said. This time Fenzel's sneeze was gigantic, knocking down trees, turning tanks upside down, and flinging Russians back across the Oder. It also blew apart his nose. Nothing remained there but a hole, and I drew myself peering through his head. Stupendous laughter! The Unteroffizier had not yet returned and the boys were falling off their chairs.

By now it was late afternoon. Perhaps to quiet us, the serving women plopped down a few more potatoes. Those glistening brown lumps, however, now filled me with revulsion. Something, permit me to explain, was beginning to happen in my stomach. A rumble, constrictions and churning, an awful sourness. The boys wanted me to continue with my comics, but the fever had regained strength, my throat was filling with acid. Dearest God, I was going to erupt. I wobbled toward the door, and asked one of the women in a madman's gibberish for the lavatory. She must have seen how green I looked, for she hustled me out of the room, to a toilet down a hallway, and there left me alone. The room stank of piss and shit, the plumbing here was like the rest of the city, not working, and this stench, dense and gagging, had an immediate effect. The herring and the potatoes, what was left of them, gushed out.

Desperate to return to the dining room, to my new-found popularity, I tried to stand but couldn't. Dizziness sent me to the floor's cold tiles. My stomach heaved, I vomited again and again, I thought my head would explode each time, it felt as if I had been turned inside out. No one entered, no one came to my aid, and for this I was mostly relieved. Exhaustion turned me into rubber, and despite the wretched odor, I fell asleep.

Sometime later I stumbled back to the dining hall, empty now. My drawings lay scattered on the table. The boys had finally been called to meet the Führer. I had missed everything. There I sat, in and out of dozing, when the same Unteroffizier burst into the room and said with anger, "There you are! What have you been doing? A terrible dishonor, an unbelievable insolence!"

"I was not feeling well—"

"There can be no excuse for not meeting the Führer! And on his birthday! Where were you?"

"In the bathroom—"

"The bathroom! Do you understand what you have done? Upset the entire number system! He wanted twenty, but got nineteen! It was vital that he got twenty! The same number as his birthday! His birthday! They are blaming me, I could be court-martialed, I could be hanged or shot, just because you decided to go play with yourself. I am a soldier, not a babysitter!"

"It was my stomach."

"Children getting the Iron Cross! Absurd. Now follow me."

We proceeded through a second hall, this one ornate and emptied of furniture, undamaged except for plaster dust that had coated everything gray. The immense chandelier, all gray, too, hung above like a giant wasp's nest. Then down a steep set of stairs, and to an iron door, where two guards peered at our identification and searched us. I assumed I was being led to a prison, though this possibility at the moment did not disturb me too much. There would be a bed.

A corridor, dimly lit. The walls were pale yellow, with green stripes on either side running the lengths, which we followed to what looked like a kitchen and mess hall. There, a stout, dark-haired woman was peeling potatoes. She turned her plain face to me, it was tinged yellow like the walls, and then said to the Unteroffizier, "Number twenty?"

He nodded and she asked me if I wanted something to eat. I shook my head, though she offered me a piece of cake, anyway, which hovered in front of my eyes as I was accosted by a pudgy, thin-lipped man, rushing up. "Finally, finally! Where have you been?"

Shameful, I muttered, "I got sick."

"Someone find him a toothbrush. You are Koertig, correct?"

"Tobias Koertig," I said, pulling out my identification, and then recognized my questioner's stiff wooden arm from my training at the Sportfeld. It was Artur Axmann, head of the boy army, the man who resembled a salesman.

"Clean your teeth, wash your face in the sink. We need a sponge, a sponge, quickly! Now stand straight, don't slouch. Yes, that's a good boy. You were up near the Seelow Heights, weren't you? Extraordinary heroism. Tell him about the tanks when he asks, but not before. And I want to hear your *Heil* spoken with assurance. Not too loud, however, because his ears are sensitive. Where's the sponge? All right, get the spot off the boy's collar, and wipe his shoes while you're at it." Axmann sniffed my mouth and then pronounced me ready.

Shivering, I followed Axmann down a spiral staircase into a narrow enclosure, where I could now hear loud voices, laughter, typewriters, the ringing of a phone, and underneath it all a forceful roar. The air had become chilly and humid. Drops clung to the walls. I was taken near the entrance of a small room and told to wait. Men and women, all in uniform, hurried past me, some clutching papers. A few peered into the doorway, scowled, and then disappeared elsewhere. Now Axmann emerged, kneeled before me, and whispered, "Raise your arm high. Do not be afraid to look directly at him. You may step inside."

In my uncertain state, I mean the swirling in my head, I still believed they were showing me to my prison cell. So I was rather shocked to encounter four women and an older, somewhat disheveled man seated at a small table, which held a half-eaten cake piled high with whipped cream. That man—who slouched in his chair, who was licking his fingers, whose puffy red eyes glanced up at my entrance—was the Führer. There, underneath the angular nose, lay the famous coal-smudge mustache, the symbol of war and fury, the symbol of everything Vati had hated, especially frightening when seen so close, even if it had collected on its left side a hard-to-miss spot of the cream. My arm sprang up like one in a mechanical toy while my throat, still full of acid, produced only a barely audible *Heil*. The women, smiling, looked at me with glassy eyes. The Führer stood, a little unsteady, and shuffled around the table to hold my shoulder.

"A hero of the Reich," he said. "Your stomach did not want to attend the ceremony."

"Yes, it was the herring, Herr Führer," I replied, feeling as if I might topple. "Mein Führer."

"I have digestion trouble myself. But I cannot resist a good cake."

I had only ever heard him on the radio, shouting out his speeches, so it was strange now to hear his voice so quiet and, I must admit, almost pleasant.

"Happy Birthday," I blurted, then inwardly cringed, for now I remembered what Vati had always done on this date. For many years, expected to give the Führer a gift like everyone else, my father sent a box of the cheapest marzipan—a candy that was produced, Vati reminded us, from a "bitter nut," the taste of which made him gag.

"You are a good boy," the Führer said. "A brave boy. Tell me about what you did."

I took a breath. It was impossible now to speak the truth. "I destroyed two tanks and killed three soldiers."

"Ha! Ha!" The Führer was almost giggling. "But how?"

I tried not to look at that bit of whipped cream clinging to his mustache. "I tiptoed behind them like a cat."

The Führer cupped me around the neck. "Did you hit them in the turrets?"

Was he testing me? Did he suspect me of lying? Had Fenzel sent him a message alerting him to my cowardice? I stammered, "One of them. The other, I aimed at the engine."

"Yes, yes! The rear drive-sprocket and the turret ring! Weak points! They don't know how to construct armor like we do. Our superior tanks will win this war. Axmann! It is time for his cross."

"Mein Führer! Mein Führer!" In the doorway appeared the same Unteroffizier, his lips now curled high enough to reveal his vampire incisors. He was panting, sweating, waving sheets of paper. "With your permission, please, you must take a look at this."

"What is it?" Axmann snarled. "You are interrupting a ceremony of the Reich."

"The boy has demeaned the German soldier. See what he has drawn. Vulgar cartoons."

"Hand them to me," said the Führer. "Where are my glasses?"

One of the women fetched a pair of green spectacles and the Führer slipped them on before peering at my comics. After a half-minute, a torture, during which I had trouble standing upright, for I was sure he would now give the order for execution, the Führer asked, "You drew these?"

I nodded, looking at the floor, wanting to weep.

"How long did it take you?"

"I did them, I did them while I was waiting, it was very quick, I did not mean to insult, I was not thinking, my fever..."

The Führer looked at me with those round green lenses, which suggested a frog. Then he pushed a bite of cake into his mouth. "They are very funny! Look how the Russians run! Very good! I must show them to Goebbels!" He gripped my shoulder once more, leaning closer. Now I could see a number of food stains on his uniform, it might have been tomato sauce on his sleeve, and maybe soup on his lapel. Dandruff lay on his shoulders like plaster dust shaken from his ears. "I am an artist, too, a painter, did you know that? When I was young, in Vienna, I made exquisite little watercolors—though of course I was destined for another life! But you—it is Tobias?—yes, Tobias, you have a fine eye, and a fast one. Your lines are graceful and bold, like Feuerbach's. You capture perspective as well as Von Alt. Remarkable! This gives me an idea. Someone get the boy a clean sheet of paper and a pencil." It was produced, and the Führer went on. "Now, draw the room for me. I will give you five minutes."

Even though it was a test, the task settled my nerves and my stomach somewhat, for this was something I knew how to do well. In the allotted time, I sketched the small space and its sparse furnishings, along with quick portraits of everyone present.

The Führer examined the result and called it wonderful, grinning. "Axmann, I have an assignment for him." To me, he said, "It is not without danger."

"Heil Hitler, mein Führer, I am very capable."

"I want you to be my eyes above ground."

"Heil Hitler," I repeated, not knowing what he meant.

"I am too busy down here planning the destruction of the Bolshevik invasion to venture into the city, too busy trying to find competent commanders who are not intent on treachery!" He had risen off his chair, like a big balloon given a blast of hot air. His eyes had begun to bulge, spittle had collected at the corners of his drooping mouth. Then he sank back down, as if a leak had developed, to slouch again. "But I want to see what is happening up there. Photography is too limiting, it is really only good for propaganda. I want an artist's interpretation, I want to see the situation's broad scope."

112

"I will do my best," I said, still not understanding.

"Very good! Now, Axmann, the medal."

Axmann pinned the cross, with its ribbon, on my baggy uniform. My clammy hand met the Führer's clammy hand, and our meeting had ended.

I was sent out into the hallway, and there I stood for a while, astonished and still woozy, not sure what had just happened. Finally, Axmann came out to give me my instructions. I was to produce sketches of Berlin every day, in various parts of the city according to my assignment, and deliver them here no later than five o'clock in the afternoon. I should concentrate on drawing avenues of approach and defensive preparations, I should note buildings that still had intact upper floors, and I was to label all locations with precision.

Axmann took me up a long, winding set of stairs and showed me another way out of the bunker, an emergency exit to what remained of the gardens. I was instructed to use it most of the time. He did not open the iron door, and I sensed his unease in doing so. To get back inside from the street, I was to rap a special knock, the opening rhythm from "The Ride of Valkyries." The Reichsjugendführer hummed it several times, tapping his knuckles on the iron, and then had me do the same. "Sing it while you work so you don't forget." Then he kneeled and said, "You understand, of course, the importance of your task. You are to supply the Führer with vital information for planning the defense of the capital. He has chosen you for your special skills. As the Reichsillustrator, you now have a great responsibility, which must be your only focus. It is life and death. We are all making the greatest effort possible to save our country." Axmann gave me a floppy salute, and I returned it. "Now remember, you are to wear the medal on formal occasions. Otherwise, you must display only the ribbon. Good luck to you!"

Because no one had expected me to stay, there was confusion about where I should sleep. In the meantime, the women who had been sitting with the Führer wanted to continue their party, even though the Führer had gone to bed. They invited me to join them, so I followed them up the way I had first come, and we went into a large room in the Chancellery, where nothing remained but a large round table and some dust-laden chairs. The prettiest lady, whose prominent cheeks glowed with rouge, who wore a blue dress that sparkled as she moved, introduced herself as Eva and explained to me that all the furniture had been taken down into the bunker. "It's not very festive, but we have booze, don't we?" Laughing, she poured everyone some schnapps, including me. Others joined us, including a doctor who resembled a pig, and a stout, balding fellow with hard, stony eyes. Someone had found a wind-up phonograph and a single record, which Eva held up like a prize. "It's Rudi Schuricke! Ah! His voice is heaven!" We listened to a love song about roses, over and over, each of us taking turns to wind the machine. Singing, dancing, mostly by themselves, sometimes with me or the stout man, the women lurched in drunken states, they shrieked in laughter, especially Eva, even as we heard explosions outside, which someone claimed was Russian artillery. The stout man, I learned his name was Bormann, Martin Bormann, he scoffed at the notion that the Russians were close enough to bombard us with their guns. "It's the British air force again," he said, coming back to the table sweaty. "A little smoke and fire. Nothing we haven't seen or heard before."

At some point giddy Eva announced that I was the Führer's illustrator and suggested that I draw everyone's portrait. Eva insisted on being first, and I produced her face with a few lines, for it was quite expressive and didn't need any help. Boosted by the schnapps, her delight in the result brought her to tears. She pronounced me a great talent, which pleased me, and urged me to do the others. When it came to the fat doctor, he waved his hands, furry with black hair so dense it looked like moss, and said, "Your pencil would break if you tried to draw me. Herr Bormann is a much better subject."

Bormann, not even acknowledging me, continued an animated discussion with the doctor. "But Bürgel's ideas are disgustingly Christian. Death is not about disappearance from the earth and some kind of mystical ascent. No, when my heart stops, I will continue to exist in my accomplishments, just as all good Germans will. Death is an outdated concept. I am often appalled at how much money we waste on funerals." As I sketched him, I softened his features, for his blocky head and his stringy, receding hair bore no trace of refinement. His skin was leather-thick, his nose a clump of putty. When I handed him my picture, he only nodded and pushed it aside. Someone wound up Rudi for the twentieth time, the women sang along in unison. Eva had one of the Führer's favorite dishes, creamed potato, brought up for me, as I had regained my appetite. While I ate, Bormann came up beside me.

"Do you know who I am, boy?"

"Herr Bormann."

"Herr *Reichsleiter*."

I began to salute him, but Bormann scowled and told me to relax. "You will be presenting your impressions of Berlin to the Führer, I understand."

"Herr Reichsjugendführer said that I will start tomorrow."

"You are very adept at flattery in your drawing. I admire that." He gave me a crooked smile. He was fiddling with his wedding ring, pulling it up and down his long finger. "So let me strongly suggest that you do the same with Berlin. The Führer is in need of good news. Understood?" He leaned closer and lowered his voice. "And since you have such an interest in art, I have an important errand for you. After you deliver your pictures, you will meet me here, at six o'clock, in this very same spot."

Another explosion shook the walls. All of us ducked, and Bormann fell to the floor, covering his head. Shortly after, a second explosion, closer, sent us hurrying down the stairs, into what I now realized was the war's headquarters, the Führer's protected bunker.

11

I did not sleep very well that night, mixed up again, guilty about the string of events that had led me here. My pictures of Stefanie had gotten Stalla sent back to Berlin in disgrace, my cowardice had earned me not only the medal but a position away from the battlefields, working for the Führer, the man my father had despised with all his soul, the man Zenzi, too, wished were dead. Zenzi! My relief in all of this was that I might be able to see her again soon. Still, I turned over and over on my cot, for the sounds of the dying were keeping me awake, too. Some adjutant had led me through a labyrinth of tunnels to find me a bed, which sat in a passage near a casualty station, and for hours moans and screams entered my ears like needles.

In the morning, after another air raid, the last one it turned out, I set off from the underground space, mostly recovered from my illness, and climbed the stairs to the emergency exit Axmann had shown me. My pocket contained the special pass, which bore my name and my new title, Reich Illustrator for Defense. In my haversack I carried a blank notebook imprinted with the imperial eagle. Ordered to begin my work in the central part of the city, in Mitte, where I was to provide pictures of east-west lines of sight, I headed out into a steady drizzle. I drew the streets carefully, noting the buildings that still had upper floors you could reach, adding other details I thought might be important—wrecked cars, rubble mounds, craters.

I wanted to believe that I was now redeeming the loss of my nerves at Seelow, that I was helping to keep the Russians out of Berlin, but as I worked, as I sketched the city, a sadness began to enfold me. Around me there was a continuous movement, slow but determined, of people looking for useful scraps. They peered into the remains of stores, they sorted through bricks, they held up their occasional prizes (an umbrella, a cooking pot) with small shouts of satisfaction. Maybe because I had not walked through the city in a while, or maybe because I had become an observer, I was a little startled to see how we had all become accustomed to the destruction. Five years before, in September of 1940, the first bombs had been shocking, but kind of thrilling, too. In the afternoons, several of us boys would gather at the wooden barriers erected by the police and marvel at the damage, not so bad back then—shop windows broken, a splintered tree, a severed sewer line sending up odors. But now these crumbled walls were appearing on my paper like something natural, as if I was capturing an ordinary landscape.

Here and there, too, I came across grim messages, nailed to fallen timber, that asked for sightings of the missing. Günther, 73, white hair, an "old-fashioned" mustache, had disappeared a month ago. Ursula, 5, wearing ballet shoes, had gone outside last June, not seen since. One notice was familiar, as it had been posted for two straight years now, all over, pleading for news of Nessel, a lost dachshund. The more I saw of these notes, the more I felt my own disconnection from everyone I had known. I soon found myself heading in a great hurry to the Schoenberg district, which did not lie anywhere near my assigned area. I had planned to go there in the evening, after my work was done, but I could not wait. I was risking punishment for going astray, maybe even piano-wire death, but the urge was too strong—to see Zenzi, or to see if she had gone among the missing.

I sprinted through the ruins. When I reached what I thought to be the right street, I wondered, as I had done with my own house—so long ago it seemed—if I had lost my way. The block was gone, or I should say flattened. There was only rubble and charred wood, all of it heaped in circles, as if volcanoes had erupted. I ran to the nearest person, a woman sweeping stones, and asked her about the Fuchses.

The woman glanced at me, then stared at her broom. "Why do you want to know?"

"I used to live with them."

She studied me. "Are you the boy that Zenzi always talked about? Who joined the army? You're on leave and anxious for love?" She laughed and I stepped back, ready to flee, for I assumed she was being sarcastic and was going to turn me in. But she just shrugged. "They went to Mitte, I don't know where."

"Yes, we do," someone else shouted, "Near the Marienkirche. Ask the pastor. He helped them."

They were not telling me everything, I thought, but I did not ask any more questions. I knew the church, my father had taken me there once to show me some paintings. I would have to go all the way back where I had come from, yet it was convenient for being the same district I had been assigned. I hurried through smashed Potsdamer Platz, then over a bridge at the Spree, where I presented my identification to a group of boys guarding the river.

They shook my hand when they saw my ribbon and learned of my high connections. Finally, coming through Kaiser-Wilhelm Strasse, I came to the Marienkirche. Toppled statues lay before it like gray, hardened corpses, a few trees were splintered, yet the stone church still stood, even the steeple, darkened by the rain. It was Saturday, so I went in to find the pastor. There in the dim light, running along the wall, was one of the works my father had wanted me to see, a medieval fresco—the *Totentanz*, he had explained, a kind of cartoon showing townspeople dancing with Death. We had come here a week after our victory in France and Vati told me that all of Germany was now doing such a dance. Then to ease his mind—I remember his chin trembling—he had taken me to eat pastries somewhere nearby.

The pastor emerged, I asked him about the Fuchses, and he, too, wanted to know my reasons.

"Zenzi," I blurted, "is my girlfriend."

"Ah, you are the Koertig boy," he said, smiling, and gave me the directions.

I rushed to the location and knocked without much force on the basement door. In a moment that seemed to come from dreaming, Zenzi wrapped her arms around me with a grip so crushing I worried she might break my ribs. "Tobias, Tobias, I was so afraid I'd never see you again," she said, her glasses pressing into my cheek. "Did you get my letter? My father didn't want anyone to know we'd moved, but I had to tell you."

"I didn't see it. The Russians came too fast. The pastor sent me here." I wanted her to know how often I had thought of her, but I could only say, "I wrote you a letter, too, but it burned."

"What's this ribbon? Did you get a medal?"

"Yesterday. I think it was yesterday. A lot has happened."

Before I could explain, a voice came from the basement, one I recognized as belonging to Herr Fuchs. "Zenzi! Who is there?"

"It's Tobias. He's back!"

A shuffling from inside, and then Herr Fuchs stood at the door. He had grown a beard, and with his usual pipe he resembled a professor or a ship captain. He squinted at me. "What is your business?"

"Vati!" Zenzi almost shouted. "He's come to say hello."

"But how did you know we were here?"

"I asked two women near your old place, and then at the Marienkirche the pastor told me."

The severest of scowls came to his dark eyebrows. He looked at me up and down. "If you're hungry, we have very little."

"I have my own rations, thank you."

Zenzi put an arm around me. "Come in out of the rain."

Inside, Herr Fuchs sat next to his wife, who lay on blankets and looked thinner. Only her eyes, heavy-lidded, moved when I approached. She murmured something I couldn't understand. Two other women, shadows, huddled in the corner.

Herr Fuchs stroked his wife's arm and said to me, "So, then, you've had a taste of battle. The ribbon of the Iron Cross. You must have been brave, my boy."

Sheepish, I nodded and explained the circumstances again as if they had happened to me, the two tanks, the three soldiers. I made the story as quick as possible, tired of it, and left out the Führer's involvement, since I was certain that Herr Fuchs would be horrified by this.

Herr Fuchs grasped my hand and said, "You distinguished yourself. Yet I'm sorry for you that it had to involve death." He brought out his map. "Tell me where you were."

"Somewhere near Seelow."

He looked at me puzzled, pulling on his whiskers. "How fast are they advancing?"

"We held them back," I assured him, though in truth I had

no idea what the Russians were doing in other areas.

"And where will you be sent next?"

"This is my new post, right here. I am Reich Illustrator for the Berlin Defense. I am making sketches of our preparations," I said, once again leaving out the man who would be looking at them.

"Sketches?" Herr Fuchs's eyes widened. He set aside his pipe. "What is your business here?"

"Well, I am just visiting."

"Yes, yes, and then what?"

"I don't know." I looked at the floor. "I need to get back. I am on duty."

"Who ordered you to come here?"

"No one." A weakness filled me, I shook my head, I tried to keep tears from coming to my eyes.

"Why are you upsetting him?" Zenzi said with sharpness. "He's come to see me, and you think he's the Gestapo, a boy!"

"Then what do you know about the enemy?" he continued, "We've heard that the Russians are coming up from the south. Zossen. Or the Americans? How far are they? The Elbe? Closer?"

I shook my head again feebly, embarrassed that I did not know these things.

"We are leaving," Zenzi announced. "He did not come here to be interrogated."

"You have to help your mother. I can't do it all myself."

"I'm tired of sitting here with these smells. I have to get out."

"I forbid you, Zenzi! You know the dangers now! The boy needs to leave."

But she took my hand and we fled down the street toward the church, into a harder rain. She pulled me over to one of the city's advertising pillars, near an abandoned apothecary with its blue sign. "I'm sorry about my father," she said. "He's full of fear. He thinks we're going to be rounded up and sent away any day. He doesn't want anyone to know we're here. The police were snooping around, asking for certain names, so he got scared. I guess you saw what that bomb did to our old place. We'd moved a few days before. Pretty lucky. Except that I'd left my records and the phonograph there, and most of my books, too. I was going to fetch them later, and it's all gone. Probably in a million pieces. Furtwängler, smashed. It breaks my heart. The Buchwalds didn't come with us, I think they must have died there. You'll be happy to know that Einbrecher is still alive. He's holding up better than anybody. I collect little shoots for him, now that things are growing. But I'm so tired of hiding, I'm so tired of being afraid, and now I think I've become a little crazy. You must have been a little crazy, too, out there in that battle! It's a miracle you didn't get hurt."

"Well, one of my ears doesn't work all that well." I made fists, trying to confess. "A friend of mine, Albrecht, he was the one..."

"Do you have anything to eat? There was a store handing out extra rations yesterday because of the Führer's birthday, but they wouldn't give me any because I'm a Mischling. Bastards! I'm ravenous."

I wanted to tell her about the Führer's party, about the cake I'd seen and everything else, but couldn't bring myself to say anything yet. I reached into my haversack and pulled out some tinned meat. "Take it," I said, "I can get more."

"You really are my favorite boy in the world."

As we stood next to an old poster, torn in the middle, warning of air-raids (*Der Luft Terror geht weiter—Mütter, schafft Eure Kinder fort!* The air terror continues—Mothers, keep your children safe!), Zenzi leaned closer, peering at me with lenses spotted by rain, then swooped in and kissed me on the mouth. "Let's go somewhere dry," she said.

"I have to go back to my sketching."

"You are always running off because of this stupid war."

"Do you think the pastor will allow me up his steeple? It will have a good view."

"Take me with you."

"I don't know..."

We both looked up there. The clock at the top said 11:30. Zenzi, catching me off-guard, put her lips on mine again, holding them there longer. I felt hot, wobbly, joyous.

Then, it was uncanny, a kiss from Zenzi was once again explosive.

The street flew apart, everything shattered, crashing booms knocked us down. The Apotheke sign burst and covered us with blue glass. We ran to the church door, terrified, perplexed, for we had heard no siren, no planes. The planes would not fly, anyway, in such rain. The pastor hurried us to the basement, and it was there that my brain forged enough logic to realize that this was Russian artillery. They had advanced close enough to shell us.

We stayed in the basement, seated on a bench close together, while the pastor and several parishioners rushed up and down the stairs checking for damage or fire. I felt that I should help, especially since I wore the Iron Cross, but Zenzi insisted that I stay with her. She clutched my hand and poured out words. "My father is insisting that we go to the Americans now. He's desperate to know where they are, and of course the Russians, too. My mother is the problem, you can see she's too sick to travel, and my father is in agony about what to do. And then those two women with us, they're unbearable. Vati used to work in the school with one of them, I guess. They smell worse than any of us and they won't dab on perfume, and all they do is pray. The same chants, over and over, it's just stupidity. Ah, I forgot, we're in a church! Well, what's going to happen? A lightning strike? That's nothing!"

The shells pounding outside had not sounded so bad while she talked. Now it was my turn to tell her everything, about my training, and Fenzel, and being punished, and the truth of the battle, and the accidental award, and the comics, and the Führer's praise. To describe all this brought back my shame. Sweat had coated my hand though she did not seem to mind. "Do you think I'm a coward?"

"No, you were brave to be there at all. But are you really working for the Kerl?"

This was a sarcastic term for the Führer. I felt more shame. "He'll be looking at my pictures, I think."

"Did you tell him about us?"

"Of course not! I hardly even talked to him."

"What if he finds out"—she dropped her voice to a whisper—"that you have a friend who's a Mischling?"

"I promised you that I would never say a word."

"We're a danger to each other now," she said, making a small sad grin. Another explosion sent something clattering onto the floor. "God, my parents must be terribly worried about me. They'll yell and yell when I get back, especially my mother. Listen to that out there. What are those idiotic Bolsheviks trying to do? The city is already dead." She squeezed my slimy hand tighter. "Come with us to the Americans."

"If I had not joined up..." I looked away. "But if I desert and they find me, they'll hang me from a lamp post."

"Yes, my God, the other day, it was horrible, I saw a boy dangling from one. Wearing a sign that said Deserter. His tongue was flopped out like a dog's." She lifted my hand to kiss it. "I'd gone very close to look to make sure it wasn't you."

I sprang up, filled with a feeling of panic. "I have to make my drawings! If I don't deliver them—"

"You can't do it when they're shelling, Tobias." She pulled me back down next to her, then closed her eyes, pushed her glasses back up her nose, and in a soft voice began to incant a long, rhyming poem, which calmed me.

"Did you learn that for school?" I asked when she had finished.

"No, I learned it because it's beautiful and true. Don't you know Schiller? 'An die Freude.' Beethoven liked it so much he wrote a symphony. I've memorized all of it." She glanced at the ceiling when another boom seemed close, repeating one of the last lines. "Und die Hoelle nicht mehr sein." And hell shall be no more.

Soon after, the pastor informed us that the church had not received much damage and that the shelling had stopped. I stood, and trying to muster strength in my voice, requested the use of his steeple to make my drawings.

In his formal attire, he peered at me. "For what purpose?"

"Defensive preparations."

"So we may continue the war." He stared at me for a moment, his mouth set firm, then thrust his finger before my nose. "I will allow you up the steeple on one condition. You will bear witness. You will bear witness to what the Führer has wrought. Draw everything you see."

He showed me and Zenzi the way, and we ascended the narrow, twisting staircase. At the top, a door opened onto an outdoor platform, just above the clock, bounded by a short rail. The rain swept over us, and so did the agonizing view. Neither of us had the seen the city from such a height since the bombing had begun. We stood there overwhelmed. The ruins were more complete than I had ever imagined. In all directions it looked as if a giant had stomped around in a rage. Almost nothing had a definite shape anymore. What remained intact—the Brandenburg Gate, the spire of another church—possessed a kind of loneliness.

In the distance I could see the needle of the Siegessäule, the victory column. Some years before, the winged figure on top had been painted black so as not to be a beacon for enemy planes and now it looked like an angel of Death.

In other spots, bombs had penetrated deep enough that I imagined I could see the center of the earth, for in gaping cellars the stored coal, burning for weeks, glowed as red as magma and turned the rain to steam. Everywhere pillars of inky smoke rose to meet the low clouds, which reflected the orange of fresh flames. And now from the shelling, bodies lay in the streets—dozens of them, parts of them—and even from our perch the puddling blood was bright. Moans and cries and a siren or two drifted up to us. Behind me, the pastor murmured a prayer and then disappeared back down the stairs. Zenzi, rain-soaked, her eyes red with weeping, crawled to the rail and shouted that same line from Schiller, "Und die Hoelle nicht mehr sein," over and over, becoming hoarse. I set aside my sketchbook, followed her to the edge, and clutched her coat, worried that she might fall. Her repeated plea did not stop. She began to shake. Slowly, slowly, to calm her, my arms went around her waist. In that moment, what came to me, I am certain, was some notion of love.

12

It took me a considerable amount of time to re-create that vision from the steeple, for getting the perspective right from such a height and angle was a challenge. But the pastor's demands and Zenzi's cries had filled me with a certain resolve—to record these visible facts, terrible as they were, for those who were unable to see, for the bunker's underground world, for the generals who sat down there staring at bloodless maps. If I could show them the way our city looked, if I could show them in superb detail what the Red Army had just done, surely they would put the greatest of effort into bolstering our defense and bringing up those all-powerful weapons as soon as possible. I would help send Ivan back to Moscow. I filled my paper with the bodies and the flowing blood, wishing that I had colored pencils to render it all the more real.

Yes, yes, so went my earnest thoughts—easily mocked now, all this time later. But it bears repeating that this skinny boy with a talent in draftsmanship—who hoped to protect the last vestiges of his home, a city reduced to little more than ash and smoke—was only thirteen, was only a few years beyond a belief in Santa Claus.

Zenzi and I arranged to meet at the church in two days, and I hurried back to the bunker, convinced of the value of my pictures. When I reached the cratered Chancellery garden, I could not quite remember the rhythm that Axmann had hummed. I knocked on the iron door, over and over, until my knuckles became red and raw. Finally the hinges creaked to allow a small crack, enough so that the guard could bellow the tune. "Daaah dah-dah *daaaah* daaaah!" He slammed the door shut, and after trying again, I was allowed inside.

"You should have let me in earlier," I said. "I have important documents!"

"Well, even so, you must be accurate," the guard said, a little drunk I suspected. "Wagner wrote a dotted eighth, followed by a sixteenth, not a straight triplet. The second note of the first beat must be quick. All my idea, by the way! I used to play trumpet in Köln's orchestra. What Russian would ever know Wagner!" He grinned at me. "You'll learn it with practice. Next time I won't be so lenient!"

Down inside, I soon found Axmann and handed him my sketches. All business, he barely glanced at them, stuffing the papers in a briefcase. "I will present these to the Führer tonight," he said before marching off. In the kitchen, that same stout woman, her name was Fräulein Manziarly, served me potatoes with canned meat and some cake and coffee. I stuffed myself, and I was so happy to have a full and settled gut that I almost forgot about my scheduled appointment with Herr Bormann.

I trotted up the spiral staircase, into the old ornate Chancellery, where I had danced with the women the night before. Larger chunks of plaster and a fresh coating of dust lay across the floor. I wandered through the room for a few minutes, until from another doorway, like a fat specter, the bulk of Reichsleiter Bormann appeared, wrapped tight in his uniform. He beckoned me to follow him, and he took me into a small room, a closet for cleaning supplies, and shut the door. He turned on a flashlight, which produced a dim glow. His square brutal face hovered above mine.

"Have you ever been to the Zoo bunker?" he asked, blunt, impatient. His voice was like gears grinding. Fumes of alcohol came at me.

I shook my head. "But I know where it is." The place was impossible to miss: near the U-Bahn's Zoo station, a giant above-ground public bomb shelter, with the anti-aircraft guns on its roof.

"Now listen to me," he said. "Dr. Schenck and Dr. Haase are performing surgery downstairs, around the clock, on our young soldiers. They are in need of medical supplies. You will find out what they require and retrieve it from the Zoo bunker, where there is a Luftwaffe hospital. Understood?"

"Yes, Reichsleiter Bormann," I said, baffled as to why he had taken me into a closet to give such an order.

"There is a secondary task." He looked at me with glazed eyes and flexed his large, rough fingers. "You are an artist, so you must be familiar with the treasures of Heinrich Schliemann. Surely your father knew of them."

I did not expect such a subject to arise, or to hear mention of my father, so I mumbled, "I think so," but in fact I had never heard of Schliemann.

"Priceless antiquities from ancient Troy. Jewelry, coins, crowns, all of them gold. They are being stored in the Zoo bunker. I have an order from the Führer"—Bormann reached into a tunic pocket and pulled out a folded sheet of paper—"to retrieve certain items. They must be protected, taken safely to another location. I am assigning this task to you. First, because you are going there already. Second, because you wear the Iron Cross, and therefore uphold the principles of the Reich. Third, because you are a keen observer of detail, and because you have a background in art. I cannot employ some idiot who does not know a pfennig from an ancient Greek coin. Your father was well known by some of us, by the way. Did you know that I acquired a painting for the Führer from him?"

I shook my head. Vati had never told me about such a thing, though he had once boasted, with cynical triumph, of shipping photographs to Göring's mansion, and had displayed several about to be sent, pictures of nude women lounging on elegant sofas.

"You will accomplish this," Bormann continued, "with the greatest of secrecy. Do not reveal your activity to anyone. There are any number of thieves who would want to get their hands on these things. Do not even mention it to Axmann. Not a word. Your regular duties will happen during the day, and this task will occur at night, starting tomorrow. You must at all times keep in mind that betraying the secrecy would be treason, and treason is punishable by death." He cleared his throat. "Now, tell me, what will you say if anyone asks what you are doing?"

"I am retrieving medical supplies."

"That is exactly right. A smart boy. You remind me a little of my eldest son, Krönzi. Not much older than you. Headstrong but obedient, and the finest example of our race. Grateful for my discipline, too, as all my children are. Now listen: the antiquities are stored on the third floor. There is only a single guard anymore. When he sees this letter, he will let you inside, but if he should give you any trouble, give him this." From his tunic, Reichsleiter Bormann pulled out a bottle of schnapps. "You will go to the Zoo bunker after midnight." He described, in detail, the items I was to obtain, and how I was to deliver them, and then he slipped out, as quietly as he had arrived.

I tried to remember if Vati had ever mentioned Martin Bormann, but couldn't. As I learned much later, after the war, most Germans had not heard of him, for he had always operated in the shadows. If I had known anything about him then, I might have left our meeting filled with suspicion and dread. But I was only perplexed by another unexpected assignment.

13

In the morning, under another low drizzly sky the color of rubble, I headed over to the remains of the Märkisches Museum, where I was supposed to deliver, by eight o'clock, two cans of beef for Zenzi, swiped from the bunker's kitchen. Searching for the spot—a crevice she was supposed to mark with bricks placed in the shape of a star—reminded me of games I used to play in the Tiergarten. It was another moment, saddening, when I was desperate to return to my old, pre-war life! I dropped the cans on the ground and pushed them into the hole with my feet.

My orders took me to the western edge of the Prenzlauerberg district, where I began my second day as illustrator by sketching a tank barricade. A charred trolley filled with stones made the centerpiece. Around it, the Volkssturm and some youth-army boys (I hoped to see Stalla but he was not among them) had dragged various junked things into a big pile, making what looked like decoration: wheelbarrows, lengths of timber, baby strollers, a milk wagon, half a piano, street signs, tables and chairs, and even a tarnished trombone. A few of the old men, straining and full of complaint, were now hauling a claw-foot bathtub into the mix. The grimiest one, his throat quivering with loose, chicken-like skin, pointed at me, and in a sneering tone asked, "How much are you charging for the portrait? It better be good!"

"I wish to know," I said, "whether you will be placing an anti-tank gun here."

The old man struck several heroic poses, flexing his biceps and pointing an imaginary sword. "Which do you like best?"

"What is the name of this street?" I asked, trying to ignore his antics. "I don't see the sign."

He and his companion, dressed in shabby suits, shook their heads. "What do we know? We're just a couple of spargel farmers from Beelitz. Talk to the guy on the corner. He knows the neighborhood."

In an alcove, a tall fellow stood there, no ordinary one, for he had painted on his withered face a fiendish black smile, like a clown's. He wore a bowler hat, too, and had looped a pair of red suspenders over his jacket. Some kind of cabaret actor, of the sort my father used to know. I kept my distance. "I am making a report," I said. "Please tell me the name of this street."

"You must first listen to a joke."

With yesterday's artillery bombardment still fresh in my head, I was in no mood for humor. "You should be helping defend the city."

"But, my boy, I am defending humanity! Let me introduce myself, I am Klingmüller the Buffoon." He extended a hand and there was nothing I could do but shake it. Then Klingmüller snapped both red straps, doffed his bowler, and stretched that black grin. "The Führer is being driven down a country road. He is passing a house when a dog leaps over the fence right into the path of the car and is instantly killed. To demonstrate his sympathy for the German people, the Führer orders his driver to apologize to the owner. The man goes up to the house and returns a few minutes later with lipstick all over his face. 'What happened to you?' the Führer asks, and the driver says, 'I can't understand it. A woman greeted me at the door. I simply said, *Heil Hitler! The dog is dead.* And she showered me with kisses.'"

I remembered that Vati, or maybe it had been one of Vati's friends, had once told some variation of the same joke. Perhaps my face betrayed the memory—a fond one—for Klingmüller gazed at me, squinting an eye. "I think I saw a smile," he said. "Yes, I am certain of it! Take this boy away! He has smiled at the Führer's expense."

A chill encircled my neck and I dropped my notebook.

"But that is a joke, too!" roared Klingmüller.

Now I heard the Volkssturm behind me laughing, and I glanced over to see that one of them sat in the bathtub while his cohort pantomimed the scrubbing of his back. There was almost nothing I hated more than to be played for a fool, and with rising indignation, I said to Klingmüller, "The Russians are only a few days away!"

Klingmüller replied, "I thank you for your time, my boy. Return whenever you want. I never charge a single pfennig, my jokes are always free, always free! Ah, look, there is a girl trying to get your attention. Quite attractive, too. Never pass up an opportunity like that!"

Suspecting a trick, I was slow to turn around. Further down the street, a mass of black hair. Zenzi was waving at me from the edge of a wrecked building. I looked around, worried that I would, once again, become the target of mockery. But the farmers had gone back to enlarging their pile of junk and the Buffoon had disappeared, so I sauntered over.

"Why are you here?" I said. "What are you doing? We were supposed to meet at the church, I thought, and not until tomorrow."

"I followed you from the museum," she explained. "I was waiting nearby. I have something very important to tell you."

"You'll get me in trouble."

"In front of these dopes? If you think they care, just pretend you are rescuing a stranger. Yank on my ankle. A stuck foot."

I grabbed her ankle, intrigued by this mutual attempt to deceive the men who had just laughed at me, but also unable to resist touching her again, unable to resist hearing whatever she needed to say.

"Now I will pretend to show you something," she said, pointing with an exaggerated gesture toward the rubble. "Follow me inside."

I did so, stepping over debris into a lobby. Part of the ceiling had collapsed, burying the lower half of a staircase under beams and plaster. Zenzi pointed upward, to the intact second floor. "No one is living there. That's where I want to go to talk."

"But how? We can't reach it. Just tell me your news now."

"No, we must go where no one can possibly hear. See that sofa? We can drag it over and stand it on one end."

Soon we had scaled the sofa's exposed springs, managing to lift ourselves onto the first landing. We proceeded up the stairs. Fire had gutted most of the apartments but we found one that had not been scorched. Zenzi, agitated, led me through the place, insisting that she wanted to make sure the rooms were uninhabited. In a partly crushed parlor, a child's spinet piano lay on its side under shattered beams. The kitchen remained undamaged but had gone unused for quite some time. Several plates, sprinkled with crumbled plaster, lay on a table. A wooden rocking horse, tipped on its side, peered at me. A pot of cloudy water rested on the stove.

Near a large black telephone, a calendar displayed a photograph of a Heinkel bomber, the month of February.

Across the hall, a bedroom door was jammed shut, locked in place by a skewed jamb. Zenzi knocked and satisfyingly got no answer. There was a second bedroom, this one open, and we entered. Here, bombs had torn away a wall's upper half, so that we could see the street below and beyond. She peered downward, then came back to the bed, the blankets still tucked and smooth. She swept off a patch of dust, so thick it looked like snow, and slouched there.

"Do you think anyone can hear us?" she asked.

"No one's here."

"Sit next to me, Tobias." She squeezed my hand over and over, and then told me, "I have found out something terrible."

"The Russians...?"

"No, no." Her voice fell to a whisper and I had to move my head closer to hear what she said. "Last night on the radio, my father and I heard the BBC, a report about a prison camp. A German camp. It's north, I don't really know where, a place called Belsen? This reporter, well, it's very upsetting...he said he saw hundreds of bodies lying in piles, most of them dead, others barely alive. The prisoners, Tobias. Mostly Jews."

"Piles?"

"Yes, yes, like trash. And all of them naked."

"Maybe there was some kind of disease that went through the camp. Maybe the BBC isn't telling the truth. Exaggerating."

"I don't want to believe it, either. But my father is convinced that it's true. He has heard about these things for a while, I told you he'd said something about it before, but now he thought it was time for me to know, so he let me listen. This is what they have been doing to the Jews. They've been sent to camps and killed."

"Maybe the British bombed it," I said. "That's why there were so many bodies. They've killed hundreds in Berlin, too."

"No, British soldiers *found* the camp. Tobias, what if it's real? Maybe now they'll start taking away the Mischlinge." She gripped my arm. "You don't hate the Jews, do you?"

"No, of course not. I never have. My parents used to help them."

"I thought they might have started teaching you. But you can't tell anyone that we heard about this. You can't tell anyone that we know. Especially not those people you work for. My God, you have to leave them. Somehow you have to come with us."

"I don't know how I would do it," I said, feeling the burden of my assignments as an ache.

"When my father sets a date, I'll tell you, and you can join us the night before. Then we'll all slip away..."

The rain fell harder, clattering something. The simplest of desires came to me, more longing for that old life: to lie in a bed and listen to a downpour, to feel that comfort. "To the Americans?"

"Yes, the Elbe. Magdeburg. Schönehausen. How far is that? I don't remember what my father said."

"I'm not sure. But I don't know if I want to leave Berlin. I don't want to give it up."

"You keep saying that, but there's nothing left. Remember what we saw from the church yesterday!" She leaped off the bed and rushed up to the shattered wall, pointing at the ruins visible beyond. "Look, look, do you really care about that? It's empty, it's the end of the world. Oh, my God, how did *he* get up there?"

I moved beside her. Across the street, on the second story, in the corner of an empty window frame, there were two pointed brown ears, and a sloped forehead, and a flickering white eye. A horse, a living horse. The strange sight put a sudden end to our meeting. We climbed down, scurried across the street—deserted now, for the heavy rain had chased the Volkssturm away—and found the animal's ruined building. He stood directly above us, emaciated, with shaky legs, on half of a charred floor.

"He must have got scared and run up," Zenzi said.

"He's stuck. The stairs are gone." I looked for a path, somewhere to climb, but couldn't spot a thing. "And he has nothing to eat."

"It's too crazy and sad," Zenzi said. "Like everything else." She gave me a light kiss. "Tobias, I have to go back to my mother. My father will shriek at me again for being gone so long."

"I have to finish my pictures, anyway."

"I think my father will decide soon. About leaving. Remember what I told you."

"Yes," I said, morose now.

"Draw something happy for me when I see you next. For both of us. All right?"

We agreed not to meet tomorrow, but on the day after, so as not to arouse suspicions, especially considering what we had discussed. Zenzi's news of the camp and her father's interest in the Americans troubled me for the rest of the day. I kept imagining bodies piled in the way she had described and wondered if Vati's artist friends had somehow ended up like that. The rain let up for a while, and at various other intersections I sketched the ruins and the barricades and the occasional gun or tank but without enthusiasm. Late in the day, when the clouds burst again and drenched the streets, I retreated to an alcove to rest. I was tired of wreckage, of capturing it, so I decided, remembering Zenzi's request, to do the opposite: I would ignore what lay around me, I would block it from my mind. Instead, I would rebuild Berlin. Soon, immense towers stretched across my pages, with spires and observation cupolas and launching pads for rocket ships...there was a zoo inside a giant glass building, with different animals on each level...people zipped between buildings in pneumatic tubes...

helicopters crowded the sky...I kept at it for too long, feeling like a boy again, and then had to hurry back to the bunker to be on time for my daily report. Underground, I waited for Axmann on a bench. The day had exhausted me and, despite the clamor of officials scurrying past me, I soon found myself nodding in and out of sleep.

Axmann poked me awake. "Koertig, I asked you to sketch defensive positions only. Buildings, emplacements, sight lines."

Groggy, I answered slowly. "But that is what I did."

"You included corpses!"

"The pastor—the pastor asked me to draw everything and I thought it would help if I showed you—"

"Who? *I* am giving the orders! The dead are not pertinent to military operations. The Führer has been under enormous stress. He cares deeply about the people of Berlin, but we cannot burden him with civilian troubles! Those drawings contributed to another terrible rage, one of the worst I have ever seen! Did you complete today's assignment?"

"Defensive positions only! In Prenzlauerberg, as requested."

"Hand them over, I'm in a hurry. We must keep the Führer calm. It's vital."

I gave him the sketches, relieved that not a single one contained a corpse. But Axmann had so befuddled me with his accusations that I had made a grave error nonetheless. He had taken the entire notebook, everything I had done that day, including, of course, all my Berlin fantasies, which in my sleepy state I had not remembered to remove. Aghast, shivering, I tried to chase Axmann down. No, my realization had come too late, he had disappeared somewhere into the labyrinth of the tunnels.

14

Nothing I had seen before—not the aftermath of air raids or artillery, not the dead Russians at Seelow, not even the body of my mother on the rubble with a hole in her neck—had prepared me for the underground casualty station, where I had gone to begin my task for Bormann. To find the place I had followed two stretcher-bearers carrying an unconscious Volkssturm soldier. I stood in the doorway and gaped. A single lamp hanging from a cord illuminated a boy lying on an operating table. His stomach had been cut open, his innards spilled out in a bright red tangle. My first thought was to hope he was not Stalla. No, not with dark hair. Above him, brandishing a small knife, stood the stocky surgeon, in an undershirt splattered with blood of several shades. His face and bare arms were smeared with it, too, and what did not cover him had flooded the floor with a sticky jellied mass, imprinted with the treads of boots. The odor here was something like steaming offal, rich and choking, and its source seemed clear.

In the far corner, I almost fainted when I saw it, a barrel held a bunch of severed limbs.

The surgeon was shouting toward the doorway. "The spleen? Is that what you said? Someone tell the bastards to shut up, I can't hear Haase!" He was speaking about the boisterous singing that had started up somewhere nearby. A nurse ran out to holler at someone, the chorus quieted, and now I could hear this Haase. Gaunt and pale, sick from something, he lay on his back near the surgeon's table and issued instructions in a wheezing voice, how and where to slice the flesh. I had to turn my head, for the shiny glop of the boy made my stomach flip. Finally I brought forth the courage to ask, "Are you Doctor Schenck?"

The surgeon did not look up. "If this is your friend, he is going to die."

"I have been ordered to find out what medical supplies you need from the Zoo bunker."

"Everything! Morphine! Plasma, iodine, splints! We are almost out of bandages. Syringes. And goddamnit, I am falling asleep! Coffee!"

After he signed the requisition form with his dripping hand, I traced a route back along the tunnel to the bunker—emptier now, it seemed—and then went up the stairs and out into the drizzling night. A reddish glow clung to the bellies of clouds. I hurried across the sea of bricks, past the shiny jagged ruins that resembled those spires in caverns, past small groups of Volkssturm huddled around small fires, then skirted the Tiergarten wasteland and came to the castle-like bunker at the zoo. Its gray walls rose before me as tall as cliffs, stained with dark tongues of rain. The place was a concrete fortress, four stories high, massively thick. I had never been inside though of course had heard the pounding, night after night, of the giant flak guns perched on the roof. Soldiers milled around, smoking, dotting the dark with their orange tips. The doorway glowed a dim electric yellow, the fortress had its own power somewhere. A muted roar came from within—machinery of some sort, I thought. When I entered, that same sound, a hundred times louder, pushed against my ears like gusts of wind. Not machines but voices, thousands of them echoing off the cavernous interior. It looked as if all of Berlin was living here. There were so many civilians that my vision went blurry. They had crammed themselves shoulder-to-shoulder, ear-to-ear, into every available space, into every corner, sprawled on top of one another, doing all conceivable human things: moaning, crying, pissing, praying, sleeping, reading, arguing, eating, shitting, copulating, and dying. Many, I think, were already dead. The stench was thick and moist. In an instant, my tongue was coated. Covering my nose and mouth, I tiptoed a path through the chaos, I tried not to step on anyone, alive or not, and made my way up the stairs to the fourth floor, the hospital.

A crowd was sprawled here, too, on tables and the floor, and slumped against the walls. After examining my requisition form, a doctor reluctantly ordered a nurse to find me the necessary supplies. I stuffed them in my haversack, and then, as Reichsleiter Bormann had ordered, made my way down a floor to retrieve the items of gold.

Here, before locked double doors, sat the uniformed guard with a propped rifle. I presented my letter and requested entrance.

"No one is allowed inside," he told me.

"These are orders from the Führer," I said.

"He must come here himself, then. The doors cannot be opened without the presence of authority."

I reached into my haversack and pulled out the bottle of schnapps. "I have also been ordered to give you this."

He inspected the bottle, making furtive glances beyond us. "Do you have anything to eat in there?"

I did have another can of meat, so I produced that for him, and now he said, "How long will this take?"

Not knowing, I said, "Half an hour."

"You have fifteen minutes." He glanced around again, then inserted the key and swung open a steel door, pushed me inside, switched on a weak light, and closed me in there. The first thing that came to me was the smell: no stench at all, only musty air, which was soothing. Left uncovered and coated in dust, paintings, vases, sculptures, and tapestries were stacked on shelves and piled against the walls. Landscapes looked haunted. Roman figures in white stone stood like phantoms. Dozens of wooden crates lay everywhere. Vati, Vati, how I wished he could be here, pointing out this and that as he used to do in the back rooms of museums and galleries, even though the details often bored me. Grief surged into my lungs, a sudden burst, and my vision went blurry. But, dearest God, my time was short and the number of things overwhelmed me. The Führer, Reichsleiter Bormann had said, wanted Schliemann's jewelry: necklaces, earrings, amulets, bracelets. I hurried from crate to crate, seeing only labels for the Kaiser's coin collection. Just as I thought my fifteen-minute limit must have expired, I discovered the one marked *Gold*. With a chisel Bormann had supplied, I pried off the top. I pulled out six things, all of them wrapped in cloth, and placed them in my bag.

I sat there with my back to the wall, relieved that I had completed this task, relieved to be in a quiet room that did not stink. I closed my eyes.

Soon I found myself stepping into a large airplane, hand in hand with Zenzi, on a flight out of Berlin. We rose into the clouds. Through the little windows we could see the flames below. The Russians were shooting but couldn't reach us. We landed near the Americans, at the River Elbe. A brass band greeted us with triumphant marches. There we boarded a sleek green ship, bound for the United States. My parents met us on the lower deck, they had been waiting all this time, and I hugged and hugged them. Just as we were leaving the dock, Stalla leaped aboard, flashing his grin, whooping. We were all delirious with happiness, and for the next few days, we cruised over calm waters, dancing, laughing, eating exorbitant meals, until one day a God-like voice, touched with anger, boomed down at us from above: "Your time is up, your time is up!"

The guard had charged into the room, brandishing the empty bottle of schnapps. "It has been an hour, do you want me to be court-martialed, do you want me to hang? I don't care if you work for the Grofaz or not! Your time is up!" He tried to swat me but missed, and I scurried out, hopping over the reeking mass as I stumbled down the stairs, hauling my bag of treasure.

I elbowed my way to the exit but somehow got re-directed by the shoving of the crowd, pushed toward one corner. Here, amid the roar, I caught sight of what I believed to be a familiar face, the fleshy jowls and the big gleaming forehead of Otto Köckler. Was it? The man, dressed in civilian clothes, was hunched over, his back against the wall.

Reaching him, I said, "Herr Köckler?"

His head rose, his eyes seemed to shiver. He did not reply.

"Are you working here now?" I asked.

He did not look at me. "You have the wrong man."

"It's Tobias! I'm back from the front."

"Go away." The words were snarled. "I don't know you."

"Tobias Koertig. Do you see?" But the man resumed his hunching and I backed off. I had made a mistake, still fuzzy-headed from my nap. I glanced again at the face, now in shadow, and became unsure. With all this noise and smell, it was easy to become confused, I reasoned.

I proceeded to my next destination, the Adlon Hotel, a grand place that had somehow escaped any significant damage. I sprinted through the Tiergarten, then under the Brandenburg Gate's bronze horses and chariot—twisted and dented, no longer so heroic—and across the debris of Pariser Platz, to the hotel's crowded dining room. The scene was precisely opposite of what I had just left. Here there was order and elegance, there was laughter and beer and plenty of food. Waiters in black hurried around, serving tables lined with soldiers, suited civilians, and grinning officers of the SS. Creamy-skinned Labor Service girls wheeled silver carts, pouring beer and coffee. Only when a shell landed nearby were there any scowls.

I spotted Bormann at one of the back tables. As he had instructed, I raised my left arm and touched my head, the signal for my success, then went out again, to wait for him at the abandoned, burned-out Reichstag. Behind it lay a vast lake, where bombs had severed a water main. Here I sat, cold but getting drowsy again, my eyes half closed, imagining that the water's surface—roughened by rain, glimmering with the reflected orange of a nearby fire—was the lake at Spiez in Switzerland, where one summer I had rowed my parents by lantern light. But soon I heard labored breathing, then saw Bormann's bulk approaching.

"Crouch low, boy," he said with sharpness, "so we can't be seen. There are traitors everywhere. What have you got? Did you have any trouble with the guard?"

"I had to give him the schnapps."

"They're all drunkards now. Drunkards or cowards." His breath, emerging in big white plumes, once again carried the sweetness of alcohol. "Open up the fucking bag so that I can see."

He pushed his wide clumsy hands inside and pulled out the jewelry. He spread the pieces on his palm, one after the other. His rubbery lips spread into a grin and he fell silent, into a kind of daze. Then he stuffed the bracelets and necklaces into the pockets of his tunic. Louder, he said, "You have told no one about this?"

I shook my head with vigor.

"You will repeat your efforts tomorrow night. Medical

supplies first, then the gold. Here, another bottle of schnapps. Bring me twice as many items. Understood? You are helping to preserve the Reich. Nothing is more honorable." He detailed a different location, nearby, where I was to meet him, then glanced around and waddled back the way he'd come.

15

Late April, and I had seen a blossom or two, but they were like memories of a far-off time—for the news was grim, despairing, it skewered my heart. The Russians, dearest God, had surrounded the city. The circle was tightening each hour around the Berlin neck—we would soon be strangled. The northern areas of Pankow and Wedding and Weissensee had been torn up, house by house, smashed with rockets and point-blank howitzers and then reduced to cinders by the dragon-like flamethrowers. In the South, Zehlendorf had fallen, some said the town hall was now surrounded by a moat of blood, boys' blood, and the Russians also controlled Templehof airport. Smoke hung above the streets now like clouds that never went away.

In the HQ bunker, I witnessed sobbing farewells and a general rush of departures. Officers drifted through as aimless ghosts, pale and sullen, or sometimes the opposite, flushed and boozy, full of jokes. Few seemed to possess duties anymore.

But Herr Axmann, clean and never drunk, remained one of the faithful. He directed his boys to the very end with bright encouragement, like those coaches in school who always tried to teach us good sportsmanship no matter what the score: never give up, always play with your best effort, be true to yourself, honor is everything.

Here he was again, speaking to me about my drawings as I received, early in the morning, my rations from Fräulein Manziarly...

"The detail was excellent," Axmann said. "Exactly what we need. Very useful. However, imagine my surprise, Koertig, when I saw the Führer inspecting certain other pictures. And of course you know what I mean. Jules Verne nonsense! Fantasy! A waste of precious time! If it were up to me, I would call this a dereliction of duty."

I cringed. "I promise not to do it again."

"But you *will* do it again. As it happens, the Führer found them very pleasing. You seem to be quite skilled in making him smile. So now you will produce both, by request from the very top: scenes of the streets according to my orders and, from your imagination, architectural entertainment. Understood? Still, despite all this, I am forced to punish you for your disobedience. For an entire week, I am prohibiting Fräulein Manziarly from giving you tarts, éclairs, or anything sweet."

I nodded and saluted. Behind Axmann, the Fräulein gave me a sad shrug. She stood beside a thickly frosted chocolate cake, which sat on the counter like a large anti-tank mine. My mouth ached for even just a taste. She had made it, she'd told me earlier, to celebrate the arrival of the Goebbels children, who were raising a racket nearby. Of course that cake would not have looked so delicious had I known that they would all soon be poisoned.

"There is something else, Koertig." Axmann's mouth became

pinched, going white. "Have you ever drawn a formal portrait?"

"A few times. That was part of my training, I mean with the pencil."

"I am happy to hear that. You may be asked to do one very soon. I cannot say more at the moment, but the request is a high honor, Koertig—be proud." He kneeled and put a hand on my shoulder as we heard the thump-thump-thump of explosions above us. "You are young, it is true, but I feel quite strongly that you are a rising star in the future of the Reich. Let us all work hard to ensure that we have one."

But even Axmann had not managed to push my mood above the gloom. Of course I wanted to believe, like those boys who had perished in Zehlendorf, that we could still turn the Russians back. But how? Though I lacked any experience in military assessment, the preparations I recorded appeared slapped-together and hodge-podge. I did not see many leaders. A few tanks waited in the streets, but they didn't have much gas, I knew. The ragged Volkssturm men hunched around their positions flinching at every crash. The barricades they had erected were just as I had seen before, full of junk dragged from homes. It looked as if you could knock them down with a good strong kick. The civilians who remained had lost their faith, too. On the city's crumbled walls, harsh graffiti appeared everywhere now, hastily painted in thin white strokes—"Beat it, Kerl!" and above a corpse "Fresh meat here" and elsewhere "Mein Führer, to plan our victory, you must remove your head from your ass." Naturally I left such things out of my illustrations, but they were further eroding my spirit. I found it hard, too, to summon enthusiasm for more Berlin fantasy, now that my creations were not intended for Zenzi.

It was my dejection, getting worse by the hour, that led me to search for Stalla that afternoon. My continued shame over the mistakenly awarded medal and the drawings that had implicated him as a scoundrel had so far kept me from making the effort. But if anyone could restore my confidence, it would be Albrecht. He had told me he'd been assigned to some sort of labor detail, and so, late in the day, I talked to a few old men from the Volkssturm, who directed me to a barber shop, where their commander was spinning in one of the chairs, gulping beer for supper. He issued a slurred dismissal when I made my inquiry, but I was experienced now with bribes and offered him my small pot of buttered spaghetti, packed for me by Fräulein Manziarly (the Führer's favorite dish, she said). He scribbled a note and told me to take it to the dispatcher of labor, nearby in a gutted bank. This man referred to a chalkboard and then said, "Stalla, Albrecht, barricade duty," and named a bridge on the Spree.

At the river, a group of boys were filling another wrecked trolley with rubble. There, in the middle of the pack, stood a wide-shouldered boy with a fuzzy beard and giant ears—grimy, sweat-shiny Stalla. In torn trousers and a jacket so small it did not come down to his waist, he was plucking bricks from a wheelbarrow. I presented myself and he flashed me a grin. "What are you doing, you lazy asshole," he said in mock disgust, "wandering around like that. Looking for something to do? I thought they'd send you back to the front."

I explained to him my new position.

"So you saw the man himself."

"He likes my drawings. He made me his special illustrator right on the spot."

"Well, good for you."

"What a place he has down there," I said, pointing at the ground. "You wouldn't believe the amount of food."

"So that's what the Iron Cross gets you," he said.

I fell into a near-whisper so the other boys would not hear. "I'd give it to you in a minute if I could." Embarrassed by the bunker's luxuries, by my sketching, I tried to muster up importance. "At night I deliver medical supplies."

"You better get plenty. From what I've heard, those Mongol bastards are going to turn this city into a bloodbath."

"Do you still think we can win?"

"Maybe so, if everybody fights."

I picked up on his meaning and said nothing.

"Fenzel's in Berlin now, too," Stalla informed me. "He said he's going to get me back in the unit. What a crazy bastard—you should see him now, he's got a leather nose—but I'd join up with him again. I want to stomp on more of those Russian worms. "This shit"—he hurled a brick into the trolley—"stinks."

An ancient, white-haired, hollow-eyed guy, his arm banded by the white Volkssturm ribbon, demanded in hoarse shouts that Stalla return to his work.

I fished a can from my haversack. "Do you want one? Beef."

"You keep it. Put some flesh on those chicken bones of yours. Say hello to the Führer for me and don't break your pencil."

With great reluctance I said farewell, promising to see him again but wondering if I would. A biting ache came to my throat, for I wanted so much to romp around with him, to tell him about my visits with Zenzi, to play Schnapsen, to ride bicycles in the Tiergarten, to shout our crazy thoughts about life, but it could not be done, nothing was normal, normal had been buried. I left him there heaving bricks.

That night, as my pessimism kept growing, I felt some comfort from Vati. Permit me to explain, Doctor Schenck had sent me across the Spree to the Charité Hospital. I knew the place from a long-ago day—it must have been the summer of 1939, just before the war had started—when Vati had surgery to remove a swollen hemorrhoid. My mother had something else to do and so Vati had taken me along to help him hail a taxi in case, later, he had trouble walking. Only seven, I clutched his hand, voicing my worry that somehow he was going to die. He broke out into laughter, flung back his head, and told me, still sputtering, that it would be too embarrassing to let his *popo* kill him. I remembered all this on the way, and there was an instant when I felt—I was certain—the warmth of his large hand on mine.

After collecting the things that Schenck wanted, I stopped on the way back at the river. It seemed almost peaceful here. The city was quiet for a change. No shells were falling, and the *tak-tak-tak* of distant guns sounded no more threatening than a barking dog. Another steady drizzle crackled on the ruins and rinsed away the dust. A few youth-army boys guarding the nearest bridge were singing. I looked into the water, and for the first time I considered an escape. The urge felt wrong, especially after Stalla's promise to continue the fight, but it persisted. I imagined a raft, big enough for me and Zenzi. I imagined floating away on the river like Tom Sawyer and Huckleberry Finn, floating undetected past the Russian line, to the west and the Americans. I thought about this for a while, long enough to consider what supplies we might need, until one of the boys shouted some insult in my direction about shirking.

At the Zoo bunker, I grabbed more pieces of the Schliemann treasure. The guard had taken the schnapps with half a grin. He whispered that such an arrangement could continue, but warned me about the SS, who had been prowling around. "There's one named Weinrich, he's come by twice," he said. "Untersturmführer. A nasty piece of shit. But if you could bring some food next time..."

Despite the bunker's smell, as awful as it was before, I did not head to the exit. I still had some time before I had to meet Bormann. At the bottom of the stairs, I edged toward that same corner where I thought I had seen Otto Köckler. I wanted to know if my eyes had played a trick before. But was this more than just curiosity? Did I also suspect that Herr Köckler had deserted his post, that he was hiding here as a civilian? On a night when I could not stop thinking about the Russian encirclement, it is possible—no, probable—that I wanted to find some fellowship in the secret act of giving up. I scanned the sea of faces, unable to focus. So I switched to looking at the wall, trying to pinpoint the location. Hadn't I seen him near that *Rauchen Verboten* sign? I concentrated. But all I kept thinking about was Netobrev, Netobrev—Dohndorf's ridiculous game had gotten into my head. A few times, since coming back to Berlin, I had found myself devilishly reversing the Führer's name...Floda...the name of a dog, I thought, which would make me smile...Floda!...which would have made Vati smile...

Now wasn't that a waving arm? Beckoning me, I was sure. I moved closer. Yes, there, not very clean, still pudgy but looking ill, seated on the floor, was Herr Köckler. This time I was certain.

"Tobias," he said, his voice almost drowned out in the human roar.

"Did you not recognize me before?"

"Crouch so that you can hear me. I don't want to shout. I'm not well."

"Were you in the hospital here?"

Herr Köckler stared at me, blank-faced. "So you're back from the front. An Iron Cross, I see. I knew you would be a good soldier."

"Now I'm assisting with the defense of Berlin. And delivering medical supplies—"

"Yes? Then you must tell me: how far away are the Russians now?"

"Zehlendorf, Pankow—but I'm not really sure. All around us."

"Too close, in any case." One of Herr Köckler's hands, black at the fingertips, rose to wipe away the sweat that dripped near his temple, then stayed there, shielding one eye. "Would you have anything to eat?"

"No," I said, then decided to test my suspicions. "But the Adlon is serving meals to officers, all night I think."

"Not possible!" He shook his head, then murmured, patting his stomach, "It's only a field kitchen there now, and the food does not agree with me, you understand." Now he motioned me closer. "Tobias, I would like you to help me with something. Do you know the Hotel Fürstenhof?"

"It's a ruin."

"Yes, yes, I am aware of that. But listen. Could you meet me there tomorrow night?"

"For what, Herr Köckler?"

"Hush, hush. Can you do it? Midnight, tomorrow. Come alone, without a light. No one can know that I have asked you. Bring a little food, if you could."

"I will try," I said, but in truth, I regretted having found him. Perhaps I was correct about his status, but here was another task and another secret, and I only wanted to sleep.

A little later, near the entrance of a U-Bahn station, I handed the collected jewelry to Bormann, who was drunk again, then descended into the bunker to deliver the medical supplies to Schenck, and then collapsed on my cot. There were no shrieks from the casualty station, the corridor was fairly quiet, yet I remained wide awake. The next morning I knew I would see Zenzi again, and I kept wondering if I would find the courage to make the decision she expected, to flee the city and the war.

16

"Sensing his death was near, Goebbels paid a visit to the Pope, hoping he might book a suite in Heaven." Klingmüller the Buffoon was telling another joke. I had been on my way to meet Zenzi in the abandoned apartment, circling around the Volkssturm barricade to avoid their pranks, but out popped the black greasepaint grin with the bowler hat and suspenders. I did not budge, for Klingmüller— lunatic, cynic, or informer, I did not know—unsettled me. "The Pope takes Goebbels into an elevator, and they rise to the top floor. There Goebbels sees a life of boredom: shapeless angels sleeping on clouds—no cabaret, no films or music halls. No entertainment at all! Goebbels now asks the Pope if he might see what Hell has to offer. The Pope points to a narrow staircase leading down, into darkness. At the bottom, Goebbels discovers a paradise, where buxom starlets in skimpy bathing suits parade around pools, serving champagne. Goebbels immediately makes a reservation. When his end finally comes, Satan escorts Goebbels to a fiery pit full of demons. 'This is preposterous,' cries Goebbels. 'Where is the pool, where are the sexy girls?' Satan smirks: "Effective propaganda!"

I had heard this joke before, too—someone had told it a few years before in our villa to good effect. But I only said, "I must go."

"By all means," said Klingmüller, broadening the grin. "Another visit with your girl, no doubt!"

I cringed and stepped back.

"But don't worry my boy, my lips are sealed! What about a small donation? Not for blackmail, but for humor. You must admit that I am funny!"

I hesitated, then handed him a chunk of soggy bread that had sat in my pocket for a couple of days. A small payment, I figured, for the memory of my parents' laughter.

"Thank you, thank you, you are helping to preserve humankind! Come back anytime!"

I scooted away, around the corner, to check on the second-story horse. There he was, now slumped against the remaining wall. I tossed up a potato, which I had brought for him, watched for a minute to see if he might try to reach it, but he seemed uninterested. So I ran across the street, slipped into the apartment building's wrecked lobby, and aimed a throaty whisper upward. "Are you there?"

"Of course I am."

Up the scorched sofa as I had done before, I found Zenzi sitting on the bed in a blue jumper, all smeared with brick dust like a baker's apron.

"I fed the horse," I said.

"You can't see him anymore from here."

"He's too weak to stand."

She nodded, scowling. "Sit next to me. I have something to show you."

"I shouldn't stay long. This guy, this clown, Klingmüller, knows we're here, I think."

"Who?"

"Down the street. But just a crazy person. Is it food?"

"A newspaper."

"The *Beobachter*?"

"Not that stupid thing."

"*Der Panzerbär*?" The Armored Bear. It was a cheap bulletin I'd seen, intended to excite everyone into defending Berlin.

"Ech. No." She reached down into her dress and pulled out the creased and wrinkled pages. "If my father knew I took it, he would strangle me. It's dangerous to carry around. He was afraid to show it, but finally he did. This is why he's known about the things I told you. It's from Geneva. You must whisper."

"The date is last year."

"He kept it from me. And it was smuggled in. That takes a while."

"What do you know about smuggling?"

"Don't be such a boy." She opened the paper with trembling hands. "I told you about that report from the BBC on the camp, and you didn't believe it. So look—here's another. This one's in Poland. Two Czechs who escaped are saying that the most horrible things are happening there. Prisoners are killed every day by some kind of poison, and then they're all burned."

"Where? What prisoners?"

"Jews. Or anyone who doesn't like the war or the Kerl." She scanned the story. "Auschwitz?"

"I've never heard of the place. How do you know the British didn't write it?"

"The paper is from Switzerland. They're not in the war. They're not spreading lies."

"The British could have dropped the poison."

"The British, the British! That's your answer for everything. Look, it says the prisoners go into showers, and they think they're going to be washed, but they're tricked—gas comes out of the spouts. That's the poison. The guards also shoot them for any reason, or starve them, or work them to death."

I leaned in to read, and the words crawled across my vision like insects: beatings...typhus...hangings...laughing...naked...gassing...furnaces...cremation...ashes...fertilizer.

"Does your father think it's true?"

"Yes, yes, that's why he was afraid to show me," she said. "Now I want to scream these things to everybody. Fertilizer, Tobias! I keep thinking about all the people I used to know who might have gone there. Frau Anders, who worked at the apothecary, who disappeared. Herr Reiner, the history teacher. Whenever he lectured about a war from another era, he always asked what good it had done. One day he didn't show up. They told us he had to go to the hospital for a while. They said the same thing about Fräulein Krukenberg when she suddenly left. But everyone knew she hated the Kerl, too."

"Fräulein Krukenberg!"

"Why do you look so afraid?"

"Do you remember, in typing class, when I discovered the secret of the number 3? When you held down the shift key..."

"It would type the SS symbol."

"Everyone started to do it. She became terribly angry. After that, she always rapped my knuckles with a ruler."

"You didn't keep your fingers curled. But she gave you the gold ribbon later. You were even faster than Sabina Rau."

"Zenzi! When that ruler hit me—I sometimes hated Fräulein Krukenberg so much I wished she'd die." I rubbed my knuckles, I closed my eyes. "I'll go straight to hell."

"No, Tobias, you sweet boy, not you, no. The people who built the camp, who run it, they will go to hell."

I fell back onto the bed, staring up at the shattered ceiling.

In the street, the Volkssturm men had started an argument, and I could also hear the thudding of distant shells, and then, very close, a bird going *crip-crip-crip*, it must have made a nest inside the wall...and now there came a smell, between the whiffs of smoke, of muddy earth and springtime, which made me think of kicking a ball across a field, and digging in the garden with my mother...

I began to tremble, first in my shoulders, and then in my jaw, and then it spread to my legs, and I could not keep still. Zenzi gripped my hand, concerned, and I wondered for a moment if I had acquired another fever, but no, it was something else, something trying to emerge, in fact I knew exactly what. I shuddered for a while longer, then released what lay inside me. "I will come with you to the Americans," I said.

There was a kiss on my forehead, but I did not return it. Though my trembling had disappeared, I had run out of strength...I closed my eyes...*crip-crip-crip*...that bird was singing to us...*crip-crip*...I wanted so much to fall asleep...

But a shrill bell began to pierce the air. We both jumped—an alarm, warning of tanks or airplanes. Then we understood that the sound was coming from the kitchen. I leaped off the bed and discovered, near the calendar displaying February and its picture of the Heinkel, that the large telephone was ringing and ringing.

"The wires still work," Zenzi said.

"It might be the Reichsjugendführer, trying to find out if I am shirking. I am supposed to be in Charlottenburg today."

"That doesn't make any sense. They could not possibly know that you're here."

The sound tore at my nerves. "Maybe Klingmüller told them!"

"We better stop it from ringing. Someone will hear it and get curious."

We both stared at the black object for one more insistent ring, and then I seized the receiver, pressing the cold thing to my ear. A feeling of strangeness surged through me, for it had been weeks since I had spoken into a telephone.

"Hello? Hello? Is someone there?" The voice on the other end, coming through crackles and hiss, came as a big relief, for it was not Axmann or the Führer. No, a woman.

"I am here," I said.

"Ah, my God! Tobias! Is that really you?"

My heart flipped. My throat became tight. I squeaked out some words. "Yes, it's Tobias—"

"What a relief! My God, my God. We have been trying and trying, we were so afraid, we had heard so many terrible things. I am thrilled to hear you! Are you in good health? Your voice sounds strange, it must be the connection."

"I am very sleepy, and a little hungry, but who is—?"

"You must come join us, then! Please don't be so stubborn this time. We have plenty of food here, plenty of room. I know we've had our disagreements, now we must forget all that. To stay there any longer is madness."

Zenzi made a gesture to ask who had called and I scowled and shook my head.

I was groggy, and so maybe that explained why I asked, "What kind of food?"

"Milk, eggs, bread—"

"Raspberry Pfannkuchen?"

"Don't start joking, you must come here at once. Are the trains still running?"

"Is this Klingmüller?"

"Tobias, we must be serious. Your father will speak to you. He knows more about the trains."

More crackles and hiss, and now a man's voice. "Tobias? Don't joke with your mother, she's not in the mood these days for anything like that."

"Vati?"

"Which lines are still operating? Is anything getting through?"

"You and Mutti are alive!"

"Don't be ridiculous. Of course we are. There are no bombs here. Are you ill? Your voice is very thin."

"You sound different, too."

"We love you, son. We only want you to join us."

"I will, I will!"

"Tobias, tell me about the trains..."

Then the crackling got louder and the connection went dead with no sound at all and I began to weep.

"Did they know you?" Zenzi asked.

"They were my parents." Tears were sprouting on my face.

"Tobias, Tobias, you sweet boy, you are dreaming."

"No, it was them, it was them, they knew my name."

I had to find out where they were. I rushed over with Zenzi to the edge of the Tiergarten, to the gravesite. Panting, sticky with sweat, I stared down at the spot. The earth was churned a little. I ignored Zenzi's suggestion that shell fragments had done it, I did not want to hear such logic. No! My parents themselves had pushed their way out and risen, they had been granted another chance at life, we would all leave Berlin together! How else could you explain what I had heard on the telephone? I dragged Zenzi over to my family's villa, which I had avoided since the bombing. Could it have been resurrected, too? Might we open the door and climb the stairs, could I introduce Zenzi as my Freundin, could we all sit in the parlor and sip Fanta?

My blood turned into lead at the vision—the same heap of bricks and pipes and splintered timber. But I was determined to find some sign of my parents and I stalked around and around. Zenzi offered comfort but also encouraged me to return to my work, fearing now that I would be punished for shirking and prevented from making the journey with her. After an hour or so, I finally saw it, a tiny miracle, wedged into a crevice where a weed had already sprouted, scorched a little but intact: my copy of Friedrich Mader's *Wunderwelten*, still wrapped in its dust jacket, which pictured scientists poking their heads out of a spaceship, marveling at the swirling cosmos. I had read it against the wishes of Vati, who considered it nonsense.

"They left it for me," I told Zenzi. "To prove that they're still here."

"Maybe," was all she said, for she had grown impatient. "Go now. Finish your sketches. Do nothing to make anyone suspect. Meet me at our apartment tomorrow, the same time. I will have news of our plan, I'm sure." She took my hand and kissed my palm. "Mein Liebster, mein Liebster," she said, "ich gehöre Dir." My dearest, my dearest, I belong to you.

For the rest of the day, I could hardly bring myself to sketch, for I became convinced that my parents were wandering through the city, looking for me. I kept seeing them on every street. That man in the suit with the fringe of gray hair, the woman in the heavy shoes...I wondered if weeks under dirt might have altered their appearances...yet I couldn't quite remember how they looked, for I had no pictures of them at all.

I followed various people through blocks of ruins, trying to examine their faces. Late in the afternoon, I became convinced that I had found my father. A man in an overcoat waddled hatless down the street, with his shoulders hunched, the way Vati had done. The strong-angled nose was the same! The baldness, too! I rushed up and shouted "Look! Look! It's me!" My skin shuddered, my hands shook. The man sped up, twisted his face toward me and growled, "Nothing to spare! Beg from someone else."

17

That night, my skull was a stewpot again, filled with boiling distress. I worried that I might betray my soon-to-happen desertion by some anxious twitch or a blurted phrase, I worried that I would be leaving my parents behind (my parents, who had begged me on the phone to join them!), I worried that Zenzi might be taken away to the camps, I worried about getting past the Russians (an impossibility, it seemed).

Yet I had managed to complete my deliveries—to Axmann and Schenck and Bormann—without revealing, I was sure, any hint of my plans. I trudged back through the muddy soup of the Chancellery's former garden, I knocked on the bunker's emergency-exit door with the Wagner rhythm, getting it right on the first try even though the half-asleep guard did not seem to care much anymore. I was very happy not to receive his musical commentary, for all I wanted was to lie on my cot. But my duties, as it happened, had not ended. When I reached the bottom of the circling steps, there stood before me a man in a long overcoat, a pair of round green glasses on his sallow face. He grasped a leather leash, which was connected to a sleek and muscular Alsatian. There stood Adolf Hitler.

"Blondi needs to go out," the Führer said, not quite looking at me. His free hand trembled and trembled. The rooms around us were quiet. It was the first time I had seen his dog.

Terrified that his authority would make me falter, I tried to disguise my nervousness by saying, too loudly, "I have just helped preserve more of the gold, mein Führer!"

"What did you say?"

"The Schliemann treasure..."

Confusion had come to his face. "What do I care about those trinkets?"

A blunder on my part! He was trying to keep the operation secret, of course, since the guard upstairs might overhear us. Now he was inspecting me, surely considering the punishment! But then he said, "Aren't you the boy who is making those sketches?"

I squeezed out an answer. "Tobias Koertig. You presented the Iron Cross to me."

He peered over the round lenses, which looked almost black in the dim light. "Koertig, you said? How bright is it outside? I would rather dispense with these damnable glasses, but I have sensitive eyes."

"It's the middle of the night."

"Is it?" He looked at Blondi with a blank expression, apparently forgetting why he stood there. There came from his pants a sharp explosion, and then another. "Where is Linge? Linge! His pills do nothing for my trouble." He stared into the hallway before removing his glasses, and then focused on me again with yellow, watery eyes. "Ah, Koertig, yes, it is you. The artist. Your work has impressed me."

"I am doing my best to help us keep out the Russians." A wretched stink like burnt rubber rose around me. I thought I might faint, I tried not to gag. "In Charlottenburg today—"

"Don't worry about those Russians. They're faltering as we speak. I'm talking about your rocket cars, your towers, your glass structures for the zoo. Giraffes four stories up! Marvelous. You'll give me more, won't you?" Once again his gaze veered away to some distant object. "I was reminded of The Great Hall. Speer and I had planned it, a massive structure, a mountain in the middle of Berlin! It would have been wondrous. But even Speer is a pessimist now. No one believes in the future anymore. I am surrounded by defeatists. Still, whenever I stand before youth my faith is renewed! You have given me confidence. We *will* rebuild. Providence is on our side. The death of Roosevelt was only the beginning. Other events will soon turn the tide. And so we must have plans in place to ensure the survival of the race. Not just architectural, you understand—also biological! Do you have a girlfriend, my boy?" I nodded meekly. "Very good! This second war in thirty years—forced on us by Jewry!—has depleted our numbers of young men. The birthrate must be increased. Ten fold! A hundred fold! If I could have given more furloughs to the soldiers! What is her name?"

"Zenzi, mein Führer."

"You must give Zenzi a child! Breed! Breed, I say! Beget! The old rules of marriage no longer matter. Illegitimacy is nonsense. Everyone must participate who is capable. To show them how serious I am, I will tax bachelors, I will tax childless marriages. The future is ours if we want it." The Alsatian looked up at its master with beseeching eyes and groaned a little. "If the people around me were half as loyal as a dog, we would have been victorious two years ago. In the last war, I had a little white terrier named Foxl, he had deserted the English, he had crossed the shell holes and come over to us. We became the closest of friends. I taught him how to climb a ladder, how to fetch my boots. He was always at my side, day or night, always obedient. That is loyalty! Then a secret Jew or Bolshevik stole him, and I fell into misery." The Führer went silent for a moment, then cocked his head upward. "What are the conditions outside?"

"There is very little fighting at the moment."

"But the weather."

"It is raining a little."

"Ah! That is too bad. I do not want to get wet. Tornow is drunk again, and there is no one else to take her out. She cannot make a mess down here. Are you fond of dogs?"

"I like all animals."

"Yes, yes! It is a shame—a crime!—that so many insist upon slaughtering them. Do you eat your vegetables, my boy?"

"I have not seen many lately—"

"Never avoid them. Manziarly is always trying to slip some meat into my meals. There are too many like her who believe that nutrients exist only in cooked flesh. But Caesar's army, one of the greatest ever assembled, was vegetarian! And Japanese wrestlers, among the strongest men in the world, do not eat meat! For that matter, a single Turkish man, who stuffs himself with lentils, grain, and eggplant, can carry a piano on his back! Compare the muscles and speed of a horse, a vegetarian, with those of the carnivorous dog. Yet Blondi has learned to love vegetables and herbs, and I think they've made her quite clever. Show him the Russian bear, Blondi!" The dog's tall ears folded down and she yawned. "The bear, Blondi, the bear!" After rising with hesitation, the Alsatian obeyed her master's signals and stood on her hind legs, lifting her front paws in a beggarly way, and walked a few steps. The Führer laughed with a snort. "The Russian bear pleads for mercy! Ha ha ha! Next time she will demonstrate how she talks!" He handed me the leash, and Blondi's tail wagged with great energy. "You don't need to take her far. Just enough for the business. She likes her privacy, so you will need to find a secluded area. And be careful she does not get away—she has a good nose for spies and Communists! I must return to work! Good night!"

I wanted only to sleep but could not, of course, decline the task. Up the steps to the iron door, where the guard gave me a sneer and said, "Why bother to let a dog piss outside when we are all pissing our pants inside." I headed out into a cold rain, Blondi keeping the leash taut. Distant rumbles, a glow in the sky of fire, still no shells falling. Blondi's long narrow snout sniffed and sniffed as she pulled me down the wet, glistening street, darting from ruin to ruin. Her mouth hung open in that way of a dog's delight with the world, a kind of laughter. She knew nothing and I envied her...I let her take me all the way to Potsdamer Platz, for I did not want to interrupt her happiness. Finally she squatted near the Columbushaus. I remembered how weird the building used to look in daylight, its glass front arcing along the street like something out of Buck Rogers. Now it was only a burned shell.

A cracking of wood or glass came from across the plaza and startled me into thinking that the Russians had already come this close. I swung my flashlight's beam around, brightening an upside-down ambulance and an upended horse cart and, further away, the brick doorways of the Hotel Fürstenof. Then with a piercing pain in my throat I realized I had forgotten all about Herr Köckler. He had wanted to meet me at the Fürstenof, at midnight. It was far past that now. What could I do? The dog needed to go back. Yet Herr Köckler was ill and had asked for my help. I dashed across the pavement, Blondi alongside me, and approached the hotel's black cavern, peering inside. I whispered Herr Köckler's name several times. Blondi was pushing her snout into the wreckage, sensing something.

Then, after a few minutes, a quiet voice from within: "Tobias?"

"I am sorry to be late."

"Why do you have a dog? Keep it away from me! Turn off the light!"

"She's friendly."

"Not so loud. Are you with a search party? The SS? Why the *dog*?"

"I am just walking her. She belongs to someone in the bunker," I said, not wanting to scare him by admitting that I had the Führer's pet, not wanting to scare myself.

"Where? What bunker?"

"Headquarters," I said. "Didn't I tell you I'm working there now?"

"My God, it'll have my scent now. They'll track me down." There was a thin, reedy sound to his voice, which embarrassed me a little. His wet, frigid hand gripped my own. "I beg you not to report me," he said.

"I won't do anything. Are you no longer staying at the shelter?"

"I have decided to make a journey. Do you understand? I am a man of God. I only want to return one day to the seminary and apply myself to the teachings of Jesus. They were going to send me to the front, I'm sure of it. A man of my age and delicate health. I'm not well. You can feel how cold I am. What use would it be? The war is lost."

To hear Herr Köckler say this—Herr Köckler!—was to feel that the end had really come. Blondi was tugging on the leash again. "But why did you want to meet me?"

"Did you bring any food?"

"No, I forgot. I forgot about coming here, there are so many things in my head."

"Tobias," Herr Köckler said, "I am asking for just a little help. A little compassion. I am placing all my trust in you. I have a fever, I'm certain. Hear me wheeze. The dampness has given me pneumonia! I need someplace dry. And some food. I stayed in the zoo shelter as long as I could, but it was awful, awful, and the SS were prowling around, yanking people out of there left and right. They're vicious wolves now. Executions everywhere!"

"Are they sending deserters to the camps?"

"Don't call me that. I am following the call of God. But what camps?"

"The prisoners are poisoned with gas, I've heard."

"Who? Who? I thought it was only Jews. Only Jews, Tobias!"

"I'm not sure. It's terrible just the same."

"Yes, yes, of course. But don't frighten me like that. I'm already in an agitated state."

"But it's true?"

Otto Köckler wheezed and coughed. "Do you hear how ill I am?"

"Do they really kill them with gas? And use them for fertilizer?"

"You're saying wild things, Tobias." The rain hissed and then somewhere a machine gun started up, hammering *clak-clak-clak-clak*. "Will you help me?"

I said, "You could go to a church."

"No, that's the first place the SS look. They tear apart every closet to find people who only want—who only want peace. Tobias, if I were young and fit—but my health has always been troublesome...if you know of a room, or a basement, somewhere I could gather supplies and recover a little before I set off..."

I pitied Herr Köckler in his current state, it must be admitted, even though I knew Zenzi had scorned his behavior. He had always been decent to me, it seemed. I considered telling him about my own decision to abandon the war, but I was exhausted and more than anything I just wanted him to stop talking so that I could return the dog and fall onto my cot, so I said, "I know of a place. An empty apartment that's not easily reached." Zenzi and I would no longer need it after I met her there in the morning. "You could go tomorrow. Tomorrow night."

"Bless you, Tobias, bless you. Fetch me at midnight, then, right here. I'm depending on you. If you could bring a little food…"

"But if for some reason I can't come," I said, "then you must go there on your own." With guilt, with the knowledge that I would never see him again, I described the street and how to climb the sofa.

Then I ran off, relieved to be free of him. Blondi led the way again, galloping, and for a few blocks, we were just a boy and a dog on an empty street, leaping over puddles, without the weight of cruelty or death.

18

Please forgive my typing and my mistakes, for my fingers are getting troubled. I mean to say that my heart is thrashing all around, and that makes it difficult to find the right keys. Also I have had three lagers, one right after the other, which I hoped would help but probably will only hinder. Permit me to explain, I know what is coming. Here is where things get more difficult, where everything changes...I wish I did not remember, but I do.

I had given Blondi a good long rub behind her ears before leaving her to settle at her master's door. But my time on the cot did not last long. At sunrise, or what passed for sunrise underground, Axmann was shaking me awake. "You must come with me at once," he said.

I assumed that he had somehow discovered that I had met with Otto Köckler the deserter and perhaps now suspected my own deceit. I was too tired to feel much terror. I followed him down a long dim corridor, then into a washroom, where an orderly brushed the mud from my pants, sponged my face, and combed my hair. There was a regulation, I guessed, that specified cleanliness for an interrogation or an execution.

"Speak only when spoken to," Axmann said, this time sterner.

Now someone pushed me along further, into the main section of the HQ bunker, and then past an iron door into a small chamber where I had first seen the Führer, and then into a room filled with the fragrance of lilac soap, cramped with ornate furniture, and crowded in the corners with luxurious gowns, coats, scarves, hats, and stoles. In the middle stood a blond woman in an elegant dress of aquamarine. Dangling from her neck, resting on her bare collarbone, a golden butterfly glimmered. She was holding a glass of champagne. "Tobias Koertig," she said after closing the door and leaving us alone. "The wonderful little artist. Do you remember who I am?"

"Eva," I replied. The same woman who had organized the party the night I had arrived in this place, who had suggested that I draw portraits, who had danced with everyone. Was she my interrogator? Was the scented air intended to lull me into a confession? A brown puppy, who'd been wriggling on the floor, was now nibbling on the toe of my just-cleaned boots. "Did Herr Axmann tell you why I wanted you here?"

"No," I said, expecting the worst.

"You're trembling. Would you like some champagne? No? Well, let me start by saying that Wolfi—ah! excuse me, a little mistake!—the Führer and I, we are close friends. Did you know that?" She giggled, colored, then sipped from her glass. "He has been admiring your talent. The drawings, I mean. He has spoken of you several times. Through all our troubles, he has never lost his love for art! What a wonderful imagination you have! Your Berlin of the future makes me giddy every time I see it. All that detail. So,

I hope this pleases you: I have decided—we have decided—to ask you to take on a special assignment."

We both ducked when a series of booms, somewhere above us, rumbled the walls and rattled her perfume bottles. The puppy had darted into the closet.

"The Russians are very tiresome," Eva said. Her plum-like cheeks, burnished with rouge, rose on a smile. "Can you keep a secret?"

"Yes, I am capable of that," I said, but didn't want another one. I was already filled with too many.

"We would like you to draw our portrait. An official, formal portrait. To be framed and displayed for future generations, so they may see us as we were. The two of us together. Do you think you can do that?"

I nodded, but only because I realized, just then, that I was not going to face a firing squad.

"We will try to supply whatever material you need," she continued, "as best we can. Herr Axmann will find you when it's time, but I wanted to tell you myself. All right, then, do not let me keep you from your regular duties. Is it rough up there?"

"It sounds like their artillery has started up again."

"Well, then, be safe."

Axmann ordered me to record more of the city's defenses, urging me not to get hurt. I was indispensable to helping create a legacy, he told me in a most serious tone—by which he meant the portrait, I guessed.

I didn't care about any of that, my single interest was to flee the bunker. But the booming above had become fierce, vibrating the floor. The guard at the top of the steps had disappeared. I stood at the iron door for a moment or two but the explosions were so loud that I had to go back down. It would not be possible to go out in such a storm of shelling. Around me, there was talk of the

Russian rockets, of thousands crashing down. I could only hope that Zenzi had not yet gone to the apartment. Already it was an hour beyond the time we were supposed to meet.

When the noise finally stopped, I ran back up the stairs, pushed open that heavy door, and beheld another planet. A yellow fog of dust blurred the air, making me choke, and above that, a thick bitter smoke swirled black and gray, oceanic. I stumbled through the freshly torn-up streets, getting lost several times because the visibility was so poor. There were bodies everywhere and I glanced at those nearest me to make sure they did not wear glasses and have a cleft in the chin.

Our building and our apartment had survived, though more of the roof had been carved away. I climbed up the sofa. She was not yet here, so I waited. Dearest God, let her be alive! I peered out the gap in the wall. Rain was falling, finding its way through the smoke. The dust was settling, which made it easier to see the street. The Volkssturm men were just starting to gather.

Then I saw that bulky coat and the dark hair hurrying through the debris. And then she was standing before me, as dirty as I was, gritty with dust and speckled with ash. We embraced and sat on the bed.

"Did your father decide?" I asked. "When do we leave?"

"The shelling," she said. "The shelling was so horrible. My mother became hysterical. Screaming, not making sense. She's in no state to go anywhere. My father, I think, has given up. I shouldn't have left them, but I wanted to see you. Coming here was very hard. You always think you've seen the worst, and then... it's the end of the world, Tobias."

"Have you given up, too?"

She looked stricken. "I don't know."

"I've heard that help is coming. From Potsdam, The Twelfth Army. There might be a path. We can try to find it."

"Then you've really quit?"

"I was given another assignment this morning," I said, "but I won't do it. I won't go back there. I'll throw my card into the rubble. My sketchbook, too." I took her by the hand into the hallway, then tossed everything into the mess below the wrecked stairwell. "You, too," I added, and she did the same with her card. Then I removed my Iron Cross ribbon and stuffed it in my pocket alongside the medal itself, both of which I intended to give to Stalla. I said, "There, we have quit."

She nodded a little. Behind her glasses tears were falling out like tiny pieces of ice. "Tobias, do you remember when we were in school and were collecting winter clothing for the soldiers? I put on that big fuzzy hat, and all the boys started calling me a Stalin girl. But you said I looked like someone Manet might have painted. It was the best thing anyone had ever told me. Manet! I knew we were going to be friends. In typing class I watched you draw little cartoons when Fräulein Krukenberg wasn't looking, and I couldn't believe how good you were. Sometimes I would think about kissing your neck. I even typed a couple of poems about you, but I was too afraid to let you see them. Then, in the shelter, when you were so nice to Einbrecher..."

"Why are you crying so hard?"

"We are not going to live much longer."

"No, you can't say that."

"No one in this city will. The Russians are raping and killing everyone."

"We'll make it out."

She managed half a smile. "What I wanted to do—what I hoped would happen later—well, it must happen now."

"What do you mean?"

"There's no time left. Please don't say No. We are going to get married."

She asked me to bring us some rainwater that she remembered had collected in the bathtub. I scooped it with one of the kitchen's dishes and we washed the grime from our faces and hands.

"So it's time," she said. "Are you ready? Stand here and look at me. Look at me like you love me. Do you?"

"Yes."

"All right. We may begin. Do I, Kreszentia Fuchs, take Tobias Koertig as my husband, even if he's still a boy and doesn't shave yet? Yes, with all my heart. Now it's your turn. Do you, Herr Tobias Koertig, take this beautiful woman called Zenzi as your wife who you will cherish forever, even if forever might be just tomorrow?"

"Yes."

"You must be definite."

"With all my heart!"

"Kiss me." She pulled my head to hers, our lips brushed, and she said, "The Mendelssohn! daa daa da-da da da da....all right, find a broom and a dinner plate."

I obeyed, searched for a few minutes in the kitchen as she continued to sing like a madwoman, and then held the requested items before her.

"Smash the plate on the floor," she said.

It shattered into a dozen pieces.

"Hold the broom with me," she instructed. "We will sweep it up together."

We did so, pushing the shards down the wrecked stairwell.

"Nothing will ever be broken in our household again," Zenzi told me. "That is what they do after weddings. Now it's the wedding *night*. Come into the bedroom. Please don't say No. Take off your boots and your pants."

She flipped off her own shoes, and then, leaving her sweater on, hiked up her skirt and pulled down her leggings and underwear.

Her bare thighs appeared before me rough with goosebumps and a little bluish, streaked here and there with short black hairs, which rose, denser, into the thick patch, far thicker than mine. I turned away, embarrassed, but she pulled me into the frigid bed and we shivered under the dusty blanket. Then she took off her glasses and said, "Lie on top of me."

"My whole body?"

"Yes, of course."

I kneeled on the bed and lowered myself onto her as if we were both fragile, as if the moment was going to disappear at the slightest wrong move. When her bare skin touched mine, I lost my mind. I mean to say, the war disappeared. The thumping of some big gun, somewhere not too far away, seemed of no consequence. We pressed our lower halves together. Awkwardly we rubbed and squeezed. Zenzi pushed my hand under her sweater, onto the 75mm softness, and I held tight, not quite knowing what else to do. Neither of us had the energy for anything more.

"Tobias und Zenzi Koertig," she said, then repeated, over and over, my name and her new name, which began to sound, in her melodious accent, like a silly children's song of gibberish. The bed was making us sleepy. That gun kept thumping but we did not flinch. My right eye lay very close to the dent in her chin, and I thought, I am looking up her nostril, it is a great privilege to do so, and these are the sorts of things you see when you are married.

"Tobias, think of something we would do if there weren't a war."

"Eat Pfannkuchen in a café."

"Yes, and then we could listen to a concert by the Philharmonic. Tell me another."

"Rowing a boat in the Tiergarten. On the Neuer See."

"Reading Balzac on the grass."

"A game of soccer."

"A warm bath..."

We went on like this for a while, dreaming, until we heard the sounds of crunching, of things being stepped on. We held our breaths to better pinpoint them: directly underneath us. "Klingmüller," I said, certain that the clown was playing a joke. I slipped onto the floor and pulled my pants on, then crawled past the kitchen's entrance to peer over the wrecked stairwell. There, covered in dust, huffing, trying to climb the sofa, was Otto Köckler.

"Tobias," he gasped, agony on his pudgy face, smeared with dirt. "I did not think I had the right place, I didn't think anyone would be here, but thank God you are...A blessing, a blessing.... Can you reach down, can you offer me a hand?"

I clutched Herr Köckler's sweaty, meaty paw and told him where to place his feet. After several grunts, he managed to roll up over the landing, where he lay full of wheezes. "The rain and the cold were too awful last night, I had to go back to the Zoo shelter... but there was an SS officer looking for someone...I was frightened, Tobias, I couldn't wait until tonight...but the rubble and the dust from the shelling, I got lost several times...I'm exhausted....you see what shape I'm in....and my foot, I stepped on something sharp, God help me if it gets infected...ah, who is that? Kreszentia Fuchs? I thought the place was unoccupied."

"We are just leaving," I said, embarrassed, needing to flee.

Zenzi, dressed but disheveled, shot me an indignant scowl. "Why is *he* here? And in civilian clothes?"

"He's ill," I said, "and needed a place to stay. He wants to leave Berlin. Just like we do. I told him he could come here, but not until tonight."

"You didn't! Why? Why? Today of all days! Our wedding day!"

Frowning, impatient, Herr Köckler hurriedly searched the

apartment, poking around the kitchen, trying to open the jammed door without success, and then peering into the bedroom. There he stiffened, then whirled. "Tobias! What has been happening here?"

I came inside. "Herr Köckler?"

"The sheets are tangled! The bed has been used. Do not tell me that you have allowed this girl to corrupt you!"

"You'll be glad to know," Zenzi said from the doorway, "that we are married."

"I see that nothing has dampened the girl's enthusiasm for satire."

"But, Herr Köckler," she said in a mocking tone, "this time I'm quite serious."

"Tobias, are you aware of her status? Do you understand what it means to be having relations with such a girl?"

"Push the fatso back over the edge," Zenzi yelled, "push him!"

"Listen to what she calls someone who saved her from death! I was under no obligation to allow a family with a background like hers into my shelter. Especially considering the mental health of the mother. It was a risk to my reputation and position, but it was my kindness—"

"You cannot say that about my mother!"

"—my kindness as a man of God."

"It was a bribe from my father! And you're not even a man. A deserter! A pig! A Jew-hating pig!"

"The devil is in you, child. Keep your voice quiet." He was standing at the bedroom's smashed wall, peering into the street. "Tobias, did you bring any food?"

"I did not expect you this early," I told him.

"Let him starve," Zenzi said. "Tobias, we must go, I don't want to spend another minute with him."

I started to leave, to go into the hallway, when Herr Köckler gasped. I turned around to see that he had ducked down into a crouch. His hands had tightened into fists. "My God, I think that's Weinrich out there. The SS officer from the Zoo shelter. Did he follow me? My God."

Zenzi and I rushed to the hole ourselves and looked. A tall, skinny-legged officer in a gray uniform, was striding toward us, past the barricade, trailed by the Volkssturm group, who were chattering, pointing, and carrying a ladder.

"Maybe they're going to help the horse," I said.

"No, Tobias, of course not," Zenzi hissed. "Come, come! We can't wait."

I chased her to the edge of the stairwell. Pale from terror, Zenzi was about to climb down, but I grabbed her. "We'll end up right in front of them. We'll go through here." I pointed to the door jammed shut, then pounded on it with my fists, then heaved my shoulder at the wood. Not a budge. Finally, after several attempts, Otto Köckler managed to smash it open. We tumbled into a dim room filled with a ghastly odor. Zenzi ran to the window, tearing aside the tattered curtains. I followed, then stopped short, too astonished to move, when I saw in the other shadowed corner the occupants of the apartment. They had been here all along. An older man with silver hair and a woman who wore a beaded evening gown. They both hung by nooses from an exposed ceiling rafter, their faces bloated like balloons. Two children, dressed in coats, lay nearby on a wooden table, curled up as if sleeping.

"Tobias, it's too high," Zenzi said. "And look how many bricks are down there. We'd break our legs."

"The bodies!" shouted Köckler. "Use their rope to climb down."

But now clanking came from the kitchen, the Volkssturm were placing the ladder. In another minute, before we could make ourselves jump, the officer, Weinrich, appeared in the doorway.

He brandished a pistol with gloved hands, brushed dust from his uniform. His face was small and pale, with a high forehead and nervous black eyes. He resembled a department-store clerk, but his grin made my legs wobble. "Follow one criminal and you always find more. Hands high! Above your heads!" He glanced at the dead family and shouted, "So is this where the cowards come to die? Berlin is teeming with cowards now! Despicable!" As he pushed us toward the kitchen, I noticed on the bedroom wall a painted message:

We wanted to spare the children a more terrible fate.
—Tobias and Ella Van Hoeven

It was not until much later, when panic no longer pulsed in my veins, that I understood with great dejection that I had not spoken to the souls of my parents on the telephone here, but to living strangers who had believed I was their grown son.

"You are under arrest," Weinrich said, waving his pistol at me. "Search him and the others," he told two of the Volkssturm men who had climbed up with him. "Search everywhere, find the gold." Then to me, "You were laughably easy to track down. I know you were taking the Schliemann treasure because the guard told me everything. And what happened to him for letting you do it? Shot in the back of his head. Where did you put everything you took, you pathetic little thief? Who got it? These two?"

I stood there dumbfounded. The only thing that could save us, I thought, would be to tell him the truth. "It wasn't stealing. Reichsleiter Bormann wanted it for safekeeping."

"Bormann! What do you know of Bormann?"

"I am Reichsillustrator, I work for the Führer and report to Reichsjugendführer Axmann."

"Show me your card."

"It fell, it fell into the rubble down there...I can find it, I'm sure."

"One more lie and I'll smash your teeth." He looked at Herr Köckler, who had turned green, who had pressed himself against the wall. "Your identification."

"Yes, yes, yes, of course, gladly." With a shaking hand, Herr Köckler presented his card—a surprise considering his intentions, but I soon understood.

"Schroeder," Weinrich said. "Are you receiving what the boy steals? Did you come here to collect it?"

"No, of course not, I will explain." His voice was faltering, sweat had sprouted on his brow. "My name is Otto Schroeder. I am simply a man who serves God. I studied at a seminary in Mainz. As you might guess, given my faith, I am greatly upset by the moral corruption in this city—"

"Yes, yes? Then why aren't you wearing a pastor's clothing, Schroeder?"

"I have not yet been ordained. The war interrupted—"

"Why are you with the boy?"

"Since that terrible shelling earlier, I have been searching for citizens trapped in the rubble. I heard voices coming from this building, one that I knew to be abandoned. And so I climbed up and had, just now, discovered this disgusting den of iniquity. Immoral acts! I don't know anything about the boy's thefts, but I was about to turn him over to the police in any case. It is painful to say"—he hesitated, looking at the floor, perhaps for dramatic effect, perhaps out of shame—"but I'm certain he is a deserter."

"He's lying," Zenzi said. "His name is Otto *Köckler*. The card is forged. He's the one who has deserted. Köckler! He came here to hide! He used to be an air-raid warden!" She glanced at me with frenzy in her eyes. "Tobias is telling the truth. He works for the Führer! The Führer gave him the Iron Cross!"

"She is a Jew," Otto Köckler said. "A Mischling. A wanton Mischling. She will say anything to save herself."

"A Jew?" Weinrich's dark eyebrows flew up, sprung loose from their scowl. He demanded to see Zenzi's card, but she told him it had been lost. "Yes," he said, "how convenient. But it's hard to miss. I could tell right away. The reek of your ass gives it away. Even from Mischlinge....Well, this is quite a catch. All of you, into the street. Volkssturm, steady the ladder!"

Shaken, stunned, I could not think. I tried to catch a glance from Herr Köckler, but he would not turn his eyes in my direction. I crawled down the ladder with the others, in front of Köckler, who had trouble lowering his bulk because of his injured foot. We stood silent in the street. The smoke, denser, was still spitting rain. Across the street, I glimpsed the second-story horse. He was standing now. His eyes were wide, glowing white. Two women had managed to push the skeletal creature into a narrow gap in the wall and were trying to overcome his last fleeting interests in life by launching him over the edge.

"Herr Schroeder," Weinrich said, "you have confirmed my suspicions about the boy."

"Thank you," Köckler said, still wheezing, "it is my duty—"

"That does not prevent you from disgusting me. You are fat and out of shape."

"I am afraid that I have never been athletic. But in God's eyes—"

"I do not care what God thinks! All of us must be physically fit now. You bear a responsibility to the Reich to lose weight. I am writing an order requiring vigorous exercise and the banishment of food from your mouth for the next 48 hours. Thereafter you will lose three kilograms each day. Anything else is treason. You will report at once to the Volkssturm, and you will begin life as a soldier. We have no further need of your efforts in discovering dying civilians or deserters. The SS handles that quite well."

"Of course, of course." Otto Köckler gave Weinrich a crisp salute, and he said, "Before I depart, Herr Untersturmführer, may I examine my foot, I believe I have injured it."

"As a soldier, you will have to endure pain much worse than that. Be quick!" He turned to glare at me and Zenzi. "Now we will take care of the others."

"Please don't do anything to her," I said. "Please let her go."

"A Jew-loving thief."

"I did not steal," I insisted. "I draw pictures for the Führer! If you go back and find my haversack, you will see my sketchbook."

"Where did you take the gold?"

"Eva will tell you who I am!"

"And who is Eva?"

"The Führer's friend. I am supposed to be drawing a portrait of them together."

"Preposterous." He raised a gloved hand and smashed his knuckles into my mouth. Down I spun into a numbing blackness. The sweetness of blood flooded my tongue. Zenzi knelt, offering a hand, uttering my name. As if to foretell our doom, that horse plunged, rolling a little in mid-air, and hit the street with a giant liquid smack.

"Do not touch the boy, Jew!" Weinrich, irritated by the minor spectacle of the horse, a distraction from his own performance, waved his pistol again as if he were swatting at bugs. "What is taking you so long, Schroeder? Soldiers must perform actions in seconds!"

"A puncture in my foot. I stepped on something very sharp."

Weinrich's eyes narrowed to black lines. "Let me see it."

"If I may have permission to remove the sock..."

"It is the sock that I wish to inspect."

"It is quite painful—"

"The sock has three size rings at the top."

"Yes, my feet are large."

Weinrich now stood over the seated Otto Köckler. "Size rings are sewn into socks issued by the Wehrmacht."

From where I knelt, pressing my jaw, I peered at Otto Köckler's lips as they contorted. He was just understanding his error. He rose slowly, his eyelids fluttered. "Yes," he stammered, "I found them, found them somewhere, I don't remember."

"You were issued those socks along with your uniform, which you have discarded. And your salute came rather easily, because the Wehrmacht taught you. You were hiding in that apartment, weren't you?"

"I am a man of God. It is true, yes, yes, I have been an air-raid warden, but the church, that is where I belong."

"You are a deserter. A fat, conniving coward. You gave me a false card, didn't you? A false name. Tell me, Jew, what did you say his name was?"

"Köckler," Zenzi muttered, shivering.

"I wanted to serve in the church," Herr Köckler said. "But I will become a soldier, I promise to do it, you can check on me later, I am very sorry for my behavior, I only want to live. Please don't harm me."

"Then show me, Köckler! Let me see you exercise! Let me see you run! In circles, right here. Go on, ten laps!"

Disbelief passed across Otto Köckler's face like a frigid wind, everything began to tremble, his eyelids, his mouth, his hands, his knees. I could hear his bowels bubbling, it seemed that he had lost control of them. He still wore a single shoe and when he started to jog, he wobbled unbalanced from side to side, saying "Bitte bitte bitte bitte."

Weinrich let him limp around a small loop three times before he lifted his pistol and shot him in the buttock. Otto Köckler crumpled to one knee, but still tried to drag himself along, pouring out yelps similar to those of a little dog.

"Continue, Herr Köckler! A soldier must learn to deal with a superficial wound! Run, run!"

Otto Köckler staggered, sobbed, and righted himself once more. Then Weinrich, perhaps getting impatient with his game, shot him three more times in the upper back. Köckler's arms reached forward as if to grasp at something none of us could see, and then he tumbled onto the glistening bricks in a heap.

Weinrich kept the pistol raised in triumph before shouting, "All cowards will be executed!" He swept his arms in grand gestures as he bellowed his words to everyone in the street. "Do not let this happen to you! Defend your city! Keep in shape! Lose weight! Fight the Russians! Preserve the Reich!"

Another voice, familiar and pleasant, echoed off the ruins: "Officer! May I lighten your mood for a moment?"

Weinrich spun toward the speaker, who had appeared in the half-destroyed, burnt-out shell across the street, in one of the empty window frames. It was none other than Klingmüller the Buffoon. He doffed his bowler and snapped his red suspenders, he raised his hand with the familiar stiff-arm salute and shouted "Heil Hitzkopf! Heil Hothead!" If I had not felt close to death I would have laughed. He ducked down, and then, after a moment, sprang into the next window, this time stretching wide his black, greasepaint grin before saluting again. "Long live the war!" he proclaimed. "Shoot everybody! Kill the world! Heil Hitzkopf!"

Like a carnival's rifle target, Klingmüller poked his head through other windows and jagged gaps in the wall. He popped in and out, doffed the bowler, saluted and cackled. This act increased Weinrich's rage, and he ordered, at first, the Volkssturm to seize the Buffoon. But the old men, who were fond of Klingmüller, only pretended to make the attempt. They shuffled about and pointed in different directions and issued a jumble of commands and observations. "Flank him on the left! No, we'll encircle him! But look, he's over there! And now he has a puppet!"

It was the puppet, a brown-eyed lion that Klingmüller wore on his hand—a lion that roared "Leibe ist Krieg! Love is War! Heil HITZkopf!"—that started Weinrich shooting again. But it turned out that this officer of the SS did not have such a steady hand when angered. For after replacing the pistol's clip, Weinrich fired several times at Klingmüller, missing him with each echoey pop. The Buffoon did not pause. The street had become his cabaret. He dashed in and out of sight, grinning. The lion roared nonsense, the bullets flew. At some point—the moment, I think, when Weinrich moved a little closer to improve his aim—the lion yelled, "Escape! Escape!"

Still dazed from the blow to my mouth, I did not immediately understand that this was a command. But Zenzi—who had been standing very still, her hair flattened into wet strings by the light rain—Zenzi bolted. Weinrich whipped around, screamed "Halt!" and fired. Immediately Zenzi fell and I thought, She is dead, she is dead. No, Weinrich's aim had been wide once more. She had only ducked because of the sound. Up in an instant, she leaped over chunks of concrete and wire and half a porcelain toilet and headed for the next block's ruins. Still, I expected to see her die, shot in the back like Otto Köckler, how could she escape, but, permit me to explain, Klingmüller had saved her. I mean to say that he had forced Weinrich to use up his ammunition. For the second time, Weinrich had to replace the clip in his pistol. He could not do it fast enough before Zenzi disappeared. The Volkssturm, ordered to murder her with their rifles, did nothing more than watch. Klingmüller had disappeared, too—hiding, wounded, or dead, I will never know, but I hope he somehow ended up having a decent life, this defender of humanity...

Weinrich, his small face no longer pale but enflamed, erupted with profanity over Zenzi's escape and then, of course, turned to me. I put my head to the ground and squeezed my eyes shut and waited for my brains to fly out. I prayed it would not be painful. Instead Weinrich grabbed my jacket and jerked me up. "Tell me where you put the gold."

"I gave it to Bormann, each night."

"You little wretch. I'll find out soon enough." Shoving me forward, he took me up through Nollendorfplatz, where Vati often visited artists, and where I liked to see the train station's glass dome, shattered now. Girders lay around next to tree stumps and the hulk of a train. He pushed me up Kleiststrasse, and then to the edge of the Tiergarten, and I thought he might be taking me to the Führer's bunker, where he could verify my story. But no, he dragged me into the cratered grounds of the zoo. We passed the wrecked aquarium and the toppled elephant cages, we passed the hippo pool, where Rosa, the mother, lay dead on her side with an unexploded shell protruding from her ribs like a dagger. The sight would have filled me with misery except that I was too numb to feel any more sadness. We ended up in front of Pongo the gorilla, still gaunt though not so sullen. His shining black face was wrinkled into a fierce glare. He was furious, I figured, because another officer of the SS lay on the floor of the cage with dried blood pooled around his head.

Soon a third officer emerged, a gangly man whose face was half-mangled. The skin of one cheek swirled around like raspberry pudding and the eye on that side, all white without a pupil, bulged as big as a boiled egg. He laughed with the undamaged corner of his mouth and said, "I thought I was going to miss it, but what luck, I am not late. Ha ha, you have brought a boy to watch. Who is fighting today?"

Weinrich produced a smile that I cannot forget, a smirk that made his eyebrows dance. "The boy is fighting."

"Ha ha ha. The boy? You're not joking?"

"He is a deserter and a thief and a lover of Jews."

"Weinrich, Weinrich, you are cruel."

Weinrich took me by the collar. "One last chance. Where is the gold?"

"Bormann," I said. "Please ask him, he will tell you."

"Put the boy inside, Nolte."

"Weinrich, I have been meaning to tell you," Nolte said, "it is funny, funny! The keeper says he is going to report us to Himmler, ha ha, for tormenting his gorilla. That should be good, that should be very good! Himmler getting a letter about a gorilla! I would love to see his expression when he reads it!" This officer laughed harder and spittle streaked his chin. "Is he still bleeding? I always thought gorilla blood would be black. Isn't that what Negroes have? Haupenhauer got him pretty good, but not good enough! I really thought Haupenhauer would win, he used to wrestle in his youth. Are you giving the boy a knife, too?"

"Yes. Put him in."

With one last hope for saving myself, I realized that Weinrich did not know of my Iron Cross because it was in my pocket. I fetched the medal and held it my palm. "The Führer gave it to me himself," I said.

"You took it off the dead," Weinrich snarled, then snatched the medal and hurled it to the ground. "Now, Nolte."

Nolte unlocked the cage door, pulled it open a crack, and shoved me inside. I stood with my back against the bars, and Weinrich threw a pen knife at my feet.

"You are cruel, Weinrich," said Nolte, "ha ha ha ha! A little knife like that! Oh, I wish I had brought my oatmeal, there is nothing better than to eat and watch a fight!"

I did not move, I did not pick up the knife. Pongo sat there in his corner, staring, breathing heavily through his enormous nose. His shoulders slumped. The contempt I had seen a few minutes before had softened, or so I thought. His vicious black eyes had gone cloudy. I could see, too, that his chest fur was wet and dark red. He was dying, I guessed. Yet I expected to be torn apart. I closed my own eyes. But nothing was happening.

"He's not moving, Weinrich!" Nolte said. "Pongo doesn't want to fight! He's tired! We need to stir him up, get him mad again! Do you want me to do it?"

"Make him mad, Nolte."

The officer began to shout and gesticulate. "Pongo, Pongo, you are the weakest gorilla I have ever seen! You are afraid of a boy! A boy with a pen knife! Ha ha ha!" Nolte hopped up and down, waving his arms. "Pongo, your mother was a whore, your father was a drunk. Pongo, you are worthless scum, you're lazier than the Poles, you stink like the Jews, you have a brain the size of a pea, you have a small cock!" From the corner of my eye, I could see Nolte unzip his fly and display his small pink member, it flapped around as he jumped. "Look, mine is bigger than yours!"

Pongo did not move.

"He is not upset," said Nolte. "Is he dead?"

"Pick up the knife, Koertig," Weinrich ordered. "Pick it up and move toward the animal. If you don't, I will shoot you."

I did not move and Weinrich did not shoot.

"Nolte, give me the key!" Weinrich shouted. After unlocking the door, Weinrich edged inside and began to kick me. I curled up to protect myself, shielding my face, and so it took me a moment to understand why Weinrich had begun to scream. The gorilla had rushed across the cage and taken hold of him. That mass of black hair had wrapped itself around Weinrich, so much so that I could see only the officer's head. Pongo was not being kind to that head. He was, in fact, slamming it onto the floor, over and over, as if he were trying to break open a piece of fruit. Weinrich's teeth went clownishly red with blood. Nolte ran off full of gibberish, and now Pongo dropped the limp carcass of Weinrich and came toward me. I was too exhausted to move. Gigantic arms pulled my body to a warm, hairy, sticky chest. Hot breath flooded my face with vile odors. The gorilla's gray, carrot-shaped fingers clutched my shoulder, and I was cradled. I had no other choice but to sleep.

19

"Get up, little boy! It is time for your prize! The ceremony will begin!" Nolte, staring at me with his blank, bulging eye, was imitating a trumpet's fanfare, buzzing and spitting through curled fingers, sounding more like a quacking duck. After one final flourish, he draped around my neck a loop of string, which held the Iron Cross. "Congratulations! It is yours again! You are the king! A boy, in the end it was a boy! What is your name?"

Through my dry throat I uttered, "Koertig."

The officer with his boiled egg of an eye danced around me, chortling. "Heil König Koertig!"

"What have I done?"

"You are the king! You have slain the gorilla! The beast is dead!"

I followed his pointing finger. I was sitting next to the dark mound of Pongo, who had finally succumbed to his wound.

He was sprawled face up in a pond of blood, not moving, not breathing. "What day is it? Where are the Russians?"

"Everywhere, everywhere! They will celebrate your victory, too!"

"I am very thirsty."

"I will fetch the wine!"

Nolte scurried away. I rose with great effort, with a piercing headache. I shuffled around Weinrich's pulpy mess, gave one last look at Pongo, who had saved me, and left the cage staggering. Out of the zoo, I stood at the edge of the Tiergarten's morass, trying to reassemble the previous day, trying to formulate some idea of what to do. I drifted toward the Spree, wondering if I might catch up with the Fuchses. Guarding a bridge, a few boys behind a brick barricade warned me not to cross, especially if I was alone and without a weapon. The Russians, they insisted, were on the other side, only a few blocks away. I stared in that direction, roughly north, where fresh smoke boiled, where frantic gunfire boomed and popped and tore the morning into shreds, thinking that it would be impossible now to get to Zenzi. I must have looked quite dazed and lost, for one of the boys asked, "Are you looking for your unit?"

They were seeing me as one of their own, a believer, a valiant fighter—I had forgotten that the Iron Cross was dangling from my neck. All I wanted was to find someone I knew, and there was only one person left now. I squinted and stared and nodded. "I am looking for Albrecht Stalla."

"Your commander?"

"A friend. Our commander is Werner Fenzel." I asked the boys if they had seen a crazy Kameradschaftsführer with lots of pimples and a leather nose, and also a red-headed 14-year-old who liked to brag about his girls. My descriptions sparked a flicker of recognition, but nothing specific except for a suggestion to head west. Another squad I encountered said they had seen the noseless one, and sent me further along. After two hours of trudging, having collected several reported sightings, I ended up pretty much where I started, following the most recent clue to a kind of cave in a rubble mountain. There I found a bivouac of seven dirty youth-army members, eating and slurping. I recognized three. Dohndorf, still looking a little goofy. Fenzel, now with a leather triangle strapped over the nub of his nose. And Stalla, who rushed up to embrace me, who shouted his greeting and pressed a fuller orange beard, all straggly, against my neck.

"Albrecht," I said and tried to smile. "Is there water?"

"You look like a pile of shit."

"What day is it?"

"April 27th? Who cares anymore?" He peered at me. "Meet up with the Russians again?"

"I slept with the gorilla."

"Don't make me laugh. Remember?" Stalla jabbed his thumb backwards. "Fenzel doesn't even let you smile."

"My throat, my throat," I said, ready to topple.

"Are you still drawing pictures for the Führer?"

"Not anymore..."

Stalla went back to the group, said a few words, and returned with a cup of water and a piece of dried horsemeat. "You can have some, but only if you join us. Fenzel's orders. We're killing tanks. Boom! Nothing like it."

"I will," I said and gulped.

"You better put the medal in your pocket. Fenzel still has fits that you got it."

"I'll give it to you," I said. "It should be yours, anyway."

"No, thanks, I don't want to carry that thing around."

Now Dohndorf hopped over and, continuing his habit, whispered "Saibot!" and then blushed.

So I returned to the youth army—reunited with Stalla and Dohndorf, commanded once again by Fenzel. Permit me to explain, if I was soon going to die, I did not want to do so alone, I did not want to be hanged for desertion. I wanted to fall next to a friend. I think, too, I had an idea that Stalla was indestructible, and that he could, with some luck, help me survive and find Zenzi. He looked much older with his full beard and a pair of silver-toed boots, which he'd yanked off the corpse of an officer. He had not lost any confidence—he'd joined up with Fenzel and his gang soon after I'd last seen him, he told me, and they'd done good work making havoc in the streets with Russian armor. "But you've got to watch out for their cooking crews," he added, using the term for flamethrowers. "Horlitz and Schwerdtfeger got caught in a basement yesterday. I found them afterwards. What a fucking sight. They looked like worms, all black and red. No faces left, everything melted. I just want revenge."

I remembered how Horlitz had winced in shame after he had mistakenly started everyone saluting over and over for SS-Hauptscharführer Drost, and could not imagine him as a worm.

Stalla shifted the mood with a grin. "What about your girl? Did you get anywhere with her?"

"We were married."

"Remember, no jokes. If Fenzel hears us laugh..."

"She and her family were trying to go west," I said, and left out the fact that I had planned to go with them.

"Like everybody else. But we'll stick it out. Good to have you back, Tobias."

"Do you think we'll cross the Spree? If there's a chance I could find her—"

"It's up to Fenzel." Stalla leaned close. "I haven't gone back to see if Stefanie's still around, but God I miss her."

Back from a scouting patrol, Fenzel issued his orders with the usual strident dramatics, slashing the air with his hands, perhaps in imitation of the Führer. We were to make our way to the edge of Charlottenburg, a few kilometers away, and attempt to knock out a pocket of enemy tanks. Stalla leaped up, joyous, and told me not to move while he fetched something around the corner. A moment later he emerged riding a bicycle. "Look! I'm an expert now!" He steered a tight figure-eight, glided with raised hands and feet, and then dismounted in motion, leaping off like a gymnast. "After the war, I'll get a nice one for myself. A motorcycle, too."

Fenzel shouted at Stalla to stop messing around, then stood before me with his leather nose, which had been cut, it seemed, from a boot. "Now the time has come," he sneered with a strange buzzing sound that came from the center of his face. "We will see how Herr Iron Cross behaves when the shit starts to fly. You won't last a day."

Stalla told me not to worry, he would look out for me, and that Fenzel said that kind of thing to everybody. "You've got to be quick, though, and alert. We don't report to anyone, so we do what we want."

We set off on our bicycles, carrying panzerfausts on handlebars, rifles on our backs, and an MG42. Weaving through the rubble, we pedaled with great earnestness. I'm not sure if any of us, even Fenzel, believed that we were saving Berlin. But the sun was beaming and spring breezes were trying their best to blow away odors and smoke, and I think we all felt a little cheerful. Gliding past the mountains of bricks, we started to act like boys. We shouted jokes, we raced each other, we bragged about what we'd do to the Russians.

At some point, I was pedaling right behind Dohndorf when I saw both of his hands come up to his face. I thought at first he was trying to pull off a trick. His front wheel started to wobble, then turned sharply. In another second or two, he was lying on the road face down. I was thinking that stupid Dohndorf had really ruined our fun, falling down like that, because now Fenzel would punish us for fooling around. Fenzel, in fact, was screaming, but he was screaming about a sniper. Stalla and I, along with the others, scrambled to the nearest building while Fenzel started shooting into the distance. He caught up to us a few minutes later, frothing and wild-eyed, not so much because the sniper had killed one of us, but because a bicycle and a Panzerfaust had been left in the street. "The next one to make a mistake like that," he snarled, "I'll gouge his eyes out, and then mash them like mice."

Through a hole in the wall, I could see Dohndorf in the street, one arm tucked under his head, as if he were dozing. Frodnhod, Frodnhod, I said to myself, over and over, hoping the incantation might reverse Dohndorf himself into life.

"That's Fenzel for you," Stalla said. "He'll send someone out there tonight to get everything back."

"Will we bury him?"

"Fenzel doesn't like to waste the time."

I hardly got a chance to mourn Dohndorf's death, for after we made a detour around the sniper, circling through Wilmersdorf, then cutting up across Hohenzollerndamm, we saw in the distance an enormous muzzle of a Russian tank. "What a cock on that thing," Stalla said. "Let's go kill it."

We ditched the bicycles in a scorched confectionary that smelled of burnt sugar, and scurried behind Fenzel from building to building, through basements and wrecked walls. We came upon a Volkssturm crew in the street, crouched and scared behind the usual roadblock of junk, for they were under heavy enemy fire from a machine-gun that sounded like a coughing giant. Fenzel screamed at us to take positions on either side of the street.

Stalla grabbed my arm and we leaped up a set of stairs to a third floor parlor with red wallpaper and smashed saucers and teacups strewn over the floor. I had been ordered to man an MG42 at the window and fire on the tank if it started advancing, to keep its commander inside and mostly blind, and to keep Russian infantry from following too close. "I'll be downstairs, waiting," Stalla said. "After I kill it, get out of here fast because once they see what happened, they'll knock the building down."

"What about the others?"

"Probst is across the street, covering that side. And Fenzel usually takes a few to intercept their infantry. He likes to kill soldiers. Me, I'd rather blow up a tank. You don't know how happy it makes me feel. Better than sex almost." Stalla shrugged. "Tobias, after the war, I was thinking, the two of us should get some motorcycles and go to Spain. I've seen pictures and the place looks great. We'll ride along the coast and screw dark beauties under the olive trees. You never told me if you did it with that Mischling."

I was trying to remember how to assemble the tripod. "Once."

"Was she wild? Did she show you lots of special tricks?"

"Yes. She was a leopard."

"What did I tell you! They do the craziest things! You've got to tell me about it later. Now, remember, keep the belt loose, don't let it jam. And don't spend your ammo all in one place."

Stalla left me and I set up my gun, the barrel pointed out the smashed window, nosed between the part in a dusty curtain. I tried to summon the confidence from my training, when I sprayed a sawdust dummy with bullets and tore apart its crotch, making everybody roar. Outside, the Volkssturm men were still huddled together, none with interest, it seemed, in the fight. But the shooting had stopped. In fact, nothing much was happening at all. I tried to concentrate on the street but my brain was filling up with Zenzi. My comic-book telepathic powers returned. Yes, she could hear my thoughts promising to find her, and I could hear her thoughts telling me she was still safe, waiting for me, her husband.

We would lie together in bed again, we would have a long happy marriage. I would try to convince Fenzel to make our next mission the crossing of the Spree...

Gunfire now. The massive Russian tank was rolling right below me. Infantry, not ours, hurried behind it like ducklings following their mother. The Volkssturm men lay dead on either side of their barricade. I heard Probst's gun chattering from his window, and then a whoosh, and a thump. Black smoke rushed at me between the curtains. Stalla had hit the tank.

I squeezed my gun's trigger. The air itself was torn. The force pushed me backward, off my chair and onto the floor. I scrambled up and tried to shoot again but I had run through the entire belt in only seconds and they had not given me another one. I remembered Stalla's warning about a quick escape, so I started fumbling with the tripod, trying to remove it from the gun, when the building shook so hard I went down again. The window's remaining glass shattered, the room erupted with dust. I was choking, I could barely see, I could not take the gun apart. Instead I dragged the whole awkward thing to the doorway, and then clanked it down the stairs. Halfway down, a dark wrinkled face. The gray fog obscured the color of his helmet—German, I assumed, the Volkssturm. I asked, "Can you help me with this?" He looked at me for a moment with narrow eyes that made me believe he did not understand the question, then he arched backward and sprayed me with blood. At the bottom of the stairs stood Fenzel. He had ripped apart a Russian with his bullets.

We retreated the way we had come, back to the confectionary, and there Fenzel had a fit. Snot poured from his leather nose as he yelled. "Were you sleeping, Koertig? We lost Winckler because there was nothing from the right side!"

"But I *did* shoot," I told him, knowing that I had been daydreaming. "I didn't hear the tank until it was under the window. Winckler died?"

"But you were supposed to be *watching* that tank!" Stalla said. "Well, that asshole's burning now."

I had failed again in a battle and felt miserable. I wanted to thank Fenzel for saving my life but I couldn't find the words. He didn't give me a chance, anyway. He was pushing his false leather nose into my face. "Yes," he said, "Winckler's guts are all over the street because of you. His liver or something like that fell out. A big gaping hole. Last I saw he was trying to stuff it back in. Don't worry, Koertig," he added, "you can still demonstrate to everyone here why you won the Iron Cross, why it was pinned to your chest by the Führer himself! I have a special mission for you."

Later that afternoon, while we were eating our lunch—pieces of smoked ham someone had found in the back of a smashed restaurant—I took the medal out of my pocket and told Stalla that he needed to take it. "All it's done is brought me trouble."

"I can't. It's not mine."

I spat out a few shards of cement that had gotten stuck in the meat. "Then I'll throw it away."

"If Fenzel found out, he'd hang you for dishonor."

I sighed and shoved it back in my pocket, knowing Stalla was right, resigned to its possession. "I am terribly sorry about Winckler."

"He wouldn't have made it, anyway. He was straggling, he already had a bad leg. When Fenzel gets mad, he'll say anything."

"What will he make me do?"

Stalla rubbed his beard. "Something at night. Something sneaky. But don't worry, around nine o'clock, Ivan starts drinking. They won't notice a thing."

20

Stalla had been correct. My special mission would be well after dark: retrieving Dohndorf's bicycle and Panzerfaust. We huddled where we had started that morning. The Russians had advanced further up, past the sniper's position, close enough that we could make out their voices. I was sure Fenzel hoped to see me die, hoped to watch me push my own innards back inside a gaping hole. Stalla saw my shivering and tried to offer comfort, assuring me again that the Russians were all too drunk to notice me. "Just keep your head down and try not to bump into anything. You're lucky you've got a full moon."

"I don't know if I can do it. I'm too scared. My legs won't move."

"Then take this. My last one." He offered me that grayish pill, Pervitin, and without hesitation, I swallowed it.

Not long after, around midnight, Stalla and everyone else except Fenzel wished me luck and I scooted along in a crouch away from the group, darting behind big pieces of debris. I did not yet see the bicycle, but when I came near to the spot where I thought it lay, I went flat on my stomach, I squirmed forward like a snake. Before me, the moon's ghost light was softening piles of jagged things into eerie visions of plant-like growths. The area was mostly quiet. The jabbering of the Russians was distinct. In years past, whenever I had heard their language, from prisoners on work detail, I had sometimes imitated their mashed-up, incomprehensible words to my schoolmates, to great comic effect, but now their gibberish sounded as if it came from otherworldly creatures. Even their laughter was odd, like gargling. I heard, too, the clinking of their bottles, and figured Stalla must be right, they were gulping vodka. When I looked back to see if he might be giving encouragement, I glimpsed only shadows.

I crept forward a little more, and then saw what I could not understand. In a single flash, the night turned into a strange kind of day. I thought at first that the pill was making me crazy. Harsh whiteness flooded the street, a million times brighter than the moon's. In the distance, giant eyes pointed their beams in my direction. I pressed myself into the rubble, shivering in wildness as if I had a fever. I tried to be logical: another Russian trick, blinding the enemy, I knew they'd done it when crossing the Oder. Had they heard me crawling? My eyes hurt, I had to squint. Before me, there was just a wall of pure blank light, like someone's idea of Heaven. But also, also, I was just glimpsing it, the outline of Dohndorf's boots. Right next to them, the spokes of a gleaming wheel, the bicycle.

Now there came a metallic roar, a vibration of the street. Emerging from the whiteness, a Russian tank in majestic silhouette, enormous, not a type I recognized, was rolling toward me. Like the cries of an infant, little squeaks slipped from my throat. They did not originate in fear but in determination, in self-preservation. I began crawling as fast as I could toward the bicycle. Reaching it, I saw that the Panzerfaust lay next to the handlebars, no longer attached. I squatted near Dohndorf's body, I shoved my hand into one of his pockets and found what I'd hoped would be there, a fuse. Then, as if it were only training, as if I were in the safety of the Sportfeld—perhaps that pill had taken effect, I do not know—I picked up the tube and went through the steps for arming the missile, and then I raised it to my shoulder, and stood, ready to fire.

My head felt as weightless as a balloon, for there was yet another weird sight. On the other side of the road, Russian soldiers stood in crisp uniforms, not firing at me because they did not carry guns. No, they were pointing movie cameras at this massive treaded thing. Movie cameras! Did they not see this German boy with the anti-tank weapon because they were peering into small lenses? Or because the tank was swirling up fog, a brilliant glittering dust bubble that blurred the air? At the top of this bubble rose the dark uniform of the brawny tank commander, topped by his black leather cap. He did not see me, either, until the tank passed right in front of my position, so close I thought the tread might crush my foot. With thick tufted eyebrows and deeply grooved skin, the commander resembled a benevolent drinker. He must have been soused on vodka, since that explained why he grinned and wagged a finger at me, as if to chastise a street scoundrel intent on mischief.

Nevertheless, I pressed the lever on the Panzerfaust, intending to destroy his tank. My missile rushed out, and I thought, I have done it, I have done it!

No, I had raised the tube too high, the missile angled right over the turret, right over the commander's head, peeling off his cap. There he stood, with bulging eyes, an open mouth full of crooked teeth, and a bald, shining pate.

He started to laugh. His brows flitted around like moles. Relief swelled in my chest, for it was clear to me that this tank commander did not hate me, he did not want to inflict death. Absurdly I began to laugh myself and raised my palms in a gesture of celebration.

Then the commander's pleasant face disintegrated into purple shreds. Not far from me, it was Fenzel again, coiled by rage, flinging his bullets.

The spotlights went off and darkness dropped in a heap, with only moonlight again. Stalla appeared at my side with a faust, told me to duck, and exploded the tank the way he liked to do. The boom was a fist in my brain. The Russians were by now shouting, their outer-space words came from every corner. Guns were barking all around us. Pushing me, Stalla said, "Go, go!" and I sprinted from the direction I had crawled, stumbling into a wrecked storefront. But Stalla had not followed me. I peered into the street, which flickered orange, colored by the burning tank and all its wretched oily smoke. I couldn't see my friend or anyone else. Tears started to flood my eyes, though I quickly blotted them with my sleeve to keep my vision clear, for now I was going back into the street. I didn't want to die alone.

I crawled on all fours like a baby, over bricks toward the tank's stench-filled fire, then rolled underneath its front lip, between the treads. Here, too, huddling in shadow, was Stalla, alive, talking to me. "Is there a way out?" he asked.

"I came from across the street. We can crawl. Did you get hit?"

"My knee doesn't work." He said this through chattering teeth and a grimace. "I think Fenzel's dead. I saw him fall. I told him not to attack while they had the lights on. But he saw the guy laughing." Stalla moaned and shivered. "I don't know about anyone else. Goddamn everything."

I tried with my limited view to locate Fenzel's body but nothing was clear. "You can't move?"

"Not very well."

"Maybe I could drag you," I said.

"I can't believe they were making a movie. In our city! What assholes. I bet that commander thought you were an actor! We gave *him* a big surprise."

"Your leg should be wrapped."

"I haven't looked at it. But let's move. They're not far away."

I pulled Stalla onto his back. Around his knee, where his pants were ragged, I could make out in the orange glow a dome of bone banded by strings of muscle swimming in blood. A machine gun started up somewhere nearby, I recognized its rhythm as one of ours, so I figured we better crawl out now and leave the bandage until later. The Russian voices had gone quiet.

"I'll pull your arm," I told him, "and you can push with your good leg."

I came out from under the tank and began to tug. We moved along even slower than I had come in. Soon my arms ached, for Stalla was no lightweight. I froze every time a gun barked, but used the moment to rest. Stalla moaned when we had to move over larger things, and I tried to tell him to keep it quiet. Once he got caught up in some kind of wire and in the five minutes I spent untangling him, I thought I saw tears on Albrecht's face. "I will get you out, I will get you out," I promised. "Dr. Schenck will help you."

Somehow we made it to the storefront without getting shot, maybe the Russians had resumed their drinking. Stalla was shivering more than ever, I had never seen him in such a state. I laid him down next to a bunch of overturned electric mixers, it looked as if the place had sold appliances. From one leg of my new uniform I tore a shred of cloth and wrapped it around Stalla's dripping knee. It was not long enough to make a knot, and so I had to tear another piece, and now my leg was bare.

"Maybe you can walk with a crutch," I said.

He closed his eyes tight, clenching his fists, writhing a little. "It's not just my knee. My ass. It's my ass, too. I feel like I'm trying to shit a bunch of nails."

"The wound you got before? Did it open up again?"

"No, it's not on the outside, it's inside. And worse, worse. All I want is a bed. Tobias, Tobias, take me to Stefanie."

I found a length of splintered wood and we set off into the rubbled street. But Stalla could not manage the makeshift crutch on the piles of bricks. He kept falling, swearing. I could really hear his sobs now. For safety, to get out of the street, I ushered him into a bombed-out restaurant. I was hoping, too, to find some scraps of food, for I was starving. Nothing edible came to my eyes, though I did find two things useful: a torn black jacket, perhaps from a waiter, and a silver cart that probably used to carry cakes and puddings. They were both for Stalla, the jacket for warmth and the cart for transporting him to Dr. Schenck.

I helped him into the jacket and then he flopped onto the cart, his legs and head hung over the edges. His face no longer bore his usual robust flush but was now the color of concrete, which scared me, but I reasoned it must be the moonlight. He said, "Take me to Stefanie, please. She'll have more Pervitin. That's what I need."

"First the doctor. Your knee is really torn up."

"But I need something now. The pill will make me better. Where are we?"

"Wilmersdorf, I think."

"Yes, yes, she's here, she's very close. Tobias, we have to go. It's too fucking painful. Not just my knee. My ass."

It did not seem the best thing to do, and from my vantage

now that is obvious, but I was only thirteen, you must remember this, and I did not know anything about medicine, and I was in a panic, and I felt too ashamed to pull down his pants and look at this other wound. So under the silver light, I began pushing the cart through the narrow routes cut into the rubble, listening to my friend, draped face-up, direct me as best he could, for I did not remember where Stefanie's building stood. But we were finally behind the front line. In windows, all down the street, white towels and sheets and even a white wedding dress hung over the sills like watchful ghosts, all of which I soon understood to mean surrender. The Russians had won.

Soon I recognized Stefanie's building with its small balconies and their French doors. Everything stood as before, undamaged. "She's an angel," Stalla muttered. His head was rolling from side to side. He looked immensely tired. I told him I would return in a minute and then hurried up the dark stairwell, dragging a hand on the wall to guide me. At the top, in the black hallway, I peered at the numbers close-up, and pounded on what I hoped was the right one. After a few seconds I grew impatient and pounded again. The door opened just a little, making a strip filled with candlelight. A silhouette there of curly hair, a small circle of a face.

"Stefanie? It's Tobias Koertig."

"What do you want? I have no food."

"Albrecht is outside. He's hurt, his knee is very bad. He wants one of those pills, I mean if you have one."

"Albrecht?"

"Stalla."

She said nothing for a moment. I smelled alcohol, and then a waft of cinnamon. "Wait."

She disappeared and I thought I could hear a man's grunt. Soon she re-emerged with a candle, stepping into the hallway, closing the door behind her. In the faint glow I could see that her flat cheeks were flushed, maybe bruised on one side. She clutched at the folds of a flimsy nightgown. "What has happened?"

"The Russians shot him. His knee. Do you have one of those pills? I'm taking him to the doctor."

"He's just outside?"

I took a step back toward the stairs. "We are in a hurry."

"No pills left, but maybe I could come down and see him."

Then her door flew open and a giant, wearing just underwear, stood in the frame, in the candle's yellow flicker. He was bellowing something at us. I did not understand a word because it was all in Russian. He was dismissing me, sweeping the air with his enormous claws.

"Stop complaining," Stefanie spat at him in German, "it's just a boy I know." She turned to me and said, "Can you come back in an hour? I don't have the time right now." She disappeared into her apartment and I bounded down the stairs to find Stalla moaning, even paler. I told him Stefanie had not been home and he closed his eyes. I continued my pushing, we rattled through the streets. Near Kurfurstendamm, a few drunken Volkssturm men shouted, "The boy has captured a Bolshevik! Bravo! Bravo!" One or two tried to catch us, demanding the enemy's silver-toed boots, but we soon lost them.

The journey was exhausting. I kept stopping to rest. Each time I checked on Stalla and each time he mumbled things as if coming in and out of dreams. "You are going over too many bumps...Stefanie, Stefanie, kiss me again...I'm freezing... Marmelade! Marmelade! Mutti always won...How much farther, we must be in Spain by now...the olive trees...I shouldn't have thrown the soup...Oh, this ache in my ass..."

"The doctor will patch you up, Albrecht..."

"Is the war over...?"

"I think it might be..."

"I don't want to surrender..."

"We don't have to...we'll just become regular boys again..."

"But the Russians won't let us..."

"We'll go to the Americans...we could leave tomorrow, after your knee's fixed..."

"The moon, it's like God, looking down..."

"Colorado...or Arizona...we'll be cowboys..."

"I have the boots...but I've never been on a horse..."

"If you can learn how to ride a bicycle..."

"Tobias, I feel a little funny...dizzy...am I dying...?"

"We're almost there..."

"Don't let him cut my leg off or anything like that..."

"No...no..."

"We'll wear big hats..."

"Hats...?"

"When we're cowboys..."

"Albrecht, here, take the Iron Cross, it belongs to you, hold it in your hand..."

"No, no, keep it, you have really earned that medal now, Tobias..."

I pushed faster, finally down VossStrasse, where the entrance to the Chancellery, covered in giant chunks of blasted cement, sat close to the casualty station. I pulled Stalla off the cart, but he could not walk up the steps because he had gone limp, he had fainted. I yelled at a soldier passing by, "Help me carry my friend!"

"Where are you taking him?"

"To Dr. Schenck!"

"A doctor? But why?"

I wanted to smash the soldier's face. "To make him better! To fix him up!"

The soldier only nodded and grabbed Stalla under the arms, and together we hauled him through a hallway, and then down the stairs into gloom and stink. My legs nearly collapsed with relief when I saw the operating room, when I saw Dr. Schenck standing there smeared in blood.

"My friend Albrecht Stalla has passed out! He's in pain! Please help him!"

"Wait your turn," the doctor snarled. Then he recognized me and came over to inspect Stalla.

"His knee," I said. "And his rear end."

The doctor shook his head. "There is nothing to do."

"Why not? Take out the bullet, get him a splint!"

Pity passed across Schenck's eyes like a bird's shadow, there and then gone. I kneeled over Stalla, whose face had gone whiter, even his lips had lost their richness. Yet his fuzzy red beard still looked vibrant, it looked very much alive, and so in a fit of love I pushed my nose into all that prickly hair and I kissed him. I kissed and kissed and kissed and kissed. And then not looking at the doctor, trying to push away the truth, I shouted, "But he just passed out, fix him up, I beg you!"

"It's not possible," the doctor told me in a somber tone, turning Stalla on his side, pulling up his shirt, soaked with a bright, bright red, so much red it hurt my eyes. "Look. There is a hole in his stomach and his buttock. A bullet went straight through. Into the bowels and out. He has bled to death."

21

Almost seven decades later, there are certain reminders of the war that will freeze my heart, such as a backfiring car or a demolished building or the firestation's noontime whoop that sounds too much like an air-raid siren. One of the strongest jolts comes to me when I occasionally see, on the beach, a brawny red-headed boy who carries a definite swagger in his hips, a suggestion of sexual braggadocio. I stop my picture-making on the easel and I stand, a little short of breath, and stare for as long as he stays in my vision. Once or twice I have followed the youth over the sand until my legs give out, a pathetic old man believing in ghosts or reincarnation.

Albrecht, may you be at peace.

On that night, underground, beneath the last of the fighting, I somehow ended up back on my cot. There, for hours, I sobbed and writhed and vaguely perceived a dying world: shrieks and shouts, massive thuds, dust falling onto my eyelids, uniformed men dragging fat suitcases, piles of papers lugged back and forth, a shirtless girl pursued by drunks, the flickering of lights, stumbling boys wrapped in bandages. The end had come. I was drained. I had lost my will. Everything had been taken from me, everything. I lay there unable to move.

Then someone was calling my name. An Unteroffizier poked me, staring down. Groggily I saluted and confirmed my identity.

"I've been looking for you for two days!" he shouted. "Where have you been? Sleeping here all this time?"

I saluted again, bewildered. "On the streets, Herr Unteroffizier."

"You were supposed to report to the Reichsjugendführer every afternoon at five o'clock. Yesterday you missed an extremely important appointment, and now it is almost too late."

"For what, Herr Unteroffizier?"

"The portrait! Why they want a child to do it, I don't know."

"Who?"

"Do you have any idea how important this is? And I find you sleeping! I will report this to Herr Reichsjugendführer. Grounds for a court-martial, I am sure!"

I now recognized this young man, the same one who had first taken me to see the Führer, who had so disliked my cartoons. "I would like to find out where they will bury Stalla," I said. "I want to give him his Iron Cross."

"You are a complete mess, Koertig! Blood everywhere."

"But the medal belongs to him."

"And dirt all over your uniform, all over your face. Disgusting. Now come with me."

I followed the Unteroffizier through the corridors. He corralled a nurse and ordered her to mop away my filth while he went in search of a uniform. It wasn't long before he returned with a perplexed messenger boy and told him to swap clothing with me.

The boy expressed his dismay, and I felt guilty for taking his gray trousers and black jacket. At the last moment, as he left wearing my soiled coat, I remembered the Iron Cross. I shoved my hand into the pocket and retrieved it.

Now we headed down a long narrow passageway. A stream of people flowing in the other direction, blank-faced and impatient, made our progress difficult. We passed under a hole torn in the ceiling, where sunlight angled down in a thick dusty beam, carrying with it a chattering of machine guns from the street, the pungent odors of death and fire. I paused there, peering up, and wondered about Zenzi, about the other boys in Fenzel's group. I was beginning to recover my senses. As soon as I discovered where they put Stalla's body, I would escape. The Unteroffizier shouted at me to hurry. There were no guards anymore asking for identification, and we descended the staircase into what was left of the hive.

In the main area, we came upon a group of uniformed men and women, dour in a semi-circle. They were giving their attention to two central figures who were exact opposites of each other— the Führer with slumped shoulders and droopy eyes, and cheerful Eva in a black dress with roses at the neck, greeting everyone with kisses. The Unteroffizier, intent on making me understand the privilege of witnessing a moment I did not yet comprehend, pointed out to me the faces of Krebs and Burgdorf, both Generals, and Admiral Voss, and Ambassador Hewel, and Goebbels and Bormann, and others he pronounced with great pride.

Eva lifted her arm like a ballerina and motioned me over. "There's our little artist," she said, giggling. "Are you ready to draw Herr and Frau Hitler? How funny it still sounds! Frau Hitler!" Perhaps she saw my confusion, for she added, "Ah, have you just arrived? Yes, husband and wife! Just today! Here, champagne for you, too!"

Never having tasted it before, I thought it might quench my thirst and accepted the glass. After I gulped, choking, I said, "My friend Stalla, a soldier, I am trying to find out where they might bury him. I have to give him something."

"My little sweet," Eva said, distracted by someone offering another somber congratulations, "let's try not to think of those things right now." She told me to wait inside the nearby chamber, showing me through an iron door. "There's no need for you to bother yourself with all this talk," she said. "You may sit on the couch, it's very comfortable. Check to make sure you have what you need. Just paper and pencil, is that right? Someone said you had disappeared, but I know a dutiful boy when I see him. The Führer and I will be with you in a few minutes."

The door was closed, and I slumped on the velvet couch, finally understanding through all my clouding grief that I had been summoned to draw the portrait Eva had requested. A wedding portrait. I put my ear to the door. Was this my chance to flee? But I could not hear a thing. The iron was too thick. There was only the occasional rumble from above. Before I had a chance to formulate any idea of escape, Eva entered with the Führer close behind, and the door was shut again.

The Führer, stiffening, turned to his wife. "I think maybe we should scrap this idea, Zaubermaus. I am in no mood for relaxing. A portrait never comes off if the subject isn't comfortable. Plus you can see that I'm perspiring. It's those pills that Linge gives me. They make me clammy. Even my feet. I have brown stains on my toes from the socks. What cheap dye! There are so many incompetents, even for the simple manufacture of clothing! Imagine if Frederick the Great had traipsed around with colored toes!"

"But he is not drawing your feet, Liebling."

"I have never liked portraits. Man was not born to sit still. Especially someone of higher powers. Posing is for the vacuous, who have no ideas! I used to give Hoffmann only a few minutes to snap his pictures. Of course he never wanted to take long, anyway, because he was always hungover."

"Let us be remembered," Eva pleaded, "as husband and wife."

The Führer scowled at me. "Köster? Krüger?"

"Koertig," I corrected.

"Be quick, Koertig. It is a very important day, a serious day, a day the world will remember." He stared into the corner of the drab room, breathing heavily. "In this hour, I have to agree with Tacitus. Do you know your Roman history, boy? Do you know what he said? 'Courage doesn't matter, luck is everything, and the strongest often die by the coward's sword.' To hell with Berlin! How do you want us to sit?"

"Whatever pleases you, mein Führer," I said, stuttering.

"Put your hand in mine, Wolfi," said Eva.

"As an artist," the Führer began, quieter, "you should *tell* your subject what to do. Exert as much control as you can to give your hand the freedom it needs. The subjects appreciate the authority, it makes them feel important. But as I always told Hoffmann, I will never smile for a portrait. It is a sign of weakness and the superficial. We will sit here with dignity. You cannot take too long. How far are the Indians from here, boy? How far?"

"The Indians?"

"The redskins!"

"A few blocks, I think."

"Savages running through German streets. It brings a terrible pain to my stomach." The Führer looked blankly beyond me toward the door. He appeared, more than ever, to be ill. His lifeless pupils swam in a liquid the color of bloody pus, while one lid twitched. Moisture trickled from a corner of his mouth. His mustache did not seem to be balanced, it was ragged on the left side, as if he had stopped trimming it there. His black hair hung across his forehead in a fringe, pasted into thick strands by sweat. His left hand jerked with spasms and he did his best to hide it. Except for his eyes, he was colorless. His skin nearly matched the gray of his tunic, and he wore black trousers, a white shirt, and a black tie—funeral attire.

Trembling, I grasped the pencil. How could I make such a face look good? How could I sketch a man who was turning Jews into fertilizer? Yet if I did not produce a satisfactory portrait, what would happen? The Führer would shoot me with his pistol, I feared. I saw it lying on a table, a Walther PPK.

I began with Eva, who did not wear a visage of death. On the Führer's left, she still produced that half smile. Her painted lips pushed up the custard-like cheeks. I drew carefully, afraid to make a mistake. I had completed an outline of her face when the Führer asked to see what I had done.

"The boy has real talent," he declared to his wife, showing her the paper. "In just a few strokes, he has captured the shape of your head. You see? Quite remarkable. It brings me back to Vienna, when I was painting with great seriousness myself—little street scenes that I sold to passersby. I might have starved to death if not for the passion of art keeping me in good health. I was quick like you, boy. Vienna! A decrepit place, a meager period, but those were the years that taught me the necessity of the will. He reminds me of myself at that age, Zaubermaus. Continue, my boy. There is not much time."

At that moment, there was a knock, and a man's voice sounded, Linge's, requesting permission to enter. But before he could, a dark-haired woman rushed inside, the woman the Unteroffizier had identified as the wife of Goebbels. For a minute or two, with frantic, high-pitched pleas, she begged the Führer to escape to the mountains. I hoped and hoped that he would be convinced, that we could all leave the confines of this chamber, damp and dim and foul with the Führer's bitter breath. But he dismissed Magda Goebbels, and Linge escorted her away. The three of us were left alone again.

Now Eva's eyes bunched up and began to squeeze out tears. The Führer pursed his lips, shook his head, tugged on one of his drooping ear lobes. "There is no need for weeping," he said. "Think of all that we've accomplished. Who else could boast of such progress for Mankind? Not even Jesus. So he cured a leper? I have performed the greatest miracle of all—I have purified the world."

"Wolfi, Wolfi, I keep thinking of how my dogs used to play on the Berghof's terrace. Even though you always complained about them, you were smiling. It was so beautiful up there, who could be unhappy? Do you remember the first time I saw the mountains in the twilight? I think I almost fainted. And the snow, and the enormous icicles. I held one up to my forehead and danced around as a unicorn, and you told me I was just as rare!"

"Yes," the Führer sighed, "I remember."

A great rumble vibrated the chamber. A lamp teetered, a glass clattered, and Eva took the Führer's arm. "Adolf! Magda is right. Let's go back. Surely there's a way. Don't we still control a bridge over the Havel? We could leave tonight."

"No, Zaubermaus. They would find us there, too. Don't let tears ruin the portrait."

"But Wolfi," Eva continued, "now that I've seen what he's drawn of me, I can't imagine...it's too distressing...what about Argentina? I know some are going there, I've heard them talking... we'll take a submarine."

"You speak as if the submarines have schedules like the railway! Going to the moon would be easier. No, it's too late for any of that. Everyone has betrayed me. Only poor Blondi was loyal to the end!" I wanted to ask him what had happened to the dog, but I did not dare interrupt him. "There is nothing to worry about," he continued. "Be strong. The world will never forget us. This portrait is a good idea, after all. I will let the order stand: it will be taken by special courier to Dönitz, who will preserve it for future generations of admirers. Wipe your eyes. That terrible ink you put around them is running. Let the boy finish."

I sketched hurriedly now, desperate to be released, to please them and run. I corrected the imbalance of the Führer's mustache. I made his expression lively, his hair tidy. I gave Eva's face a kind of blooming openness, and pitched her shoulders forward a little to erase the fear that possessed her.

The Führer pushed out a hand, the one that did not shake, and demanded once again to see what I had done. It was not my best work but he nodded with approval.

"The boy knows how to flatter," he said. "I am impressed. If these idiots in the high command hadn't ruined the war, I would have had time to turn Linz into a marvelous city of art and music, and you, my boy, would be exhibited there! Especially being such a fine example of our race. Himmler, that traitor, was forever sponsoring these ridiculous expeditions to discover evidence of Nordic ancestry—Lebanon, Sweden, the Antarctic!—but we need to look no further than a talent like yours! Passed down through the generations, it is embedded in the blood. Compare work like this to the trash of Jewish painting. Primitive dabs, like a child's effort! No skill whatsoever in portraying the human figure. Their brains are only good for cunning. They cannot see things as they are. Yes, yes, what you've done with my face, I feel stronger just looking at it. I have always been a man of vigor and stamina, it's these pills that Linge gives me that make me weak! Linge, too, I suspect! A deceiver!"

"In the mountains," Eva said, "you were healthy, there was

a good color in your face. You strode ahead of the others on those jaunts up to the tea house."

"Some slothful reporter, I think from America, once asked me how I could walk up steep slopes without breaking a sweat. Don't hunch like a Jew, I told him. Keep your back straight as if you are walking on level ground and you won't notice the difference. He was astonished at the result, but it's a principle of life: to overcome apparent difficulty is merely a matter of changing your perspective. That is how we cut into France like a saw through the finest butter. Avoid common beliefs—religion begins that way. With Russia, the staff ignored me, they adhered to standard maneuvers in the way a baby clutches its bottle. It is the Bolsheviks, sadly, who have demonstrated the greatest imagination. Throughout my life, I have specialized in thinking at a much higher level than those around me. Others are examining the dirt, while I am considering the cosmos! Some may have scoffed at my plans to give every town an observatory so that the citizenry, too, could expand their interests beyond simple entertainments. Yet let a man glimpse the glories of astronomy and he becomes a more productive member of society. At the Berghof, of course, the sky was incredible. All that glowing cosmic ice, almost within reach! Horbiger, I would tell everyone, not only explained the universe but discovered the origins of Nordic man, of Nordic dominance! There is our evidence, the sky! We descended from the heavens like snow, frigid crystalline cells from the outer reaches, seeding life on this earth. I am often subdued when snow is falling, and people mistake it for anger. No, I am simply sensing the birth of our race on this planet. Heat, on the other hand, makes me irritable. The cold produces a pleasing rosy shine and mental clarity. From heat, however, there comes sweat, odor, lethargy, and rage. The Jew of course emerged from a hot, stinking, lazy climate, and his theories are conceived in delirium. Einstein is the prime example of crackpot science.

Relativity is gibberish, it is pure trickery! Zaubermaus, I may have life left in me yet. My hunger is returning. I would not mind some more spaghetti. Did you know, boy, that if my generals hadn't been such idiots, I would have been able to build spaghetti factories all across the East, fed with endless grain? Now finish the portrait!"

I moved my pencil with painstaking effort because my head felt full of stones, my arms were leaden. There were murmurings between the married couple, things I could not make out. I completed the rest of their faces, the gray one and the pink one, and I was starting to sketch in their bodies, working on the Führer's arm, when he snatched the paper away. After an intense study, he looked up and grinned. I swear there was a kind of demon presence that entered his eyes, for they brightened, and the jagged crimson veins spreading from the dark centers held a fiery glow.

"You are right, Zaubermaus," he said, "seeing myself like this, a proud defiant leader in his prime, drawn with such skill, the skill of a boy who carries the Reich's rich spirit—it becomes difficult to consider an end."

"Then not today," Eva said, "not today!"

"I don't want the fate of Mussolini."

"He was a fool, you said so yourself. We could leave tonight."

"If the Indians capture me, I would be tortured. They would scalp me and put hooks in my flesh."

"No one will catch us, Wolfi."

"Twenty years ago they threw me in jail and I came back to crush those who opposed me! Why not again? Why not? I will have to consult those who know the situation. Bormann might be able to get a helicopter..."

"I'll have the bags packed in a minute."

"Let Linge do it." The Führer covered one side of his mouth

and whispered to me, "She can't even get a purse together in under an hour." Louder, he proclaimed, waving the portrait, "I have often said that the actor and the officer are the two professions that most readily allow men to reach old age. Why? Both are in the presence of youth. I have been spending far too much time with the frail and the feeble-minded. You have restored me, boy! You will receive another medal for this! In fact, you must accompany me! You will remain by my side and sketch more portraits! Just like Hoffmann. Zaubermaus, get your things together, we can be there tomorrow. The clean cool air will let me think clearly, I can plan, I can plan! We won't let the Jews win the war! I'll call ahead so someone can prepare a screening of *King Kong*. The ape always fills me with such energy! You may carry my maps, boy."

It was all too much for me. I wanted nothing more to do with the war, I did not want to go to the mountains with him, I did not want to carry maps, I did not want to draw any more portraits of Adolf Hitler. My brain heated up. I would do anything to prevent all this from happening, anything! And there, before me, I perceived an opportunity: the Walther PPK. I would use it to prevent the Führer or Linge or anyone else from apprehending me. I would escape this bunker.

I snatched it and held it high, backing toward the door like a comic-book criminal. I did not know if it was loaded, and yet the weight of the thing in my hand, the authority of it, confirmed my crazy attempt to flee.

There was screaming now. A terrible pressure inside my skull made me wobble, and a white, blinding fog came to my eyes. I stumbled this way and that. That pressure increased a hundred times, my skull began to crack or so it felt, and dearest God, permit me to explain, I am afraid to type it, perhaps few will believe me, possibly it was an accident though I cannot know, possibly I dreamed it, possibly the moment exists only in my imagination, but what I remember is a blast, one that sent a stabbing pain into my bad ear and made my vision poor, and then a blurry sight: the Führer slumped on the couch, rich bright blood gushing from his head. Eva was shouting, though I could hear only a giant ringing. The distress on her soft face filled me with remorse and I wanted to apologize. Before I could do so, she put something in her mouth and appeared to faint. No, not fainting. She seemed to have died, too.

A stench of sulfur and other bitterness choked me. At some point I must have dropped the pistol. Too much death, too much shooting! I staggered away from the two bodies into a hall, to see if there might be another way out, a back entrance into the labyrinth. But there wasn't. Instead, I found a bedroom. I shut the door. Before a mirror, I wiped the Führer's blood off my hand and my chin. I wiped and wiped and wiped.

22

One summer afternoon when I was seven, I went out into the street with a friend, Herbert Höhn, to fire off a Gene Autry Repeating Cap Pistol, a prized toy that my father had managed to find in a Berlin department store. After shooting at imaginary enemies—the war had not yet started—Herbert and I decided to cause a little trouble by scaring a horse. We hid behind an advertisement kiosk and leaped out like cowboys when a delivery wagon appeared. Our shots cracked the air and that horse bolted, knocking the driver to the ground and smashing the cart into a parked car. Terrified, we ran, separating. I went home, to the villa, and scampered all the way up to the attic. There I stayed for much of the afternoon, in the quiet dark, worried but feeling protected, feeling beyond the reach of the world I had just disturbed. In fact, nothing ever came of our misbehavior. My father found me and I produced an effective lie, that I had come up here because I'd been upset after an argument with Herbert.

In that bedroom underground, was I thinking of this incident? It is doubtful. But I relate it now to present some similarities: a gun, a shot, a shocking event, my fright, my escape from the scene into a small enclosure, and my lie.

The lie was given to Bormann. He had burst into the bedroom. In his gray uniform, he stood over me, sending down waves of heat, reeking of sweat and booze.

"The others forgot about you but I did not," he said. "What did you see? Why are you in this room?"

I sat on the edge of the bed and looked at the floor, and then invented the reason. "I was drawing the portrait but then the Führer told me to leave. He had become angry."

"What about?"

"He did not want the Jews to win the war."

"What else did he say? Tell me, boy."

My thoughts were all broken up. "He wanted to let everyone see the stars...."

"What do you mean? Out with it."

"With telescopes...and he wanted to eat spaghetti, he wanted to watch *King Kong*."

Instantly I regretted this, knowing Bormann would find it insolent. But he backed away from his looming posture of violence and gave a kind of grunt, as if he had expected my answer. Then his eyes narrowed and darkened and he asked with a lower pitch, "After your dismissal, you came in here?"

"Yes."

"It is the Führer's bedroom. Why didn't you go out into the hall?"

"Eva sent me here," I said, expanding the lie. "She was hoping I could come back and finish the portrait."

"You could be court-martialed for being on the Führer's bed."

"I am very sorry."

"Are you aware of what has happened?"

"I am not sure..." I said, trying to stay calm.

"The Führer is dead. Given no other choice, he took his own life."

I tried to demonstrate surprise, though I did not have much to invent, for I did feel a jolt, not dread but a renewed desire to survive. There seemed to be a chance, a chance Zenzi's father would call infinitesimal, that I would not be put to death. Bormann, too drunk, too dismissive of anyone below his rank, did not consider, I am guessing, that a boy of thirteen could have fired the pistol, did not notice with his glazed eyes the blood on my jacket's collar.

Now tension stiffened Bormann again, his mouth twisted into a grimace, and he grabbed my jacket the way he had done before, roughly jerking me. "Why didn't you meet me the last two nights?"

"I was fighting the Russians, and before that, I was with the gorilla..."

"Sober up, you little shit. I can smell the champagne. Think straight and listen to me. From now on, you will take orders only from me."

But Bormann issued just a single order, which was to stay with him for the remainder of the day as he wandered unsteadily through the halls sending messages and trying to obtain updates on the Russian positions. What did he want of me? The Führer and Eva, I'd overheard, had been given a funeral of fire, but no one, including Bormann, seemed to suspect my involvement in their deaths. He kept sucking on a bottle of brandy, and shoved me this way and that. All I desired to do was to find where they buried Stalla but I could see that would be impossible now.

In the early evening, an officer gathered those of us left in the bunker to announce that we would soon attempt to break through the enemy lines, and then head northwest to Schwerin, which lay near the Baltic Sea and sounded far away. It was, he added grimly, our only hope. Bormann stood next to me, drunk and swaying. Unlike other officers who had ditched their uniforms for civilian garb, he was still wearing his gray tunic, but had torn off his insignia with an animal's ferocity. Now, slurring and mashing up his words, Bormann finally revealed to me my new duty: because he had never learned the streets of Berlin very well, I was to be his guide.

We were divided into three or four groups and ordered to sleep so that we could build energy for the journey. Bormann was making sure I remained close. I tried to find comfort on the hard floor while the bulky Reichsleiter lay face up on a cot. His arms dangled to either side, his giant snout roared like a tank's engine. But every so often, one beady eye, squinting, would check on my presence.

Around nine o'clock the next evening, May 1st, 1945, the call came to assemble. Officers, soldiers, boys like myself, and a few women, we all trooped in silence down the dim corridors to an underground garage. Flaming wooden torches stood in the corners, sending long shadows, as jittery as us, to stretch across the walls. It reminded me of *Frankenstein*, which I had seen with Vati some years before and had given me nightmares for a week. Deeper in the gloom, black limousines faintly gleamed, and I thought they might be bussing us somewhere. No, a strained voice outlined the immediate plan: run to the nearest U-Bahn entrance and proceed through the tunnels northward, under the Spree, and eventually to the Stettiner Bahnhof station, which would bring us outside the Russian encirclement. My own private plan, formulated soon after, was to flee Bormann at the first opportunity and—dearest God, if she was still alive—try to find Zenzi.

Soldiers smashed away bricks that had walled-up an old window, and we all looked without a word toward this framed vision of the street, an orange glow blackened by swirls of inky smoke, our portal to the future.

Bormann gripped me, and breathing on me with hot sweet gas, he growled, "Where are we supposed to go?"

"To the Kaiserhof station, he said."

"Where? How far?"

He was not testing me, I sensed. He did not, in fact, know the city. "We will come out on Wilhelmstrasse," I said. "We go right and then left down Voss Strasse to the station. It is only a short run. He said to stay close to the walls because of sharpshooters."

"You will lead me to the Lehrter station."

"It's across the Spree," I said, brightening a little, for crossing the river was exactly what I wanted to do. "Near the Charité hospital."

"We must head north," he said, unfolding a scrap of paper. "We must follow this."

I looked at a hasty sketch of lines and dots. "The Big Dipper?"

"Yes, yes, the North Star. Always keep it in sight!" Knowing he was drunk, I said nothing and so he raised his voice, his words a little garbled and cracking. "You will always be in front of me, understood? Understood?" He pulled a pistol from the pocket of his tunic, even though we had been advised not to carry weapons in order to better pose as civilians. "But never beyond arm's reach. Don't even think about deserting me."

At eleven o'clock, the first group clambered up through the opening. I heard the cracking of gunfire, though nothing heavy. The rest of us whispered that it seemed possible they had reached the station. Bormann breathed rapidly, still clutching me. Twenty minutes passed before the next group left, and another twenty in slow agony before we got the signal for ours.

I climbed on a table, hoisted myself to the window, peered around, and crawled out, keeping close to the Chancellery wall. No longer even a pathway, Wilhelmstrasse stretched out like a public dump, filled with wrecked cars, severed pipes, tangled wires, a few bodies or parts of them, and a thousand other things under heaps of mud and bricks. Not far away, long pointed flames were stabbing upward. Red-hot sparks swarmed above me, as if the devil had released a plague of glowing wasps. I covered my mouth with my jacket and waited for Bormann to heave himself up behind me. Backs against the wall, we sat with others in terror, trying to spot Russians. We heard shots, but they seemed further away.

"We should go now," I told Bormann. After he grunted in reply, I darted through the rubble. I recognized almost nothing. My skin quivered. I slipped on concrete shards, cracking my knee. But there—the battered entrance to the Kaiserhof station. Over chunks of granite, I tumbled down into darkness. Others landed near me with groans and finally there came Bormann's bulk, rolling across the U-Bahn platform. We had survived the first dash. Beyond us lay blackness.

Bormann barked out a question. "Boy, where are you?"

Here it was, then, a chance to flee, for his eyes had not adjusted, and he was in no state to chase me, but I did not know where to go, and feared that pistol, and simply said, "I am here."

"Goddamn you, don't get so far ahead, don't go so fast. Stay with me." He crawled over, carrying a heavy satchel I had not noticed before. "Have you seen Baur?"

He meant the pilot, the Führer's pilot, who was in our group. I told him I hadn't and he spat out profanity, the darkness echoed with it. Then we both went silent when we heard a bang, something had been dropped, perhaps across the tracks. The

Russians were in the tunnel! We remained still, trying to see something. A flashlight sent its beam into the black. Forms became visible, people huddled against a wall. Someone near me said they must be Germans, for a stench of shit overpowered our noses and the Russians would not have had time to create such a pile. Indeed, after a few questions shot out into the dark, we discovered that there were civilians here, dozens of them, maybe hundreds. Protect us, give us water, they pleaded, now assured that we weren't Russians, either. Another flashlight surveyed their sprawl, and I could see their pitiful state—bodies hunched, shivering, wrapped in foul blankets, voices hoarse and weak, faces covered in dirt or red sores. "Zenzi!" I shouted, wondering if she could be here, but the only answer I got was Bormann's, a snarl ordering me to shut my mouth.

We hooked up with Baur, an intelligent-looking man with deep-set eyes. We climbed down onto the tracks with a number of others and set off underground for the Friedrichstrasse station, which sat close to the river Spree. The going proved difficult. Baur was trying to hurry us along so that we could stay close behind the group in front, for the tunnel's darkness was rich. Bormann had a flashlight he'd snatched from a civilian, but he was filled with too much alcohol and burdened by his satchel, and could not keep up, lurching along and slashing the walls with his beam. He yelled at me to slow down and Baur urged us to walk faster, and I was caught between. Worries about the third rail had us all nervy, for we wondered if it was charged and, if controlled by the Russians, whether they would zap us.

We made it to the Stadmitte station, where more civilians lay on the platform and begged us for supplies, where surgeons operated inside a lantern-lit U-Bahn car parked on the tracks. We rested here for a short while before moving beyond, discovering that in all of our confusion and concern and tentative creeping, we had lost sight and sound of the other group. We were not certain of our direction. Bormann, anxious, croaked his complaints: "Baur, I thought you knew what you were doing."

"I know the sky, not the tunnels."

"Boy," Bormann said, "where do we go?"

I thought for a minute. "We came into Kaiserhof, and then Stadmitte. We should have gone left there, up the line to Friedrichstrasse. If we go back, we can find the way."

"Then why didn't you say anything, you idiot!"

"I was not thinking about it," I said with truth, "I was just walking."

Baur's voice was calm. "The boy is right, I believe. We'll find the other tunnel and go as far as we can underground. That way, we might emerge outside the ring. That was Mohnke's idea."

"It will take us all night in this fucking darkness," Bormann said. "Mohnke left an hour ago, but we don't have time. The Russians will be in the tunnels soon enough. And if we're caught down here, we are dead, Baur, you must understand that, even for someone whose head is in the clouds."

Baur ignored the insult, sticking to logic. "The only other way is on the street."

"Yes," Bormann agreed, "at least we'll know where the hell we are."

"We'll have to be quick. We won't survive if we're not. I suggest you drop that satchel, it's no good lugging such weight."

"I can handle myself. You worry about the plane."

This was the first time I had heard any mention of a plane—all the more reason to find my chance to flee them, for surely they would find me dispensable once they located it. We returned to Stadmitte, climbed the wrecked stairway, and started making our way across Unter den Linden. In the distance, under the Brandenburg Gate, in the orange glow of a large fire, Russians were roasting what appeared to be the carcass of a steer. We could hear the cascading circus notes of an accordion and a messy kind of singing. The city was no longer ours, it belonged now to a strange tribe. "It's May first," Baur said as we huddled behind a crushed Volkswagen. "May Day. I only just realized. The Communist celebration. They're drunk." Behind me, Bormann muttered, "Barbarians."

But lucky for us, the barbarians were not shooting. From a distance, if we could be seen at all, we must have resembled civilians. Now we came within sight of the black iron spires of the Weidendammer Bridge, which lay across the Spree. The Volkssturm had erected a tank barrier across the width, visible in silhouette, a tangle of wires stretched between a frame of wood, with iron rods emerging to face in our direction. I did not think it would stop a tank for very long, though it made crossing the bridge by foot nearly impossible. The bodies of those who had already tried lay there, a heap of them, it was hard to tell in the dark how many. We'd been joined now by a narrow-faced doctor I had seen in the bunker, but somehow we had lost Baur.

"You are supposed to keep him in sight at all times," Bormann said. He was fiddling with his wedding ring. "Where is the Lehrter station from here?"

"Across the river and then to the left and north a little, I think."

"How far?"

"Two kilometers?"

"The fucking bridge is blocked." Mortar shells began to fall close by. The Russians were not going to be so quiet, after all. We ducked and pushed ourselves against the wall, not knowing what to do.

The answer seemed to come out of nowhere. Five Tiger tanks, the sight was a miracle, were rumbling and groaning toward the bridge. Tigers! For the moment, the spirit to win returned in me. Reinforcements had arrived! We would smash the Russians! The massive boxy tanks were like dragons, real dragons, they were indestructible, they lined up and rolled onto the bridge. Of course they mashed those bodies into a pudding, I closed my eyes for that, but then, hurrah, they demolished the roadblock beneath their treads. The shelling had stopped, no doubt because the tanks had surprised the enemy, too.

In another minute, I don't know who gave the order, all of us rushed onto the bridge. I slipped on slimy guts, though I hardly noticed as the tanks had begun to fire. My ears almost burst, the explosions vibrated my bones. Russian searchlights tunneled through the smoke and dust with their yellow tubes and waved crazily from side to side, as if it were a carnival. Crouching, we scurried and darted, and then we were over the Spree! Several of us hid in a doorway, panting like dogs. I checked myself for wounds, but I had not been hurt. Bormann with his awkward running had arrived without a scratch, too, cradling his satchel as if it were a baby.

A flare floated down with the serenity of Christmas Eve. It spread a strange green light over the jagged remnants that lined the river, now more or less quiet. Bodies of several Russians with their round helmets sprawled near us. I felt instant contempt, satisfied to see agony frozen on the enemy's gaping mouths, an enemy who had killed Stalla. Under the glow, glancing around, I got my bearings. We were not too far from the basement where Zenzi and her family had been staying.

Maybe Bormann sensed my interest in escape, for now he grabbed my jacket and pushed his square head close to mine, his eyes watery and unfocused. "Now which way?"

"We need to find the railroad and follow it along the river."

"Where is the Big Dipper?" We both looked up, but the bright flare and the drifting smoke prevented any good view of the stars. "All right, go. You better be right."

Not far down the road, we came across the same Tigers, and I thought we might follow them again until I saw that this time they were facing several giant Russian tanks. Furious blasts came in our direction. We threw ourselves on the ground and

Bormann began to moan. In a matter of minutes the Tigers were burning, all of them, and heartbreak filled me. There was nothing we could do about the Russians, nothing. Bormann and I crawled into a vestibule, where we found the doctor, whose name was Stumpfegger, and also Artur Axmann, his pudgy body squeezed into a civilian suit. The doctor, a towering man, attended to Bormann, who had been wounded in the shoulder—a big tear in his coat, a glimpse of bone. Twisted by pain, the Reichsleiter ordered me to carry his precious satchel, and then we were off, heading to a railway embankment, to the Lehrter station.

We scurried for a while along the elevated rails, but on Axmann's suggestion, to limit our exposure, we jumped down beneath a bridge. Here we discovered, to our great shock, a strange Russian platoon. They all had blond, shoulder-length hair. Several wore puffy pantaloons and frilly shirts. One held a shield and a spear. Another stood in a wide ballroom dress. Drunk and grinning, they started shouting a few phrases of German. "Hitler kaput! Krieg kaput! Rauchen zigarette!"

It turned out—as Axmann discovered, knowing a little Russian—that they had found a storehouse of opera costumes. Having mistaken us for pitiful members of the Volkssturm, they shared their bitter cigarettes. Even I was offered the chance. When I began to choke, they laughed so hard the biggest of them fell over and singed his wig in the flames. Then they began crowding Axmann, fascinated by his wooden arm. He removed it and performed the rumored act of comedy that I had hoped to see at the Sportfeld—so long ago, it seemed—pressing the stiff hand against his neck to mimic strangulation. Inspired, the Russians took the arm themselves and raised it in the Nazi salute, shouting their mangled German in mockery of the Führer's raging speeches.

Meanwhile, Bormann was sulking in the shadows. Eventually he flagged me over and told me that he and the doctor were going to make a run for it, and that I was to go with them. When the platoon started using Axmann's arm to scratch their backs, laughing like children, the three of us scampered off. The Russians did not seem to care.

We continued along the railway line, following the Spree. We kept glancing to our left, for there lay the inconceivable, an astonishing sight when viewed from afar: the center of Berlin reduced to mangled forms and frantic blazes, a volcanic landscape, a pit of death and ash. The smoke, grown thicker, twisted upward in funnels, curling around a bright three-quarter moon. Just across the river the Reichstag's blackened dome rose like a tomb.

But ahead, we could see the outline of the Lehrter station. Though Bormann still talked of a rendezvous with Baur there, he had slowed, staggering and listing to the side of his wound. He kept asking the doctor for assurances that he was not seriously hurt, and Stumpfegger, more and more annoyed, kept telling him it was not mortal. I, too, was struggling to keep up, burdened by the weight of the satchel, losing energy, and disheartened about any chance of escape. We were heading further and further away from Zenzi's basement.

We managed to scramble over to Invalidenstrasse, and here, in the roofless ruins of a church, Bormann insisted that we rest. He clutched his shoulder, he grimaced in a way that made him resemble a pig. Seated on a splintered pew, I listened to the night's continuous booms, which sounded to me like the anger of God.

Meanwhile, Stumpfegger, who had a young mild face with devious eyes, was examining me. "So this is the boy who drew the Führer's wedding portrait? The last person to see him alive? How strange that he wanted such an amateur."

"The Führer maintained some odd affections, especially with art," Bormann said. "He even wanted the picture brought to Dönitz."

"You have it?"

"No, it was covered in blood. I tore it to pieces. Unfinished, in any case."

"Unfinished? But why?"

"The Führer went into another rage, the boy said. Booted him out. I found the kid sleeping in the Führer's bedroom. Eva was hoping he might come back and finish. Naïve to the very end, that girl. But what does it matter? We must find Baur. I've rested enough."

Stumpfegger was still staring at me. "Come closer, boy, into the moonlight. Closer. Yes, now tilt your head back. Bormann, take a look at this."

"We're going to miss Baur."

"I believe there is blood on the boy's collar," Stumpfegger said. "Speckled. Splattered."

"What's the matter?" Impatient, Bormann groaned as he struggled to stand. "He doesn't look injured. He will continue to carry my satchel."

"Yes, exactly what I mean. He has no significant wound. A scratch on his forehead, nothing more. But the blood is splattered. Look, a few spots on his neck, too."

"What are you suggesting? All the kids I've seen are covered in blood."

"The pattern is from a shot, I'm sure—a close-range shot. What I'm suggesting is that the blood might be the Führer's."

"The boy was sent away."

"I'm not so sure."

I was listening to this speculation while nervously shifting on that pew, knowing I would have to run, and I did. I leaped up and sprinted out through the church's ruins, out to the road. There was a shot, I assume it came from Bormann. Perhaps because of his wounded shoulder, the bullet did not find its mark. I continued underneath a bridge but did not get much beyond it. Tired and clumsy, I stumbled on debris and fell. And the doctor, with his long legs, caught me. He was gripping my ankles. Bormann lumbered up and kicked me in the ribs so hard that I lost my breath, and then said, "What happened in that room, you fucking little liar." He brought out a knife and pressed its tip into my chin.

The doctor held my shoulders. "The portrait! A plot! A plot all along. Who put you up to it?"

Bormann was lowering his boozy, sour-smelling mouth as if to kiss me. "Tell us or you will writhe in the worst agony."

I looked into the night sky, and there, between the swirls of shadowy smoke, I saw the Big Dipper, sparkling, fiercely beautiful. The sight of the stars, the certainty of my time to die, they gave me a moment of bravery, and I said, "I did it for everyone who became fertilizer."

"Puncture his gut and twist," the doctor said. "It will be slow but deadly."

"No," said Bormann. "I will jam it in his ear."

I closed my eyes as tight as I could and remained still, not struggling at all, I do not know for how long. I assumed that I must have died already, for I felt no pain from the knife that must have plunged into me. Was my soul now speeding into the furthest reaches of space, beyond Pluto, beyond the stars and the comets, where I would soon meet all the dead?

At the sound of a moan, I peered around. Bormann was on his stomach making noises. The doctor, no longer holding my ankles, was sprawled face-up. From where I lay, on the road, I could see those Russians in their wigs prancing inside the church, full of fresh laughter. It seemed that they had shot at us.

"Stumpfegger," Bormann mumbled, "I think my lung has been pierced."

The doctor did not answer.

Quieter, Bormann said, "Boy!"

I said nothing.

"Boy, help me."

"I cannot." Then stated, "I will not."

Bormann remained face down. His moans produced a rough hissing. "Gerda, Gerda, my mommy-girl," he whispered, "take care of the children." More laughter from the Russians, and then they moved out of the church, out of sight. With great effort, Bormann said, "You will be discovered. You will be executed." Then he struggled to find something in a pocket, and then pressed a hand to his mouth, and I did not hear another breath from him. Stumpfegger appeared to be dead, too.

So there I was, dazed, free again, and oddly grateful to the Russians. They had brought me agony in these last few weeks, and they would soon bring more, but in this moment, they had, by happenstance, saved my life. Their bullets did not find a skinny boy lying flat in the dark. But this is how you survive a war, that giant machine designed for killing. You encounter an occasional flaw.

After a while, I managed to rise, though with a stinging pain in my ribs and one leg. I left Bormann's pistol and knife where they lay, not wanting the Russians to catch me with them, but grabbed his satchel. Inside, I discovered two small sausages, a canteen of water, and a bottle of brandy. The rest of the contents, inedible, were a great surprise, though familiar. Necklaces, bracelets, pins— all the gold jewelry I had obtained from the Schliemann treasure, from the Zoo bunker. Bormann had never sent them away to preserve them, he had kept everything for himself. I considered dumping it, for the weight was considerable, but wondered if I might be able to trade these things for food.

Then I hobbled off, back the way I had come, in hope of finding Zenzi.

23

The dawn of May 2nd was bone-cold, and I could not stop shivering as I made my way to the neighborhood of Mitte. My nerves were making it worse. It was clear that Berlin now belonged to the Russians. Around me, things were strangely festive. In the ruined buildings all remaining window sills, and even holes in the walls, had been draped in the white of surrender. Booming voices, projected from loudspeakers, blared announcements in poor Russian-accented German about the Führer's death and the end of the war. Soviet soldiers were grinning, singing, dancing, barking orders, and everywhere setting up bivouacs. The smoky smells of cooking made my mouth ache. On one street, I saw the roasting of a whole pig. The reddened carcass with its pointed ears turned and turned atop the flames like a demon on a spit.

As much as I could, I slipped in and out of the ruins. The civilians I passed warned me that the Russians were arresting or killing anyone they thought was a soldier, anyone who possessed a weapon. They weren't tolerating anything. In fact, I saw an older man hauled off because his son was brandishing a toy pistol, one that shot only bits of potato. The black jacket I'd taken from the messenger boy was not of military style, but I ditched it, anyway, in case it might be mistaken for a uniform, which of course made me colder. At one point, my shivering forced me to take a risk. I crouched at the edge of a bivouac's fire. My eyes were so fixed on a large pot of Soviet soup that I did not notice when a burly soldier strode over to me. He began to speak sharply in his gibberish. He pointed at his hairy wrist several times. I thought he wanted to know the time, and I shook my head. "No watch," I said in German. He became angry, I could not understand why, and then he rummaged through the satchel. He snatched the brandy, took one bite from a sausage but spat it out, left everything else, and shoved me away.

Finally, I came to Zenzi's building. I rushed inside, stumbling in my anxious state down the short set of stairs, and entered darkness, met by a rank and sweetish odor, the one of death. "Zenzi? Are you here?"

The blackness eased away, and now I could make out the interior, the same as I had seen it before, a few pieces of furniture, some crates. But there was no one. They had left. They had gone to the Americans. In the next building, I questioned a woman about the Fuchses and she told me that she thought one of them had died, but didn't really know because she herself had been hiding. Back in the Fuchses' basement I began a frantic search, following those death vapors, throwing things aside. Near the wall, the smell was strongest. I flung away some crates and found a hole. There I saw a human form, stretched across the dirt. I steadied myself from dizziness, which came from both the smell and my terror. I covered my mouth and nose. In dreamy slowness I crouched, I drifted toward this body. Now I could see the wide cheeks and the dented chin, all smudged, and the glasses, too, and I reached an arm out to touch Kreszentia Fuchs.

"Tobias," that body said, and then rose to embrace me.

While the Russians shouted orders in the street, we sat there silent for a long while, just clutching. Then Zenzi whispered, "Is it true that you're really here?"

"It's hard for me to believe, too."

"I left you. I'm so sorry. The way that officer shot Otto Köckler, I was so afraid, I had to run."

"You were brave to run."

"My husband. We will never be separated again."

"But where are your parents? Why didn't you go with them?"

"Tobias, they died." Now tears came. "I think, I think you can smell them. My God, let's go to the doorway."

"Was it the SS?"

She shook her head. She squeezed my hand. We sat on the steps breathing fresher air. She took a minute or two to begin, and then the story flowed out, as if it had been collecting in her throat.

"After I ran, I came back here and begged my father to help me find out what had happened to you. He was very angry at me because I'd left again and said there was nothing anyone could do. My mother was still weeping after all the shelling that morning. She had really lost her mind. In her eyes you could see that her spirit had just gone. She started screaming about wanting to die. Her jaw was shivering. And then, when a few more shells started to fall, we could not stop her, she ran out into the street. She looked up, held out her arms, and in a minute she was hit." Zenzi took several large breaths before continuing. "My father went to find her after things quieted down and brought back—he brought back an arm. He knew it was hers because of the pattern on her sleeve. My mother was nothing more than an arm. We were in disbelief. He put it in a box and clutched it all day. He stopped talking. He told me it was time for him to die, too. I remember, he said, 'The odds for life no longer exist. We are dividing by zero.' I yelled at him for even thinking it, but he only tried to convince me to do the same thing. Tobias, I cannot tell you how horrible this was. He found a packet of rat poison. We will take it together, he said. I considered it for a minute, no longer, and then refused. He smoked one last pipe, he had stashed some tobacco for a special occasion. While he puffed, he looked at me and said he hoped that I could find my way in the world, and I could see that he was no longer interested in being a father or anything at all, and right after he finished the pipe, he stood at a distance from me so I could not grab his arm, and he spooned the powder, the poison, into his mouth. It was not quick. He had convulsions for a long while, he foamed at the mouth, he kept coughing up blood. I poured water into his mouth, I tried to wash out the poison, but it continued. I rushed out to find a doctor, but nobody would help. When I came back, the convulsions had stopped, everything had stopped. His eyes were red, he looked like one of those space creatures you used to draw. I dragged his body behind the wall, where you found me. My mother's arm is there, too. I did not have the will to bury them, or the strength. I was hiding because I didn't know where else to go, and the Russians are coming after girls at night."

After a moment, I said, "I can help you dig a grave."

She nodded. "For Einbrecher, too."

"I had forgotten about him."

"He just gave up and stopped breathing. He got tired of the war."

"Well, it's over now. The war."

"Everyone's saying that Hitler is dead."

I could only nod as my heart wildly jerked.

"But how did you get here?" she asked. "Look, you have blood on your pants."

"I was chased," I said, "and I fell. I got kicked in the ribs, too. That's a little worse."

While Zenzi inspected my wound and dressed it with a strip of bedsheet, I tried to explain what had happened to me, but the words that emerged from my mouth hardly seemed to make any sense.

"Do you have anything to eat?" Zenzi asked. "Yesterday I had to make do with beer, but I drank the last bottle."

"Half a sausage," I said, taking it out of the satchel. "And this jewelry."

"Where did that come from?"

"I had been collecting it from a special storehouse for a man named Bormann. An official. I don't really know what he did. He died in front of me. I'm sure they're valuable. They're old. Ancient Greece. We could trade them."

"Ancient Greece? Everything is so strange now." She draped a necklace across her hand. "It's beautiful, but all the Russians want are wristwatches."

"That explains what one of them was demanding from me."

"They behave like children or animals. I hear them yelling all day. I bet they don't even know how to tell time."

"Zenzi, do you still want to find the Americans?"

"It's too late. We're trapped. We'll all be slaves soon. Tobias, you can't let them know you were a soldier! Or that you worked for that madman! They'll take you away."

Then I remembered that I still had the Iron Cross in the pocket of my pants, and so I took it out and buried it behind the wall, in the space where Zenzi had hidden. We split the last piece of sausage, savoring it slowly, and then slept in restlessness on a dirty mattress until dusk.

Strengthened a little, we decided that night to bury the remains of Zenzi's parents. We managed to place her father on a torn metal sheet, and then dragged him to a nearby garden that was sprouting weeds. Using pieces of broken pipe, we began to dig, but soon a Russian soldier, waving a flashlight, ordered us to stop. He shouted a command to a comrade. This same shout was repeated, soldier to soldier, down the street. After a while, a stocky, dark-haired young man, who had as few whiskers as I did, appeared before us, pulling a child's wagon and carrying a lantern. The first soldier then ordered us to lift the body of Herr Fuchs onto the wagon. Zenzi and I both assumed that we would be led to an official burial site, so we did as we were told. The young soldier began to roll Herr Fuchs away when Zenzi rushed up with the box containing the arm and the rabbit. The soldier started to wave her away until she opened it and said "Meine Mutter." He froze, he said something soft in his language, then took the box and placed it on the body.

"Levka," he said, pointing at his chest. "Levka."

Through narrow corridors of rubble we followed the young dark-haired Levka, who looked like a boy playing a strange game, carrying his lantern, pulling his wagon and its body. I told Zenzi that he must be taking us to a small graveyard behind a church, or a former garden plot, but this was wrong, all wrong, for when we turned a corner, we saw a giant bonfire blazing in the middle of the plaza. And we could see, with a great shock, that bodies lay inside it on wooden planks, wrapped by flames. Rushing up, Zenzi tried without success to wrest away the wagon. Levka just shook his head and pointed at the fire.

"I don't want them burned!" she screamed. "Tobias, they want to make us disappear! Look what they're doing! It's just like the camps, like the Jews!"

An old German woman emerged, gripped Zenzi's arm, and explained above the fire's roar that the Russians were trying to prevent the spread of disease. Zenzi sank to her knees and said, "I don't care, I don't care, I don't want them turned to ash, they'll be mixed together with everyone else."

But there was nothing she could do. Levka placed Herr Fuchs and the mother's arm on a plank and then carried it to the fire. He tried, I think, to show his sympathy by being gentle. The heat was too much, however, and he could not get close enough. Then another soldier, older and impatient, took the body himself and from a safe distance threw Herr Fuchs and the box into the flames like someone heaving garbage. Zenzi and I both turned our heads away from the sight, and remained where we stood only because the fire warmed our backs.

24

The next day, morose from the previous night, Zenzi and I stayed in the basement. She slept while I sat near the open doorway, where I hoped to catch any rumors of food distribution or discovered storehouses. Before me, Berliners moved slowly. Everyone was gray, sullen, drooping. They shielded their eyes from the foggy concrete dust, and some wore rags around their mouths. They avoided looking at the Russians, who veered between kindness and rage, who comforted a child injured in a fall, and then soon after threw men down or smashed things in the street they had removed from apartments. I saw one soldier hammer away at a rocking horse—someone said he thought it mocked the Russian cavalry. Though we did not fear shelling or shooting anymore, we held no desire for anything but food and water. It was a time of numbness and nothingness.

In mid-morning, that same young private who called himself Levka appeared before me. Tentative and awkward, he gripped a helmet under his arm and kept his hands clenched. He looked even younger in the daylight. He had a delicate nose and thin lips. His hair, thick and black, was sticking up on top, as if tar had been spilled in it. Zenzi, who had awoken, joined me to help ward him off, twirling her wrists and declaring, "No watches."

But Levka seemed encouraged by her gesture. He took a few steps inside, still nervous, and then held out his fists and opened them, revealing in his palms two lumps bundled in paper. Gently nodding, he urged Zenzi to take them but she only shook her head. I grabbed the lumps myself and discovered, with quick unwrapping, that they were a pair of cooked potatoes, still pretty hot. I looked at Levka with openmouthed gratitude.

Zenzi remained guarded. "He wants something."

"It's an apology," I said. "For what happened last night."

"Then tell him we need more. Water, too. And blankets, and matches for the lantern."

"You do it."

"I will not speak with imbeciles."

"Zenzi! He might know German."

"That's just the point. Look at him, he stands there and smiles. He doesn't understand a word of what we're saying. To think that we must live with them now. People who throw my parents into a fire. Who know nothing about Furtwängler or Goethe. All they care about is cows and pigs and wristwatches."

"You better quiet down or they'll take you away. Here, I'll try drawing it for him." I thanked Levka for the potatoes with a nod, hoping he had not understood anything that Zenzi had said, and then gestured to him to wait a moment. I found the pencil and paper Herr Fuchs had used to plan his hoped-for journey, and sketched as fast as I could some simple illustrations: someone collecting water from a street pump, sleeping under a blanket, and lighting a lantern, with arrows indicating the needed things. Levka took the sheet, studied it, nodded rapidly, and then disappeared into the street.

It was not long before Levka returned with the requested items, a green blanket that smelled of horses, a steel pot of water, and a handmade lighter constructed from a bullet casing. I thanked him in German, mirroring his own broad smile. Zenzi stayed quiet, still wary, for Levka did not seem to be in any hurry to leave. Now he pulled out the sketch I had made, pointed to it, and then jabbed his own chest. Grinning, he began to babble in Russian.

"I do not understand," I said.

But Zenzi did. "He wants you to draw *him*."

When I confirmed the request, pointing at Levka and drawing in the air with my hand, he slapped his leg several times and broadened that grin. He straightened his back and brushed his smooth cheeks clean, as if I were going to photograph him. In a few minutes, I had finished my quick sketch on another of Herr Fuchs's papers. Levka stared at this portrait—I had flattened his hair and thinned out his face—and laughed with a throat-clearing sound. Then he shook my hand several times before leaving with his prize.

"You made the farm boy happy," Zenzi sneered.

"Maybe he'll bring us more potatoes. He seems all right."

"What does it matter? There is livestock in the street, and all night they sing those stupid country songs. I should have swallowed that rat poison."

"You can't say that. I want you to live. I want you to be with me. Anyway," I added, trying to ease her growing bitterness, "the Russians made music you like."

"You mean Tchaikovsky? He lived a long time ago, before they killed the aristocrats. So did Pushkin and Chekhov and Tolstoy. In any case, none are as good as German artists. Tchaikovsky is an amateur compared with Strauss or Mahler. But when will we ever hear that music? It'll be accordions and folk tunes from now on."

Very soon, another Russian soldier showed up, this one gaunt with furtive eyes. I feared some punishment for having sketched one of his comrades. Maybe it was against their rules to fraternize. But this soldier pointed at his cheeks, which were scooped out and pockmarked, and then, from his pocket, fished out a chunk of bread and offered it. I understood that he wanted a portrait, too. So I proceeded to draw his bony, angular face. Zenzi, meanwhile, had darted into the corner, rummaged around, and produced a book. She stood next to me, announced, "I will demonstrate how the Russian has no interest in art," and began to recite lines from Schiller. She spoke with great care, emphasizing the rhymes, and the soldier stared at her the whole time. When I handed him the finished sketch, he examined it like a shy boy, then guffawed with his yellowed teeth and shouted toward the door, where a third soldier appeared.

Just like that, we were in business. Soldier after soldier visited us, each bringing payment—more bread, a teacup filled with butter, fresh eggs, strips of pork, two candles, a canteen of vodka, and even a spoon engraved with words in Cyrillic. For each man, I drew his portrait. Soon I ran out of paper, yet the next sitter brought sheets of German military stationary, souvenirs from a command post. The soldiers, both young and middle-aged, were quiet and serious, their eyes fixed on Zenzi as she recited the poetry. She stood like a girl auditioning for the lead part in a play, she read with perfect enunciation and with a certain haughty tone to her voice. Partly I was happy that she had resumed her snobbishness, a sign she was regaining her interest in life. But really it was only an extension of her anger. Between visits she whispered to me, "They sit there as dumb as sheep" or "Not one of them appreciates it" and other such comments. Nevertheless,

I could see that the soldiers thought the poetry was a kind of blessing that accompanied the capturing of a face.

After almost a dozen visits, a Russian major, a bullish man whose shiny seashell ears were peeling from sunburn, came in for his turn. He did not bring any kind of payment, he merely indicated that I should begin. When Zenzi, who did not seem to realize this was no ordinary foot soldier, started reading the poetry, the major signaled with his hand to stop, told her in poor German not to read such fascist propaganda in his presence, and gestured at me to hurry up. He snorted at my finished sketch, snatched the book of Schiller from Zenzi's hands, and marched out. At the doorway, he shouted, "Where are guardians for you?"

"They are dead," I told him.

"Then you must find others. It is not safe without them."

The portraits had come to an end, but, by candlelight, we stuffed ourselves with the Russian food, passing spoonfuls of butter to each other. It was the first good meal either of us had eaten for a long time. Euphoric with our full stomachs—I barely noticed the aches in my leg and ribs—we did not discuss reaching the Americans at all. Instead, we talked of taking our portrait business to another section of the city, another platoon, who would give us new gifts. "Strawberries," Zenzi said, listing the items we'd request. "A new pair of shoes. What else? A phonograph! Next time I will dance for them." She kissed me on the cheek, and I heated up. "I want to check on a mother and her child just down the street. We'll take some food. My father and I had helped them on occasion." She dropped her voice to a whisper. "They are Mischlinge, too."

After nightfall, despite a curfew, we grabbed hunks of bread and a few slices of pork and slipped out. Somewhere a spotlight, aimed in a different direction, let us see enough of the street. There seemed to be no Russian patrols, so we darted through a snaking path in the rubble to a shattered basement staircase. "Typhoid, typhoid," the mother said as we entered, but embraced Zenzi once she understood who had come. Behind her a five-year-old boy slept with raspy snoring. Zenzi handed over the food and explained about her parents, as if it had happened months ago. "What will you do? Terrible, terrible," the mother said. "Zenzi, you in particular must protect yourself. It is dangerous for someone with your qualities."

"The SS cannot still be operating here."

"No, I mean the Russians. They are having their way with everyone, no matter how young." She patted her chest. "They like it big here. Excuse me for being so blunt, it's the truth. You must hide. Or make yourself look sick."

"We had lots of visitors today," I said, "and no one tried to touch her."

"They come at night."

"I have a secret place," Zenzi assured her.

"You can stay here," the mother suggested. "When they see a child, they move along."

"We'll be all right."

"Yes, I hope so. We've all had enough suffering. Enough for a whole century."

Zenzi sighed in a particularly sad way. "You must have heard about the camps, too."

"There have been a lot of rumors."

"Not rumors. I have a real report of the killing. From a Swiss newspaper. Visit tomorrow and I will show it to you."

"I don't need to see it."

"But you should. Everyone should."

"Zenzi, who tells the truth in a war? No one."

"I read it myself," I said. "The Jews were used for fertilizer."

"Don't be ridiculous. You are both young, and you are

living with the worst kind of grief. But when all this calms down, you will see that these are only exaggerations. Do you really think that we could do that? Germans?"

"Yes," Zenzi said, too loud, "of course I do! It's been going on for years. Open your eyes."

"Don't try to earn sympathy from the Russians by turning on your own people!"

Awakened by the raised voices, the child began to cry, and Zenzi tugged me to the doorway and into the street. "What an idiot," she whispered. "Another ignorant housewife. And to think that I wasted that food on her."

"Maybe it *would* be safer there," I said, and repeated what the Russian major had said about finding guardians.

"The child is malnourished and cries too often. You heard it. The noise is awful, it makes me crazy."

Further away, flashlights sent out yellow cones in the dust, a patrol. We hurried back to our own basement. As soon as we entered, a bright white beam, coming from the corner, blinded us. We froze, shielding our eyes. Then came laughter. Then words, German with a Russian accent, "Good book." The beam turned to shine on the speaker's hand, which gripped Zenzi's copy of the Schiller. Up the light traveled, onto a reddened globe, the face of Levka. "Not fascist," he added, laughing once more. "No trouble!"

Even from where I stood I could smell the alcohol.

"Of course not," Zenzi said, showing little fear. "It's just poetry."

"Yes, yes! Here, a gift. For you." He held out a worn volume. "Pushkin." He thumbed to a page, and in his language, in slow, sweet, lilting cadences, he read something neither of us could understand. Yet, I could hear the beauty of the rhymes, and I could tell, from Zenzi's silence, that she was not unhappy with this surprise, this boy with his book.

"Now you," Levka said. He pointed to the Schiller. "Read for me."

"Why did they have to throw my parents in the fire?"

"The fire? So the sickness does not travel. But I am very sorry. There's no one else for you?"

"Only Tobias," Zenzi said.

"The Russians are not so terrible." He turned the beam on his boyish face. "We like nice things, too. Will you read?"

"Yes, all right," Zenzi said. "I'll light the lantern."

"No, no. If they see me, they order me away."

I stood there uneasy. His German was not good, but I wondered how many of Zenzi's insults he had understood earlier. The beam was transferred, and Zenzi began to recite stanzas about a dreamy, melancholy boy. "Wonderful," Levka said when she'd finished. "Pushkin again."

They traded several poems in this way, trying to outdo the other, it seemed, with their own language and literary hero, their own music of words, pronounced with great delicacy and care. I had grown jealous, not only because of Zenzi's transfixed state, but also because she was sitting next to Levka now, and this young man, I could tell even in the dark, was shifting closer to her after each recitation. When it came to Zenzi's turn again, she said, "Something a little different." With greater drama, she began Schiller's "The Fight with the Dragon." It was not always easy for me to follow, even knowing the language. But I saw that the poem was her sly protest against the Russian invasion. She was brave to read it, but I worried again how much Levka might understand. Her voice, singing out, rose and rose as the battle became more ferocious—the youthful knight swung his sword at the dragon's hide to little effect, the dragon swept the knight to the ground with his giant tail. All seemed lost, if not for the knight's hounds leaping on the monster's back. Now it was staggering, wounded, and here Zenzi paused and took a breath and moved the light across Levka's face. Did she want to detect his anticipation of the dragon's defeat? His head looked almost fragile despite its heft. His young polished skin was like glass. His thin lips resembled ribbons. He still seemed to me a gentle young man. But when Zenzi made a grand and thrusting gesture with one hand—the knight was taking advantage of the moment, he was plunging the sword into the dragon's guts to kill it—I thought, She is too dramatic, her act is too dangerous for this Russian soldier who has conquered us.

"Wonderful, wonderful," Levka repeated. Then he spoke her name for the first time. "Zengee. Very pretty. No other will touch you."

"Yes, keep them away."

"Because you are the most pretty in all Berlin, in all the world."

"Will you read another by Pushkin?"

"The boy goes away."

"What do you mean?"

"Send him out."

"Tobias," she said, "is a friend."

"Zengee." The flashlight switched off, it was dropped on the floor. I heard gasping, a scream from Zenzi, a torrent of Russian words. I fumbled for the light, I pointed it at them, and saw that this dark-haired Russian soldier was kissing her, was pawing her, he had wrapped his arms around her waist.

"You can't do that," I said. My voice was feeble. "Let her go."

Levka's efforts grew more violent. He tore at her dress and underclothes, one of Zenzi's breasts flopped out, its whiteness was almost supernatural, I could not believe in its existence here. Zenzi was shouting my name, over and over. The Russian's pants had fallen to his knees, his pale buttocks floated in front of my eyes, another apparition. I failed to twist his arm away from her as he swatted me to the floor. Now I ran to the basement entrance, shouting into the street for help.

Behind me there came shrieking, "*TOBIAS TOBIAS!*" then more muffled cries because Levka had pressed his forearm against her mouth.

My head swirled, I begged Levka to leave. No one came from the street, so I rushed to Bormann's satchel and dumped it out and said, "Look, you can have all of this, it's treasure, it will make you rich, please take it and stop." But Levka would not stop. The light revealed him in a state of grotesque adult excitement. He was curved there and giant. Zenzi's torn dress enfolded her head, and Levka was rubbing himself on her bare middle. In desperation, I took a brooch from the Schliemann treasure, a long oval-shaped piece, and held it close to Levka's face. "Please, please, please, you can have this and everything else, see how beautiful it is, do not hurt her."

He smacked me away again. On the floor, I looked for his gun, he must have entered with one, but found nothing. I stood, returned to his writhing body, to Zenzi's muffled cries, still holding the brooch, and this time, it was an impulse I could do nothing to prevent, I raised my arm like Schiller's knight and with all the force I could muster, I jabbed the brooch's pin into Levka's neck. Now he was the one to scream, arching backward. I jabbed it again. He staggered sideways, then dropped to his knees. I stood away from him for a moment but when he didn't rise I moved closer and held the light near his face. Blood had coated an ear, it was soaking his collar. I had succeeded in severing something. This young soldier who had given us potatoes sank further, onto his stomach, and lay there moaning.

"Are you hurt?" I asked Zenzi.

"Take the light off me, do not look." I could hear her struggling to dress herself, sobbing. Finally, she asked, "Did he leave?"

"No," I said, tracing the flashlight beam across Levka's figure. "He is here. He might be dying."

"Why?"

"I stabbed him."

"Good, good." Dressed, she cautiously moved toward Levka to stand over him. "Is he breathing?"

"A little."

"I don't want him to breathe." She began to kick the young soldier in the mouth, in the eyes, in the nose.

"He will die on his own," I said, pulling her back. "We have to leave as soon as we can. The other soldiers will look for him."

"There is no place to go."

"The Americans."

"There is no future! I want the rat poison."

"No, I do not want to give up now." Now I aimed the flashlight at her. In its glow, red smears bloomed on her cheeks, from her own veins or Levka's I did not know. "Are you cut? Do you need a bandage?"

Zenzi shook her head and turned away.

I told her, "We should put him in the place where you hid. If they find him, they will want revenge."

"He has bled all over the floor. They will see that."

"We can cover it with boxes, with the blanket."

"You really stabbed him?"

"I did," I said, shaking. It was my second killing, but this one wasn't dreamlike, this one had left me feeling lucid and logical, it had given me a kind of maddened energy, had galvanized me into a singular purpose, to flee the Russians, to flee Germany. "Help me carry him."

"I will not touch that body. It is not human, the Russians are pigs. And I must wash myself. I am covered with bacteria, probably with manure."

While Zenzi poured water from the steel pot on her private area, I managed to drag Levka to the corner. But I could not lift him myself. "Help me, Zenzi."

She sobbed a little more. "Only if he is dead."

I put an ear to the soldier's smashed mouth. "Nothing is coming out."

We cleared away the board that covered the crawlspace, lifted the body through the hole with considerable effort, and then rolled Levka into the darkened crevice. We placed a blanket over the blood. Soon after, we heard Russian shouts, and so we flattened ourselves, trying to keep still, to keep our breathing shallow. Several soldiers entered the basement, searched quickly with flashlights, shouted their mashed-up words, laughed, and left. I whispered, "Is there any way out through here?"

"I don't know." Her soft voice, trailing off, suggested that she did not care. Then she added, "During the day, you can see light coming from the far corner."

"We cannot go out through the door. Someone would see us, come after us."

"You mean come after me."

I nodded though Zenzi did not see it. "I will look for an opening."

Keeping the flashlight in my fist to douse the brightness, I wriggled my way around blocks of concrete and under splintered beams and then saw a glimmer of red, from the bonfire of the dead, making a glow in the sky. Zenzi was right, a gap existed here. I crawled up a loose mound of something, then slowly raised myself, first into a crouch, then into a taller position. My eyes went above the rubble, and I could see the street, or part of it, tinted crimson. We would only have to squirm out, and then dart to the next ruin. The Russians had gone elsewhere or so it seemed.

When I returned to Zenzi and told her of the plan, I found

her less resistant to escape. "If I die running or die from poison," she said, "what difference does it make?" She gathered the last of our food given by the Russian soldiers into Bormann's satchel, along with that jewelry, while I searched the floor for Levka's gun, discovered a rifle, and decided it was too heavy. I searched Levka himself, too, for any useful item and found a wristwatch and a torn photograph of an older woman, probably his mother. I told this woman, the photograph, that I was sorry for killing him and put her back with her son. Then I did something that I know sounds odd, I retrieved that Iron Cross from where I had buried it, wrapped it in a piece of cloth, and put it back in my pocket. Of course it was too late to give the cross to Stalla, wherever his body had ended up, but another notion had come to me: that this medal—mistakenly bestowed by a tyrant I had slain—had given me special powers to ward off death. It was another comic-book fantasy, but you must remember that I was only thirteen.

Now I made a suggestion to Zenzi that embarrassed me a little. "It will be easier if you look like a boy."

"Yes," she said, "I have already thought of that. We can try to flatten my front. Tie a string across my bra to tighten it. You can get it from my mother's sewing box."

She turned her back to me and took off her blouse. I fumbled with the string, my cold knuckles making Zenzi flinch when they brushed her bare skin. We found a shirt and a pair of trousers that had belonged to her father and though they were baggy they would help with the disguise. Clothed, Zenzi said, "My hair. Tobias, you will cut it off. There are scissors in the sewing box, too."

She held the light and I snipped away at her long thick strands. "You must make it short on the sides, like a soldier's," she said. She was resolute but held the fallen hair and softly wept.

"It will grow back," I promised. "It will be long again when we're safe."

Inside the crawlspace, we pulled a box up to cover the hole, then made our way to the corner.

"I have forgotten the newspaper," Zenzi whispered. "We have to go back."

"No, no, it's too late."

"But who will believe what I tell them?"

"Everyone will hear about it now. Look, the street is close. No more talking."

We found that a splintered joist made the opening too narrow for us to squeeze our shoulders through, so I pushed it with all my strength. Something clattered, and we braced for Russian shouts. None came. We edged out through the wider gap onto the rubble, sucking in the chilly air, seeing no soldiers. The billowy shirt that Zenzi wore got tangled on a wire before we raced across the street into the jagged remains of the next building.

25

We did not possess any clear ideas about what might happen to us once we reached the Americans, but they had become fixed in our heads as welcoming angels. It was a strange thing to want the embrace of a country that had helped destroy Berlin and the rest of Germany, but permit me to explain, I saw them as gum-chewing cowboys who only wanted adventure and fought only when necessary, who bore us no hatred. For her part, Zenzi envisioned some kind of audition at the Elbe—if she could demonstrate her love of dance and music and poetry, and I could show them how well I could draw, they might let us go to New York, a place she had imagined as one vast stage. In truth, neither of us talked in detail of our future, for mostly we just wanted an ocean between us and Germany, a distance that would keep away the bombs, the Bolsheviks, and the SS.

That night, we managed to find our way further west, following the Spree for a while. The streets themselves remained quiet, except for distant crashes. The Russians, it seemed, were busy with booze and women. Female shrieks, making us cringe, sometimes emerged from the caverns that surrounded us. A steady rain fell. At one point I removed the cap from a dead civilian and gave it to Zenzi to keep her head, so strangely shorn, from getting wet and to help with the disguise. We passed through the railyards of the Lehrter station, where Bormann had wanted to go. We crept between overturned trains, and then across a canal. Here a sleepy Russian patrol met us, and when I told them that my brother and I were trying to find our Mutter, their officer waved us on. "Hitler kaput," he said, "Fatherland kaput. Motherland now."

After another hour or so, we found ourselves in a factory area, all torn up, with blackened metal slashed and twisted. I had taken Herr Fuchs's map and as best I could tell we were in Siemensstadt, where electrical devices had been manufactured. Now we could hear the sounds of shelling and machine guns. The war was still not over. Beyond us, fires dotted the ruins. Soon we discovered a group of wet, ragged civilians, who shared some bread with us. Clutching suitcases, they told us that even though Berlin had surrendered, there was still a chance to get out. German forces, General Wenck's Twelfth Army—the one I had heard about—were pushing out of Ruhleben, just south of us, across the Havel River into Spandau. From there, they could escort us to the Elbe.

Anxious but a little hopeful, we filed south with the others over the Spree on a railroad bridge that had not been wrecked, and then into Ruhleben. It soon became apparent that thousands had the same idea. I had not seen so many in the streets since the days of torchlight parades. Many people must have been secretly hoarding gasoline for years, for we were threading our way past every conceivable vehicle...ancient automobiles belching blue smoke, most with flat tires...bulky motorcycles from the previous war...two fire trucks bearing dejected Volkssturm...brightly painted three-wheeled delivery vans...limousines that looked as if the well-dressed passengers inside had polished them that morning...and dozens, too, on bicycles, all with bare rims, and horse-pulled wagons, the animals reduced to skeletons...and then, also, the army...the giant tanks, Tigers and MkIVs...halftracks full of young soldiers.

The noise of engines and orders being screamed and clanking equipment and wailing babies and increasing gunfire forced me to give hand signals to Zenzi, for she could not hear my shouts. I pointed to the west. We did not see any bridge, only a burning tower in the distance, candle-like. We clutched hands and elbowed our way through while the rumors flew at us. "The Russians have captured Spandau...our boys are holding it...they're going to blow the bridge...if you carry a bottle of liquor they will not shoot."

After edging up the sloping roadway, where the crowd was so jam-packed we could hardly move, we finally saw the span, the Charlotten Bridge, a two-lane path with a simple arch. An overturned truck burned in the middle, launching black balloons of smoke. Bodies lay there, too, piles of them, like cargo that had spilled—the sprinters who had not made it. The crowd stayed back a hundred meters or so, gauging their chances, watching attempts. At one point, a young man zigzagged with frantic energy toward the bridge. Everyone cheered him and shouted encouragement as he managed to survive the first volleys of gunfire. At the span's center, he slipped on the wet surface and careened into the wrecked truck. A groan from the crowd. But now another dash. More shouts, it was like a soccer match. Soon, however, the Russian bullets found him, chewing him up. A collective gasp.

"There must be another bridge," Zenzi said.

"The next one is wrecked." I pointed. "You can see it."

"Yes, but what about further down the river?" Her glasses kept slipping onto her nose, and she kept pushing at them with her nervous hand. "It can't be worse than this!"

"We'll go with the tanks," I said. "When the army goes, we'll follow them. They'll blast the Russians to the moon."

"I don't want to cross. I don't think I can do it, Tobias. I'm so tired, I just want to sleep."

"Yes, sleep now," I said. "When you wake up, we'll follow the army."

But she could not close her eyes, for in another minute a diaper service van, with a smiling baby printed on the side, rolled to the edge of the crowd. The baby, blond and pink-faced, was declaring "*Sauber, weiss, und frisch!*" and then it zoomed onto the bridge, as happy as ever. The Russians again fired everything they had, that baby made a good target, and with the shattering of glass, the sad little vehicle swerved and overturned before it reached even the middle. Despair soaked us like the rain. Zenzi had begun to shiver, and so I clutched her to keep her warm. Still, great vibrations shook her whole body. "Please, let's not die like that," she said, her eyes red and wild behind the streaked glasses. "Let's go somewhere else, away from all these people. Why should we assume they know anything more than we do?"

"If we all go together, we will have a better chance," I said, and then hugged her, pulling her close so that she would not see the doubt on my face as I peered through the gray downpour at the opposite bank, where the *pok-pok-pok* had re-established its rhythm. "If we make it across that bridge," I said, "we will make it all the way to New York, I promise."

"I don't want to wait. I don't want to watch any more of this. I want to be there now."

Then she was running. Not away from everything here, but toward the bridge, across the empty space beyond the waiting masses. It was lucky, permit me to explain, that she wore the oversized men's clothing that had come from her father, for their wetness made the pants heavy and awkward, and it slowed her down, she ran as if her ankles were tied. I was slow, too, because

I still carried Bormann's satchel, with the jewelry rattling inside. Yet before she got very far I managed to tackle her like they do in American football. Exhausted, pinned by my weight, she ordered me to free her and kicked a little until two men helped me drag and carry her to the shelter of a ruin. There, in the crux of two smashed walls, she finally slept.

I waited for the army to advance. I guessed they would do it at nightfall. I could not see the bridge from this spot, though I could hear the Russian guns. Occasional shells came crashing down nearby. There must have been several more civilian attempts to cross, for the crowd groaned and cheered and gasped. Every so often I would check to see what was happening and then return quickly, fearing that Zenzi might wake and run for the bridge again. Darkness came, and still no movement from the tanks. The rumors were flying: They had run out of ammunition, they were searching for gasoline, the Russians were going to surround us and let us starve, we were waiting for the delivery of a super weapon. Hearing all this, I was gripped by an urge to reveal the one fact about the end of this war that I alone possessed.

I leaned over Zenzi and pressed my mouth to her ear. "I have a secret for you," I said.

Roused, she turned to glare at me, and whispered back, "Good or bad?"

"I don't know." I felt the wet chill of her ear on my lips and said, "What they say about the Führer is not true."

"What do you mean?"

"He did not kill himself."

"You're saying he's alive?"

"No. Someone else fired the shot."

"Who told you?"

"I saw it."

"But how?"

"They told me to draw his portrait. He had just gotten married. A wedding portrait. I was there in the room with him and his wife. Just the three of us."

"You're testing me."

"There was a pistol, I think he meant to use it on himself. But I took it, and I fired."

"Tobias, you're testing me to see if I'm still crazy. But I'm better. My head is clear. I just needed to sleep. I promise I won't run again. I won't be like my mother."

I inhaled the smoky air. "I'm glad you're better."

Her hand squeezed mine. "Thank you for getting that Russian boy off me. With everything so far, it was the worst. If only he had just kept reading the Pushkin! I want to be sorry for what I did to him, but I don't feel that way. Not yet. Maybe that makes me as bad as anyone else."

"No, because you don't want to do anything like that again. I don't, either."

She nodded and offered a faint smile. "I will go with you across that bridge."

Somewhere in the middle of the night, great booms shook the ground. We pushed our way through the mob, now full of shouting and jostling, and moved to its edge. The Tigers were firing on positions beyond the river. Flames had erupted in buildings there, lighting up jagged silhouettes. Tracers cut green streaks through the rain like horizontal fireworks, bricks shattered, shells had begun to land around us, a few people fell. The Russians were hollering, madly firing at the bridge. The structure shook and swayed from the biggest shells, and in another moment, our tanks began to move. The human mass roared, surging forward like a reservoir breaking a dam. I grabbed Zenzi's hand and we watched the people flow. We worked up our courage, second by second, calculating when to dash. Then we nodded to each other and joined the stampede.

Though we were faster than many, we had great trouble once we reached the bridge, not so much from gunfire, but from our ability to remain upright. The biggest of men were trampling anyone in their way. Worse, we had to slosh over the shiny innards of those who had perished, as slippery as ice. The entire structure, too, shook even more from the explosions, from the weight of the Tigers. We wobbled, slid, and fell. The noise was horrendous. A fat member of the Volkssturm, shot in the eye, tumbled onto us. Now we were crawling, crawling. When we reached the lead tank, crouching behind its back end as it edged toward the middle of the span, we looked as if we had just been born, smeared with blood and gray gluey stuff. The human pile was accumulating. Women and children staggered toward us, the machine guns cut them down. Frozen, with terror in my bowels, I watched a girl of about four, I cannot forget her, she stood dazed and splattered with blood, not crying, because she was trying to put a shoe on her mother's foot. The mother lay there shot and twisted up. I held out my hand, urging the girl to take it, but she would not budge. Someone else snatched her, and then leaped with the wailing child into the water.

Others, too, were diving off the bridge. Zenzi had covered her ears with her hands from the relentless booms, her mouth was misshapen, I could see she was considering the river, too. We were both sliding into panic. The advance was jammed, the lead tank had stopped. Tracers streaked above our heads and mortar fire started to land around the bridge's eastern end, smashing more people under puffs of smoke, like a magician's trick.

Now panic came to a tank. Behind us, this giant gray machine was driving crazily, wild with impatience, it crumpled a stalled limousine, it crushed bicyclists, cracking bones. It was heading for us. To get out of its way, Zenzi and I leaped onto the rear end of the lead tank along with several others. The commander, who had

266

been peering out the hatch, screamed, "Get off, get off, you are not allowed to sit there!" Then the crazy tank slammed into us from behind and sent all of us toppling back into the glop. That is, all but Zenzi. Part of her baggy clothing had caught on something, maybe an exhaust pipe, I do not know what, and there, like a figurehead on a ship traveling backwards, she dangled, moving away from me, into ferocious Russian fire, for the entire column had begun to move again. "Jump, jump," I screamed, but she could not, she was stuck. So there was nothing I could do but follow, chasing this tank that carried Zenzi, my wife.

Maybe the Russians did not kill us because they were laughing too hard, or maybe they were just aiming at the bridge and not worrying about the few that got through, or maybe that medal that still sat in my pocket really did have some magical good-luck power. In any case, the two of us received no fire, as far as I could tell, and just after getting to the other side, Zenzi's pants broke, releasing her. We scrambled to the nearest rubble. Around us, a few German soldiers had established a defensive position. We sat there breathless, filthy, depleted, unable to convey any thought at all. It took me a while, in fact, to realize that Zenzi was wearing only briefs on her lower half. With quiet determination, I removed the trousers from a nearby dead soldier, who lay with his mouth open as if still trying to say one last thing, and handed them to Zenzi. But she refused the offer. She pointed out the swastika on the belt buckle and, with sudden force, loudly denounced Adolf Hitler. Behind those glasses speckled with rain, there was rage in her eyes. Yet she received no reprimand. Later, one of the soldiers even procured her a skirt.

26

Some hours later, Zenzi and I found ourselves in the back of an open-topped Opel truck. We had crawled into it because there seemed no other place to go. We were squeezed in amongst other dispirited passengers, military and civilian, it was difficult to tell the difference anymore. The rain sliced down like threads of ice, but we held our faces up to rinse away the smears of other people's blood.

The truck moved with agonizing slowness. But the jittery fires of Berlin began to recede. We did not know where we were headed, caring only that our direction was westward. For the rest of the night, huddled together, shivering and shivering, we fell in and out of sleep. Occasionally we woke to shouts about our progress—someone had spied a road sign, a name of a town in the truck's headlights. Falkensee, Brieselang, Bredow, Nauen. Nothing sounded familiar, I had never been this way before. In the pale wash of dawn, we could see that the land had opened up—farms and forests and lakes. The greenery—thick, shiny, gleaming on this clear morning—was a joyous sight. Still, cheer did not come easy. The Russians were sending out patrols to chase down those who had made it beyond the Havel. Now that the rain had stopped, Sturmoviks strafed some fields near us. We ducked, as if it would do any good. A few Russian tanks, too, were firing in the distance. The truck, undamaged, not a target it seemed, kept rolling.

Somewhere just past Retzow, we sputtered to a halt, out of gas. The driver, morose in defeat, expressed no hope for finding any more, and so with a few others, Zenzi and I continued on foot, following a rail line. For much of the morning, we trudged over the tracks, sprinting when they emerged into open fields. After the path began to cut through dense woods, the sounds of machine guns and rifles and mortars faded. Maybe we were finally leaving all that. By now, we had lost the rest of the group, they had lagged behind us from exhaustion. Though we found a stream or two for our thirst, hunger was starting to make the journey painful. Some hours before, we had eaten the last of the stuff given to us by the Russian soldiers. As soon as we found an opportunity, we would trade the jewelry for food. The weight of it in the satchel was giving me plenty of aches. When we came across a farm, with a house at the end of a dirt road—peaceful and bright red—we decided to try our luck there.

We crouched at the edge of a grove of trees, watching for any Russians. We saw no one, so we ran up, past an old tractor and a gray sedan, and knocked on the front door, calling for some help. There was no answer, and we entered. A few empty bottles lay on the floor. A strong smell of wine, but thankfully, not of death. The place appeared to be abandoned. In the kitchen, Zenzi held up a small rectangular box and screamed—not in fright but joy. She spoke some English words printed on the side: *Breakfast. Ration K.* "Tobias, it's food for the U.S. Army. They've been here. We must be close. God, I'm starving!"

There were several boxes, others marked as "Dinner" and "Supper," with specific instructions that Zenzi recited in the English: "Open inner bag carefully...for security, hide the empty can and wrappers so that they cannot be seen." We tore at the boxes and first found toilet paper and cigarettes, but then crackers, powdered coffee, chewing gum, cans of meat and cheese, sugar. We devoured the food, we made cold sweet coffee from rainwater that had collected in a bucket, we chewed the first gum we had ever tasted and swallowed it, not knowing any better.

After our little feast, we sat at the kitchen table, covered in crumbs. Our bellies were full and we were not in danger and we were a little delirious, I think. Zenzi was leaning back and smiling, and I was looking at her through a pair of green binoculars I had found upstairs near the window.

"How far is it to the Elbe, do you think?" Zenzi asked.

"I don't know. Your father's map doesn't go past Berlin."

"But a lot of walking."

I nodded, framing her magnified face in the lenses, seeing only a dreamy blur.

"Then we should get some rest," she said. "There's that bed upstairs with sheets and a blanket. I can hardly keep my eyes open."

I laughed, giddy, this time peering at her through the wrong end of the binoculars. "Now you are very far away."

"Use that for something useful and see if the Russians are close."

I aimed them out the window and saw only a distant spiral of smoke and said, "No one."

"Then let's sleep for a little while. I'm going to rinse myself with that rainwater and you can do the same. Arms, legs, and, well, everything. Then come upstairs."

I did as she asked. I washed off the last of the blood, and then dropped my pants and washed down there, too. And as I stood outside half-naked, under a great dome of blue, before all the lush green trees, before a few flowers that had bloomed, with a house all to my own that had given me food, that had provided a bed, in which I was to sleep with a lovely girl, my wife, I believed more than ever in the power of that medal, still nestled in my pocket.

I galloped up the stairs. Zenzi, without her glasses, had tucked herself under the blanket. Only her bare pale shoulders poked out. "The Americans slept here with their boots on," she said, making a face, "but I swept it off as best I could."

"Do you want me to take off all my clothes, too?"

"Yes, they're too dirty."

I flung off everything in a kind of madness, crawled in next to her, and wrapped my arms around her warmth. In boyish fashion, I fell asleep very quickly, but Zenzi nudged me awake.

"Tobias," she said, "you told me something about the Kerl, back at the bridge, before we crossed. Were you just making it up?"

I stared at the ceiling and took several breaths. "No."

"But it must be a dream."

"I don't think so."

"Were you really alone with them?"

"Yes. But I didn't want to be."

"What kind of pistol?"

"What does it matter?"

"I'm testing you," she said.

"A Walther PPK."

"Did he beg for mercy?"

"It happened very quickly. I'm not sure how. But I am too afraid to talk about it."

"Tobias, Tobias, even if you only dreamed it, I am happy that you wanted to do it, I am happy that man is dead, I am happy to be here with you." With her soft fingers she took my chin and turned my face so that she was looking directly at me. "You are all the gardens I have ever gazed at."

I blushed, hot and ebullient.

"Rilke wrote that," she said, "and it is how I feel, too."

We heard then a mechanical growling, a plane above us. We braced for bombs or bullets, not wanting to move from the bed's luxury. Nothing came. The noise thinned out and disappeared, memory-like, drawing our thoughts to the past, to the war's past, to what the war had done. We began to sob a little, then with greater force. And then neither of us could stop. We lay next to each other shuddering and named everyone we once knew. It was like having stones laid one by one on our lungs, they pressed and pressed until we could hardly breathe.

After a while, Zenzi whispered, "If you add a positive number to a negative number, it lessens the negative."

I nodded, believing that she was thinking of her father and his mathematics.

She slipped one hand to my lower back. Her eyes were ringed in red, as if they were burning. "There are too many dead," she told me. "But we can *make* life."

The sobbing had cleared my head a little. That growling we'd heard, a Russian sound, had stayed with me. "We should not stay here too much longer."

"I think you are old enough," Zenzi said. "I think it is possible..."

"What?"

"A child."

"I am not a child."

"I know," she said. "That is what I mean. When you looked with those binoculars, you didn't see any Russians?"

"No, but they're probably not so far."

"It doesn't take long, I think." Zenzi touched her choppy hair. "Do I look too much like a boy? I was afraid to stand before the mirror there."

"Not without your clothes."

"Do you want to be a father?"

"I am thirteen years old."

"No, not anymore."

As you might imagine, Zenzi convinced me to remain in the bed. She kissed my neck and my eyelids and my nose. I wrapped myself around her nudity, around her unearthly heat. I wanted to get as close as possible to her living presence. Everything was magnified—her black-marble pupils, a large crevice running the length of her tongue, two freckles dotting her shoulder like accidental ink spots, a single dark hair sprouting from a nipple. Impatient, thrilled, scared, awkward, we struggled for a while to get things right, but eventually I moved in the way she wanted. She winced several times, trying not to cry out. Then a shiver raced up and down my back, my mouth pushed out a gasp.

"We have lessened the negative," she said.

We wanted to sleep but couldn't. Our thoughts were too jumbled, our nudity embarrassed us now, it seemed. We both quickly dressed, in clothes still damp, and went downstairs to finish the American rations. Under the lid of a gramophone, Zenzi discovered a record and wound the thing up, and we both danced, I mean we skittered back and forth across the room, aching from happiness, absorbed with ourselves. The song was something the Americans must have left, something about cowboys, Zenzi told me. We listened to it again and again, I did not understand most of the words but it sounded like a tune for children, and it made me feel like a child even though I was now a husband and maybe a father. Then, wanting to capture all this, perhaps knowing it would not last much longer, I found a pen and a sheet of letter paper left by the Americans and sketched Zenzi posing with an American cigarette dangling from her mouth. "Like a gangster," she said, grinning. "Perfect for New York!" On the bottom I wrote,

"Zenzi Fuchs, meine Frau." But she crossed out Fuchs and added, right underneath, "Zenzi <u>Koertig</u>. Trotz der Umstände ist sie sehr liebevoll." Despite the circumstances she is full of love.

We laughed and laughed, the silly cowboy music putting us in a frenzy, until we heard the front door crash.

A bearish American soldier stood before us with a rifle. Unshaven, his hair askew, his fly unbuttoned on his dark green pants so that we could see his underwear, he barked, "What the hell are you doing? Hands in the air! Up! Up!"

"We were hungry," Zenzi said in English. "We are civilians."

He lurched over to the gramophone and stopped the music. Then he switched to German. "Deutsch?"

Zenzi nodded. "From Berlin."

"You ate all my food, God damn it to hell. Where are your parents?"

"They are dead."

"Who else is here?"

"Only us. We are sorry about the food."

"What's the matter with your hair? Some kind of disease?"

"To make me look like a boy. I did not want the Russians to rape me."

He searched both of us, running his hands along our clothes, even Zenzi's. "If you scratched that record, I'll kill both of you. I took that all the way across the ocean, and not a mark on it." He removed the 78 to inspect it, and grunted. "OK, drop your hands." He fumbled with his pants, buttoned them, then went to the window to peer out, keeping his rifle aimed in our direction. "What are your names? Show me your identification."

"Tobias Koertig and Kreszentia Fuchs," I said. "We lost our cards."

"Just like everyone else."

"We are going to Schönhausen," Zenzi told him.

"You and a thousand others. We're not letting civilians

across the bridge, do you know that? You might as well turn around. Go on, get out of here. This is U.S. Army property and you're trespassing." He rubbed his wide, squared-off head and his whiskery face, mumbling things in English, and glanced at his watch. Now he scowled, stared at that watch, tapped its glass, and then glared at us. In German again, he shouted: "What day is it? This says Friday! It has to be broken. Bulova, too. God damn it. Is it Friday?"

I thought about it for a moment or two, trying to remember the days and nights, hoping that agreement with his watch might make him friendlier, and said, "Yes, it is Friday, May 4th, I think."

The soldier stomped around and spat out angry words in both languages. I realized that I could smell the odor of wine more strongly, that it was coming from the soldier himself. "God damn it to hell," he said. "Come on, clear out!"

Zenzi stepped forward and said, "If you take us across the bridge, we will give you some jewelry."

"A bribe? Some cheap necklace from your grandmother? Not interested."

"Look in the satchel," I said. "It's all gold."

He picked up his rifle, carried it to where the satchel lay, and inspected the contents. He placed several things in his hand, one after the other, grunting after each. "Where did you get this?"

"I found it."

"You're a looter."

"No," Zenzi said, "he took it from a German officer, a dead one."

"Reichsleiter Bormann," I added.

"Bormann? Martin Bormann? What the hell do you know about him?" He had said this in English, and Zenzi translated it for me, then urged me to tell him.

I gave him the truth: my time as a soldier, the medal (I fished it from my pocket), my visit to the HQ bunker, my illustrations for the Führer, Bormann's scheme for making me a thief, the Greek jewelry, Bormann's death, our encounter with the Russians. I left out my two murders.

I wasn't sure if the American believed anything. He prodded me with questions, asking, for example, the names of my superiors, the details of the bunker, and also about the kinds of weapons and vehicles I had seen of the Russians.

"Now listen," he said, still speaking reasonable German, "what you're telling me is pretty crazy, but I don't know how a kid like you would know all this if it weren't true. So we're going to do each other a favor. It's the American way, right? Give and take. You understand?"

We were baffled but we nodded.

"I'm here doing recon. We didn't get to advance beyond the Elbe, bullshit if you ask me, but it came straight from Eisenhower. Still, we like to know who's coming our way. Russians, Germans, Nazis, criminals. Especially the Russians. I'm trying to see how far away they are so we don't get hammered by their rockets and mortars and the rest of the crap they put into the air. I was supposed to report back to the captain yesterday. I forgot. I mean, I found some refreshment here. I passed out in the barn. A whole day went by. The captain is going to kick my ass to Hong Kong. Unless, that is, I bring him someone who can give us some insight from the inside, not to mention news on the Russian position—then maybe he won't be so hard on me. What you get out of it is a river crossing. I'll take you on our ferry, over to HQ for questioning. HQ happens to be on the other side. Considering you already ate all my food, I don't think you have much choice in the matter. Corporal Hartley, by the way."

"We agree," Zenzi said.

"I don't know about the girl," he said.

I shook my head. "I will not go if she cannot. We are married."

Hartley's mouth exploded with laughter. "Newlyweds! Both of you then!" He reached into the satchel and pulled out a handful of jewelry—"My commission"—and then snatched his record from the gramophone. "Cow-Cow Boogie," he laughed, "Ella Mae Morse, what a peach." We followed him to the barn, where he'd hidden his jeep. We were just about to climb in when Zenzi ran back to the house, telling us she'd forgotten something. She returned with her portrait, the one I had drawn, and stuffed it into the satchel. "A little souvenir," she said.

As we sped away, Russian artillery vibrated the air, a distant storm now, hardly troubling at all. The corporal raised a hand, middle finger extended, and aimed it behind him. "Those sons of bitches," he said, "they fire those things off as often as they fart."

Zenzi turned around and translated this for me, and I laughed so hard I nearly fell out of the jeep. But anything, absolutely anything, would have struck me as hilarious just then. Joy filled my throat. I put a hand on Zenzi's shoulder and she kissed my knuckle. We plunged through more farmland, the most beautiful I had ever seen. My eyes watered from the wind, then pushed out real tears. We had finally met an American, and he was our escort.

Before long, from a rise, we saw the river's silver glimmer. The corporal said, "It will be slower now with Wenck's army and all the refugees. But I'll get you over there soon enough."

So here was Wenck, who had, the American informed us, cleared a path for everyone before surrendering. The road grew cluttered with weary and wounded German soldiers, army trucks, tanks, skeletal horses, and masses of civilians, staggering and dirty. It was an undulating sea. We were crawling along. On either side, arms stretched up for food, and I could only say, over and over, "Nichts zu essen." I searched the faces for anyone I knew but it was all a blur.

We came within sight of the bridge. Bombed, twisted and crushed, the span traced a crazy path of metal across the water and led our eyes to the most gorgeous vision, that bank on the other side, the western side, safety. We gripped each other and grinned. The jeep approached the American perimeter and Corporal Hartley greeted the first guards. After a brief and heated discussion, most of which Zenzi could not understand, the Corporal turned around to speak to us.

"There's a problem with permission. Someone wants to hear what the hell's going on, why I'm a day late, so I've got to explain the situation to my CO. You understand? They're not letting you come across on the ferry until all that's cleared up. It's the rules. You'll stay here for a while, the guards will take care of you, and I'll be back in a couple of hours. Tobias, you hang on to that medal and the jewelry. It's evidence for your story, and it's your ticket for getting across the river."

Another soldier drove us between pockmarked stretches of farmland to Schönhausen, the nearby village, also wrecked by bombs, where he ushered us into a small building. We sat in two hard metal chairs in a blank room, guarded by sleepy soldiers playing cards. After a while, ignored and given only a few unkind glances, we asked for water. Our guards did not speak German, but Zenzi translated their dismissive words. "You have to wait. This is not a café."

Our request had provoked them. They put aside their cards and began to look at us, joking amongst themselves. Soon they were speaking to us directly. Though Zenzi did not translate their words for me, I understood that they were taunting us, they were calling us Nazis. It was not long before they were goose-stepping, springing out their arms, shouting *Heil*, and impersonating the Führer with screams and the pounding of fists. They were young and bored, relieved that the war was over, and all these years later I cannot judge them harshly. But at the time, Zenzi and I sat there stiff and frightened, bracing for a blow. I clutched the satchel, worried that they would steal it. Frustrated by our silence, the men became louder, more belligerent. *Nazi! Nazi! Nazi!* they chanted, sometimes inches from our faces.

Zenzi had reached her limit, she leaped up, her hands pressed tight into fists. I thought she might assault these soldiers, but instead she began to shout, mixing German and a stuttering English. "You don't know what we have gone through to get here! It is not a joke! We are not Nazis! We are gute Leute! But I will tell you about the Nazis! Unlike others I will tell you the entsetzlich things they have done! Sending away the Jews! Poisoning the Jews! Killing the Jews! Turning them into ash! You cannot laugh at this, you cannot laugh! I am a Jew, I am a Jew!"

Trembling, sobbing, she fell back into her chair and spoke to me in German: a lot of time had already passed, we were prisoners, we were not going to get across the river, that Corporal had grabbed what he'd wanted of the jewelry and would not return, we had to do something.

The men ordered us to keep quiet but, brazenly, Zenzi requested the use of a toilet, for both of us. First there was refusal, but Zenzi told them, even I could understand this from her gestures, that we would piss in our pants and all over the floor if they did not show us where to go. At this, one of the soldiers motioned us out the door. I grabbed my satchel, afraid again of theft, and they took us outside and around the back, where they pointed to a wall.

I was fumbling with my pants while Zenzi was yelling, "Run, Tobias, run," and in a moment, we were off, racing in blindness down a street and into the crowd of refugees. The soldiers did not fire and did not give chase. They laughed in higher pitches.

Of all the decisions we made during that time, it is our escape from the American soldiers that brings on the biggest regret, one that still stings—especially since it occurred at the end, when we were so close to crossing the last river. I wonder now what might have happened if we had waited a little longer for Corporal Hartley, if we might have been taken across the Elbe for calm questioning—if our futures would have been very different. But there are too many days like this in a lifetime, too many, and it is only a sadder and sadder thing to consider.

We huddled that evening in the crowd, sharing some dry bread with a family who'd come from Prussia. Around us rumors ran wild again, we did not know what to believe...Anyone who'd fought against the Allies would be allowed to cross but harshly interrogated and thrown in prison...The Russians would soon be taking control of Europe....Their raping of women was part of their plan to populate Germany with Bolshevik children.... The Jews were all still alive in Norway, living in comfort....The Americans were going to put everyone to work in chewing-gum factories. All we knew for sure was that civilians were not being allowed across the Elbe.

We drifted down to the river's edge, where a few groups were constructing rafts from scraps of wood. The river was wide here, and its flow was swift. The western bank, a modest rise with trees, was excruciatingly clear, every detail of it, I felt I could distinguish the rocks, the flowers, the young pale leaves on thin trees. Overhearing the men, we understood that some who had made it across had been sent back, ferried by the Americans. Yet others, they said, had stayed. It was simply a matter of luck, it was luck that determined the course of lives now, nothing more, and perhaps we had already used up our share.

The hammering of the boat builders clanged and clanged, and we watched them in a state of stupefaction. The sun fell, making the water pink. "A pfennig for my passage, Charon." Zenzi placed a stone in my hand and then clasped my fist. "Do you think we could build something, too?"

"Yes, maybe. But what if we return to the bridge and ask the guards where Hartley is."

"They would lock us up again."

"I could tell them what I did in the bunker."

"They would never believe you."

"Why did you tell them you were a Jew?"

"I don't know." She stared at the western bank, at the last of the sun. "Because to say it makes me feel like I have not lost everything, it makes me feel like I still have some little thing to hold."

"In the morning," I promised, "we will look for some wood. We'll build a boat, too."

"Tobias, do you see that beautiful little tree on the other side? That silhouette? We will be standing next to it. I have never been more sure of anything."

"I hope they don't send us back."

"No, no, they would not. Not us. We'll tell them we've dreamed of nothing else. My God, I would swim across if I could!"

Later, after nightfall, when we were huddling under a blanket borrowed from the same Prussian family, watching the headlights of vehicles, American vehicles, on the far bank, Zenzi said to me, almost in a whisper, "Tell me what names you like. How about Isolde? Or Rodolf?"

"I'm too tired. Who do you mean?"

"Isolde is my favorite, it's from the Wagner opera. I think it will be a girl."

27

At dawn, my plan to build a raft did not look so appealing or possible. Ravenous again, I felt weak, and I could not even imagine collecting wood or finding tools. Zenzi and I wandered past the builders, asking if anyone might be willing to take us as passengers, for we were not so heavy. Each group sent us away, claiming they had no room.

I fell into the grass to stare at the tantalizing river, at that tree on the other side, when Zenzi said, "Let's buy one."

"Where? How?"

"We'll offer some of that jewelry."

"We were going to save it for New York."

"What good is it if we stay on this side of the river?"

The idea took hold of us. We traipsed the bank, shopping for the one we wanted. After an hour, we saw it: a real vessel, an old green row boat a man was patching up. We wandered over and explained our proposition, opening the satchel to let the gold gleam in the sun. I told them it had come from the family safe, for they would surely not believe the truth. We asked for a small amount of food as well, since I had seen them nibbling on something brown. The man, joined by his wife, inspected each tassel, ring, and brooch, and then after conferring at a distance from us, they returned to make a deal. They wanted all the jewelry. I started to shake my head, remembering how far I had taken everything, but Zenzi immediately agreed, insisting only on keeping the satchel, so that she could protect that portrait I'd drawn.

We sat there in the boat, ours now, afloat in shallow water at the river's edge, smiling because we saw no leaks, eating strips of dried brown meat—from a horse, but not so bad.

"What should we do first when we get to New York?" Zenzi asked.

"I don't know. A movie. Or an amusement park. They have a big one, don't they?"

"A concert by the Philharmonic."

"I'd rather sit in a café and eat raspberry Pfannkuchen."

"I think they call it a doughnut there."

"I want to buy a doughnut," I said, trying out my poorly remembered English, and we both laughed.

A fair amount of strength had returned and I gripped the oars, eager to push off. I would have to put in all my effort to fight the current. But I had rowed my parents on that lake in Spiez, and I knew what to do.

Then the promise of this day, the promise of that tree on the opposite bank, the promise of New York, was gone.

The Russians, it turned out, were not far from the bridge now, they had advanced more easily than we had in France five years before. They wanted to obliterate all that was left of the German Army, and, I think, the civilians, too. It was an easy thing to do, for thousands of us sat in the open, on the green banks, without any protection except prayers. When their artillery began to fire, soon after dawn, we were torn apart. The springtime earth sprouted red, chaos came to the crowd. Many, rushing into the water, were swept down the river, their arms flailing and then sinking. Others launched their unfinished rafts, which did not take long to sink or come apart. One man tried to ride a stallion into the river and make it swim but the animal, I could see, had already broken its leg, and it floated like a log. Terrible shrieks sliced the air. I have never heard such agonized noise since, pouring as it did from the gut of the soul, for we had all believed—stupidly, stupidly—that we had come to safety here.

Zenzi and I were crouching in the boat. The water around us shot up in frothing spouts. I tried to row but we were rocked from side to side as if in a storm and then, dearest God, one of the oars leaped from its support into the river. I jumped out, waded over, and threw it back in. I began to climb inside as bullets started to spray the water. It could not be possible, they seemed to be coming from the other bank, from the Americans. I tried to lift myself in, Zenzi was pulling one arm. But I kept slipping back, gulping the river. The boat, out far enough now to catch the current, was moving away from me. I waded further, then tried to swim, thrashing my arms under still more bullets when a Russian shell, too close and roaring, took away my consciousness.

28

There's a teenaged girl behind the counter at Margo's Bakery who greets me by name, for I am a regular there. This morning, she dropped an extra jelly doughnut into my bag because she thought that I looked distressed. She was right, I was trying to get away from the Elbe. To thank her for the kindness, I sat at one of the tables, and using some crayons provided for children, I sketched her face on a napkin. She was delighted with the result and then, needing to share her own trouble, confessed that she and her boyfriend had broken up the night before. I told her that my own sorrow had a similar origin: a separation that had occurred almost exactly 71 years ago. That probably wasn't a comfort to her— suggesting, I mean, that Time does not always erase an ache—but my mood had improved a little. Back at home I consumed those doughnuts like a wolf, and then returned to the river.

The bullets had stopped. The artillery was silent. The birds were going *crip-crip-crip*. Night had come and gone. The heavy sun was having trouble rising through a yellow haze of distant smoke. I lay sprawled on the river's bank, wet and frigid. My head felt as if someone had struck it with a hammer.

I stood, wobbled, and then started to skitter here and there to look for any sign of Zenzi. A few boats were still trying to cross the water, struggling against the current. I ran back and forth, called out her name, and asked survivors about a green boat. I did this for a long time, that is, until hunger forced me to sit, until my belly ached as if I'd swallowed dirt, until dizziness spun the sky. I had found no trace of her—only smashed rafts and bodies and the digging by families of shallow graves in the grass and moaning everywhere. Zenzi must have gone to the other side, in our boat, or another, or swimming. I refused to consider anything else.

At some point there was jubilant shouting. "The Americans have pulled back! The bridge is free to cross!" A crowd began to run along the bank. I looked around one last time for our boat, and then joined the rush. The mangled girders and railroad track, twisted like strands of licorice, were covered with civilians and soldiers, crawling thick and slow. A few American sentries were demanding to see identification and ordering everyone to discard their weapons and other military equipment. Rifles, pistols, helmets, and mess kits lay in a big gleaming pile.

When the Russian artillery found us again, raining down shells on the eastern bank, the flow became frantic, the sentries abandoned their posts. I climbed past the elderly in their suits and wool dresses, past despondent German soldiers, past mothers lugging suitcases held together by rope. Up and down the rails and ties, clutching girders, over a partially submerged section, the going was not easy. The shells kept coming down behind me, but knifing hunger drove me onward, for someone who had come back across the span to help said the Americans were serving stew, and I believed that I could smell beef.

And then, and then, I clawed the final stretch of wooden ties, almost vertical like a ladder, a ladder to the other side of the universe, and I was across, I had reached the western bank. The exploding shells and the screams seemed a great distance away now. Around me men and women collapsed on the ground to kiss it, to pray.

I staggered over to a steaming pot, where I got a ladle of that beautiful stew and gulped it so fast I almost scalded my throat. Soon after, at a registration table, a Yank soldier asked me for my name. I almost said Koertig, I almost said it, but I feared discovery of having fought in the army, I feared discovery of what I'd done, and so I replied, "Tobias Frankfurter." It was the first thing that came to me because someone Vati and I knew with that surname had owned a bakery and still crazy with hunger I had been imagining, what else, the Pfannkuchen full of jelly he used to serve us on a winter afternoon, when nothing else tasted so good.

The soldier shouted *hot dog!* and guffawed—for I am sure he was desperate to laugh like everyone else at the end of a war—and then wrote down Frank, just that, because the Americans were as hurried then as they are now. He wanted to know about family members, and I said there were none still alive, and so he gave me a bed number in an area for orphans. I asked him, then, if he had registered a girl named Kreszentia Fuchs. He studied his list, shook his head, and told me to check a nearby bulletin board. When I looked at all the names listed on that board, none of them hers, it occurred to me that I had made a terrible mistake, because if Zenzi were looking for me, she would be asking about Koertig, not Frank, but how could I change it back now?

For the next several days, this new boy—Tobias Frank— wandered in desperation past tent rows and field hospitals of the haggard, the wounded, the diseased, the suicidal, asking again and again if anyone had seen Zenzi. I wished that I had that portrait I'd drawn in the farmhouse, but the satchel had disappeared with her. I tried to do another picture from memory, but my memory was too shaken and the result was not so good. No one had heard of her. A note I left on the bulletin board was not answered.

Soon we learned that all of Germany had surrendered, and this proved to be the final blow to my spirit. My will for life was falling close to zero, and I felt no impulse to complain when, as an orphan, I was not shipped to New York, as I had so fervently hoped, but sent to a nearby American camp for displaced persons—DPs, as they preferred to call us. Yet here it was worse than the ruins of Berlin, an enclosure surrounded by wire and full of stench and rot and muck and the insane and the dying.

In this prison, for that was what we all called it, I kept quiet, I answered only the occasional questions from doctors about my health. I still had my medal, which had somehow remained in my pocket, and every morning I squeezed it for good luck, hoping the powers I believed it held would get me through another day. Nothing warranted my faith anymore except that piece of iron, and I went to great effort to keep it hidden, often stuffing it in my underwear.

More often than not, anger burst into my head as if a valve had broken. I fought with other children over food rations, books, writing paper, clothing, and attempted theft. We had come from everywhere, I mean Germany and Poland and Finland and Norway and Lithuania, and speaking to each other was nearly impossible. Maybe we were reenacting the war, I do not really know. From them, gradually, I came to learn more about the death camps, confirming what Zenzi had told me, but I was too hungry, dirty, and miserable to feel any more shame. One afternoon, a tall Polish boy who resembled a skeleton with giant ears, who had spent years in a camp himself, he wrestled me to the ground for having passed through his imaginary perimeter, pinning me in the mud. In poor German he called me a stinking Nazi. He threatened to stop my heart with a blow from his knee, and believing he would do it and wanting to prove that I was sympathetic to his suffering, I blurted, "I shot the Führer, I killed him." Sparing me the heart destruction, his knee smashed into my face. "Nazis will say anything to save themselves."

In August, we heard about the end of the Pacific War, and the secret (which camp officials tried to prevent children from hearing) of the real super weapon, the atomic bomb. I wished for a while that Germany had been able to invent it until I heard the details of how the thing made cities disappear in a flash and left the few survivors with melted brains. Death, I imagined, was spreading across the planet in a kind of flood.

I had been hoping that Zenzi, herself an orphan, would appear in the camp one day. I kept begging the camp commander to find news of her location, but no word came, and Zenzi did not show up. As the cold of autumn and then winter hardened the ground and bit into our thinning skin, my longing for her, it is painful to say, my longing began to fade. I believed, more and more, that like everyone else I had known she had died. The river had swallowed her. There was a peacefulness, I understood, to drowning, and that gave me a measure of comfort, for I did not want to think of Zenzi bleeding.

My grief floated on a sea of boredom. The quarrels lost their meaning. We existed in a kind of zoo without spectators. We all just sat around or slept through the hours between the meals. Like the caged antelope who longs for the savannah, where the jaguar will chase him again, I began to miss the days of scurrying through ruined Berlin, dodging bombs and Russians. Christmas came and went with practical gifts like soap, socks, and candles. A little less than a month later, now in the year 1946, I turned fourteen on a snowy morning. I was presented with a square of tasteless cornbread (made, many of us suspected, with a portion of sawdust), which held a leftover Christmas candle, a sad sight that led me to remember how my mother used to spend my birthday morning baking me a Geburtstagskuchen with cherry custard and how Vati gave me a special prize for correctly answering a series of riddles, equal in number to my age.

Now, on most days, I retreated into a corner so that I could journey, on paper, into deep space. I created more of my rocket ships, distant planets, fiery stars, strange civilizations, and grotesque creatures. It kept me calm, it kept me from declining as others had into the darkest despair, and for that reason the camp's supervisors supplied me with paper. One morning, in early spring, I was sketching another fantasy, astronauts battling a behemoth as big as the Earth, when I heard a whining voice behind me: "So Koertig still makes his little pictures."

I turned around to see a teenaged boy with a metal nose that resembled a joke-shop gag. His eyes were glassy, one lower than the other. It was Fenzel. He had survived our night battle, after all, crawling away after the enemy had marched right past him, though with additional disfigurement (an arm held at a funny angle). He bragged about being indestructible, about his killing of Russians— "I went after the bivouacs," he sneered, "where they thought they were safe"—and told me he'd been picked up and sent here after a doctor, who'd treated his arm, had turned him over to the "orphan brigade." He didn't mind—it was an "opportunity to find recruits."

"For what?"

"The Werewolves!" he whispered. "We work like ghosts, at night, killing Russians one by one, sabotaging their command and communication. And German traitors." He made the motion of slashing his neck. I did not quite know whether to believe him. He asked me if Stalla was still alive.

"He got shot and I took him to a doctor," I said, "but he did not make it."

"Too bad. He was good with the tanks." He snickered, and I could hear a vibration in his golden nose. "I didn't think *you* had a chance."

"Because you wanted me to die."

"I was just trying to toughen you up, Herr Iron Cross. Still have the medal?"

"No," I said, emphatic.

"I can see that you're lying. Show it to me, or I'll tell the commander you worked for the Führer."

With some hesitation, and keeping my movements slow and furtive, I pulled the medal from my pocket, holding the black cross in my palm so that Fenzel could see. He stared and stared with an expression that almost suggested tenderness. His lips twitched, and I could hear measured breaths coming from his brass nose piece. After another moment or two, he said, "There was nothing I wanted more than to meet the Führer. But you ruined it. You didn't die at Seelow. Even so, if not for my nose, they would have chosen me. Stalla had his perversions, so he was not eligible. But you have those Nordic looks, those pink cheeks and blue eyes. I look at you and I see a girl. I tried to convince them that you had not destroyed those tanks or killed those soldiers, and they dismissed my claims. Admit that you did not! Admit it!"

"I did not."

"Then it belongs to me," he said, and snatched the cross from my hand.

I lunged for him and we tussled in the mud. Neither of us had much strength, but I managed to retrieve that medal from his fingers before one of the guards separated us.

That afternoon, Fenzel approached me again. His nose-piece was crooked from our wrestling, augmenting the skewed nature of his eyes. "I'll let you keep that medal," he said, "if you redeem yourself."

"I don't need to do anything."

Fenzel surveyed the decrepit expanse of the camp. "Aren't you tired of this place?"

"Of course."

"Then pledge to be a Werewolf and I'll get you out."

"When?"

"In a week."

"I will," I said.

I suppose it must seem insane that I had agreed to join up with Fenzel again, a boy who despised me, who wished that I had died, who called me a coward, yet I wasn't going to pass up any opportunity to escape the wretched camp. I had no interest in being a soldier again. No, my plan was to ditch Fenzel at the first opportunity and find my way to New York: maybe, by some miracle, Zenzi was waiting for me there.

Fenzel made good on his word. He paid off a few boys to stage a big fight a week later so that four of us—including the Polish bully who had threatened to stop my heart—could slip over the fence during the commotion. Several kilometers away, in a burned-out factory, Fenzel ordered us to swear an oath to the Werewolf, a meandering tract he'd written himself in which we promised to free Germany from the barbarians. At one point, Fenzel pointed to the pale moon, stuck way up there on a washed-out sky, and set us to howling. Then he put us to work making small bombs with gunpowder, pencil fuses, and, from captured British supplies, Heinz Cream of Tomato Soup cans. I pretended to work on the devices until the next morning, when—with Fenzel on reconnaissance somewhere—I found my way to the center of the nearest village. Here, the military police caught me trying to steal some bread and then, smelling gunpowder on my fingers, became suspicious. Under questioning, and threats to stick me in a real prison, I revealed the location of Fenzel's HQ and then promptly got returned to the orphan camp. Rumor had it that Fenzel had been rounded up himself and, because he was older, sent to a place for what the Americans were calling denazification.

To my surprise, the episode with my former Kameradschaftsführer actually led to a successful escape, a sanctioned one. Permit me to explain, informing on the Werewolves got me placed at the top of a list for "family placement." The new President of the United States, Truman, had ordered someone in charge of European clean-up to find homes for DPs, with children given priority. I was labeled "a sensitive, artistic boy who likes to draw," and was selected, along with a dozen other children, for one of the first excursions to adoption. America, at last.

We did not yet know where and when we'd be going, and the wait was difficult. My worries piled up. Was I really getting a new family, or would I become a slave laborer in a chewing-gum factory? How could I love my new parents when I still longed for my real ones? If Zenzi were alive, maybe she was going to stay in Germany...

One day a letter arrived for me, by Allied Military Post—the official notice of transport, I assumed. Instead, I discovered a single scrawled line, in German, apparently not checked by any censor: "Coward! Traitor! Next time, you will die, and I will claim what is mine." The note, signed with the initials WF, brought on a fresh wave of fear, and I kept looking around to see if Fenzel had been re-admitted to the camp.

Then, on a morning in May, Fenzel and the war were behind me. For here was the day—bright, thrilling, dreamlike, mournful, all at the same time—that I left Germany, my disgraced and ruined country. I stood on the deck of the S.S. *Vivienne*, a passenger ship bound for the United States, to a place called New Jersey.

29

We ended up in a town near Hoboken, in an abandoned building that used to be a YMCA. Neglected and crumbling, the place reminded me somewhat of the Berlin I'd just left, and for that reason it offered me a little well-needed comfort. For I felt lost in the sights and sounds here—the torrents of English from the staff of the supervising Christian organization, the mishmash of languages from the other children, the eerie quiet of the nights, the rushing blur of the streets during the day, as if everyone were trying to flee something. In our first week, on a bus tour of Manhattan intended as entertainment, I was stunned by the immense buildings, not so much by their size but by the fact that they had not been damaged. I had assumed, somehow, that America had come under bombardment, too. When the staff took us out—to a park, to a bookstore to find something in the appropriate language—I found myself staring at every dark-haired girl who walked past me, hoping she might be Zenzi.

The adoption routine, too, was wearying. Married couples—middle-aged, over-dressed, childless—visited regularly to take us out to lunch, stacking hamburgers and ice cream before us. Through a translator, they asked endless questions to determine our temperaments. They smiled and smiled, they made stumbling attempts to speak German themselves, but I could not imagine any of them becoming my parents.

The feeling was mutual, it seemed. As the weeks passed, other children marched off into fresh lives, but I wasn't chosen. The staff gave me tips on my appearance, and my manners, and what to say, making greater efforts to tutor me in English. But it was the war, I figured, that was making me unattractive. It was always in my head, more so now than ever with all the quiet, with all the time for contemplation. At night, in that heavy muggy air, the plaintive chirping of crickets was like the crying of lost souls. I had nightmares about the Führer's ghost. The Fourth of July terrified me with its explosions, I thought the Russians had come across the Atlantic. Several of us raced through the school's aisles, looking for the basement. The frequent thunderstorms, too, gave me the shakes. The staff tried their best to keep our minds on joyful things—music and games, mostly. I learned the tunes of American folk songs and how to swing a baseball bat. Supplied with pencils and paint, I drew more of my outer-space adventures. Still, despite efforts to keep us away from newspapers, to block knowledge of the worst horrors, the gruesome details managed to trickle in about death camps, the burning of villages, mass rapes. When I heard the reports of the Führer's suicide or of Bormann's escape, I didn't say a thing. Yet hope for adoption brought such strains to my hours that when a pleasant couple, whose German was passable, showed interest in me and came back for a second interview, I became so anxious to please them that I announced, in a whisper, "I killed Hitler." They recoiled in embarrassment, excused themselves, and never returned. I was sent to a psychologist.

One Saturday afternoon, when I had grown despondent over my future, I decided it was time to find Zenzi, *now or never*, *make or break*, as I was learning to say. I gathered the pocket money I'd been given for doing a few odd chores and fled to Manhattan on the train. I managed to hail a taxi and have myself deposited in front of Carnegie Hall, where I knew orchestras performed. There I would wait for Zenzi. If she had survived and gone to New York, she would come here eventually. My logic was slapdash but I was desperate.

A crowd formed that evening and I searched and searched for the glasses and the dark hair and the dented chin, all of which I had not seen for well over a year. Would I even recognize her anymore? A dozen brunettes, on the arms of men, seemed to suggest Zenzi except when I got close enough. I asked the box office if they knew of her name but received, once again, a quick American shrug. Late in the evening, after examining the same crowd when they exited, I resigned myself to returning to the YMCA. I thought the subway might be faster, but ended up on a train going the wrong way, and became utterly lost. The heat down there felt like a poisonous gas. I sat against a pillar and, for the first time since I'd arrived in the United States, I wept.

Soon a man in a hat was stooping over me. Summoned by a policeman who had somehow figured out I was German, he spoke to me in my language, calming my despair. A smell of alcohol but also of coffee clung to him and this mix, which reminded me of my father's artist friends, also helped put me at ease. He introduced himself as Gerhard Reisner, a former resident of Augsburg, and then offered to take me to an all-night diner, where we spoke, bit by bit, of the war. I told him about my days as a soldier, omitting my duties as the Führer's illustrator. He told me about his years as a political prisoner, starving in a camp near Dachau, forced to work in a Messerschmitt factory. To have a conversation in

German and to talk about these things with someone who had lived in my country was to feel a great burden dissolving minute by minute. It turned out that Gerhard himself lived and worked in New Jersey. He helped roast coffee at the Maxwell House plant, which accounted for his pleasant smell, and had an apartment in Weehawken with his American wife Betsy. They'd been married only a few months, having met in the U.S. Occupation Zone, where she'd been a secretary for a translator. He took me back to the YMCA, delivering me after midnight to the worried staff, and claimed the fault was all his—he had taken me to a concert, he said, to lift my spirits. Two days later he showed up to request an adoption, and by autumn I became Tobias Reisner, son of Gerhard and Betsy.

Their apartment was small and spare, not at all like my real family's Berlin villa, but the closeness suited me. I was struggling at the local public school, where I'd been enrolled, finding it difficult to understand the teachers and sometimes getting jeered by other students for my accent. At home I found a degree of happiness. We avoided any more discussion of the war. I spoke freely in German, for Betsy knew the language pretty well herself. In the evenings, Gerhard settled on the couch with a beer and I sat near him sucking on coffee beans and we listened to the radio, to shows like *Inner Sanctum* or *Fibber McGee and Molly*, which Gerhard helped me understand. "Tain't funny, McGee," Betsy often said, mimicking with perfection Molly's famous reply to Fibber's jokes. On weekends, my new parents took me to movies and museums, they bought me books and a bicycle and a baseball glove, they bulked up my skinny frame with hamburgers, sliced bread, and potatoes. They encouraged my drawing, though neither had much interest in art beyond the *Saturday Evening Post*. America was starting to turn out all right for me. Sometimes it seemed as if the war had never happened.

But then, on a night in December, a week or so before Christmas, when Gerhard was out at a company party, Betsy sat me down on the couch to tell me some news.

"Your father has spoken to you about his time in prison, how the Nazis locked him up for his politics," she said. "Well." She fumbled for a cigarette, and with shaking hands lit it. "Do you know what they call a man who likes men?"

I knew only the German term. "Warmer Bruder," I said, perplexed.

"Here it's homosexual. Did you know that the Nazis put homosexuals in prison, too?"

I nodded. "My father's friend Herr Romling went to prison because he liked to wear stockings."

"Well." She switched to German to make me understand. "Your new father does not wear stockings. But he was not political."

"He is always complaining about Truman!"

"Tobias, things between us have not been right. I mean, in the important ways, the private ways. I didn't understand why. But finally I needed to know, and finally he has told me the truth. Your father was arrested in Germany because he liked men. Because—forgive me for being so blunt—because he slept with men. It was not a passing phase. When he comes home late...do you understand? The night he found you, I didn't know it then, but he'd been drinking in a place..." She inhaled deeply on the cigarette, then pushed out a big cloud of smoke to settle herself. "This does not take away from his suffering." Then she added, quieter, "But it adds to mine."

Tain't funny, McGee. My life, I knew, was about to change again.

By the time 1947 greeted us, Betsy had moved out. Soon after, Gerhard's single, nightly bottle of beer became four or five, fueling an anger that grew hotter each week. He started blaming me for the divorce that his wife had demanded. I had never accepted her as my mother, he claimed, even after all she had done for me! I'd been ungrateful! I'd ruined us all! Perhaps, I thought, he was right. His drinking got worse. Sometimes he struck me. He stayed out later and later. He often called Maxwell House to tell them he was sick. The plant put him on probation for too many absences, and then in March, he got fired. For a while we were forced to return to a wartime kind of life, hungry, scrounging food, often stealing it from grocery stores. One night, searching for something, he found my medal, which I had made every effort to keep safe, for I still considered it a kind of amulet. He screamed at me for being a Nazi, raising his fists. I protested, I insisted that I had deserted the army, but when his threats became ferocious, I told him, screaming back, that I had killed the Führer while all he'd done was sleep with men. He lunged at me, putting his hands around my throat, and if not for his drunkenness, he probably would have strangled me to death.

I dropped out of school the next week and found a middle-of-the-night cleaning job in the shipyards, where no one seemed to care about my age. It gave me another place to stay, for Gerhard frightened me now. The last I saw of my would-be father, he was staggering around, drunk again, hollering about the fascist landlord with an eviction notice crumpled in his fist.

The following years were not kind. At the shipyards, I didn't earn enough money to get a place of my own so I remained there as a kind of slave laborer, sweeping and mopping. I was ridiculed for my "enemy" accent and pummeled by longshoremen ten times my size.

A lonely teenager, shy around the few girls I happened to meet, I often thought of Zenzi and made attempts to locate her. In local papers, I placed ads, Tobias Seeking Kreszentia Fuchs. In subway stations, I taped signs to pillars. I wrote letters to the American military government in Germany, to the refugee organization that had arranged my trip to the United States, and even to the New York City police for any information. Official replies came back, all of them stating that hundreds of such requests came in every day and they could not offer, at the moment, any assistance.

Eventually I left the shipyards and found work in the railway, and by age twenty I had gathered enough money to feel confident enough to marry a red-headed Catholic girl I met in Atlantic City. But permit me to explain, my long hours in the yards, my smells of grease and coal, displeased her. Worse, my sexual approaches were awkward and quick. I was too eager, I performed (the way I'd learned) as if bombs would interrupt the lovemaking. She divorced me after less than a year. I mention it only to say that I did not have children.

A little later, New York presented another chance to alter my life. At a coffee shop one evening, I was eating a fruit pie while entertaining myself by sketching another cosmic fantasy. An older man with shaggy, unslicked hair, sat next to me smoking. He leaned over and said, "That's really very good. Who are you working for?"

"Penn Central."

"Huh? No, the drawing. Who's paying you?"

"It's a hobby."

"Well, how would you like to earn some money doing that?"

He handed me his card, and the next day I called in sick and showed up at the offices of *Astro Spectacular*, a new comic book chronicling the conquests of Victor Invincible throughout the galaxy and beyond. The pay wasn't great but it was just enough to cover my needs—I stayed with the editor until I found a basement apartment of my own near the Bowery—and all I had to do was sit at a desk and draw what I loved. At first, the shaggy editor had me pencil backgrounds of planets, moons, and stars. Then, a few months later, he fired the other artist for missing deadlines and designated me as the guy to keep Victor Invincible flying across the universe on schedule, strapped to his atomic jetpack.

For a while, I was content to maintain *Astro Spectacular*'s flat simple style, but after almost a year, I wanted to demonstrate my skills, and so I began introducing shadow and shading. Though he resisted these changes at first, saying they made the pages too dark—"Victor's outlook is always bright!"—the editor relented when dozens of fan letters applauded the realism. Encouraged, I directed similar efforts to ray guns, missiles, volcanoes, and exploding stars, and in particular, to their violent effects—ragged wounds, flowing blood, burned faces, screams. The editor grew nervous, but figuring they might give him an edge over the competition, he approved these changes, too. "But keep it light," he warned me. "Nothing more than what a Band-Aid could fix. Can't upset the kids."

In the manner of all young men, I became cocky and charged forward blindly, holding my convictions high. Like Victor Invincible, I sought to use my powers. When the editor, a heavy smoker, caught a drawn-out, debilitating infection of his lung, he assigned his wife, who managed the operation's finances, to monitor my work. She confessed that she knew little about art or the tastes of boys, and she left the pictures to me.

While the editor languished in the hospital, sleeping much of the time, I went wild with ideas and concocted a story of ferocious war. A race of giant hairy cave-men—who resided on a distant planet and who, despite their sub-human intelligence, had assembled a fleet of starships—was invading the Earth. They were rampaging through cities, smashing everything, burning everything, throwing women and children into the flames! Their hordes were endless. If you killed ten, a hundred more would appear. The world's armies had done little to stop them. Only Victor Invincible, man of atomic strength, could save humanity! He streaked through the sky, strafing the brutes with uranium rays. He stood bravely before their vicious mobs and blasted the Neanderthals into pieces. The battle was furious. Buildings crumbled, buses were crushed, trains and cars melted! Bridges twisted into corkscrews! Carnage and mayhem! I drew all this in a frantic rush, in a fever state, I could not put the action on the paper fast enough. New York City became a smoldering ruin. Bodies of civilians lay in the streets with gaping holes in their heads and chests, leaking rivers of blood. In every corner of my panels, there were piles of mangled cave men. Finally, to ensure the defeat of this evil alien race, Victor had to kill King Dirt, the Neanderthal leader. Victor fueled up his jet pack, streaked to the enemy planet, dodged the flak, descended to the deepest of caves, and dropped the Super-Gamma X Bomb onto Dirt's HQ, engulfing it all in a fireball! Burned, blackened, and minus one hand, Victor returned to Earth a hero.

The rheumy-eyed old guy who inked *Astro Spectacular* told me it was some of the most inventive stuff he'd ever seen. "But," he added, "it's gonna kill us."

"How?"

"They'll call it indecent."

"It's what they want," I said. "They'll ask for more, you wait."

The old man shrugged, he inked it, the story was printed, and the outrage began. Hundreds of letters poured in, all from parents. The scenes were depraved, disgusting, satanic, sure to turn children into killers and maniacs. I was a creep, a criminal. Victor Invincible was denounced by priests and politicians. Subscriptions were cancelled by the dozens. The editor, recovered, told me I had ruined him, and then gave me the boot. I learned later that the U.S. Senate summoned him to appear before a committee investigating juvenile delinquency. In a matter of weeks, *Astro Spectacular* folded. It was the end of my comics career, and I never drew such things again.

Over the next decade I did my best to forget Berlin. My accent often provoked questions about the war, but I told everyone that I'd stayed in Switzerland during that time. I avoided the newspapers, which depressed me with their constant talk about the Iron Curtain, East and West, the extent of ruins, the discovery of bones. As best I could figure, the grave of my parents, which I hoped had somehow not been disturbed, lay inside the Western half, and this gave me some degree of relief. Never once did I consider a return, for I feared being recognized, feared discovery of what I had done, or believed I had done.

I left New York City, which reminded me of Zenzi, and drifted back across the Hudson, into New Jersey again, to work in a shoe factory, and then, for fresher air, in the fishing business, though never on the boats themselves. Boats, bringing my thoughts back to the Elbe, did not make me seasick, but heartsick. In the following years, especially after a few beers, I often railed against Fate, which had led me to Zenzi in the first place, and which had taken her away. Yet sometimes I felt a wave of satisfaction by remembering that we had been essential to each other for three months. Who could expect anything more when the world was at its end? On the shore, I settled into a solitary and decent life, happy enough in my spare time to keep sketching my pictures, lighthearted ones now.

In November of 1965, Berlin did return. Twenty years had passed since the war had ended, and five months earlier there had been brass bands and fireworks to celebrate the occasion, though I had closed my eyes to all of it. One afternoon, bright and cold, a visitor came to my door. A gaunt man far older than me, or so it seemed, stood there in a gray suit. He had a pale, narrow, wedge-like face with a tiny thin nose that looked like pinched clay and that also whistled when he spoke. He held one arm across his shabby jacket as if it were in a sling. "Are you Koertig?" he said in German.

"I am not," I said with weakness. "Reisner."

"You used to be."

"What's your business?"

"I am Werner Fenzel."

I backed away, my heart flipped. The nose was a poor reconstruction. The arm was still damaged, the glassy eyes still sat uneven. His hair had gone thin.

"It took a while, but I tracked you down," he said.

"What do you want?"

"Let me sit."

Warily I motioned to a chair.

He looked around my apartment. It was nicer than the one I live in now, for I had a salary then and the world was not so unforgiving. He peered in the direction of the kitchen. "Do you have something to eat?"

I made him a sandwich of cold cuts. Fenzel ate rapidly, like a dog, as he had done before. He asked for another, and with this one I served him a beer. His hand trembled when he lifted the bottle. He appeared ill, lacking good color. But when I asked him why he'd come to the United States and how long he'd been here, he became animated. Ignoring my questions, he leaned forward and began to talk as if we had already been conversing for hours.

"When I was young and it snowed in Berlin," he began, "I would sit on the roof of our apartment building as the forward observer for Karl Vogel. A boy with muscles, Vogel had the arms of a wrestler. He would stand behind me, on a lower roof, and on my command, he hurled snowballs over my head and into the street below with incredible accuracy, exactly where I directed. He was a human mortar." Fenzel laughed in a kind of spasm, grimacing.

"We bombarded the Sunday strollers, we hit cars and trolleys. A few meters to the right, I'd say—make a shorter trajectory—and wham! We got one guy right on the top of his hat. When he looked up, I had Vogel fire ten more in succession! What a sight! That was Berlin! Or in the Tiergarten, Koertig, a summer night, we had swiped and gulped some wine, and after swimming naked in a pond, Johanna Hellberg, what great tits on that one, she let five of us screw her, she was laughing the entire time. That was Berlin!"

I tried to resist Fenzel's nostalgia, but it sideswiped me, and after a second beer, we were soon swapping escapades and hijinks of boyhood. There was my attempt, after reading *The Hound of the Baskervilles*, to unearth the carcass of a dead dog several of us believed to have been demonic. There was the time a schoolmate and I interrupted a brass band's summer concert by using slingshots to pelt the tuba with cherry pits. Fenzel remembered the year he had dropped bullets into a fireplace at a Christmas party, and also the day policemen chased him down Kurfürstendamm for stealing chocolate. During our talk I was marveling at Fenzel's friendliness, thinking he had come only to chat. The beer had relaxed him. He was sitting back in his chair, flushed, without as much trembling to his hands. That tiny nose, not really human, gave him the delicate look of a puppet. We were winding down, and it seemed that Fenzel was preparing to leave when he said with bitterness, "The Soviets have it now."

"Half," I said.

"Half is too much for despicable scum. Every year they ruin it more! It makes me sick. When I was there, I saw what ugly Communist things they were putting up. They're improving their wall again, too. I tried to organize resistance to it, but they ban everything. It was impossible. That's why I have come to this country. Here you can do anything. Here you can make speeches and hold meetings and buy guns, and no one will ask questions."

"What are you getting at?"

"An operation, Koertig. The same thing we did twenty years ago. Take the battle to the streets. Destroy the Russian force. I will bring a band of men with me, along with a shipment of arms. We'll infiltrate the eastern sections and we will kill them one by one. Just like old times."

"You must be kidding."

"You dismiss it. I expected that you would. Do you know what's happened to the country of your birth? Have you seen what they've done?"

"I have not been back," I said. "I do not want to see the ruins again. And I am not interested in joining, if that's what you want. I finished with war two decades ago. In any case, your plan is fantasy, it's ridiculous."

"Then you are not a true German."

"I have spent more of my life here than there. I am a citizen of *this* country."

"So a true American," Fenzel sneered, "in love with cars, potato chips, and television."

"I enjoyed talking with you about old Berlin. We should leave it at that." I stared at his thin frame and his gray skin, then reached for my wallet. "I can give you ten dollars."

Fenzel scowled, waving away the offered bill. "Is that why you think I've come here? A hand-out?" After a moment, Fenzel stood, stiffened his spine, and began to sing. The melody and the lyrics were not distinct at first, for he was wobbling and his voice was quivering, but soon I recognized the Horst Wessel tune, the one the boys all used to sing while Fenzel marched us around. By the last verse, Fenzel's off-center eyes were gleaming, glazed with tears. Then he said, "The Iron Cross. Show it to me."

"What makes you think I still have it."

Fenzel grinned, baring little fangs. "Your pride in Germany."

"I am not proud. I am full of regret. I do not want to revisit the war."

"I am simply asking to see the medal."

There was no use in pretending I did not still own it. I retrieved the cross from the drawer of a dresser.

Fenzel fondled the thing in his red, dry hands. "If not for you, if not for my nose...I will keep it."

"Fenzel, do not cause trouble. You know as well as I do that thousands, probably millions, of these medals were issued. You can find one for yourself at any surplus store."

"Yet you, so full of regret, treat yours as a treasure."

"I have my reasons."

"I will take what is mine."

"Is this why you wanted to find me? Don't make me notify the police."

"To tell them someone has stolen your prized Nazi medal?" He pulled a small pistol from his overcoat pocket, a surprise, but not out of character, at least the character I had known all those years before. "Goodbye, Koertig the Coward," he said in English. I did not know whether he meant to shoot me, or meant to leave, but I did not give him the chance for either, for I lunged at him. The gun did not fire, and after a brief struggle, Fenzel collapsed into stillness. Not dead, just unconscious, whistling through his nose. I called for an ambulance, hid the gun, and lied to the medics when they came. "He thought he knew me but didn't. I took pity on him and gave him something to eat. And then he fell." Fenzel left on a stretcher, under the spinning red light, and it was the last I saw of the former Kameradschaftsführer.

The next day, I stood on the beach in a cold wind, holding the sharp-edged medal in my fist, intending to hurl it into the ocean. I reached back, copying the style (long familiar to me now) of a baseball pitcher. A single forward motion would finally release me from the past. But that was why I could not bring myself to do so. Permit me to explain, that hunk of iron was all that I had taken from Berlin and it had come to mean too much. Discarding it would be, I realized now, an act of cowardice, a denial of all that I had seen and done, a denial of having joined that army in the first place, a denial of all the dead, a denial of Jews becoming fertilizer. I took it back home and put it away.

My fingers are sore from typing, there is little ink left on the ribbon, and so here I will end my story, which I hope has made it clear why I want that stolen medal returned, why I am certain that Fenzel is the thief. But if all I have accomplished is the stirring up of memories, then maybe that is enough.

Let me say, for the record, that I am sorry I did not search with greater effort for Zenzi. Time diminishes sorrow and resolve in similar measure. A tight bond formed in war loosens after the shooting stops. The quicker and brighter world overwhelmed me. These are my only explanations.

One day, I should add, one day I thought I found her. I was standing on a subway platform in Manhattan during the Christmas rush of 1974. My attempt to land a holiday job in the department stores had been unsuccessful, and I was glum. A train arrived, covered in the crazy painted scrawls of the time, jam-packed, and I managed to squeeze inside, facing the door. We did not immediately move, and I happened to glance through the window at the platform crowd, startled by the sight of a particular woman. She was draped in a brown, ankle-length coat. She wore stylish glasses. Her dark hair was cut short, maybe streaked with gray. She was clutching a red shopping bag. And her chin displayed a beautiful little dent. I tried without success to pry apart the sliding doors, I tried to open the nearest window but couldn't reach the latch through all the bodies, I rapped on the glass, and then pressed my mouth there and yelled "Zenzi! Zenzi, meine Frau! Meine Frau! Sehen Sie mich, Zenzi? Tobias! Ich bin Tobias!" The woman scowled, not in my direction. Embarrassed by my outburst, I said nothing more, glancing at that dent and convincing myself that my sullen mind had played a cruel trick. The car lurched forward. The woman traveled backward and backward and I plunged into the tunnel. But I did not feel a crush of disappointment. No, what came to me was a wish, deeply deeply felt, that if you had made it across the river, Zenzi, that if you had survived, you should be just like that, a woman clutching a red shopping bag and scowling only for having missed a train.

Tobias Kruse

Afterword
by Christopher Voss, Ph.D.

If not for an absurd marital spat, Tobias Koertig's extraordinary account of love and war in the ruins of Berlin might have ended up in the trash at a grubby New Jersey police station. As Koertig himself often writes, permit me to explain: how I came to read it, and how I came to meet the man himself.

On the morning of Sunday, May 8th, 2016—ironically, it was the date, 71 years earlier, on which Germany officially surrendered to the Allies—my wife and I had an argument over the arrangement of bowls in the dishwasher, an exchange of idiocy that soon became heated. I stormed out, furious, and drove a half-hour at top speed to the sanctuary of my office, a cramped room in the History department of Lovell College, where I am employed as a tenured professor of Twentieth-Century Studies.

Almost as soon as I arrived, the telephone rang—a policeman from nearby Misty Hook, a town on the Jersey shore. My heart, still in agitation, lurched. But as soon as Sergeant Toomis revealed, with some exasperation, the reason for his call, I came close (I must admit) to laughter.

An 84-year-old "male nut job" (the sergeant's term) had reported a minor burglary five weeks ago—so minor that Toomis had dismissed it. The same man had now shown up at the police station and was refusing to leave until a "history guy" (the sergeant's term again) promised to read his typewritten statement—a document that apparently connected the theft with a former Nazi! My Germanic surname Voss, found on the college directory, on a Sunday no less, had suggested to Toomis a good match for the job. Just my luck, I thought at the time—I'd be forced to listen to one of those wacky claims, something about the Luftwaffe's flying saucers or a Hitler clone in Argentina. But it did lighten my mood, and hoping an amusing tale would help restore good relations with my wife, I agreed to come in as soon as possible. Fish and chips at one of the shore's ubiquitous seafood shacks, a guilty pleasure, beckoned as a reward.

Less than an hour later, the young, muscular Sergeant Toomis greeted me with his monotone—"Appreciate the help in getting the old man off my back"—and then led the way into a blank room, where, under a stinging fluorescent light, I first met Tobias Koertig. Clutching a manuscript, squinting, seated with his knees together, he appeared nervous and timid. There was a fragile quality to his cherubic face. Freckles no darker than tea-stains dotted pink, almost translucent skin. His hair—yellow-white, still full at his age, uncombed—rose in a brittle, straw-like pile. Toomis introduced me as a "college historian" and I presented my credentials.

Koertig leaned forward. "My medal was stolen," he said with a slight German accent, rushing his words. "Did they tell you already? My medal. It is very important to me, but not for the reasons you may suspect. I have never been a warrior. I have never been a fanatic. The police won't do a thing because they think I'm an old fool, crazy in my head. But if you read this you will understand. Then you can convince them to find the thief, his name is Fenzel. Fenzel is the fanatic. After all these years, he has come back. I am so very thankful for your arrival."

Koertig's frail, earnest manner disarmed my readied sarcasm. I shook his chilly hand, made a half-hearted promise to help, and sheepishly offered to drive him home. He refused, insisting on a taxi. Toomis gave me a shrug and a wink, and I left with Koertig's document tucked under my arm.

Over on the main drag, I slipped into a booth at the grungy Clam Down, ordered the deep-fried special, and thumbed through what I estimated to be well over two hundred pages, all of them creased, stained, unnumbered, and, God Almighty, single-spaced.

The text, which ran as thick as mud, had been typed on some old machine with a malfunctioning H, T, and R (an odd coincidence of letters, considering Koertig's story). It all appeared, I won't deny it, like the efforts of a nut job. Yet I couldn't help being curious: at the station Koertig had specifically mentioned the end of the Second World War, when he would have been only thirteen years old.

So I began to read, and by the time my greasy filets arrived, I was hooked, pulled into the apocalypse of 1945 Berlin, with a boy as my guide. Sparked by the theft of his medal, Koertig had written his confessions—a fantastical story of war and survival and love, kept secret for over six decades. Koertig insists at the beginning that everything is true, though of course I had significant doubts. Many scenes and facts corroborate the historical record, yet what to make of a boy sketching sci-fi pictures for Hitler, or the rescue of Tobias by the gorilla, or the ancient Greek jewelry, or the marriage portrait in the bunker, or (most astonishing) his claim to have killed the Führer himself? All of it is plausible, to a degree, but rather dream-like, to put it mildly. And if the story, or most of it, is true, then there are other burning questions: Whatever happened to Zenzi Fuchs? And did Fenzel actually re-appear? Intrigued by everything, I decided I would try to find out.

Drive a half-mile south of Misty Hook's central strip—past Margo's Doughnuts, the Clam Down shack, and several purveyors of salt-water taffy—and after making a left at the abandoned Sunoco station, go to the end of a narrow road paved with stones and crushed shells. At the edge of bleak marshland, you come to a sagging, motel-like apartment building. There, behind the door marked 203, lived Tobias Koertig.

On the morning I finished reading his confessions, I stood before that same door and knocked. My first three taps did not receive an answer. But I persisted and finally heard a voice, faint though resolute: "Give me your name."

"Christopher Voss. We met last Sunday, at the police station."

After a moment, the door opened a crack, held by a chain. Two shadowed eyes, watery and red, peered out. "You have news?"

"Not really."

"You were not able to convince the police?"

"I don't think they'll be pursuing the case." When I'd called Toomis to follow up, the sergeant made it quite clear that he had no interest in dealing anymore with a "demented old fart," muttered something about a string of real robberies that needed his attention, and then handed me Koertig's address, hoping I'd convince him to stay clear of the station.

"But I've read your document," I added, "and I will help you find Fenzel."

The chain fell, the door opened, and with a little wave of his hand, Koertig motioned for me to come in. The apartment did not contain the degree of squalor the sergeant had described. There was, indeed, a faint smell of garbage, and in one corner the ceiling had crumbled, the hole surrounded by fingers of water stain. A window was cracked, and a threadbare oval rug looked as if it had been recovered from the dump. Yet the place was actually quite cheery, for on every wall Koertig had tacked up sketches of life on the shore, in all seasons—beachcombers, boaters, kite-fliers, all richly detailed and rendered in a light, spirited style. "They must be yours," I said. "Very accomplished."

A sigh, a shrug, and Koertig fell back onto a tattered sofa. "My hand wobbles too much anymore."

His diffident pride reminded me of the lanky boy I had envisioned, making expert pictures of outer space while the bombs fell, accidentally impressing the Führer with his cartoons. I eased into a chair near the ancient typewriter, an Underwood. I placed his document on a table between us. "I must ask you some questions about this."

"To test me. To see if I'm not crazy."

"To clarify."

"What is your motivation?"

"If what you wrote is true, then you are a man with a remarkable past. Deserving of recognition."

Koertig shook his head. "No. I was a boy who stumbled into things. Chance, nothing but chance. I do not want to be known for anything and I forbid you from making it public. I simply want to have my medal returned."

"All right. Let's talk about the robbery. You're sure nothing else was taken?"

"A block of cheese from my fridge. A carton of milk."

"You haven't mentioned that before, have you?"

"It would have convinced that policeman even more that it was petty theft."

"It remains a possibility, doesn't it? A burglar might have mistaken the Iron Cross for jewelry."

"No, no," Koertig insisted, "a thousand times no. The thief went through the entire apartment before finding the medal. And he took only that. Who else but Fenzel knew I had it?"

"Wouldn't he be eighty-eight years old now?"

"Age does not eliminate certain obsessions."

"Will you show me the word that you found?"

Straining a little, Koertig pushed himself up, shuffled over to the single closet, and pointed at the back wall. The scrawl, made with one of Koertig's charcoal pencils, was frantic: *Feigling!* The exclamation point was heavily marked, and the word itself—meaning coward, of course—underlined three times.

Koertig glared at me. "If you like, I will print the word myself to prove the handwriting is not mine."

"That's not necessary."

"Then what other questions do you have?"

I won't transcribe the entire interview here—largely an attempt to confirm his story's details—but I will relate the inquiry I made about Koertig's central act, the one, I figure, that few will believe:

"In all the accounts of the bunker," I said, "from Speer, Von Loringhoven, and Traudl Junge, from Trevor-Roper and other historians, no one mentions a boy making illustrations for Hitler, let alone his wedding portrait. How do you explain that?"

"I have not read anything about the war. I have not needed the reminders." He paused, looking with his watery eyes into the corner. "There were many boys coming in and out of the bunker. Messengers, soldiers, the wounded. Nobody paid any attention to us except when something was needed. If these writers don't mention me, it is because I was dispensable. And that made me invisible. My pictures, too. They were unimportant."

"A couple of times in your chronicle, you mention the possibility that what you recall doing in the bunker was really a dream."

"I had hoped it was." He saw my quizzical look, and added, "Because of the terror that followed."

"But you held that pistol and pulled the trigger?"

He sighed, irritated. "Do you want me to tell you that I invented it out of my guilt? Maybe I did. But I have recorded what I remember."

"May I keep your manuscript?"

"If it is of use in finding Fenzel, then yes."

I thanked Koertig for his time, promising to keep in touch, and returned home, a bit dazzled. I was intent now—selfishly, I must admit, thinking of the honors I might earn—to prove the truth of his claims.

First, I sent copies of Koertig's confessions to two experts on the Third Reich's last days. Then I turned my attention to finding a witness. Werner Fenzel would of course be useful. There also might be the possibility of the American corporal, the Elbe escort who'd disappeared. But what intrigued me most was a needle-in-a-haystack search for the person who might offer a far more trustworthy eyewitness testimony—Kreszentia Fuchs.

Corporal Wade Hartley, I soon discovered from U.S. Army records, had died in the Korean War, in 1951. Though identified as a corporal, he'd actually been an agent in the CIC, the Counter Intelligence Corps, which explained his interest in Tobias's story. It wasn't a surprise, given the secrecy of his organization, that his frail widow, now confined to a nursing home, did not remember him ever mentioning an encounter with a German boy and girl in a requisitioned farmhouse—or, for that matter, bringing home gold antiquities.

For Fenzel and Zenzi, to keep the effort reasonable, I would initially limit my search to New York; if nothing turned up, I would try Berlin. Either, of course, could have left their surnames behind. Either could be dead. If Zenzi had married, it might be impossible to track her down. Even if she hadn't, she could be anywhere in the world. And yet I decided to give it a shot, both for the sake of history and for a notion of pure romance: reuniting Tobias with Zenzi.

A quick glance through phone books of the five boroughs revealed only seven Fenzels. I called each one myself, asking about my "old friend" Werner. All claimed no knowledge of the man. Though few would admit to an association with a die-hard Nazi, I found their statements credible. Not giving up, I paid an ambitious undergrad named Derek to plow through public files.

At the same time, I assigned a group of my best students to track down hundreds of Fuchs listings in marriage records, immigration records, death records. After three months, we came across just one promising lead. When I went to the family's home in Queens, it turned out that their distant cousin had been named Kristiana, and had been born in 1940. Not a single Kreszentia or Zenzi, Fuchs or otherwise, had turned up. Derek's efforts, too, were encountering only dead ends.

Meanwhile, some good news, of a sort, had come back from the Third Reich experts: they could not deny the possibility of any event that Koertig described. But in no way did they endorse the document as factual. One of them warned me to step away from the manuscript immediately: did I want to ruin my reputation, as Trevor-Roper had, by confirming the authenticity of what turned out to be a hoax?

By now, it was late August, and I needed to prepare my classes for the first semester. Continuing the search, in either New York or Germany, seemed almost impossible. "If she survived, she could have settled anywhere or married anywhere," I complained to my wife. "Lost to history."

"But you are forgetting something," she said. "You know where and when she got married. She and the boy..."

"Oh, come on. A silly game they played to comfort themselves."

"They seemed to take it seriously. According to Tobias, anyway."

I shrugged. "Hard to believe it would have carried beyond the war for her."

"But after they were separated, if of course she survived, Zenzi might have felt the bond more deeply. She was fifteen. Her emotions were high. She'd gone through a terrible ordeal. And exaggerating her age and claiming to have a husband would have helped protect her from, shall I say, horny American soldiers. I think she could easily have registered herself as Kreszentia Koertig."

Yes, of course. A wild hope gripped me. But the phone books listed no Koertigs. A search on the Internet, across a wider area, turned up nothing useful.

A month or so later, after having pretty much abandoned the project, I attended a concert by the New York Philharmonic. The featured piece, I will note, was Tchaikovsky's Symphony No. 4, which begins with a fanfare signifying Fate. Browsing the program notes, I happened to glance at one of the last pages, a list of the symphony's donors and their amounts. The names, printed in small type, appeared as a kind of gray blur—that is, until my eyes found two initials, in a list for $1500, right in the middle: K.K. I made some sort of exclamation, loud enough to turn heads, embarrassing my wife. It could be anyone, but it also could be Kreszentia Koertig, lover of classical music.

After the concert, I hurried out into the lobby and explained the situation to a woman in the ticket office, begging her to relay to this K.K. a brief message, along with my phone number. Finally, seeing that I wasn't going away easily, she agreed, though warned it might be impossible to find the person, if the patron wished to be anonymous.

A sleepless week passed without a word, a hundred doubts kept rolling through my head. Then on a Wednesday evening, my phone rang, displaying Private on the ID display. The caller's voice, from an older woman it seemed, bore an unmistakable touch of German. "I received your note. What is it that you want?"

"Kreszentia Koertig?"

She repeated her question. I tried to compose myself, to keep from sounding like an over-enthusiastic idiot. "I am, as I mentioned in my note, Christopher Voss, a professor of history, and if you are formerly Kreszentia Fuchs, who once lived in Berlin, I have, as I mentioned, information about Tobias Koertig—"

"What kind of information?"

"Everything. His life."

"How did you obtain this—whatever it is you claim to have?"

"Tobias recently finished writing a kind of memoir, and I have spoken with him, too."

"Then you have contacted the wrong person. The Tobias I knew died in 1945."

"He didn't. He survived. He is living in New Jersey."

"I may be old, but I am perfectly capable of recognizing a racket."

Sensing she was about to hang up, I blurted, "Your father committed suicide with rat poison." Silence from the other end, yet she had not ended the conversation. I went further. "You were a Mischling, you escaped from a murderous SS officer named Weinrich, you crossed the Havel hanging from the end of a tank."

A long pause, with stuttering breaths. Then, almost whispered, "Tell me what you want."

"Only to speak with you. To confirm Tobias's story." I explained my involvement—the robbery, the request from the police, the reading of the manuscript. "Perhaps we could meet. Take your time to consider. Bring someone else along, if you like."

She called the next day and named a delicatessen in the Williamsburg section of Brooklyn. Several hours later, I stood in front of an old-fashioned storefront, under a Coca-Cola sign that might have dated from the '50s. Appropriately, it appeared as if I'd been transported back in time. I entered, surveying the booths. In the back, below a wooden cane hung on a hat rack, a woman with short gray hair and a pair of large, stylish glasses returned my gaze. I became lightheaded, unsteady. I had only read Koertig's descriptions of her—descriptions of a girl 71 years ago—yet I recognized the wide, and still striking, face of Kreszentia. She had come alone, which surprised me somewhat, so I tried not to appear overly solicitous as I shook a hand that still held considerable strength. "Zenzi," I said, then realized my mistake. "I'm sorry. Does anyone still call you that?"

"A few. You may, if you like."

I told her about Koertig's years after the war. Zenzi, solemn, kept nodding, telling me she did not remember a man named Fenzel and smiling only when I told her that Koertig had never stopped sketching.

"What does Tobias know of me?"

"Nothing yet."

"You must understand," she said, "that I am rather stunned by all this."

But with little coaxing, Zenzi told her own story, picking up where Koertig had left her, in that final maddened rush to cross the Elbe under Russian bombardment. She remembered, she said, being in the green row boat. There were so many shells coming down, it seemed like the sky had shattered. There was an explosion very close. Tobias reeled backward into the water. She reached for him and fell into the river herself, but he was floating face up and someone was pulling her onto another boat, screaming, *Let him go, you can't help him, the boy is dead!*

"The Russians were intent to kill every last one of us," she said, "and so I believed it. He wasn't moving. There was no time to think. Confusion, terror, panic. We could not run because we were on the river. So I floated away, insane with grief. I did make it to the other side. And then the boat was going back, to get others, and I crossed the river again to find Tobias. There was more confusion. I'm not sure if we returned to the same spot. In any case, I did not see him. By then, I was exhausted, and in such a state of trauma I could not speak. The next day I realized that three of my toes had been shattered by a bullet or something. The cane became necessary."

She admitted to the American authorities to being a Mischling, and was later grouped into a Jewish contingent of refugees, perhaps given greater protection than others, which may explain why Tobias couldn't locate her. Likewise, her efforts to find him didn't go anywhere, either—probably, I suggested, because he'd changed his name to Frankfurter, which then became Frank. She remained in the camp—"a godawful place"—for almost three years, sometimes helping the Americans with translations of Nazi documents, and hearing from others the disgusting details of the Jewish extermination. By 1948, in another Truman-directed initiative, she was given a choice to emigrate to either the U.S. or the newly-formed state of Israel. "The desert sounded too harsh a place, and I had heard about the strife there at that time. Skirmishes and things. I was tired of war. I still had the dream of New York, so that's there we went."

I cut in here, repeating her pronoun. "We?"

Zenzi gave me a scowl, flustered for a moment. "I meant the refugees."

Though sensing there was something she did not want to discuss, I did not pry. I was lucky, I figured, that she was talking to me at all.

In New York, she struggled. She took jobs sewing or cleaning, and lived in a tiny, illegally-crowded apartment. She often went hungry, "but I was used to that." She worked for a while, too, for a relief agency, helping to repatriate displaced European Jews. In 1952, encouraged by co-workers, she converted to Judaism. "I had immense sympathy for all of Hitler's victims, which is probably not the best reason to become a Jew. Still, I felt a need. It was a close community, a comfortable one." She soon found steady work in translation, which helped bring her out of poverty, and she later edited a German-language journal. A poem of hers appeared in *The Partisan Review*. But a career in the arts, as she'd once dreamed about, never developed. "I couldn't dance because of my foot, it never healed properly, and I didn't have the body for it, anyway. I went to concerts and plays, dabbled with some verse, and that was enough. I had other responsibilities. I was good with numbers, and I ended up in the banking industry, if you can believe it. European investments."

"Let me ask you about your name. Tobias described the wedding you staged as children in Berlin—a kind of playacting, but you ended up taking it quite seriously."

"Yes, it was a teenager's little fantasy, a death fantasy, a desperate attempt to imagine a different life. But it meant a great deal to me. It still does. A wedding does not need the blessing of an observer, only the trust of husband and wife. Even as children, our bond was as legitimate as any other, considering the circumstances. If you brought it up to find out if I ever married again, the answer is no."

I nodded, took a sip of my iced tea, and prepared for a bigger question. "In the manuscript, Tobias reveals an astonishing act, one that revises the historical record."

"So he has written about that, too."

"Can you tell me what it was?"

"You sound like a courtroom lawyer. Of course you are talking about the death of Hitler."

"He writes that he had confessed this act to you just before you crossed the Havel, and then at a farmhouse, an American observation post."

"The farmhouse!" Zenzi nodded and smiled, her eyes pooling with tears. "It felt like a kind of miracle. It *was* a miracle."

"Did you believe Tobias? I mean, about Hitler?"

"He had an incredible amount of courage for a boy of thirteen. Yes, he might have imagined it. His father, like mine, had hated Hitler. But his claim seemed possible. Anything was possible then."

"Did you ever mention the act to anyone else?"

"An American official who was managing the refugees. He laughed, thinking that I was trying to earn some privilege. Maybe I was. More than a decade later, I told a rabbi. He suggested the idea was a delusion that my subconscious had created to substantiate the conversion. I never spoke of it again. There was so much from that time that did not seem real. It was hard to distinguish those days from my nightmares."

"Would you like to see Tobias?"

Zenzi took a breath. "I was waiting for you to ask, and I want to give you an unequivocal Yes," she said, sounding a bit coy, "but it is difficult, and very strange. I really had believed he had died. And to know now that he has lived in New Jersey ever since I have lived here, that is almost tragic. It *is* tragic."

"He did look for you, by the way. I mean, when he first came here. He was hoping. Put notices in the newspaper, in the subway."

"I never got out much back then. And I never listed my name in any directory. My fears of discovery, of avoiding arrest, remained fresh." She scowled, looking away. "To be honest, Mr. Voss, I am very afraid of taking my head, my memory, back to that time. But I think a meeting may be necessary now."

I did not want to push things. I told her she could call me whenever she wanted. "It was an honor to have met you," I said.

Leaning on her cane, she squeezed my arm before stepping into a taxi. "Is he in danger, by the way? From this Fenzel?"

"I doubt it. Fenzel or not, the burglar seems to have taken what he wanted and disappeared."

Like a matchmaker, I soon went back to Koertig. We had not spoken for several weeks, and he assumed that my interest in seeing him meant that I had recovered what had been stolen. "No," I said, "but there's something else you will be very pleased about. I have found Zenzi herself."

"What do you mean? Don't be ridiculous."

"In Brooklyn."

"Someone else with the same name."

"She has a different name," I said. "She is Zenzi Koertig."

He gripped the chair's armrests. "You're making this up."

"She confirmed a great number of details from your story. Her features match the ones you described."

Koertig stared at the floor with glassy eyes. For a minute or two, he seemed to have forgotten that I was in the room. His mouth twitched as he drummed his fingers. "How long has she lived in New York?"

I took a deep breath. "Since 1948."

He nodded as if he had expected the answer. "She made it across the river, too."

"She thought you had died." After I told him what I now knew of Zenzi's life, all he said was, "I am sorry to hear about her foot." He rubbed his head for a minute or so. "Why did you track her down?"

"It took time. She never listed herself in the phone book. But I wanted someone else to verify your story. I also thought, perhaps I was mistaken, that you'd want to see her again. She has expressed interest in a reunion."

"I see." He clasped his hands together, unclasped them, closed his eyes, and kept them closed as he spoke. "You have interfered with private history. I am not pleased about that. But now, of course, you must arrange this."

Not long afterwards, on a warm October day, I returned to Koertig's apartment to escort him to his past. He'd asked that I bring him his original manuscript, and when I handed it over, he took out a pen and on the first page wrote "To Zenzi." He wanted to give it to her. He remained subdued for the ride to Brooklyn, nodding or shaking his head to supportive statements I'd hoped would relax him. He had dressed himself in a wrinkled suit jacket, and kept pulling at the knot of his narrow red tie. After we crossed the Verrazano Bridge, he asked me to stop at a florist. In front of Zenzi's building, clutching both the boxed manuscript and the modest bouquet, squinting, he looked like a nervous boy on his first date. He trembled a little as we rose in the elevator.

That first moment between the two of them did not turn out quite as I expected. The flowers, thrust forward, delayed an embrace. Zenzi, who wore a plain blue dress, pottered about the kitchen looking for a container, eventually choosing a plastic pitcher. She dropped her cane, which clattered on the floor. Finally they hugged, but without a kiss. In the small living room, they settled opposite each other, on a sofa and armchair, and exchanged pleasantries. A mixture of sweet perfume and aftershave hung a bit too heavily in the warm air. The manuscript, which had brought them together, sat on a coffee table in its box as if it were nothing more than a gift of pastries. I had planned to stay, to witness what I had arranged, and yet I could see that I was only making the situation more difficult. I excused myself and assured Koertig, who appeared glum, that I would return in a couple of hours.

On my way out, passing through a hallway, I happened to see a drawing, framed and hung on the wall, that stopped me, throwing a hiccup into my heart: the sketch Tobias had made in the farmhouse. The square of paper, a faded pink, was an old Victory Mail sheet, issued to U.S. soldiers and sailors for the writing of letters. It once had belonged, of course, to Corporal Hartley. Underneath the address lines and the circle for the censor's stamp, a girl stared out at me, a cigarette pushed into one corner of her grinning mouth. Zenzi, aged fifteen. The pencil had faded, the lines were rushed, but here were the wide eyes and broad cheeks and the prominent, graceful chin with the hint of a cleft, that "dent"—a lovely face, and somehow modern with the hair shorn to make her look like a boy.

Over lunch, feeling confident now of the reunion's success, I took out my muted cell phone to call my wife, and discovered several notifications for missed calls, along with a text message from Derek the undergrad. "PCM, PCM," it read, "great news." I'd learned a few of these abbreviations from students and knew PCM to mean "Please call me."

Derek's voice was breathy, clipped. "Professor Voss! I've been trying to reach you all day. Do you remember what you asked me to do?"

"Yes, yes, of course."

"Well, I found him. I found Werner Fenzel."

The details were few: an old man with the same name living in a flophouse hotel, one of the last of its kind, on the lower east side. He'd been there a long time, twenty years or more, didn't go out much. The information had come by way of the hotel's manager, who had not permitted Derek to go upstairs for an interview.

"Anything else?" I asked.

"Well, the manager let it slip that he's got all these war pictures tacked on his walls."

It was a day of surprises. When I returned to Zenzi's apartment, I found a third person had joined the reunited couple—a trim, handsome woman, a little beyond middle-age, dressed in jeans and a loose white blouse, whose presence appeared to have broken up the awkward formality I'd witnessed earlier. Zenzi, falling into that coy tone again, introduced her: Isolde Koertig, a painter.

"Koertig?" I said.

"My daughter," Zenzi replied. Then, putting her arm around Tobias, she added, "Our daughter."

Because I spluttered something unintelligible, Zenzi wanted to make sure I understood: Isolde had been born in February of

1946. I glanced at Koertig, who appeared calm. This was the secret that Zenzi had not wanted me to know—a daughter fathered by a thirteen-year-old boy. She had his features, no doubt: delicate cheekbones, an angular nose, fair skin, bluish-gray eyes that were large but somehow timid, never quite holding your gaze. I wanted to stay, I wanted to ask a hundred questions, but both Tobias and Zenzi appeared quite tired. I briefly spoke with Isolde, mostly about her art (she had just opened a show in the Chelsea district), and then escorted Koertig to the parking garage.

While the attendant was retrieving my car, I asked Tobias how he felt.

"It is difficult to say," he said. "I have imagined all this for many years. But now it is real...and I have missed everything."

"If I can assist in bringing the three of you together again..."

"Yes," he said with a single nod. "Thank you."

"Tobias, I have some other news. A student of mine told me just today that he has found a man by the name of Werner Fenzel. There is a possibility—a strong possibility, I think—that he is your Werner Fenzel."

"Well, then. The past rushes back all at once."

On Koertig's request, we drove to the hotel, an old building of sagging bricks, squeezed between restaurant-supply stores on the Bowery. Behind a caged window, the manager considered us with distrust. "Is this one of those human interest stories? A kid came around and asked about the same guy. Every six months the papers want to write some amusing shit about the folks who live here. Don't mess with their dignity, because that's all they got anymore."

I assured the man that we weren't journalists and that my friend was only trying to find someone he knew decades ago.

"Well, I don't normally allow visitors, but I could make an exception."

I slipped him a twenty-dollar bill and we were given the room number. On the second floor, the battered hallway smelled of disinfectant. Clothes, boxes, suitcases, and bits of junk were scattered across the floor. The specified door had no knob and so I peered through the hole. There was someone inside stretched out on a narrow bed. I knocked and we heard a grunt.

"Werner Fenzel?" I said.

Another grunt, and so I pushed the door open. The space, kept dim by a torn yellow shade yanked down over the window, was no bigger than a walk-in closet. The walls were, indeed, filled with pictures from the war—all of them of German soldiers, as far as I could tell, and no doubt snipped from library books, which sat here and there in waist-high stacks.

On the bed (a plank and a mattress supported by cinder blocks), the man appeared to be little more than a skeleton: a bald head, a sliver of a nose, arms as thin as broom handles, papery skin. Wart-like beads of sweat had collected on his forehead. Any lingering doubt about his identity disappeared when I realized that the stain on the front of his dark T-shirt was nothing of the kind: it was a black cross, the medal.

"Who is it?" the former Kameradschaftsführer asked, raising his head with effort.

Now Tobias spoke, but only his name: "Koertig."

"So you've found me," Fenzel said, switching to German. "Welcome to my...luxury home." His breathing was labored, but he managed a raspy laugh. "Have a seat...you will enjoy...watching me die."

"I don't know what you mean."

"Then they haven't told you...that's why I've always... liked this place, everyone leaves you alone...I see you...brought a bodyguard...fear not, I am in no condition for a fight...the Bolsheviks couldn't kill me, but cancer...a tough one to defeat... good at hiding...in the lungs, I'm told..."

"I am sorry to hear that."

"No, I do not think...you are...but still, I must thank

you...for extending my life...a year ago, some young doctor at Bellevue...told me I had six months...I wish I could have gone back to Germany...but they had kicked me out a long time ago... my unlawful behavior...all I did was hate the Communists...so I decided that I would finally get this medal...my last mission, it gave me strength...a pleasure to plan...you were still around...a boy under my command staked out your place...told me of your doughnut habit...that made it easy...he slipped through your window, and then let me in the door...all those pretty pictures... could only be your place...take some coins from the jar in the corner there if you wish to be re-paid for...what the boy took from your fridge...let me keep the medal until I expire...well, if you could...hand me a pill from that bottle...and that glass of water... yes, thank you...now if you will kindly take your leave...I do not want my dreams of Berlin to be ruined...by the face of a coward..."

Koertig shuffled out and I followed him back down the stairs. He stood before the office's wire cage, asked the manager for a pad of paper and a pen, then wrote his name and his phone number. "Please notify me when the man in room 14, Werner Fenzel, has died."

"He's sick or something?"

"Yes. Not much time left, I think."

"Friend of yours? Funny old coot, that one."

"No. He has something of mine that I wish to retrieve."

The manager shrugged. "OK, but you gotta come right away. If the heat keeps up, situation like that gets cleaned out quick."

Two weeks later, Koertig called and asked me to meet him at his apartment. When I arrived, he appeared somewhat agitated. He wanted me to accompany him to the beach. He took me close to the waves, which were crashing rather dramatically, as there'd been a recent storm. He fumbled in the pocket of his sport coat and extracted the object that had led, across all the years, to this moment: the Iron Cross. He'd been notified, as requested, of

Fenzel's death and had traveled to the hotel and back on his own—a considerable effort and expense for a man of his age without a car. Now he placed the medal in his palm, staring. Against his pale skin, the black-and-silver symbol took on a sinister Gothic character, especially as the bright sun was making its central swastika gleam.

"Toss it for me," he said.

"Where?"

"Into the sea. But I don't mean toss. I mean hurl. As far as you can. I would do it, but I don't have the strength."

"You're sure?"

"I have never been more sure of anything."

The waves smashed down, emphasizing his conviction. I took the medal, held it as if I were about to skip a flat rock, and then threw the thing—hurled it—with a sidearm motion, with all my might. We witnessed the distant splash and Koertig thanked me. Then he made another request, handing me a scribbled Manhattan address, a gallery in Chelsea. "My daughter's exhibit," he said. "Could you drive?"

I was glad to oblige, hoping to help further exorcise his demons, if that's what he'd just done. He was quiet for the entire trip. In Chelsea, on a street of converted warehouses, we entered the gallery through tall glass doors, into a white-walled cave, where a sullen young receptionist didn't bother to look up from her computer. A dozen paintings lined the walls, all by Isolde—dark and dense abstraction edged by skeletal figures who appeared to be falling. We did not remain long, though Koertig studied each work, his jaw set by pride. "Even if I don't understand them," he said as we left, "I see they are done with a lot of care." My offer to buy lunch was declined, and I deposited him that afternoon at his sad little apartment.

Three months passed without a word from him. I called a couple of times to check in, hoping that I might earn his permission to do something with his document, but he never picked up the phone. I didn't try to visit, afraid to intrude on the solitude he seemed to prefer, but also because I got caught up in my classes. I had been developing a new theme around the assumed truths of history.

One December evening at home, I received a call from Sergeant Toomis. He spoke in the usual monotone: That morning, a few blocks from his apartment, Koertig had just left his favorite bakery, carrying two jelly-filled doughnuts, when he was struck by a delivery van. According to witnesses, the driver had ignored the stop light. Koertig, 84 years old, died on the asphalt, still clutching his paper bag. Could I identify the body? I expressed my disbelief and hurried over to the morgue. Koertig's expression was one of peace, and for that I was grateful.

The funeral, in Misty Hook, attended by Zenzi and Isolde, was short and spare. My sorrow deepened when Zenzi revealed that Koertig had not contacted them since the reunion, and had not answered their calls. Afterwards, the three of us went to his apartment to collect his things. We started taking down his sketches from the walls. The scenes were so pleasantly innocuous that I hadn't given them much more than a few glances. Once again I admired his attention to detail—the rigging on a sailboat, the shadow of a beach umbrella. But it was Isolde, seeing them for the first time, who noticed what I had overlooked: three figures, never quite central, but always there, always delighted with life and each other—a tall, thin father, a full-figured mother wearing glasses, and a daughter. In boxes, there were dozens of other drawings, each one with the same trio, pictured season to season, each labelled according to the month and year. Now, of course, I understood what Koertig had meant when he told me that he had "imagined all this." It looked as if he'd worked on the series for decades.

Though Zenzi later granted me permission to publish Koertig's confessions (with some necessary tidying), she and Isolde decided that the drawings were too personal—"too overwhelmingly sad"—to be included here. They are, I must say, quite remarkable, almost like snapshots. With great skill, he gradually aged the family throughout. In an early scene, the young couple is pointing out a horse to their curious toddler. When the girl has become a teenager, the three of them often appear in animated conversation as they traipse through a field, slip across a lake in a row boat, or, in several, stand near a churning sea. At the end of the series—the last one is dated 1987—bodies sag a little, hair has thinned, faces are grooved. The settings have become interiors. In one, my favorite, the trio sits in the back of a crowded café, at the lower edge of the frame. A cluttered background (tables, chairs, customers, waiters) keeps their figures rather inconspicuous. But you can see, once again, that they're all at ease. The mother and daughter are grinning, while the father—whose mild, pensive expression suggests no experience with war—is pressing a thumb onto his plate, picking up, no doubt, a few stray grains of sugar.

Acknowledgements

Let me express my profound thanks to:

Bonnie Jo Campbell and the Association of Writers and Writing Programs (AWP) for selecting *To Zenzi* for the 2019 AWP Prize for the Novel

Bonnie again, along with Jaimy Gordon, for keen editorial insights

Kimberly Kolbe at New Issues for smoothly ushering the novel through the publication process, Kaitlyn Fisher for the cover concept, and Nicholas Kuder for developing it, all during a difficult time in the world

Sheryl Johnston for her book-business knowledge and guidance

The James Jones Literary Society for its generous First Novel Fellowship

Ilona Karmel and Elzbieta Ettinger, Holocaust survivors from Poland who both published acclaimed novels on the subject, for teaching me how to write and tell a story in their fiction workshops at M.I.T.

Fanny Howe, also at M.I.T., for further valuable studies in the craft of fiction

· Joyce Thompson for her literary wisdom

Deena Madnick for her high school English class, which opened my eyes to great literature, most memorably the classics of war

My mother Helen Shuster for instilling an appreciation for a good tale by letting me, at age 11, read her Alistair MacLean spy novels

My brothers Richard Shuster and Stephen Shuster for their WWII military expertise

Roger and Rosemarie Binggeli for their help with the German language

Michael Olson for our enriching hours together in bookish conversation

My father, the late James Shuster, for taking pride in my work

And so many more over the years, individuals and organizations, from Seattle to New York, for their critiques, encouragement, opportunities, and inspiration that kept this writer afloat